A point of utter blackness formed in the center of the fiery sphere. From far within it, a voice filled Mannoroth's mind, a voice as familiar to him as his own.

Mannoroth . . . it is you . . .

But not that of Sargeras.

We have waited too long . . . it said in a cold, analytical tone that made even the huge demon shrink into himself. *The way must be made completely open for him. I will see to it that it is finally done. Be ready for me, Mannoroth . . . I come to you even now.*

And with that, the blackness spread, becoming a huge emptiness above the pattern. The portal was not quite as it had been when first the night elves created it, but that was because the one who spoke from the other realm now also strengthened it. This time, it would not collapse.

"To your knees!" Mannoroth roared. Still under his sway, the sorcerers had no choice but to immediately obey. The Fel Guard and night elven soldiers in attendance followed suit a moment later. Even Captain Varo'then quickly knelt.

The demon was the last to kneel, but he did so with the most deference. Almost as much as he feared Sargeras, he feared this one.

We are ready, he informed the other. Mannoroth now kept his gaze on the floor. Any single act, however minute, that could be construed as defiance might mean his painful demise. *We, the unworthy, await your presence . . . Archimonde . . .*

THE DEMON SOUL

WARCRAFT

WAR OF THE ANCIENTS

TRILOGY

BOOK TWO

THE DEMON SOUL

RICHARD A. KNAAK

POCKET STAR BOOKS
New York Toronto London Sydney

An *Original* Publication of POCKET BOOKS

A Pocket Star Book published by
POCKET BOOKS, a division of Simon & Schuster, Inc.
1230 Avenue of the Americas, New York, NY 10020

ISBN: 0-7434-7120-2

First Pocket Books printing November 2004

10 9 8 7 6 5 4 3 2 1

POCKET STAR BOOKS and colophon are registered trademarks of Simon & Schuster, Inc.

Cover art by Bill Petras

Manufactured in the United States of America

For information regarding special discounts for bulk purchases, please contact Simon & Schuster Special Sales at 1-800-456-6798 or business@simonandschuster.com.

For Thomas "Sonny" Garrett,
Accomplished Writer and Friend

THE DEMON SOUL

ONE

The voices whispered in his head as he moved through the huge cavern. Where once they were but an occasional occurrence, now they never ceased. Even in his sleep, he could not escape their presence . . . not that he wanted to do so anymore. The huge black dragon had heard them for so long that they were now a part of him, indistinguishable from his own twisted thoughts.

The night elves will destroy the world . . .

The Well is out of control . . .

No one can be trusted . . . they want your secrets, your power . . .

Malygos would take what is yours . . .

Alexstrasza seeks dominion over you . . .

They are no better than the demons . . .

They must be dealt with like the demons . . .

Over and over, the voices repeated such dire things, warning him of duplicity, betrayal. He could trust no one but himself. The others were tainted by the lesser races. They would see his decision as a danger, not the only hope for the world.

The dragon unleashed a puff of noxious smoke as he snorted at such treachery from those who had once been his comrades. Though he had the power to save everything, he had to be careful; if they discovered the truth too soon, it would mean calamity.

They must not know its secret until it is beyond their altering, he decided. *It cannot be presented until the spell must be cast. I will not let them destroy my work!*

Huge claws scraped fresh the rock floor of the cavern as the scaly behemoth entered his sanctum. As massive as the dragon was, the rounded cavern dwarfed him. A molten river flowed through the center. Massive crystal formations glittered in the walls. Huge stalactites hung like swords of doom from above, while stalagmites grew from the ground so sharp that they looked as if they waited for someone to be impaled upon them.

And, in fact, such was the case with one.

Teeth bared, the great black dragon peered down at the puny figure struggling to free himself despite the stony spike thrusting up through his heaving chest. The remains of a tattered, black and bloodred robe and fragments of ornate, golden armor hung around his oddly-shaped torso. High, goatlike horns thrust from his skull and the crimson visage resembled most to the dragon a long skull with a wide, fanged maw. The eyes were pits of darkness that immediately tried to suck the behemoth in, but they were no match for the will of the creature's captor.

In addition to being impaled, the horned figure was bound by thick, iron chains to the cavern floor. The chains had been set especially tight, pinning the demon to the stalagmite and keeping his limbs spread downward.

Constantly the captive's mouth moved as if he furiously shouted something, yet no sound emerged. That did not keep him from trying, however, especially when he saw the dark leviathan approach.

The dragon mulled over his prisoner for a moment, then blinked.

Immediately the cavern chamber filled with the venom-laced, rasping voice of the creature. "—is Sargeras! Your blood will flow! Your skin he will wear for a cloak! Your flesh will feed his hounds! Your soul he will keep in a vial, ever to torment at his pleasure! He—"

Blinking again, the dragon silenced once more his captive. Even still, the demonic figure continued mouthing threats and obscenities until, finally, the dark behemoth opened his huge jaws and exhaled, enveloping the prisoner in a searing plume of steam that left the latter shaking in renewed agony.

"You will learn respect. You are in the presence of my glorious self, I, Neltharion," the dragon rumbled. "I am the Earth Warder. You will treat me with the reverence which I deserve."

The demon's long, reptilian tail slapped at the rocks below. The mouth opened in what was obviously more silent blasphemies.

Neltharion shook his crested head. He had expected better from the Eredar. The warlocks were supposed to be among the commanders of the Burning Legion, demons not only skilled at casting spells but well-versed in battle tactics. The dragon had assumed that he would hear far more intelligent conversation from such a creature, but the Eredar might as well have been one of the brutish Infernals, the flaming, skull-headed behemoths who acted like fearsome battering rams or airborne missiles. The one he had tested before capturing the Eredar had only the wit of a rock, if even that much.

But then, Neltharion had not sent his flight out to pluck the demons from their rampaging horde for conversation.

No, the captives had another purpose, a grand one that they, unfortunately, could never come to appreciate.

And the Eredar was the last, the most significant. His innate magical abilities made him the key to fulfilling the first part of the Earth Warder's quest.

It is time . . . the voices whispered. *It is time* . . .

"Yes . . . " Neltharion answered absently. "Time . . ."

The dragon raised one huge paw palm up and concentrated. Immediately a golden aura flared to life in his palm, growing so brilliant that even the captive demon paused in his tirades to stare at what Neltharion had summoned to him.

The tiny disk was as golden as the aura that had presaged its coming, but otherwise it was an astoundingly simple-looking piece. It would not have even quite filled the hand of a much smaller creature—say a Night Elf, for instance. The disk resembled a large, featureless gold coin with rounded edges and a gleaming, untarnished shell. Its very unassuming appearance was all by Neltharion's design. If the talisman was to perform its task properly, it had to seem entirely innocent, harmless.

He held it toward the warlock, letting the Eredar see what awaited him. The demon, however, appeared quite unimpressed. He stared from the disk to the dragon, mockery filling his eyes.

Neltharion noted the reaction. It pleased him that the Eredar did not recognize the strength of the disk. That meant that others would also fail to realize the truth . . . until it was too late.

At the Earth Warder's silent command, the object rose gently from his palm. It floated above the paw for a moment, then drifted over to the captive.

For the first time, a hint of uncertainty colored the warlock's monstrous visage. As the disk descended, he renewed his futile struggles.

The golden talisman alighted on the demon's forehead. A brief flash of crimson light bathed the Eredar's face—and then the disk sealed itself to his flesh.

Speak them . . . urged the voices as one. *Say the words* . . . *seal the act* . . .

From the savage, lipless maw of the dragon erupted words from a language whose origins lay not in the mortal world. Each one was tinged with an evil that made even the demon quiver. To the Earth Warder, though, they were the most wondrous sounds he had ever heard, perfect musical notes . . . the language of gods.

As Neltharion spoke them, the disk began to glow again. Its radiance filled the vast chamber, growing brighter and brighter with each syllable.

The light suddenly flared.

The Eredar warlock stretched his mouth as wide as it would go in a noiseless cry. His horrific eyes rained tears of blood and his tail slashed madly against the rocks. He tore at his bonds with such fervor that he scraped away the flesh from his wrists and ankles. But still the demon could not escape.

Then the Eredar's skin started to decay. It crumbled from his still-twisting body, his still-shrieking countenance. The demon's flesh became as if a thousand years dead, dropping from him in dry, ashy bits.

The eyes sank in. The tail shriveled. The warlock swiftly reduced to a cage of bone surrounding rapidly-putrefying entrails. Yet throughout the macabre ordeal, he continued to scream, for Neltharion and the disk had not so far permitted him the comfort of death.

But at last, even the bone gave way, collapsing inward and

fragmenting. The jaw fell loose and the ribs rolled away with a clatter. With terrible efficiency, the power unleashed by the disk absorbed the demon's remains from the bottom up. The trail of dry dust spread fast from the feet to the legs to the torso until only the skull was left.

And only then did the Eredar grow still.

The sinister light ceased. The chains once holding the demon dangled empty.

Like a doting father reaching for a cherished offspring, the black dragon used two claws to gently lift the talisman from the skull. As Neltharion did this, the skull, too, turned to ash. The gray powder scattered over the ground.

He stared with admiration at what he had wrought. Neltharion could not even sense the extraordinary forces now residing in the disk, but he knew that they were there—and when the time came, they would be his to command.

No sooner had he thought this than another presence touched his mind. The voices subsided abruptly, as if they feared discovery by this intruder. The Earth Warder himself immediately smothered his own desires.

Neltharion knew the touch well. Once he had believed it to come from a friend. Now the dark leviathan understood that he could trust her no more than he could the rest.

Neltharion . . . I must speak with you . . .

What is your wish, dear Alexstrasza? The Earth Warder could imagine her. A sleek, fire-colored dragon even slightly more imposing than himself. As he was the physical Aspect of the world's innate strength, so was she the Aspect of the Life that flourished in, on, and above it.

There are dangerous forces again playing around the palace of the night elves' queen . . . we must come to some decision and soon . . .

Fear not, Neltharion replied soothingly. *What must be done will be done . . .*

I pray it will be so . . . how soon can you make the journey to the Chamber?

The Earth Warder imagined that other place in his mind, a mammoth cavern that made his own seem but the burrowing of a single worm. The Chamber of the Aspects, as the lesser dragons respectfully called it, was also perfectly round and smooth, as if at some point in the past—before even the coming of the dragons—someone had set some great sphere into motion, completely shaving away the ripples and outgrowths found normally in caves. Nozdormu, to whom all things involving history were fascinating, believed that the creators of the world had made it, but even he could not prove so with any certainty. Hidden by a field of magic that kept it from the mortal world, the Chamber was the most trusted and secure of places anywhere.

Thinking that, the black dragon hissed low in anticipation. His crimson gaze shifted to the disk. Perhaps he should go there now. The others would all be there. It could be done . . .

No . . . not yet, said the voices just barely audible in the back of his subconscious. *The timing must be right or they will steal what is yours . . .*

Neltharion could not let that happen, not when he was so near to triumph. *Not now,* he finally told the red dragon, *but soon . . . I promise it will be soon . . .*

It must be, Alexstrasza replied. *I fear it must be.*

She left his thoughts as quickly as she had entered them. Neltharion hesitated, trying to determine whether or not he had left to her some hint of what was going on. The voices, however, assured him that he had not, that he had done very, very well.

The black dragon held high the disk, then, with a satisfied look in his blazing eyes, conjured it back to where he kept it hidden from all others, even his own blood.

"Soon . . . " he whispered as it vanished, a toothy grin stretching across his monstrous visage. "Very soon . . . after all, I *did* promise . . ."

The mighty palace stood on the edge of a mountainous precipice overlooking a vast, turbulent lake whose waters were so dark as to be utterly black. Trees augmented magically by solid rock created tall, spiral towers that jutted up like fearsome warriors. Walls made of volcanic stone that had been bound by monstrous vines and tree roots surrounded the huge edifice. A hundred gargantuan trees had been drawn together by the power of the builders to create the framework of the main building, then the rounded structure had been covered with stone and vine.

Once, to any who gazed upon it, the palace and its surroundings had been one of the wonders of the world . . . but that had changed, especially in recent times. Now the foremost tower stood shorn of its upper half. The blackened stone fragments and dangling bits of vine spoke of the intensity of the explosion that had destroyed it. That alone had not turned the palace into a place of nightmare, though. Rather, it was what now surrounded the once-proud edifice on all sides, save where the foreboding lake demanded dominion.

It had been a magnificent city, the culmination of night elf rule. Spread out over the landscape and very much a part of it, the high tree homes and sprawling habitations built into the earth itself had created a wondrous setting for the palace. Here had been built Zin-Azshari—"The Glory of Azshara" in the old tongue, and the capital of the night elves' realm. Here had stood a teeming metropolis whose citizens had risen every eve to give homage to their beloved queen.

And here, save for a few select, walled regions flanking

the palace, had been a slaughter of innocents such as the world had never seen.

Zin-Azshari lay in ruins, the blood of its victims still staining the broken and burnt shells of their homes. The towering tree homes had been ripped to the ground and those built into the earth had been plowed under. A thick, greenish mist drifted over the nightmarish landscape. The stench of death yet prevailed—the corpses of hundreds of victims lay untouched and slowly rotting, a process made all the slower and more grotesque by the absolute absence of any carrion creatures. No crows, no rats, not even insects nibbled at the chopped and torn bodies, for they, too, had either fled with the few survivors or fallen to the onslaught that had claimed the city.

But although such carnage surrounded them, the remaining inhabitants of Zin-Azshari seemed not to notice it one bit. The tall, lanky night elves remaining in the city went about their tasks in and around the palace as if nothing had changed. With their dark, purple skin and extravagant, multicolored robes, they looked as if they attended some grand festival. Even the grim guards in forest-green armor standing watch at the parapets and walls appeared out of place, for they stared out at wholesale death without so much as batting an eye. Not one narrow, pointed visage reflected the slightest dismay.

Not one registered fear or horror at the grotesque giants moving in and among the debris in search of any possible survivor or spy.

Hundreds of armored, demonic warriors of the Burning Legion scoured Zin-Azshari while hundreds more marched out of the palace's high gates to supplement those moving beyond the capital. At their hand had this fair realm fallen and, given the chance, they would scour over the rest of the world, slaying all in their path.

Most were nine feet high and more, towering over even the seven-foot-tall night elves. A furious green flame perpetually surrounded each, but did not harm them. Their lower bodies were oddly thin, then expanded greatly at the chest. Their monstrous countenances resembled fanged skulls with huge horns atop and all had eyes of red blood that peered hungrily over the landscape. Most carried massive, pointed shields and glowing maces or swords. These were the Fel Guard, the bulk of the Legion.

Above them, with wings of fire, the Doomguard kept watch on the horizon. Similar otherwise to their brethren below save for a slight difference in height and a look of deeper intelligence, they darted back and forth over Zin-Azshari like prospecting vultures. Now and then, one would direct the efforts of the Fel Guard below, sending them wherever someone or something might be hiding.

Hunting alongside the Fel Guard were other fiendish creatures of the Legion, most of all huge, horrendous, four-legged monstrosities with a vague resemblance to either hounds or wolves. The scaled abominations, coarse fur atop their backs, sniffed the ruined ground not only with their massive muzzles, but also with two sinewy tentacles with suckers on the end. The felbeasts raced along through the carnage with extreme eagerness, occasionally halting to sniff over a ravaged corpse before moving on.

But while all this continued beyond the palace grounds, a quieter, yet no less horrific, scenario played out in the southernmost tower. Within, a circle of the Highborne—as those who served the queen of all night elves were called—bent over a hexagonal pattern etched into the floor. The hoods of their elegantly-embroidered, turquoise robes hung low, all but obscuring their silver, pupilless eyes . . . eyes now tinged with an unsettling red glow.

The night elves loomed over the pattern, muttering repeatedly the great words of their spell. A foul, green aura surrounded them, permeating their very souls. Their bodies were wracked with the continual strain of their efforts, but they did not falter. Those who had shown such weakness in the past had already been eliminated. Now, only the hardiest weaved the dark magic summoned from the lake beyond.

"Faster," rasped a nightmarish figure just beyond the glowing circle. "It must be done this time . . ."

He moved about on four titanic legs, a gargantuan, tusked demon with broad, clawed hands and huge, leathery wings now folded. A reptilian tail as thick as a tree trunk beat impatiently on the floor, leaving cracks in the sturdy stone. His toadlike head nearly scraped the ceiling as he moved among the much tinier Fel Guard—who wisely scattered from his path—for a better view. The green, fiery mane running from the top of his head to the tip of each of his squat hooves flickered wildly with every earth-shaking step.

Under a heavy, hairless brow, sinister orbs of the same baleful green gazed unblinking at the dark tableau. He who commanded the night elves in their unsettling task was one used to *spreading* fear, not feeling it. Yet, on this tempestuous night, the demon called Mannoroth was afflicted with the disturbing emotion. He had been given a command by his master, and he had failed. Never before had this happened. He was Mannoroth, one of the commanders of the Great One's chosen . . .

"Well?" the winged demon growled to the night elves. "Must I rip the head off another of you pathetic vermin?"

A scarred night elf wearing the forest-green armor of the palace guard dared to speak. "She won't approve of you doing that again, my lord."

Mannoroth turned on the upstart. Fetid breath washed

over the pinched face of the helmed soldier. "Would she complain as much if I chose to give her *your* head, Captain Varo'then?"

"Very likely," returned the night elf without any sign of emotion flickering over his own face.

The demon thrust out one meaty fist more than large enough to engulf Captain Varo'then's skull, helmet and all. The clawed fingers encircled the elf—then withdrew. Mannoroth's master had decreed early on to him that the queen of the night elves and those important to her were to be left untouched. They were valuable to the lord of the Burning Legion.

At least for now.

Varo'then was one whom Mannoroth could especially not touch. With the death of the queen's advisor, Lord Xavius, the captain had become her liaison. Whenever the glorious Azshara opted not to gift those working in the chamber with her magnificent presence, the guard captain took her place. Everything he saw or heard, Varo'then reported succinctly to his mistress . . . and in the short time that Mannoroth had observed the queen, he had determined that she was not so empty a vessel as some might have imagined. There was a cunning to her that her oft-languid displays hid well, but not well enough. The demon was curious what his master intended for her when he finally stepped into this world.

If he finally stepped into this world.

The portal to that other place, that realm between worlds and dimensions where the Burning Legion roamed between their rampages, had collapsed under a magical assault. That same force had also ripped apart the original tower, where the Highborne and demons had worked. Mannoroth still did not know what exactly had happened, but several survivors of the destruction had hinted of an invisible foe in their midst, one who had also slain the counselor. Mannoroth had his suspicions as to who that invisible intruder was and had already dispatched hunters to seek him out. Now he concentrated only on restoring the precious portal—if it could be done.

No, he thought. *It* will *be done.*

Yet so far the fiery ball of energy floating just above the pattern had done nothing but burn. When the tusked behemoth looked into it, he did not sense eternity, did not sense the overwhelming presence of his master. Mannoroth only sensed *nothing.*

Nothing was failure and, in the Burning Legion, failure meant death.

"They're weakening," Captain Varo'then remarked blandly. "They'll lose control of it again."

Mannoroth saw that the soldier spoke the truth. Snarling, the monstrous demon reached out with his mind and thrust himself into the spellwork. His intrusion shook the Highborne sorcerers, nearly upsetting everything, but Mannoroth seized control of the group and refocused their efforts.

It will be done this time. It will *be . . .*

Under his guidance, the sorcerers pressed as never before. Mannoroth's determination whipped them into a manic state. Their crimson-edged eyes widened to their fullest, and their bodies shook from both physical and magical stress.

Mannoroth glared grimly at the recalcitrant ball of energy. It refused to change, refused to open access to his master. Yellow drops of sweat poured down over the demon. Foam formed on his broad, froglike mouth. Even though failure meant being cut off from the great one, Mannoroth felt certain that somehow he would be punished.

No one escaped the wrath of Sargeras.

With that in mind, he pushed even more furiously, tearing from the night elves whatever power he could. Moans arose from the circle . . .

And suddenly, a point of utter blackness formed in the center of the fiery sphere. From far within it, a voice filled Mannoroth's mind, a voice as familiar to him as his own.

Mannoroth . . . it is you . . .

But not that of Sargeras.

Yes, he reluctantly replied. *The way is open again.*

We have waited too long . . . it said in a cold, analytical tone that made even the huge demon shrink into himself. *He is disappointed in you . . .*

I did all that was possible! Mannoroth protested before common sense warned him of the foolishness of doing so.

The way must be made completely open for him. I will see to it that it is finally done. Be ready for me, Mannoroth . . . I come to you even now.

And with that, the blackness spread, becoming a huge emptiness above the pattern. The portal was not quite as it had been when first the night elves created it, but that was because the one who spoke from the other realm now also strengthened it. This time, it would not collapse.

"To your knees!" Mannoroth roared. Still under his sway, the sorcerers had no choice but to immediately obey. The Fel Guard and night elven soldiers in attendance followed suit a moment later. Even Captain Varo'then quickly knelt.

The demon was the last to kneel, but he did so with the most deference. Almost as much as he feared Sargeras, he feared this one.

We are ready, he informed the other. Mannoroth kept his gaze now on the floor. Any single act, however minute, that could be construed as defiance might mean his painful demise. *We, the unworthy, await your presence . . . Archimonde . . .*

TWO

The world he had known, the world they all had known, was no more.

The central region of the continent of Kalimdor was a ravaged plain. Spreading out in every direction, the demons had wreaked carnage on the complacent, jaded night elf civilization. Hundreds, possibly thousands, lay dead and still the Burning Legion pressed on relentlessly.

But not everywhere, Malfurion Stormrage had to remind himself. *We've stopped them here, even pushed them back.*

The west had become the place of greatest resistance to the monstrous invasion. Much of that credit went to Malfurion himself, for he had been the principal agent in the destruction of the Highborne spell that sealed off the Well of Eternity's power from those outside Queen Azshara's palace. He had faced Lord Xavius, the queen's counselor, and destroyed him in epic combat.

Yet, although Lord Kur'talos Ravencrest, master of Black Rook Hold and the commander of the night elf forces, had acknowledged his part before the gathered leaders, Malfurion did not feel like any hero. He had been tricked more than once by Xavius during the encounter, and only the intervention of his companions had enabled him to overcome the sinister counselor and the demons Xavius served.

His loose, shoulder-length hair a startling dark green, Malfurion Stormrage stuck out among the night elves. Only his twin brother, Illidan—who shared his narrow, almost lupine features—garnered more notice. Malfurion had eyes completely silver, as was most common among his people, but Illidan had gleaming orbs of amber, said to be the portent of great things to come. Of course, Illidan tended to dress more with the flamboyance most accepted of his kind, while Malfurion wore simple garments—a cloth tunic, a plain leather jerkin and pants, and knee-high boots. As one who had turned to the nature-oriented path of druidism, Malfurion would have felt like a clown had he sought to commune with the trees, fauna, and earth of the forest while clad like a pretentious courtier about to attend a grand ball.

Frowning, he tried for the thousandth time to put an end to such superfluous thoughts. The young night elf had come to this lonely spot in the hitherto untouched forest of Ga'han to calm and focus his mind for the days ahead. The huge force massed under Lord Ravencrest would be on the march soon—to where, no one knew just yet. The Burning Legion advanced in so many places that the noble's army could travel hither and yon for countless years, facing battle after battle without ever making any true progress. Ravencrest had summoned the top strategists to discuss the best way to gain a decisive victory, and quick. Each day of hesitation cost more and more innocent lives.

Malfurion's brow furrowed as he struggled harder to find his inner peace. Slowly, his mind relaxed enough to sense the rustling of leaves. That was the talk of the trees. With effort, he could speak with them, but for now the night elf satisfied himself with listening to their almost-musical conversations.

The forest had a different sense of time, and the trees especially reflected that difference. They knew of the war, but spoke of it in an abstract manner. Although aware and concerned that other forests had been ravaged by the demons, the woodland deities who watched over them had so far given the trees here no reason to be truly worried. If the danger neared, they would surely know soon enough.

Their complacency jarred Malfurion again. The threat of the Burning Legion to *all* life, not just the night elves, was obvious. He understood why the forest might not fully comprehend that yet, but surely by now its protectors should.

But where *were* Cenarius and the rest?

When he had first sought to learn the way of the druid, a life which none of his kind before him had ever chosen, Malfurion had journeyed deep into this forest outside the city of Suramar in search of the mythic demigod. Whatever made him think he could find such a creature when no one else had, he could not say, but find Cenarius the night elf had. That in itself had been astonishing enough, but when the forest lord had offered to indeed teach him, Malfurion could not believe it.

And so, for months, Cenarius had been his shan'do, his honored instructor. From him, Malfurion learned how to walk the Emerald Dream, that place between the mortal plane and sleep, and how to summon the forces of nature to create his spells. Those very same teachings had been a tremendous part of the reason for not only Malfurion's survival, but that of the other defenders as well.

So why had Cenarius and the other woodland deities not added their own prodigious strength to the desperate defenders?

"Ha! I thought you'd be here."

The voice so similar to his own immediately identified

the newcomer for Malfurion. Giving up on his quest for balance, he rose and solemnly greeted the other. "Illidan? Why do you search for me?"

"Why else?" As ever, his twin kept his midnight blue hair bound tight in a tail. In contrast to the past, he now wore leather pants and an open jerkin, both of a black identical to that of his high, flaring boots. Attached to the jerkin and hanging just over his heart was a small badge, upon which had been etched an ebony bird's head surrounded by a ring of crimson.

The garments were new, a uniform of sorts. The mark on the badge was the sign of the house of Kur'talos Ravencrest . . . Illidan's new patron.

"Lord Ravencrest will be making an announcement come dusk, brother. I had to get up early just so I could find you and bring you back in time to hear it."

Like most night elves, Illidan was still used to sleeping during much of the day. Malfurion, on the other hand, had learned to do just the opposite in order to best tap into the latent forces permeating the natural world. True, he could have studied druidism at night, too, but daylight was the time when his people's link to the Well of Eternity was at its weakest. That meant less chance of falling back on sorcery when casting a spell for the first time, something especially necessary during Malfurion's earliest days as a student. Now, he felt more comfortable in the light than in the dark.

"I was just about to head back, anyway," Malfurion said, going toward his twin.

"It would've looked bad if you hadn't been there. Lord Ravencrest doesn't like disorder or delay of any kind, especially from those integral to his plans. You know that very well, Malfurion."

Although their paths in the study of magic had gone in

opposing directions, both brothers were adept at what they had chosen. After having been saved from a demon by Illidan, the lord of Black Rook Hold had appointed him personal sorcerer, a position of rank generally given to a senior member of the Moon Guard, the master mages of the night elves. Illidan, too, had played a pivotal role in the crushing of the demon advance in the west. He had seized control of the Moon Guard after the death of their leader, and guided their power effectively against the invaders.

"I had to leave Suramar," Malfurion protested. "I felt closed in. I couldn't sense the forest."

"Half the buildings in Suramar were formed from living trees. What's the difference?"

How could he explain to Illidan the sensations more and more assailing his mind each day? The deeper Malfurion delved into his craft, the more sensitive he became to every component of the true world. Out in the forest he felt the general tranquillity of the trees, the rocks, the birds . . . everything.

In the city, he felt only the stunted, almost insane emanations from what his own people had wrought. The trees that were now houses, the earth and rock that had been shifted and carved to make the area habitable for night elves . . . they were no longer as they had been in nature. Their thoughts were confused, turned inward. They did not even understand themselves, so transformed had they been by the builders. Whenever Malfurion walked the city, he sensed its wrongness, yet he also knew that his people—and, in fact, the dwarves and other races, too—had the right to create their civilizations. They committed no crime by building homes or making the land usable for them. After all, animals did the same thing . . .

And yet the discomfort he felt worsened each time.

"Shall we return to our mounts?" Malfurion asked, pointedly forgoing any reply to his brother's question.

Illidan smirked, then nodded. The twins walked side-by-side in silence up the wooded rise. Often of late they had little to say to each other, save when matters concerned the struggle. Two who had previously acted as one now had less in common with each other than they sometimes did with strangers.

"The dragon intends to leave us, likely by the time the sun sets," Illidan abruptly remarked.

Malfurion had not heard that. He paused to gape at his brother. "When did he say that?"

Among the night elves' few powerful allies was the huge red dragon, Korialstrasz. The young but mighty leviathan, said to be a mate of the Dragon Queen, Alexstrasza, had come to them along with one of a pair of mysterious travelers, the silver-haired mage known as Krasus. Korialstrasz and Krasus were somehow linked deeply to each other, but Malfurion had not yet discovered in what way. He only knew that wherever the gaunt, pale figure in gray went, the winged behemoth could be found. Together, they proved an unstoppable force that sent demons running in panic and paved the way for the defenders' advances.

Separated, however, they both seemed at death's door . . .

Malfurion had decided not to pry into either's affairs, in part due to their choice to aid the night elves, but also because he respected and liked both. Now, though, Korialstrasz intended to leave, and such a loss would be disaster for the night elves.

"Is Master Krasus going with him?"

"No, he's staying with Master Rhonin." Illidan spoke the last name with as much respect as his brother did Krasus.

Flame-haired Rhonin had come with the elder mage from the same unnamed land, a place they sometimes briefly spoke of when relating facts about their own experiences against the Burning Legion. Like Krasus, Rhonin was a wizard of high learning, although much younger in appearance. The bearded spellcaster wore dour blue travel clothes almost as conservative as Malfurion's, but that alone was not what offset him from those around. Krasus could pass for a night elf—albeit a very sickly, pasty one—but Rhonin, equally pale, was of a race no one recognized. He called himself a *human,* but some of the Moon Guard had divulged that their studies indicated he was some variation of a dwarf who had simply grown much taller than his fellows.

Whatever his background, Rhonin had become as invaluable as Krasus and the dragon. He wielded the Well's magic with an intensity and skill even the Moon Guard could not match. More important, he had taken Illidan under his wing, teaching him much. Illidan believed it was because Rhonin saw his potential, but Malfurion understood that the cloaked stranger had also done it to rein in his twin's impetuousness. Left to his own devices, Illidan had a tendency to risk not only his own life, but those of his comrades.

"This isn't good, Illidan."

"Obviously not," retorted his amber-eyed twin, "but we'll make due." He raised his hand for Malfurion to see; a red aura surrounded it. "We're not without strength of our own." Illidan caused the aura to cease. "Even if you seem a little reluctant to make full use of what Cenarius taught you."

By full use, Malfurion's sibling meant unleashing spells that wreaked havoc not only on the enemy, but the landscape and anything else caught in the path. Illidan still did not understand that druidism required working *with* the peaceful balance of nature, not against it.

"I do what I can in the way I must. If you—"

But Malfurion got no further, for, at that moment, a figure out of nightmare dropped down before them.

The Fel Guard opened his grisly maw and roared at the pair. His flaming armor did not make Malfurion in the least hot, but rather chilled the night elf to the very core of his soul. Sword raised, the horned demon swung at the nearest foe—Illidan.

"No!" Malfurion shoved his brother aside, at the same time calling upon the forest and heavens to come to his aid.

A sudden, intense wind slammed into the demon, flinging him like a leaf several yards back. He fell against a tree—cracking the trunk—then slid to the ground.

As if the tentacles of some huge squid, the roots of every tree within reach squirmed over the stunned attacker. The demon tried to rise, but his arms, legs, torso, and head were suddenly pinned to the earth. He struggled, but only succeeded in losing what remained of his grip on his weapon.

Their victim secure, the roots then immediately sank back into the ground—and, in the process, *through* the demon.

A hissing gasp was all that escaped the monstrous assassin before the roots severed his head from his body. Green ichor poured out of the horrific wounds. Like a puzzle someone had just spilled, the parts of the demon tumbled back toward his would-be targets.

Yet, even as Malfurion dealt with the first, two more Fel Guard dropped from the trees. Cursing, Illidan rose to his knees and pointed at the nearest.

A demon in the midst of lunging at him abruptly turned his mace on his comrade, caving in the unsuspecting victim's skull with one terrible blow.

Malfurion suddenly detected something amiss. The hair on his neck rising, he started to look over his shoulder.

A humongous, four-legged beast leapt upon him. Two wriggling tentacles with toothy suckers at the end drove into his chest. Row upon row of yellowed, fanged teeth filled his gaze. A stench like rotting flesh assailed him.

Somewhere beyond his own ghastly predicament, he heard Illidan cry out, the shout cut off by a sound vaguely reminiscent of a hound's howl.

They had been deceived, put purposely off-guard by the frontal attack so that an even worse foe could come at them from behind. The felbeasts had been set to spring the moment the opportunity arose.

Malfurion screamed as the vampiric suckers literally tore the magic from his body much as the teeth would soon tear his flesh. To any spellcaster, felbeasts were an especially insidious foe, for they hunted those with the gift for magic and drank from them until nothing but husks remained. Worse, given enough energy to devour, the demonic hounds could multiply themselves several times over, creating an epidemic of evil.

He tried to tear the tentacles free, but they had clamped tight. The night elf felt his strength waning . . .

. . . And then what sounded like the patter of rain filled his ears.

The felbeast shook. The tentacles released their hold and flailed about until, with a ponderous groan, the demon fell to the side, almost collapsing on Malfurion's arm.

Blinking away his tears, the night elf discovered more than a dozen sharp bolts sticking out of the felbeast's thick hide. Each shaft had been expertly aimed to strike the most vulnerable areas. The demon had been dead before it had even dropped.

From the forest above came more than twoscore riders clad in gray-green armor and sitting atop huge, black saber-toothed panthers called night sabers. The massive cats darted between the trees with an agility and swiftness unmatchable by almost any other creature.

"Spread out!" called a young officer whose voice sounded familiar to Malfurion. "Make certain there are no more!"

The soldiers moved out quickly, but with caution. Malfurion could appreciate their care, for he knew that, this being daylight, they were not at their best. Still, the druid could not deny that their skills were admirable, not after they had saved his life.

Riding up to Malfurion, the officer reined the hissing cat to a halt. The night sabers, too, did not like this switch from dark to light, but they were gradually growing to tolerate it.

"Is this to be my fate, then?" asked the somewhat round-featured night elf. He seemed to be studying Malfurion very intently, though the latter knew part of that was simply due to the sharper slant of the officer's silver eyes. "Trying to keep from getting yourselves slaughtered? I should've begged his lordship to let me keep my posting in the Suramar Guard."

"But then this might've turned out different, Captain Shadowsong," Malfurion replied.

The soldier exhaled in frustration. "No . . . it wouldn't have, because Lord Ravencrest would've never let me go back to the Guard! He seems to think I was anointed by the Mother Moon herself to protect the backs of his special servants!"

"You came back to Suramar in the company of myself, a novice priestess of Elune, a mysterious wizard . . . and a dragon, captain. I'm afraid we marked you in the eyes of

Lord Ravencrest and the other commanders. They'll never see you as a simple Guard officer again."

Shadowsong grimaced. "I'm no hero, Master Malfurion. You and the others slay demons with barely the wave of a hand. I just try to preserve your heads so that you can continue to do it."

Jarod Shadowsong had had the misfortune to capture Krasus while the latter had tried to enter Suramar. The mage had used the captain to gain aid for himself, which in turn had resulted in bringing Malfurion and the others, including Korialstrasz, together at last. Unfortunately for the good officer, his dedication to duty meant that he had accompanied his prisoner through the entire incident; that, most of all, had stuck in Lord Ravencrest's mind when he determined that his spellcasters needed someone to watch over them. Jarod Shadowsong soon found himself "volunteered" to command a contingent of hardened soldiers, most of whom had far more military experience than himself.

"There was no need for all this charging about," Illidan snapped as he joined his brother. "I had this situation in hand."

"My orders, Master Illidan. As it is, I barely caught sight of you leaving on your own, against his lordship's commands." Shadowsong swung his gaze back to Malfurion. "And when I discovered how long *you* had been missing . . ."

"Hmmph," was all Illidan responded. For one of the few times in recent days, the twins were in agreement—neither cared for Lord Ravencrest's demand that they be constantly watched. Doing so only made them more eager to escape. In Malfurion's case, it was due to the nature of his calling; in Illidan's it was because he had no patience for the endless councils. Illidan did not care for battle plans; he just wanted to go out and destroy demons.

Only . . . this time it had almost been the demons who destroyed him. Neither he nor Malfurion had sensed their nearness, a new and frightening aspect. The Burning Legion had learned how to better cloak its assassins. Even the forest had been blithefuly ignorant of the taint in its midst. That did not bode well for the future of the struggle.

One of the other soldiers rode up to Shadowsong. Saluting, he said, "The area's clear, captain. Not a sign of any more—"

A bone-shivering cry echoed through the forest.

Malfurion and Illidan turned and ran in the direction of the source. Jarod Shadowsong opened his mouth to call them back, then clamped it shut and urged his mount after.

They did not have far to go. A short distance further into the woods, the gathered party paused before a gruesome sight. One of the night sabers lay sprawled across the ground, its torso ripped open and its entrails spilled out. The huge cat's glassy eyes stared sightlessly skyward. The animal had been dead no more than a minute or two, if that long.

But it was not the beast that had been the source of the blood-chilling cry. That had been the soldier who now hung skewered on his own sword against a mighty oak. The night elf's legs dangled several feet above the earth. Like the cat, his chest had been methodically torn open—that despite his armor. Below his feet lay most of what had fallen free. His mouth hung open and his eyes were a perfect copy of the panther's own empty orbs.

Illidan eagerly looked around, but Malfurion put a sturdy hand on his brother's shoulder and shook his head. "We do as the captain said. We go back. Now."

"Get his body down," ordered Shadowsong, his face losing some of its violet pigment. He pointed at the twins. "I want an escort around them this instant!" Leaning down to the pair, the captain added with some impatience, "If you don't *mind*, of course."

Malfurion prevented his brother from making any remark back. The pair dutifully marched up the rise toward their mounts, the bulk of the escort constantly circling them like a pack of wolves surrounding prey. It was ironic to Malfurion that he and his brother wielded more power than all the soldiers put together and yet they would likely have died if not for Jarod Shadowsong's intervention.

We've much to learn still, the young druid thought as he neared his night saber. I *have much to learn still.*

But it seemed that the demons were not going to allow anyone the precious time needed for that learning.

Krasus had lived longer than any of those around him. His lanky, silver-haired form gave some indication of the wisdom he had gathered over that time, but only by gazing deep into his eyes did one garner any hint of the true depths of the mage's knowledge and experience.

The night elves thought him a variant of their own race, some sort of albino or mutation. He resembled them enough, even though his eyes were more like a dwarf's in that they had pupils. His hosts accepted his "deformities" by marking them as evidence of his powerful links to magic. Krasus wielded the arcane arts better than all the vaunted Moon Guard combined, and with good reason.

He was neither a night elf nor even merely an elf . . . Krasus was a dragon.

And not any dragon, but the elder version of the very leviathan with whom he spent much of his time, *Korialstrasz.*

The cowled mage had not, as he had indicated to others, come with red-haired Rhonin from a distant land. In fact, both he and the human wizard had come from far, far in the future, from a time after a second and decisive battle against the Burning Legion. They had not, however, come by choice. The two had been investigating a curious and unsettling anomaly in the mountains when that anomaly had swallowed them, tossing both through time and space into ancient Kalimdor.

They were not the only ones, either. An orc—the veteran warrior, Broxigar—had also been swallowed. Brox's people had also fought the demons that second time and his Warchief had sent him and another to investigate a troubled shaman's nightmare. Caught on the edge of the anomaly, Brox's companion had been ripped apart, leaving the older orc to fend for himself when he arrived in the past.

Circumstance had gradually thrown the dragon, the orc, and the human—all former enemies—together. But circumstance had *not* given them a way back to the future and that, most of all, worried Krasus.

"You are brooding again," rumbled the dragon.

"Merely concerned about your coming departure," Krasus told his younger self.

The red dragon nodded his huge head. The pair stood at the wide, solid battlements of Black Rook Hold, the imposing citadel from which Lord Ravencrest commanded his forces. Contrary to the lively, extravagant homes of his contemporaries, Ravencrest kept a very martial residence. Black Rook Hold had been carved from thick, ebony rock, as solid a structure as any ever made. All the chambers above and below ground had been chiseled out. To many, Black Rook was a fortress impenetrable.

To Krasus, who knew the monstrous fury of the Burning Legion, it was one more house of cards.

"I do not wish to depart," spoke the red dragon, "but there is a silence among our kind. I cannot even sense my beloved Alexstrasza. You of all should understand my need to discover the truth."

Korialstrasz knew that his companion was a dragon like himself, but he had not made the connection between past and future. Only his queen and mate, the Mother of Life, understood the truth and she had not told her new consort. That had been a favor to him—or rather, to his *older* self.

Krasus, too, felt the emptiness and so he accepted that his younger version would have to fly off to discover the reason why, even if it meant risk for both of them. Together they were an astonishing force, one most valued by Lord Ravencrest. While Korialstrasz sent showers of flame down on the demons, Krasus could expand that flame into a full firestorm, slaying a hundred and more of the foe in a single breath. But when they were divided, illness struck them, rendering both nigh impotent.

The last vestiges of sunlight disappeared on the horizon. Already the area around the edifice bristled with activity. The night elves dared not grow complacent at any time, day or evening. Too many had perished early on because of habit. Still, the darkness was always welcome, for as much as they were tied to the Well of Eternity, the night elves were also strengthened by the moon and stars.

"I have been thinking," said Krasus, letting the wind caress his narrow features. Because of his immense size, Korialstrasz could not enter Black Rook Hold. However, the solid rock structure of the keep enabled him to stay perched atop it. As such, Krasus chose to sleep there, too, using only a thin woven blanket for comfort. He also ate his meals and spent nearly all his waking moments on the battlements, descending only when duty called. For other matters, he turned to Rhonin, the only one here besides himself who truly understood his situation.

"There may be a way by which we can still journey alongside one another," he continued. ". . . So to speak."

"I am eager to hear it."

"There is on you at least one loose scale, yes?"

The dragon spread his wings and shook like a huge dog. His scales clattered in rhythmic fashion. The behemoth's great brow furrowed as he ceased and listened, then twisted his serpentine neck to investigate an area near his rear right leg. "Here is one, I think."

Dragons generally lost scales in much the way other creatures lost fur. The areas exposed generally hardened, eventually becoming new scales. At times when more than one broke free, a dragon had to take care, for the soft flesh was, for a time, susceptible to weapons and poison.

"I would like to have it . . . with your permission."

For anyone else, Korialstrasz might have refused, but he had come to trust Krasus as he did himself. Someday, Krasus hoped to tell him the truth, providing that they lived that long.

"It is yours," the crimson giant replied readily. With his back paw, Korialstrasz scratched at the spot. Moments later, the loose scale fell to the floor.

Quickly retrieving it, Krasus inspected the scale and found it to his liking. He looked up at his companion. "And now, I must give you something in return."

"That is hardly necessary—"

But the dragon mage knew better; it would bode him ill if anything happened to his younger self because of Krasus's interference with the past. "Yes, it *is*."

Putting aside the head-sized scale, he stared at his left hand and concentrated.

The slim, elegant fingers suddenly gnarled, becoming reptilian. Scale spread across the flesh, first from the fingertips, then racing down the hand until just past the wrist. Sharp, curved claws grew from what had once been flat nails . . .

As the transformation took place, a sharp agony coursed through Krasus. He doubled over and nearly collapsed. Korialstrasz instinctively reached for the tiny figure, but the mage waved him back. "I will survive it!"

Gasping for breath, still doubled over, Krasus seized the hand he had altered and tore at the tiny scales. They resisted his efforts. He finally gritted his teeth and tugged on two as hard as he could.

They tore free, leaving a trail of blood pooling on the back of his monstrous appendage. Swallowing hard, the gaunt figure immediately let the hand revert, and, as it did, the pain receded.

Ignoring his self-inflicted wound, Krasus inspected his prizes. Eyes sharper than any night elf's looked for the slightest imperfection.

"You know that what afflicts us both does not allow you to transform to your natural shape any more than it lets me change into other than a dragon," Korialstrasz chided. "You risk yourself terribly when you attempt such an act."

"It was necessary," Krasus replied. He turned the bits over, frowning. "This one is cracked," he muttered, letting the scale in question fly away in the wind, "but the other is perfect."

"What do you intend to do with it?"

"You must trust me."

The dragon blinked. "Have I ever done otherwise?"

Taking the tiny scale, the mage went to where Korialstrasz had scratched free his own. The area was still red and soft and large enough for any good archer to hit.

Whispering words older than dragons, Krasus pressed the scale directly on the center of the open region.

The scale flared a bright yellow as it touched. Korialstrasz let out a gasp, but did not otherwise react. The dragon's eyes gazed intently on what his companion did.

Krasus chanted the elder words over and over, each time increasing the speed with which he spoke them. The scale pulsated and with each pulsation seemed to grow a little larger. Within seconds, it had become almost identical to those surrounding it.

"It will adhere to your flesh in a matter of seconds," Krasus informed the leviathan. "There will be no chance of losing it."

A moment later, he stepped back and inspected his handiwork. The dragon's head came around to do the same.

"It feels . . . normal," the leviathan commented.

"I hope it does more for you. As I now carry a part of you with me, so you, in turn, carry a part of me with you. I pray the synergistic magics involved will give us some of the benefit we receive when actually with each other."

Korialstrasz spread his wings. "There is only one way to find out."

Krasus agreed; to discover whether the spell had worked, they would have to separate. "I bid you farewell, then, good Korialstrasz."

The huge beast dipped his head low. "And I, you."

"Alexstrasza—"

"I will tell her of you and your wishes, Krasus." The dragon eyed the tiny figure carefully. "I have suspicions about our links, but I respect the need you have to keep your secrets from me. One thing I discovered quickly, though, is that you love her as much as I. *Exactly* as I."

Krasus said nothing.

"As soon as I can, I will tell you how she fares." Moving to the edge of the battlements. the dragon looked to the sky. "Until we meet again, my blood . . . "

And with that, the crimson titan leapt into the air.

My blood . . . Krasus frowned at the choice of words. To dragons, such a term meant close ties. Not mere comrade or clan, but closer yet, such as brothers from the same clutch of eggs or offspring and parent . . .

Or . . . the same being in two bodies . . .

Krasus knew himself better than anyone. He had no doubt as to his younger self's intelligence. Korialstrasz almost had the truth in his grasp and the mage had no idea what that might mean for both of them.

Weakness suddenly overtook him. Through quickly watering eyes, Krasus sought out Korialstrasz's scale. The moment he seized it, some of the pain and weariness left him. But touching it was not enough; he had to keep it closer to him for the effect to be worthwhile.

Exposing his chest to the cool night wind, the dragon mage planted the large scale against his flesh. Again he muttered the ancient words, stirring up forces no night elf could understand, much less wield.

The same golden aura flared around the scale. Krasus shook, fighting to keep his balance.

As quickly as it had appeared, the aura faded. He stared down at his chest, now covered in the center by his younger self's parting gift.

A slight hint of weariness still pervaded his being, though both it and the tinge of pain also present were nothing Krasus could not readily suffer. Now at last he could walk among the others and not feel their pity. Now he could stand beside them against the demons. The mage wondered why he had not thought of this plan much earlier—then recalled that he had, but only bothered to put it into action once Korialstrasz had declared his intention to seek out the other dragons.

It is hard to part with one's self, apparently. How Rhonin would have laughed at his conceit. The irony made even Krasus chuckle. How Alexstrasza would have enjoyed the jest as well. She had more than once suggested that his continuous intrusion into the matters of the lesser races had a touch of vanity involved, but this act now more than topped that in every—

A sudden wave of vertigo struck him.

It was all he could do to keep himself from slipping over the battlements. The attack ended swiftly, but the repercussions kept Krasus leaning against the stone wall and breathing heavily for more than a minute.

When he could at last stand straight, the dragon mage immediately looked far beyond Black Rook Hold, far beyond Suramar.

To distant, dark Zin-Azshari.

Krasus continually had many secretive spells in play, several designed to keep track of what other sorcerers might be casting. He was, without conceit, perhaps more attuned to the shifts in the intensity of the world's magical forces than anyone—but even he had not been prepared for a change of such magnitude.

"They have done it . . ." he breathed, staring at the unseen city. "The portal is again open to the Burning Legion."

THREE

The pain of his death had been unbearable. He had been destroyed in more than a dozen horrific manners simultaneously, each one sending through him such torture that he had embraced oblivion as a long-yearned-for lover.

But the agony of his death could not even compare to that which followed.

He had no body, no substance, whatsoever. Even *spirit* was not the right word for what was left of him. He knew that he existed by the sufferance of another, and understood that the anguish he constantly felt was that other's punishment for him. He had failed the other and failure was the ultimate sin.

His prison was a nothingness without end. He heard nothing, saw nothing, felt nothing other than the pain. How long had it been—days, weeks, months, years, centuries . . . or only a few horrible minutes? If the last, then his torture was truly monstrous, indeed.

Then, without warning—the pain ceased. Had he a mouth, he would have shouted his relief, his joy. Never had he felt so grateful.

But then he began to wonder if this respite only signaled some new, more horrendous terror.

I have decided to redeem you . . .

The voice of his god filled him with both hope and fear. He wanted to bow, to grovel, but lacked the form with which to do either . . . or anything else, for that matter.

I have decided that there is a place for you. I have looked into the darkness within you and found that which once pleased me. I make it the core of what you are to become and in doing so make you a far superior servant than you were . . .

His gratitude for this greatest of gifts was boundless, but again he could do nothing.

You must be reshaped, but so that others will mark in you the glory I give and the punishment I mete out, I return that by which they will know you best . . .

A crackle of energy shook him. Tiny specks of matter suddenly flew into the center of the energy storm, gathering and condensing, creating of him substance once again. Many had been bits of him when he had been destroyed and, like his soul, had been taken by his god at the moment of death.

Slowly, vaguely, a body formed around him. He could not move, could not breathe. Darkness covered him, and he realized that the darkness was actually his vision returning to him.

And as he truly began to see for the first time since dying, he noted that he had arms and legs different from those which he had formerly worn. The legs bent back at the knee and ended in cloven hooves. Like the legs, his arms and hands were covered in a thick fur, and his fingers were long and clawed.

He felt his face mold differently and sensed the bent horns sprouting from his forehead. Nothing about him reminded him at all of his previous incarnation and he wondered how he could still be known to others.

Then, with hesitation, he reached up and touched his eyes . . . and knew that they were the mark. He felt the innate forces within them growing more powerful, more precise with each passing second. He could now make out the very strands of magical energy recreating him, and saw how the invisible hand of his god restructured his body to make him far greater than that which he had once been.

He watched as his god's work continued, marveling and admiring the perfection of it. He watched as he became the first of a new kind of servant, one which even the others who attended the master would envy.

And he watched with artificial eyes of black crystal, across the center of which ruby streaks coursed.

The mark by which those who had once known him would recall his name—and know new fear.

Lord Kur'talos Ravencrest stood in front of the high, stone chair where he usually held court and faced the assembled commanders. A tall figure even among the seven-foot-high night elves, he had a long, narrow visage much akin to that of the black bird whose name he bore, even to the downward turn of his nose. His tufted beard and stern eyes gave him an appearance of both wisdom and might. He wore the gray-green armor of his troops, but also marked his superior rank with a billowing cloak of gold and a mighty, red-crested helm from which the stylized head of a raven peered down.

Behind the chair hung the twin banners of his house, square flags of rich purple with the ebony silhouette of the avian in the middle. The banner of House Ravencrest had become the de facto symbol of the defenders, and there were those who spoke of the noble in terms once reserved only for the queen.

But Lord Ravencrest himself was not among those and as Malfurion listened, his anxieties concerning the direction in which the counterattack was headed increased.

"It is clear," stressed the bearded night elf, "that the point of focus *must* be Zin-Azshari! There is where these abominations originated and there is where we must strike!"

Rumbles of approval swept over the night elves gathered to listen to him. Cut off the foe at his most critical point. Without Zin-Azshari to strengthen them, the demons already on the field would surely fall to defeat.

Ravencrest leaned toward his audience. "But it is not merely monsters from beyond we face! In Zin-Azshari, we confront a most duplicitous foe—our own kind!"

"Death to the Highborne!" someone shouted.

"Yes! The Highborne! It is *they*, led by the queen's advisor, Lord Xavius, who have brought this calamity upon us! It is *they* who now must face our swords and lances and pay for their crimes!" The noble's countenance grew even more grim. "And it is *they* who hold our dear Azshara prisoner!"

Now roars of anger burst forth. Several cried, "Blessed is our Azshara, the Light of Lights!"

Someone next to Malfurion muttered, "They remain blind even now."

He turned to see the red-haired mage, Rhonin. Although a foot shorter, the odd-looking figure was broader of build and looked as much a fighter as a master wizard. The only human among them—the only human *anywhere* as far as Malfurion knew—Rhonin caused comment merely by existing. The night elves, haughty and prejudiced when it came to other races, treated him with deference because of his power, but few would have invited him into their homes.

And even less likely to receive such an invitation was the grotesque, brutish figure next to him, one almost as tall as Malfurion but built like a bear. Slung on his back was a huge, twin-edged battle ax that appeared made of wood, yet somehow gleamed like steel.

"Those who do not see the truth in battle march willingly to defeat," grunted the tusked, green-skinned warrior, his philosophical words belying his savage form.

Broxigar—or Brox, as he preferred to be called—shook his head at the night elves' unwavering devotion to their queen. Rhonin's cynical smirk in response to the orc's words only added to Malfurion's discomfort at how his people appeared to the outsiders. They could readily see what few of his kind other than himself could—that Azshara *had* to know what happened in the palace.

"If you knew what she has been to us," the night elf muttered, "you would understand why it is so difficult for them to accept her betrayal."

"It doesn't matter *what* they think," Illidan interjected from in front of him. "They'll attack Zin-Azshari either way and the end result will be the same. No more demons."

"And what if Azshara comes out and tells them that she's seized control of the demons from the Highborne, and that everyone's now safe?" Rhonin countered pointedly. "What if she tells her people to lay down their arms, that the battle's over? And then what if the Burning Legion falls on Ravencrest and the rest while the queen laughs at their folly?"

Illidan had nothing to say to that, but Brox did. He gripped the hilt of his dagger and muttered under his breath, "We know her betrayal. We know. We make sure this queen plays no tricks . . ."

Rhonin tilted his hooded head to the side in consideration of this suggestion, while Illidan's face masked whatever opinion he had on the dread subject. Malfurion frowned, caught between the remnants of his own devotion to Azshara and his realization that eventually someone would *have* to put an end to the queen if the world hoped to survive this monstrous invasion.

"If and when the time comes, we do what we have to," he finally replied.

"And that time approaches swiftly."

Krasus slipped into the back of the chamber to join them, an arrival that left all of them silent. The pale, enigmatic wizard moved with more assurance, more health, yet obviously the dragon from whom he seemed to draw strength could not be out in the hall.

Rhonin immediately went to him. "Krasus, how is this possible?"

"I have done what I have done," the latter said, absently touching the three small scars on his face. "You should know that Korialstrasz has departed."

While the news was unexpected, it still struck them hard. Without the dragon, the night elves would have to depend upon their small band even more.

At the other end of the room, Lord Ravencrest continued his speech. "Once there, the secondary force, under Lord Desdel Stareye, will then pull in from the south, squeezing them in from the two sides . . ."

Next to the dais, a very slim night elf—clad in the same armor as Ravencrest but wearing a cloak of intertwining green, orange, and purple lines—nodded to the speaker. Stareye's helm had a long, shimmering crest of night saber fur. The helm itself was decorated with a multitude of tiny, gem-encrusted stars. In the center of each had been set a golden orb—an overall gaudy display to the outsiders, no doubt, but well-appreciated by Stareye's compatriots. The night elf himself seemed to be constantly staring down his long, pointed nose at anyone he looked at—anyone other than his host, that is. Desdel Stareye knew the importance of attaching himself to the House of Ravencrest.

"We must move swiftly, surely, yes," Stareye added uselessly. "Strike at the heart, yes. The demons will cower at our blades, grovel for our mercy, which we shall not give." Reaching into a pouch on his belt, he took a white powder and sniffed it.

"May the heavens help us if that popinjay ever becomes leader," murmured Rhonin. "His armor gleams as if newly-forged. Has he ever fought a war?"

Malfurion grimaced. "Few of our kind have. Most prefer that 'distasteful' duty to Lord Ravencrest, the Moon Guard, or the local forces. Unfortunately, bloodline dictates who is granted a high rank in troubled times."

"Not unlike humans," Krasus said before Rhonin could respond.

"Strike at the heart and quickly," Lord Ravencrest agreed. "And we must do so before the Highborne succeed in re-opening the way for more of the monsters—"

To the surprise of Malfurion and the others, Krasus stepped forward and dared interrupt. "I fear it is already too late for that, my lord."

Several of the night elves took affront at this interruption by one not of their own kind. Ignoring them, Krasus strode toward the dais. Malfurion noted that the mage still showed subtle signs of strain. Whatever he had done to enable him to walk free of the dragon had not completely rid him of his mysterious malady.

"What's that? What do you mean, wizard?"

Krasus stood before Ravencrest. "I mean that the portal is already open."

His words reverberated through the assembly. Several night elves lost a shade or two of their purple color. Malfurion could not blame them. This was hardly welcome news. He wondered how they would react when they discovered that they had also lost the one dragon who had been aiding them.

Desdel Stareye looked down at the outsider. "And you know this *how?*"

"I felt the emanations. I know what they mean. The portal is open."

The haughty noble sniffed, his way of indicating his distrust of such questionable evidence. Lord Ravencrest, on the other hand, accepted Krasus's dire pronouncement with grave faith. "How long?"

"But a few minutes before I entered here. I verified it twice before I dared come."

The master of Black Rook Hold sat back in his chair, brooding. "Ill tidings, indeed! Still, you said it was but a short time ago . . ."

"There is some hope yet," the mage said, nodding. "It is weak. I can sense that. They will not be able to bring through too many at once. More important, their master will be unable to physically enter yet. Should he attempt to do so, he will destroy the portal . . ."

"What does it matter if he stays where he is and simply directs them?" asked Stareye with another sniff.

"The Burning Legion is but a shadow of his terrible darkness. Trust in me when I say that we have hope even if every demon who serves him comes through, but *no* hope if we destroy all only to have him step into the world."

His words left silence in their wake. Malfurion glanced

at Rhonin and Brox; their expressions verified Krasus's warning.

"This changes nothing," Ravencrest abruptly declared. He faced the audience again, expression resolute. "Zin-Azshari remains the focus, now more than ever! Both the portal and our beloved Azshara await us there, so there is where we march!"

The night elves rallied almost immediately, so trusted was the elder commander when it came to war. Few night elves had the reputation that Lord Ravencrest held. He could draw people to his banner almost as well as the queen could to hers.

"The warriors are already set to march! They have but been awaiting our decision! I give you all leave to depart after this gathering and prepare each of your commands! By the fall of day tomorrow, we push on toward the capital!" Ravencrest raised his mailed fist high. "For Azshara! For Azshara!"

"For Azshara!" shouted the other night elves, Illidan included. Malfurion knew that his brother added his voice because of his position as Black Rook Hold's sorcerer. Whatever Illidan believed concerning Queen Azshara, he would not jeopardize his recently-gained status.

The night elven officers nearly stormed out of the chamber in their eagerness to return to their soldiers. As they poured into the hall, Malfurion thought to himself how mercurial his people could be. A moment before, they had been lamenting the news of the portal's resurrection. Now they acted as if they had never even heard the terrible report.

But if they had forgotten it, Rhonin and Brox had not. They shook their heads and the red-haired wizard muttered, "This bodes ill. Your people don't realize what they're marching into."

"What other choice do they have?"

"You must reconsider sending messengers as I suggested," Krasus suddenly insisted.

The wizard still stood before Lord Ravencrest, who now was accompanied only by a pair of dour guards and Desdel Stareye. Krasus had one foot on the dais and his expression was as animated as Malfurion had ever seen it.

"Send out messengers?" scoffed Stareye. "You jest!"

"I accept your anxiety," their host replied, "but we've hardly sunk so low. Fear not, Master Krasus, we *will* take Zin-Azshari and cut off the portal! I promise you that!" He adjusted his helmet. "Now, I think we both have plans to make before the march, eh?"

With Lord Stareye and the guards in tow, the noble marched out of the room as if already the victor. Illidan joined his patron just before the party vanished. Krasus watched Ravencrest depart, his countenance anything but pleasant to behold.

"What was that you tried to convince him of?" asked Rhonin. "Messengers to whom?"

"I have been trying—in vain, it appears—to persuade him to ask for assistance from the dwarves and other races—"

"Ask the *other* races?" blurted Malfurion. Had Krasus asked him beforehand the odds of success, the young night elf would have immediately tried to dissuade him from even suggesting such to the master of Black Rook Hold. Even with Kalimdor under siege and hundreds or more already dead, no lord would ever demean himself by even thinking of contacting outsiders. To most night elves, dwarves and such were barely one step above vermin.

"Yes . . . and I see from your expression that attempting to speak later with him about it will be just as futile."

"You know how hard it was to convince the dwarves,

orcs, elves, and humans to work together in our—where we came from," Rhonin remarked. "Not to mention the complexity of getting each of the factions and kingdoms within those groups to trust one another."

Krasus nodded wearily. "Even my own kind have their prejudices . . ."

It was as close as he had ever come to identifying what he truly was, but Malfurion did not press. His curiosity concerning his ally's identity was a slight thing compared to the potential holocaust they all faced.

"You didn't tell them about the dragon leaving," he said to Krasus.

"Lord Ravencrest knows of it. I sent word of it to him as soon as Korialstrasz declared his decision."

Rhonin frowned. "You shouldn't have let Korialstrasz go."

"He shares a concern with me about the dragons. As should you." Some wordless communication passed between the two wizards, and Rhonin finally nodded.

"What do we do?" asked Brox. "We fight with the night elves?"

"We have no choice," Rhonin answered before Krasus could. "We're trapped here. Things've become too tangled *not* to take an active part." He stared deep into the elder mage's eyes. "We can't just stand by."

"No, we cannot. It has gone beyond that. Besides, I find I will not abide waiting for assassins to come targeting me. I *will* defend myself."

Rhonin nodded. "So it's settled."

Malfurion did not understand all that they said, but he recognized the end of what had been a long, stressful argument. Evidently, despite all he had done for the night elves, Krasus still had reservations about aiding them. An irony, so the druid saw it, after how much effort Krasus had spent pushing for Lord Ravencrest to approach the dwarves and tauren.

It occurred to him then that they had all decided to join the host marching on Zin-Azshari. With those last doubts erased, Malfurion realized there was one other person with whom he needed to speak before that happened. He could not leave Suramar without seeing her.

"I must go," he informed them. "There—there is something I need to do."

His cheeks must have flushed, for Krasus kindly nodded, adding, "Please give her my greetings, will you?"

"I—of course."

But as he started past the elder mage, Krasus took hold of his forearm. "Do not steel yourself against your emotions too much, young one. They are a part of your calling, your destiny. You will need them greatly in the days ahead, especially as *he* is no doubt here now."

"Here?" Rhonin's brow furrowed. "Who? What else haven't you told us?"

"I am only using logic, Rhonin. You saw the beast Mannoroth guiding the Legion when it first swept out from the city. You know that, despite him, we were able to not only cut off the portal, but also inflict serious damage to the demon army."

"We beat Mannoroth. I know. We did it in the—back home, too."

Krasus's eyes had a veiled look to them that stirred Malfurion's anxiety anew. "Then you should also recall what happened *after* his defeat."

The night elf saw Rhonin blanch. Brox, too, seemed disturbed, but his reaction was more like Malfurion's. The orc understood that something dire was about to be revealed, but did not know just what.

"Archimonde." The human whispered the name so quietly that he almost appeared worried that its bearer might hear it even in Ravencrest's sanctum.

"Archimonde," repeated Brox, now understanding. He gripped the hilt of his dagger and his eyes darted back and forth.

"Who—who is this Archimonde?" asked Malfurion. Even saying the name brought a distaste to his mouth.

It was Rhonin who answered him, Rhonin with his eyes unblinking and his mouth set in utter hatred. "He who sits at the right hand of the lord of the Burning Legion . . ."

Captain Varo'then brought the news to his queen as he always did. With Lord Xavius dead, he had become her favored . . . in more ways than one. His new uniform—a resplendent, glittering emerald green with golden sunbursts across the chest—was the latest gift bestowed upon him by Azshara. His title remained that of captain, but in truth, he commanded more than some generals, especially as even demons followed his orders.

Varo'then swept aside his glittering golden cape as he entered the queen's sanctum. Her attendants immediately curtsied, then stepped away.

Azshara herself lay draped across a silver couch, her head resting perfectly on a small cushion. Her hair, more silver than the couch, cascaded gracefully down her back and shoulders. The queen had long, almond-shaped eyes of pure gold and features of perfection. The gown she wore—a wondrous, translucent blue and green—displayed her curved form magnificently.

In her hand, Azshara held a view globe, a magical artpiece that displayed for its user a thousand different exotic images of night elven creation. The image that faded away as the soldier knelt appeared to be that of Azshara herself, but Varo'then could not be certain.

"Yes, my dear captain?"

Varo'then forced his cheeks not to flush from desire. "Radiance of the Moon, Flower of Life, I bring important tidings. The Great One, Sargeras—"

She immediately sat up. Eyes wide, full lips parted, the queen asked, "He is here?"

A pang of jealousy struck the officer. "Nay, Light of Lights, it is not yet possible for the portal to hold the magnificence of the Great One . . . but he has sent his most trusted to finally make the way ready."

"Then I must greet him!" Azshara declared, rising. Attendants immediately darted out of hiding to take her train. The long, silken gown trailed for some distance. The skirt was cut so that the queen's long, smooth legs briefly revealed themselves as she walked. Everything about Azshara spoke of seduction and although he knew that she toyed with him as she did others, Varo'then did not care.

The instant that she started forward, several new figures lurched out of the shadows. Despite their huge forms, the Fel Guard who acted as her personal bodyguard had remained unseen until now. Two stepped in front of the pair while the rest lined up behind. The demons waited patiently, emotionlessly, for the queen to move again.

He raised his armored forearm so that she might place her perfect, tapering fingers upon it. The captain led her through the gaily-painted marble halls of the palace to the tower where the surviving Highborne sorcerers had restarted their efforts. Sentries both night elf and demon stood at attention as they passed. Varo'then had studied the Legion enough to understand that while Mannoroth and Hakkar seemed astoundingly oblivious to the queen's beauty, the lesser demons appeared not so immune. Her bodyguard had become especially protective of her, even keeping a wary eye on their own brethren at times.

It did not do for even demon lords to underestimate the ruler of the night elves.

A pair of felbeasts guarded the outside door. The tentacles on each houndlike demon twitched toward the pair.

Immediately the Fel Guard created a protective wall between Azshara and the hounds. Felbeasts drained magic the way some insects drank blood, and Azshara had, contrary to appearances, a great aptitude for sorcery. To the creatures, she would seem a feast.

Varo'then had his own weapon out and ready, but Azshara touched his cheek gently and said, "No, dear captain."

With a wave of her hand, she parted the Fel Guard, then walked up to the felbeasts. Ignoring the menace of the tentacles, the queen knelt before the pair and smiled.

One monster immediately planted his fearsome head under her outstretched hand. The other opened a mouthful of rows of jagged teeth and let his thick, brutish tongue loll out the side. Both acted as Varo'then had seen three-day-old night saber kits do around Azshara.

After petting both on their coarse heads, the queen urged the monsters aside. The felbeasts readily obeyed, sitting down near the wall and looking as if hoping for some tiny treat.

The captain sheathed his weapon. No, it would not be good for *anyone* to underestimate his beloved monarch.

The way opened for Azshara as she stepped past the felbeasts. Following close behind, Varo'then saw immense Mannoroth look over his shoulder at the new arrivals. As much as he could read the demon's expression, the captain noted some distress. Mannoroth, at least, was not so pleased with the coming of the Great One's second.

And as the night elves entered, they could not help but notice that Archimonde had already arrived.

For the first time, Azshara momentarily lost a bit of her cool composure. The brief, open-mouthed gasp vanished swiftly, but it still startled Varo'then . . . almost as much as the demon himself did.

Archimonde stood as tall as Mannoroth, but that was where the likenesses ended. By any standard, he was far more handsome and in some ways resembled the night elves over whom he towered. His skin was a black-blue, and it took Varo'then a moment to realize that Archimonde surely had to be related to the Eredar warlocks. His build was similar and he even sported a fearsome tail like theirs. No hair covered any part of his body. His skull was huge and his ears wide and pointed. From under a narrow brow ridge, orbs of deep green stared out. He wore armor plating on his shoulders, shins, forearms and waist, but little else. An arresting display of lines and circles tattooed over his body radiated high magic.

"You are Queen Azshara," he said in smooth, articulate words, a vast contrast to Mannoroth's more guttural speech or Hakkar's hiss. "Sargeras is pleased by your loyalty."

The female night elf actually flushed.

His steady, unblinking gaze turned to Captain Varo'then. "And the Great One always approves of the capable warrior."

Varo'then went down on one knee. "I am honored."

As if no longer acknowledging the pair as anything of interest, Archimonde turned to where the sorcerers worked. A black gap hung in the midst of the pattern they had created, a gap that, despite its tremendous size, had surely disgorged the huge demon with difficulty.

"Hold the way steady. He will be coming through now."

"Who?" Azshara blurted. "Sargeras is coming?"

With utter indifference, Archimonde shook his head. "No. Another."

Varo'then chanced a glance Mannoroth's way and saw that the tusked demon, too, was puzzled.

The edges of the black gap suddenly shimmered. The Highborne maintaining the portal immediately shook as their efforts demanded more than ever from them. Several gasped, but wisely did not falter.

And then . . . a shape coalesced in the portal. Though smaller than the demons, it somehow radiated a forceful presence nearly on par with Archimonde or Mannoroth even before it put one foot out onto the mortal plane.

Or rather . . . one hoof.

On two legs like those of a shaggy goat, the figure stepped toward the demon commanders and night elves. The lower half of his body was pure animal in design. The unclad torso, however, while so deep a purple that it was nearly black, was otherwise identical to that of a night elf, save far more muscled. A long mane of black-blue hair hung loose around the narrow visage. The huge, curled horns contrasted sharply with the elegant, pointed ears. The only clothes the newcomer wore was a wide loincloth.

But if any thought because of the lower half and horns that this was only a beast sent by the lord of the Legion, they had only to look into its eyes and sense the deep, cunning intelligence within. Here was a mind sharper and quicker than most, devious and adaptive where it needed to be.

Only then did the eyes themselves register on the soldier. There could be no mistaking the black, crystalline orbs—clearly artificial—and the streaks of crimson running across the centers.

Only one being he had ever known had possessed such fantastic eyes.

Captain Varo'then stood, but it was not from his mouth that the identity of the other was uttered. That came instead from Queen Azshara, who leaned forward, studied with pursed lips the leering visage that was and was not the face both she and the officer had known, and said, *"Lord Xavius?"*

FOUR

The night elven host assembled by Lord Ravencrest was truly impressive to behold, but Malfurion found no comfort in their great numbers as he waited for the noble's signal to begin the march. The young night elf looked to his right, where his brother and companions also awaited astride their mounts. Rhonin and Krasus constantly discussed some matter between themselves, while Brox stared ahead at the horizon with the clear patience of a seasoned warrior. Perhaps of all of them, the orc understood the overwhelming task they faced. Brox held the ax Malfurion and Cenarius had created for him as if already seeing the endless tide of enemy.

Despite Brox's clear knowledge of combat, Ravencrest and the rest of those in command of the host had not once turned to the orc for his experience and knowledge. Here was a creature who had fought hand-to-hand with the demons, yet no one asked him of their weaknesses, their strengths, or anything else that might give those on the front line a further edge. True, Krasus and Rhonin had provided some such insight, but theirs was tempered by a more familiar use of magic. Brox . . . Malfurion suspected that Brox could have taught everyone far more when it came to true fighting.

We are a people whose downfall may yet come because of our own arrogance . . . Malfurion frowned at his own pessimism, then lost the frown as the only sight that could cheer his heart came riding up to him.

"Malfurion!" Tyrande called, her expression pensive and worried. "I thought never to find you in all this!"

Her face was as he always remembered it, for he had long ago burned it into his memory. Once a childhood friend, Tyrande had now become for him a desire. Her skin was a smooth, violet shade and her dusky blue hair was tinged with silver. She had a fuller face than many of their kind, which added to her beauty. Her features were somehow delicate yet determined, and she had veiled silver eyes that ever pulled Malfurion inside. Her lips were soft and often wore a hint of a smile.

In contrast to the previous times that they had met, the novice priestess of Elune—the Mother Moon—wore an outfit more befitting the way of war than the peace of the temple. Gone was her flowing, white robe. In its place was a form-fitting suit of armor with layered plates that allowed much mobility. The armor covered Tyrande from neck to foot, and over it, almost as an inconsistency, was a shimmering, gossamer cloak the color of moonlight. In the crook of her arm, the young priestess held a winged helmet that would protect the upper portion of her face as well.

To Malfurion, she looked more like the priestess of a war god and evidently Tyrande could read such in his expression. With a bit of defensiveness, she admonished him, "You may excel at your new calling, Malfurion, but you seem to have forgotten the elements of Mother Moon! Do you not recall her aspect as the Night Warrior, she who takes the courageous dead from the field and sets them riding across the evening sky as stars for their reward?"

"I meant no disrespect to Elune, Tyrande. It was more that I've never seen you dressed so. It makes me greater fear that this war will forever change us all . . . providing we survive it."

Her expression softened again. "I'm sorry. Perhaps my own uneasiness makes my temper short. That, and the fact the high priestess has declared that I myself shall lead a group of novices into this conflict."

"What do you mean?"

"We are not going to ride with the host simply to offer our healing powers. The high priestess has had a vision in which the sisterhood *must* actively fight alongside the soldiers and the Moon Guard. She says that *all* must be willing to take upon themselves new roles if we're to keep the demons from victory."

"That may be easier said than done," Malfurion responded with a grimace. "I was just thinking how hard it is for our people to adjust to change of any kind. You should have been there when Krasus suggested that they call upon the dwarves, tauren, and other races to work with them."

Her eyes widened. "It's a wonder they work with him and Rhonin, much less tauren. Doesn't he realize that?"

"Yes, but he's as stubborn as one of us, possibly more."

He quieted as his brother suddenly joined them. Illidan gave him a cursory glance, then focused his attention completely on Tyrande.

"You look like a warrior queen," he told her. "Azshara herself could appear no finer."

Tyrande flushed and Malfurion wished that he had made some compliment—*any* compliment—for which the priestess might remember him before the host set off.

"You are the Night Warrior herself, in fact," Illidan continued smoothly. "I hear you've been put in charge of a band of your sisters."

"The high priestess says that my skills have much increased of late. She says that in all her years of guidance, I'm one of the swiftest to attain such levels."

"Not a surprise."

Before Malfurion could say anything similar, a horn suddenly blared. It was followed by another, then another, and so on as each segment of the mighty army signaled its readiness for departure.

"I have to return to the sisters," Tyrande told them. To Malfurion, she added, "I came to wish you well." Instinctively, the priestess turned to Illidan. "And you, of course."

"With your blessing, we're certain to ride to victory," Malfurion's sibling returned.

Again Tyrande flushed. Another horn sounded, and she quickly donned the helmet, turned her panther around, and rode off.

"She looks more suited for battle than either of us," Malfurion commented.

"Yes. What a mate she'll make for someone, eh?"

Malfurion looked at his brother, but Illidan had already urged his night saber toward Lord Ravencrest. As the noble's personal sorcerer, Illidan had to ride near the elder night elf. Malfurion and the others had been ordered to remain within shouting distance, but otherwise they did not have to stay with Ravencrest. The master of Black Rook Hold did not want all of his strongest weapons clustered together. The Eredar already knew to focus on the druid and the wizards whenever possible.

Jarod Shadowsong and three soldiers rode to him. "It's time to go! I must ask you to come with us!"

Nodding, Malfurion followed the captain back to the rest. Rhonin and Krasus wore almost identical dour expressions. Brox's had changed not one bit, but under his breath the orc appeared to be chanting.

"A march at night," commented Krasus, turning to watch the last vestige of day vanish. "How very predictable. Archimonde will note it. Despite their best to adapt, your people are still inclined to fall back to comfortable tendencies."

"With such numbers, we'll still be able to push the demons back," Captain Shadowsong insisted. "Lord Ravencrest will sweep the monsters from our fair land."

"So we can only hope."

A final horn sounded and the night elven host moved as one in the direction of Zin-Azshari. Regardless of his misgivings, Malfurion swelled as he watched the armed force cover the landscape. The banners of three dozen major clans highlighted a collection of alliances spanning the width and breadth of most of the realm. Foot soldiers marched in perfect unison like a swarm of dedicated ants heading to a feast. Night sabers leapt along in great prides a hundred strong and more, their helmed riders staring wearily ahead.

The bulk of the soldiers wielded swords, lances, and bows. Behind them came siege machines—ballistae, catapults, and the like—drawn by teams of the dark panthers. Most of those operating the machines were of Lord Ravencrest's clan, for in general night elves did not work with such devices. Only Ravencrest seemed to have the foresight necessary to lead his people to victory. That he had not sought the aid of the dwarves and others was bothersome to the druid, but in the end it would not matter. Despite his misconception that Azshara was innocent, the noble would still see to it that the Burning Legion fell to bloody defeat.

After all, there was really no other choice.

• • •

Urged on by Ravencrest and their own belief in certain victory, the night elves made good distance that first eve. Their commander finally gave the order to halt two hours into daylight. Immediately the host set up camp, a long line of sentries marking the front to ensure the demons would not catch them by surprise.

Here the land had not yet been touched by the horror of the Burning Legion. To the south, forest still stood. To the north, high, green hills dotted the landscape. The elder night elf sent out patrols to investigate each direction, but no foes were found.

Malfurion was immediately drawn to the woods, almost as if they called his name. When chance came, he separated from his companions and turned his mount toward them.

Jarod Shadowsong immediately noted his act. The captain rode after him, calling out as he approached, "I must ask you to turn back! You cannot go out there by yourself! Remember what happened—"

"I'll be all right, Jarod," Malfurion replied quietly. In truth, he felt that this particular patch of wilderness was shielded even from the demonic assassins who had so often preyed on him and his companions. How this could be, Malfurion could not say, but he knew it with the utmost certainty.

"You cannot go alone—"

"I'm not. You're with me."

The soldier gritted his teeth, then, with a look of resignation, followed the druid into the forest. "Please . . . just not so long."

Promising nothing, Malfurion continued on into the deeper part of the forest. A feeling of trust, of faith, over-

whelmed him. The trees welcomed him, even seemed to recognize him—

And then he understood why he felt so at home in this
place.

"Welcome back, my *thero'shan* . . . my honored student."

Captain Shadowsong looked around for the source of the
stirring voice, a voice reminiscent of both the wind and thunder. Malfurion, on the other hand, waited patiently, knowing
that the speaker would reveal himself in his own fashion.

The wind abruptly picked up around the duo. The officer
held tight to his helmet while the druid bent his head back to
better feel the breeze. Loose leaves began rising up in the
wind, which grew stronger, fiercer. Yet, only the captain appeared dismayed by this; even the night sabers raised their
snouts up to inhale the fresh wind.

A miniature whirlwind arose before the riders. Leaves,
brush, bits of stone and earth . . . more and more they gathered within, compacting together to form something solid.

"I have been waiting for you, Malfurion."

"By the Mother Moon!" Jarod gasped.

The giant moved on four strong legs akin to those of a
stag; the bottom half of his torso was indeed the body of one.
Above that, a barrel-chested form similar in coloring and
shape to a night elf peered down at the two intruders with
orbs of pure golden sunlight. A hint of forest green tinged the
otherwise violet flesh and the fingers ended in gnarled but
deadly talons of aged wood.

The newcomer shook his head, sending his thick, moss-
green mane fluttering. Leaves and twigs appeared to be growing naturally within both the mane and the wide, matching
beard, but they were not as astonishing as the huge, multilay-
ered set of antlers rising high over the giant's head.

Malfurion bowed his head in reverence. "My *shan'do*. My

most honored teacher." He looked up. "I am happy to see you, Cenarius."

Although both night elves stood a good seven feet tall, Cenarius towered over them and their mounts. At least ten feet in height himself, his antlers gave him at least another four feet. He was so impressive, in fact, that the captain, who had conversed face-to-face with a dragon, could only gape.

With a slight chuckle that seemed to make all the nearby birds decide to sing, Cenarius declared, "You are welcome here, Jarod Shadowsong! Your grandsire was a true friend of the forest!"

Jarod shut his mouth, opened it again, shut it once more, then merely nodded. Like all night elves, he had grown up hearing the tales of the demigod, but like most of his people, he had assumed that they were simply that—tales.

The forest lord gazed down at his pupil. "Your thoughts are in crisis. I felt it even in the Emerald Dream."

The Emerald Dream. It had been some time since Malfurion had walked it. In the Emerald Dream, one saw the world as it might have been in its earliest creation—no animals, no people, no civilization. There was a tranquillity to it; a dangerous one, in fact. One could become so caught up in it that one forgot how to return to the mortal plane. The walker might instead wander forever while his body finally perished.

Taught to travel it by Cenarius, Malfurion had used the dreamscape to enter the palace prior to his struggle with Lord Xavius. Since that event, however, the young druid had been afraid to return, the vague memories of the aftermath still haunting him. He would have drifted through the Emerald Dream for eternity if not for his teacher just barely noticing him.

Cenarius saw his anxiety. "You must not be afraid to walk

it again, my son, but now is not the time. However, there are other parts of your training that have lagged and that is why I chose this pause to come to you."

" 'This pause'? What do you mean?"

"The others are still divided as to what to do about the demons. We will fight them, yes, but we are creatures of individual spheres of power. It is difficult for us to work in harmony, for we all feel we know what is best to do."

The news did nothing to temper Malfurion's uncertainties. First the dragons had failed to show any inclination to battle the Burning Legion, and now even the demigods, the guardians of the natural world, could not agree on the proper course of action. Truly, it was all up to the night elves . . . likely Malfurion and his comrades, in particular.

"Our time together will not be long. There are some things that I must quickly try to teach you. We will need use of the entire day—"

"Out of the question!" blurted Captain Shadowsong, surprising himself. "My orders are—"

With a benevolent smile, the woodland deity trotted toward the soldier. Jarod's face paled as Cenarius loomed over him.

"He will be protected while he is with me and will be back when he is needed by your commander, Jarod Shadowsong. You will not be shirking your responsibility."

The officer shut his mouth, already clearly dumbfounded that he had dared interrupt Cenarius in the first place.

"Return to your other charges. I will see to it that Malfurion comes back safe and sound."

The druid felt as if the pair discussed a child, but the demigod's words were evidently what Jarod had wanted precisely to hear. He nodded to Cenarius, turning the nod into a bow at the last moment. "As you say, my lord."

"I am not your lord, night elf. I am Cenarius only! Go with my blessing!"

With one last awed glance at Malfurion and his teacher, the captain turned his night saber and rode off toward the night elven host.

Cenarius turned back to his student. "Now, my *thero'shan*, we must begin in earnest." All congeniality vanished from the deity's expression. "For I fear we will need all the knowledge we have if we are to save our world from the demons . . ."

At that moment, another who feared they would need all that they could gather to defeat the Burning Legion flew over the realm of the dragons, seeking the lofty mountain peak where his kind made their homes.

Korialstrasz had spent his long flight considering many things. The silence of his brethren was one. Dragons were reclusive, but never had he encountered such utter quiet. No one responded to his summons, not even his beloved mate, Alexstrasza.

This caused him to think of the demons. He could not believe that they could have attacked and destroyed the dragons, but the lack of communication left that fear alive. He almost wished that Krasus had accompanied him, for at least then there would have been one other red dragon with whom to discuss the dire thoughts.

But Krasus himself was a subject on par with all else. More and more, Korialstrasz had begun eliminating the possible theories concerning this enigmatic dragon to whose words even Alexstrasza paid close attention. She did so as if Krasus were the equal to her consorts, even perhaps *was* one. Yet, this could not be . . . unless . . .

No . . . that is not possible, the soaring behemoth thought. *It is too extraordinary . . .*

Still, it would explain so very much.

He would confront Alexstrasza with his thoughts once he found her. Korialstrasz banked, turning toward the familiar, mist-enshrouded mountain. Unlike all times past, there were no sentinels keeping watch, yet another ominous sign.

The great red dragon descended toward the high cavern mouth used as one of the main entrances to the sanctum. As he alighted, he turned his massive head back and forth, seeking some sign of his fellows. The area was deathly silent.

But as he folded his wings and moved forward, he collided with a sudden, distinct force invisible to all his other senses. It felt as if the air had taken on a thickness akin to honey. With great determination, Korialstrasz threw himself forward, barreling into the unseen wall as he would against a rival dragon.

Slowly it gave way. He felt it press around his body as he advanced, almost enveloping him. The dragon had difficulty breathing, and his view became as if he saw the world from under water. Yet still Korialstrasz did not falter.

And suddenly, without warning, he was through.

Sounds instantly filled his ears. Bereft of any barrier, the leviathan fell forward. He would have landed headfirst, but huge paws caught him.

"It is good that you are back," a deep voice rumbled. "We feared for you, young one."

Tyranastrasz lifted him up, the reptilian countenance of Alexstrasza's senior consort filled with concern. Behind him, other dragons moved about through the system of tunnels . . . and what surprised Korialstrasz most about the activity was the fact that there were dragons of *other* colors. He saw blue, green, bronze, and, of course, red. The dragons intermingled constantly, all seeming on some task and all obviously quite anxious.

"Alexstrasza! Is she—"

"She is well, Korialstrasz. She gave word that she would speak with you the moment that you returned . . ." The larger male glanced at the younger's shoulder, seeking something. " . . . and Krasus, too, but I see that he is not with you."

"He would not leave the others."

"But your condition—"

Flexing his wings, Korialstrasz replied, "He has devised a manner by which we are both *nearly* whole. It is not perfect, but it is the best we could do."

"Most interesting . . ."

"Tyran . . . what happens here? Why are the other flights among our own?"

The elder consort's expression grew veiled. "She has commanded that she be the one to tell you all and I will not disobey her."

"Of course not."

With Tyranastrasz in the lead, the pair wended their way into the lair of the red flight. Korialstrasz could not help but eye the other dragons as they passed among them. The greens were mere flitting shadows, gone before one realized they were even there, and made more disconcerting by the fact that they ever kept their eyes closed, as if sleepwalking. The bronze figures of Nozdormu's flight seemed not to move at all, but somehow were elsewhere whenever he blinked. As for the blues, they appeared here, there, everywhere in almost random fashion, darting about through the use of magic as much as physical movement. The more Korialstrasz saw of them, the more he welcomed the stable, solid presence of his own kind. When they moved, they moved. When they rushed to one destination, he could follow their every step, see their every breath.

Of course, in all fairness, he suspected that the newcomers felt the same way about their respective flights.

So many different dragons, and yet we all fit in here, he suddenly thought. *Are we so few as all that, then?* Had they tried to crowd the night elves or dwarves in this mountain, either lesser race would have filled it to overflowing, yet the dragons ever found room to maneuver.

Thinking of the endless horde that was the Burning Legion, Korialstrasz wondered if even the dragons had the strength to stop them.

But as he entered the next chamber, his fears melted away. She stood there as if waiting for him in particular. Her simple presence filled the male with calm, with peace. When she looked his way, Korialstrasz felt confidence. All would be well. The Queen of Life would see that it was so.

"Korialstrasz . . . my beloved." Only her eyes gave indication of how much force that simple sentence had. The lesser creatures might often see dragons only as savage beasts, but even the best of them could not possibly match the intensity of emotions Korialstrasz's kind wielded.

"My queen, my existence." He bent his head low in homage.

"It is good that you are back. We feared for you."

"As I feared in return. No one answered my summons, or explained the sudden silence."

"It was necessary," the huge female responded. Despite the sleekness of her form, Alexstrasza outweighed her consorts by half again as much. Like all of the great Aspects, she commanded forces that dwarfed those of even her mates. "The demand for secrecy is paramount."

"Secrecy? For what?"

She studied him. "Krasus is not with you?"

He noted her tremendous concern. She worried about

Krasus as she would have Korialstrasz. "He chose to stay behind. He managed a trick that enables us to spend our time apart from each other without suffering . . . much."

A brief smile spread across her scaled visage. "Of course *he* would."

Before Korialstrasz could pursue the line of conversation to what he desired to know about Krasus, another entered the high chamber from the right. Korialstrasz looked at the new arrival, and his eyes widened.

"It is necessary that *all* dragons take part in this ritual," the black giant rumbled, his voice like a smoldering volcano. "Mine have already done so. The other flights must now do the same."

Neltharion filled the other end of the chamber, the only one who could possibly match Alexstrasza in size and power. The Earth Warder radiated an intensity that made Korialstrasz a bit uncomfortable.

"My final consort is here," Alexstrasza returned. "The bronze flight has come and although Nozdormu is not with them, they have brought that which is part of his essence so that he, too, will be joined with us in this struggle. That leaves only Krasus, a single entity. Is that so terrible a thing?"

The ebony dragon tilted his head. Never had Korialstrasz seen so many teeth. "One dragon only . . . no . . . I think not."

"What is this about?" the younger male dared ask.

"The demons have reopened the way to our world," Alexstrasza explained. "Once more, they flow through like water, doubling their strength with each passing day."

Korialstrasz imagined the monstrous army and what its numbers had already accomplished. "Then we *must* act!"

"We are. Neltharion has devised a plan, possibly the only hope for our world's survival."

"What is it?"

"Neltharion must show you."

The ebony behemoth nodded, then closed his eyes. The air shimmered before him. A sense of astounding power touched Korialstrasz's magical senses. He felt as if the chamber had filled with a thousand dragons.

But instead, a tiny, almost insignificant little golden disk materialized in the air, hovering just below eye level for the gathered leviathans. Korialstrasz sensed nothing within it, yet somehow knew that very fact meant the disk was much, much more than it seemed.

The Earth Warder opened his eyes, an expression of exaltation spreading over his reptilian features. To Korialstrasz, it was as if Neltharion worshipped his creation.

"Behold that which will exorcise the demons from our world!" the black leviathan thundered. "Behold that which will cleanse the lands of all taint!"

The tiny disk flared bright, suddenly no longer insignificant to the eye. Now, the young red male felt the full extent of the powers within . . . and understood why even Alexstrasza believed it to be their best recourse.

"Behold," Neltharion roared proudly. *"The Dragon Soul."*

FIVE

aptain Varo'then was not one to be made ill at ease by shadows and noises. He confronted all such things with the same dour earthiness with which he did everything else in his life. The scarred soldier had been born to the role of warrior and, despite his inherent cunning, never saw himself in any other role. He had no desire to be king or consort save that it would then place him even closer to Azshara. He commanded his forces in her name and was satisfied with that. The political machinations he had always left to Lord Xavius, who understood and savored them far more than Varo'then ever could.

But of late, his mind had been forced to turn to paths other than those of battle. That had to do with the return of one he had assumed quite dead . . . Xavius himself. Now the queen's advisor, brought back from the afterlife by the astounding power of the great Sargeras, again guided the will of the Highborne. That should have not bothered Varo'then, but Xavius had changed in ways even the queen did not see. The captain was certain that the advisor—or this thing that had once been the advisor—concerned himself not with the glory of Azshara, but with other matters. Varo'then, whatever his loyalty to the lord of the Legion, was ever first and foremost his queen's servant.

"The ever-efficient captain. Of course I find you stalking the halls even when not on duty."

The officer jumped, then silently cursed himself for reacting so.

As if pouring out of the shadows themselves, Xavius stepped out in front of the night elf. His hooves clattered on the marble floor and he breathed in snorts as he moved. Archimonde had called Xavius a satyr, one of Sargeras's blessed servants. The unnatural eyes that the noble had himself put in place of his own stared out from under the deep brow ridge. They snared the captain's own, drawing him inexorably into some unsettling place.

"Sargeras sees much promise in you, Captain Varo'then. He sees one whose status could be great among those who serve him. He sees you as a commander of his host, set up there along with Mannoroth—nay—*Archimonde*, even!"

Varo'then saw himself at the head of a horde of demons, his sword thrust out before him as they poured over their foes. He felt the pride and love of Sargeras as he rode down those who would defy the Great One.

"I am honored to serve," the soldier murmured.

Xavius smiled. "As are we all . . . and we would serve in any way we could, if it would make the dream come true sooner, is that not so?"

"Of course."

The hooved figure leaned close, his face nearly touching the soldier's own. The eyes continued to pull Varo'then in, both tantalizing and unnerving him at the same time. "You could serve in a manner better suited for you, in a role that will lead you sooner to the command you desire . . ."

Excitement coursed through the officer. He again pictured himself leading armies in the name of his queen and Sargeras. He imagined his conquest of their enemies, the blood of the foe flowing so much it created rivers.

But when Captain Varo'then tried to imagine himself doing all this, he could not see his own form distinctly. He tried to draw forth an image of himself as a warrior, an armored and armed commander such as in the old epics . . . but another shape persistently pushed itself on him.

A shape much like that worn by Lord Xavius.

That, at last, enabled him to pull free of the advisor's gaze. "Forgive me, my lord, but I must be about my duties."

The artificial eyes flared briefly. Then Xavius nodded ever so politely and with a sweep of his hand bid the soldier to move on. "But of course, Captain Varo'then, but of course."

At a quicker pace than he would have preferred to display before the horned figure, Varo'then marched away. He did not look back. His hand clutched the hilt of his sword as if about to draw it. The night elf did not slow until he was certain that Lord Xavius had been left far behind.

But even then he could still hear the beguiling words of the satyr . . . and Varo'then knew that where he had managed to deny them, others would not.

As night fell upon Lord Ravencrest's forces, the Sisters of Elune spread out among the night elves to give their blessings. Even clad like warrior maidens, the priestesses brought peace and comfort to the soldiers. Elune offered the night elves strength and confidence, for she was always there in the heavens, watching down on her favored children.

Although her expression did not reveal it, Tyrande Whisperwind felt none of the peace or strength she passed on to her people. The high priestess seemed to think that she especially had been touched by the Mother Moon, but

Tyrande sensed no great presence within herself. If the Mother Moon had chosen her for something, she had failed to inform Tyrande.

The last bit of daylight fled beneath the horizon. Tyrande hurried, knowing that soon the horns would sound and the host would move on toward Zin-Azshari. She touched the heart of one more soldier, then strode to her waiting panther.

But before she reached it, another night elf confronted her. Out of reflex, Tyrande put a hand to his chest—only to have him take her hand by the wrist.

The priestess looked up and her own heart at first leapt with joy. Then she noted the dark uniform and the hair bound back in a tail.

Most of all, Tyrande noticed the amber eyes.

"Illidan . . ."

"I'm grateful for your blessing, of course," he responded with a wry grin. "But I'm comforted more by your near presence."

Her cheeks flushed, though not for the reason he thought. Still gently holding her wrist, Malfurion's twin leaned close.

"Surely this is fate, Tyrande! I've been looking for you. We're entering fast-moving times. Decisions must be made without hesitation."

With sudden anxiety, she understood what he intended to ask—nay, *tell* her. Without meaning to, Tyrande pulled back her hand.

Illidan's face immediately grew stony. He had missed neither her reaction nor the meaning behind it.

"It's too soon," she managed, trying to assuage his feelings.

"Or too late?" The wry grin returned, but to her it now

appeared to be slightly hollow, more of a mask. After a moment, though, Illidan's face relaxed. "I've been too impetuous. This isn't the right time. You've been trying to comfort too many. I'll speak with you again, when the moment is more appropriate."

Without another word, he headed toward where a mounted guard in the garb of Ravencrest's clan awaited with the sorcerer's own night saber. Illidan did not look back as he and his escort rode off.

More troubled than ever, Tyrande sought her own panther. Yet, even as she mounted, another came to interrupt her thoughts. This time, however, it proved to be a more welcome soul.

"Shaman, forgive this intrusion."

With a gentle smile, she greeted the orc. "You are always welcome, Broxigar."

Only she was allowed to call him by his full name. To all others, even Lord Ravencrest, he was merely Brox. The massive orc stood a good head shorter than her, but made up for it with a girth three times her own and nearly all of that muscle. She had seen him wade into enemies with the ferocity of one of the huge cats, but around her he acted with more respect than many of those who asked for her blessing.

Thinking that a blessing was what the orc had come for, Tyrande reached down to touch his chest. Brox looked startled, then welcomed the touch.

"May the Mother Moon guide your spirit, may she grant you her silent strength . . ." She continued on for a few seconds more, giving the orc a full blessing. Most of the other priestesses found him as abhorrent as the rest of the night elves did, but in Tyrande's eyes, he was no less one of Elune's creatures than herself.

When she had finished, Brox dipped his head in gratitude,

then muttered, "I am not worthy of this blessing, shaman, for that is not why I've come to you."

"It isn't?"

The tusked, squat face twisted into what Tyrande recognized as remorse. "Shaman . . . there is something that burdens my heart. Something that I must confess."

"Go on."

"Shaman, I have tried to find my death."

Her lips pursed as she struggled to understand. "Are you telling me that you tried to kill yourself?"

Brox pulled himself up to his full height, his expression darkening. "I am an orc warrior! I've not guided my dagger to my own chest!" As abruptly as his fury had arisen, it now vanished completely, replaced only by shame. "But I've tried to guide the weapons of others to it, true."

And the story came flowing out. Brox told her of his last war against the demons, and how he and his comrades had held the way while they awaited reinforcements. Tyrande heard how, one by one, all the other orcs had perished, leaving only the veteran. The actions of Brox and the others had helped save the battle, but that had in no manner made him feel any less guilty about surviving where others had not.

The war had ended soon after, leaving Brox with no proper method by which to atone for what he saw as a tremendous failing on his part. When the Warchief Thrall had requested that he hunt down the anomaly, he had seen it as a sign that the spirits had finally granted him an end to his misery.

But the only one to die in that search had been his young comrade, which added to Brox's already heavy burden. Then, when it became clear that the Burning Legion would invade Kalimdor, the orc had once more hoped for redemption. He had thrown himself into the struggle and fought as hard as any warrior could be expected. He had always been at the forefront, daring any foe to take him on. Unfortunately, Brox had fought too well, for even after slaying a score of the demons, he had survived with barely a scratch.

And as the gathered host had set out from Suramar, the graying orc had finally started to think that he had committed a different sin. He realized that the shame that he had felt in surviving his former comrades had been a false one. Now Brox felt a new shame; everyone around him fought for life while he sought to *escape* it. They went to battle the Burning Legion for reasons opposite his own.

"I accept that I might die in battle—a glorious fate for an orc, shaman—but I am filled with dishonor for seeking it at the possible cost of those who fight against evil for their lives and those of others."

Tyrande stared into the eyes of the orc. Beast he was to the rest, but once more he had spoken words of eloquence, of meaning. She touched his rough cheek, smiling slightly. How arrogant her people were to see only the image, not the heart and mind.

"You need not confess to me, Broxigar. You've already confessed to your heart and soul, which means that the spirits and Elune have heard your remorse. They understand that you have realized the truth of things and regret your earlier thoughts."

He grunted, then, to her surprise, kissed her palm. "I give thanks to you even still, shaman."

At that moment, the horns sounded. Tyrande quickly touched the orc on the forehead, adding a slight prayer. "Whatever fate battle holds for you now, Broxigar, the Mother Moon will watch over your own spirit."

"I thank you for saying so, shaman. I will trouble you no more now."

Brox raised his ax in respect, then trotted off. Tyrande watched the orc vanish among the other fighters, then turned as a signal she recognized as coming from the sister-hood alerted her to her own need for haste. She had to be ready to lead her own group forward as soon as the host began to move. She had to be ready to meet the fate that Elune had planned for *her*.

And that, she understood, included matters other than the coming battle.

"They added soldiers from two more settlements in the northwest," Rhonin commented as he and Krasus rode. "I heard as many as five hundred."

"The Burning Legion can bring forth such a number in but a few scant hours, perhaps even less."

The red-haired wizard gave his former tutor a sour expression. "If none of this helps, then why bother? Why not just sit on the grass and wait for the demons to slit our gullets?" He took on a mock look of surprise. "Oh, wait! That's not what happened! The night elves *did* fight—and they won!"

"Quiet!" hissed Krasus, giving Rhonin as sharp a glare as the human had given him. "I do not downplay the additions, only point out the facts. Another fact to be recalled is that our presence here and the existence of the anomaly through all time means that what *has* happened in the past may not be what *will* happen this time. There is a very, *very* good chance that the Burning Legion *will* triumph now . . . and all we know will never have been."

"I won't let that happen! I *can't*!"

"To eternity, the fates of your mate Vereesa and your unborn twins are nothing, Rhonin . . . but I will fight for their sakes as much as I fight for my own flight's future, however monstrous that may still be even with victory."

Rhonin quieted. He knew as well as the dragon mage what fate would eventually befall the red flight. Even if the Burning Legion was defeated in this period, the dragons would still suffer terribly. Deathwing the Destroyer would see to it that the orcs gained control of them, especially Krasus's own red flight, and used them as beasts of war. Many, many dragons would die for no good reason.

"But there was just beginning to be hope for us again," Krasus added, his stare drifting momentarily. "And *that*, more than anything else, gives me another reason to see that history does not change."

"I only know what happened from the histories preserved by the wizards of Dalaran, Krasus. You know them from living this time—"

The gaunt, almost elven figure hissed again. "Your recollections based on the writings are likely more accurate than my own riddled mind. I have come to the conclusion that Nozdormu's intrusion into my thoughts, while helpful in setting us on this mission, also were too much for me to absorb completely without the loss of other memories." Nozdormu, the Aspect of Time, had been the one to call upon Krasus and warn him of the crisis. The huge, sand-colored dragon now could not be contacted even in this period, and Krasus feared that he was, in all his incarnations, trapped in the anomaly. "I fear that I will never entirely recall this time period—and what is missing is enough to fuel my uncertainties as to the outcome."

"So we fight and hope for the best."

"As has been done by everyone in battle throughout history, yes."

The bearded human nodded grimly. "Suits me just fine."

On and on the night elven forces traveled, advancing

miles without pause or delay. Most of the soldiers marched
with high spirits, for it seemed that the enemy was not at all
eager to match blades with them. With ears sharper than
any of the creatures around him, Krasus heard soldiers
pointing out that much of the destruction and death caused
by the demons had been on unsuspecting and ill-prepared innocents. Once they had faced an organized resistance, the
demons themselves had been slaughtered. Some even specu-
lated that if the night elves had pursued the Burning Legion
back to Zin-Azshari after that first battle instead of with-
drawing to gather more strength, then the war would have
already been over.

Such comments bothered Krasus; it was one thing to go
into battle with confidence, another to believe the foe so easily defeated. The night elves had to understand that the
Burning Legion was death incarnate.

His gaze turned to the one night elf who seemed to realize some of this. Krasus recalled that Malfurion would be a
key to winning this struggle, but he could not remember exactly how. That he was the first of the druids was a significant point, though not the only one. The dragon mage had
already determined that everything must be done to protect
him.

With nearly most of the night spent, scouts suddenly returned from the southeast. Ravencrest had organized a
steady stream of outriders to ensure the most up-to-date information possible.

The three night elves looked quite bedraggled. Clearly,
they had ridden their heavily-panting night sabers at a swift
pace for some time. Sweat covered their faces and grime colored their garments. Pausing only to sip water, they reported
their findings.

"A small column of the fiends is moving methodically

through the region of Dy-Jaru, my lord," said the senior scout. "We've seen smoke and fire and sighted refugees heading away."

"Estimate of the enemy's numbers?"

"Difficult to say for certain, but far less than this host, definitely."

Ravencrest tugged on his beard, considering. "Where are the refugees heading?"

"It looks to be Halumar, my lord, but they'll not make it. The demons are on their heels."

"Can we come between them?"

"Aye, if we hurry. There's just enough of a gap."

The noble reached out a hand to one of his aides. "Chart."

Immediately the proper map was handed to Ravencrest. He unrolled it, then had the scouts point out the locations of the refugees and the Burning Legion. When he saw them, he nodded. "We must move up the pace and prepare to meet them in daylight, but it can be done. We will still be on the path to Zin-Azshari. We can afford this minor detour."

"Especially as it might save a few innocent lives," Rhonin muttered under his breath to Brox.

Krasus leaned forward. "Did you mark the demons? What kind did you see?"

"Mostly those called the Fel Guard."

One of the other scouts added, "I saw a couple of the hounds and one of the winged demons, the Doomguard."

The dragon mage frowned. "A meager assortment."

"They no doubt ran far ahead of the rest in their zeal," Lord Ravencrest announced. "We shall teach them the benefits of restraint . . . not that they'll live long enough to appreciate the lesson." To his officers, he commanded, "Give the order! We head to meet them!"

The army shifted almost instantly. The night elves moved with eagerness, ready not only to save their kin, but to taste the first victory in their grand march to the capital.

Illidan and the Moon Guard shifted position, taking up areas along the width of the host. The Sisters of Elune did likewise, their groups poised to aid in whatever way necessary, be it healing or war. As the only outsiders, Rhonin, Krasus, and Brox remained together, although the two wizards had already agreed that Rhonin would watch Illidan once the battle began. Neither still trusted him to be cautious.

Malfurion stayed with them, in great part because Ravencrest was still uncertain over how best to use his unusual abilities. With Captain Shadowsong's unit guarding the four, the noble felt satisfied that the druid would be protected well enough for him to decide on his own what attacks would work against the demons.

Between having studied with Cenarius all day and riding most of the night with the prospect of battle imminent, Malfurion felt his exhaustion growing. The demigod had taught him how to better draw strength from the natural world and Malfurion hoped that he would be given the opportunity to do so before the night elves met the Burning Legion.

The sun rose over the horizon, vanishing quickly into a thick, low cloud cover that actually benefited the host. The spells that Krasus and Rhonin had used on both them and Brox enabled their vision to immediately adjust to the changing light, but the soldiers for the most part had let their eyes grow accustomed in the normal fashion. The cloud cover gave the nocturnal race some relief, further stirring their enthusiasm for the coming conflict.

The scouts continued to ride in and out gathering information. The demons had not yet caught up to the fleeing night elves, but they were close. Encouraged, Ravencrest urged his warriors on. Sending forth a large contingent of night saber riders, he planned to come at the Burning Legion from two sides.

When word came that the host had begun to cut between the refugees and their pursuers, the noble had the horns sounded. The signal set the soldiers into battle readiness.

And at last, as they flowed over a series of low hills, the night elves came upon the foe.

The fiery demons had laid waste to every inch of the land, leaving all scorched. No life existed behind them. The dead lands that Krasus witnessed while astride Korialstrasz spread to the horizon and the horror of it steeled the defenders more.

"It's as the scouts have reported," the master of Black Rook Hold muttered, drawing his sword. "All the better. Now we show them the folly of ravaging our fair land."

Krasus studied the horde. Still a great enemy, but nothing the night elves could not destroy readily. "My lord, caution is still suggested . . ."

But Ravencrest did not hear him. The elder night elf twice waved his sword back and forth, and every horn in the host blared at once.

With a single shout, the night elves descended upon the demons.

The Burning Legion did not falter at the sight of the superior force. Rather, the armored demons roared lustily, eager to add to the carnage that they had already wreaked upon Kalimdor. The refugees forgotten, they surged toward the night elves.

A set of two high notes was followed almost instantly by

a wave of arrows that filled the sky. Like shrieking banshees, the bolts dropped among the monstrous warriors, piercing throats, limbs, and heads. Dead and wounded demons toppled over everywhere, forcing others to slow to clamber over them.

A bolt of golden lightning struck the center of the horde, tossing Fel Guard left and right. Gobbets of flesh and the ooze that was the demons' blood rained down upon the survivors. Krasus looked to his left and saw Illidan laughing at the successful results of his first attack. The young sorcerer immediately directed several of the Moon Guard into a pattern akin to the one used during their first battle against the Burning Legion. Illidan planned to draw from his comrades and amplify their power through him.

The dragon mage frowned. Such tactics tended to drain those providing the power more than the one who cast the spell. Should he not pay attention to the condition of his companions, Illidan threatened to weaken them to the point where they could not defend themselves if personally attacked by the Eredar.

But concern for what Malfurion's brother might cause because of his negligence gave way to concentrating on the enemy alone. For the first time, Krasus cast a spell without the aid of Korialstrasz's presence. He did not know what to expect, but when he felt the power build up inside him, the elder conjurer smiled.

A fearsome wind swept over the center of the demons' front ranks. It threw the horned warriors together, even directed their weapons against one another. Mayhem arose among the enemy there.

The chaos gave the night elves a perfect opportunity. As the first of the soldiers reached the demons, they quickly slaughtered those they faced. The Legion's front lines could not maintain any organization. Fel Guard dropped by the scores as they sought in vain to regroup.

Another flight of arrows decimated the ranks further back. Within minutes, a good quarter of the horde lay either dead or dying. Krasus should have felt more confident, but he still found the battle moving much too easily. The Burning Legion had never fallen with so little trouble.

Not that he could discuss his uncertainty with the others. Brox had slipped in among the fighters and somehow gotten all the way to the front. Astride his night saber, he swung the huge ax around and around. Wherever the weapon's blades cut, the orc left death. The head of a demon flew over Brox as the green-skinned warrior shouted his challenge to the enemy.

As for Rhonin, he cast spells whose intensity made Krasus envious. Touching upon the green flames that were an inherent part of the demons, the red-haired wizard made them truly fiery and, in a sense, caused the demons to consume themselves. One after another they fell, quickly reducing to ash and a few bits of armor. Rhonin's expression was among the grimmest that Krasus had seen among the defenders; the dragon mage had no doubt that his former pupil thought constantly of his wife and un-born children, whose future literally hung on victory in this war.

Where was Malfurion? At first the lanky wizard could not spot the druid, but then he saw the young night elf at the rear of the host. Malfurion sat quietly atop his mount, his eyes closed in concentration. Krasus felt nothing at first, but then he noted a pressure in the earth, a pressure that moved toward the Burning Legion. With his magical senses, he followed its path, curious as to what would happen.

And suddenly, beneath the first few rows of the horde,

roots sprouted up. Tree roots, grass roots . . . any and every sort of root that one could imagine. Krasus realized that Malfurion had caused them to not only stretch forth from the untainted ground, but to grow as most could never possibly do under natural conditions.

A horned warrior stumbled, then, with a startled roar, fell forward into the waiting blade of a night elf. A felbeast growled and snapped as its massive paws became entangled. Everywhere demons tripped, twisted, and battled just to keep standing. They made for easy prey and scores more perished because of the roots. However, none of the night elves, Krasus saw, had even the slightest difficulty with the tendrils. In fact, several times the roots cleared paths for the soldiers, further aiding their cause.

With less than half of the demons still fighting, victory was surely at hand . . . and yet Krasus did not trust in the host's success. He surveyed the entire scene, finding nothing to add credence to his concerns.

Nothing, that is, save one lone winged demon flying up into the cloud cover. Krasus watched him ascend, then quickly tried to cast a spell.

He caught the demon just before the creature would have vanished into the clouds. The mist itself wrapped around the Doomguard warrior like a shroud, sealing his wings to his tall, armored form. The demon struggled, but could do nothing. A moment later, he dropped like a deadly missile toward his own comrades.

Krasus did not congratulate himself for his quick action. Urging his mount toward Lord Ravencrest, he sought the noble's attention. Unfortunately, Ravencrest moved away from him as he, in turn, attempted to give commands to some of his soldiers.

The dragon mage peered up at the clouds. There was still

a chance. If the night elves were warned quickly enough, disaster could yet be averted.

Then a tingling coursed through his body. Krasus lost control of his limbs. He slumped over the shoulders of his panther, and would have fallen off if not for the girth of the beast. Too late did Krasus realize that his fears for the host had left him momentarily open to the attack of an Eredar warlock.

And as he struggled to overcome the spell, Krasus's gaze twisted skyward. The clouds had thickened, darkened. They seemed to sag from their immense weight . . .

No . . . all that he saw was illusion, and he knew it. Fighting both the warlock's attack and the vision above, Krasus finally pierced the facade the demons had cast on the stormy sky. The swelling bottoms of the clouds vanished, revealing the truth.

From out of the heavens, the Burning Legion rained down upon the defenders.

SIX

Malfurion sensed something amiss even as his spell took full effect. The plants had been all too pleased to be a part of his desire, for they found the demons an abhorrence. With silent coaxing, he made them expand to lengths far greater than normal, then manipulated them so that they were more like the squirming, seeking tentacles of a kraken than simply roots. By doing so, he had enabled the soldiers to slay many of the demons.

But from another point far from the battle, his heightened senses detected a wrongness which he realized had to be a protective spell. Without opening his eyes, Malfurion reached out and discovered that the source lay not anywhere on the ground, but rather high above.

In the clouds.

Still seeing with the powers taught him by Cenarius, the druid delved into the cloud cover and sought what attempted to be hidden.

And in his mind Malfurion saw hundreds of airborne demons.

They were Doomguard for the most, so many that Malfurion could only assume that they had been gathered from other parts of the horde just for this. With their savage weapons and horrific faces, they were terrible to behold. Alone, they would be a terrible enough foe to confront.

Even more unnerving, however, were those that flew among them. There were Eredar warlocks, scores of them. They had no wings, but kept aloft through spells. Watching them, Malfurion knew that some kept the illusion consistent while others already sought out weaknesses in the night elven forces.

But as terrible as all this was, what soared toward the battle, from behind the Doomguard and Eredar, shook Malfurion the most. As if launched by a thousand catapults, huge, fiery rocks descended with terrible precision through the clouds. The druid pressed harder, avoiding the warlocks' senses as best he could, and saw the missiles for what they truly were.

Infernals.

Eyes snapping open, Malfurion shouted to any who could hear, "Beware the skies! They attack us from the skies!"

He caught Lord Stareye's attention briefly, but the noble simply sniffed his direction, then focused again on the demons' decimated ranks. Malfurion pushed his mount forward and seized one of the sentinels.

"Sound the warning! The demons attack us through the clouds!"

But the soldier only looked at him in befuddlement, not understanding. The illusion above still held, and any who looked upward surely thought the druid mad.

Finally, Malfurion saw another who seemed to understand. Krasus crossed his field of vision, the mysterious and pale mage seeming frantic about something. As their gazes met, both realized that the other understood. Krasus pointed, not at Ravencrest but rather at Illidan. Malfurion nodded, catching his meaning immediately; the druid had to warn one of the few who could quickly react to the threat above.

"Illidan!" Malfurion shouted, standing in the saddle in the hopes that his twin would see him. Illidan, though, was far too caught up in his spells to notice anything.

Concentrating, Malfurion asked the wind to aid him. When it agreed, he had it concentrate its efforts. Guiding it with his finger, the druid rubbed his own cheek twice.

His brother abruptly touched his cheek in turn, the wind having imitated Malfurion's touch. Illidan glanced over his shoulder and saw his twin.

Pointing skyward, Malfurion made a warning expression. Illidan almost turned away, but Malfurion grew angry and glared. His brother finally looked up.

At that moment, the first of the demons dropped through the illusion.

The Eredar struck the moment that they were visible, casting spells in unison that swept over the night elves' lines. Heavy droplets fell upon the soldiers, causing no major concern until the first began burning through armor and flesh. Cries arose from those struck as the shower became a monstrous downpour. Night elves fell writhing as their faces were seared away.

Malfurion spoke with the wind again, asking it to blow the torrent away from his people. As he did, he sensed Illidan and the Moon Guard casting their own spells.

One of the warlocks exploded with a shriek, one of the Doomguard nearby also perishing. However, when the night elven sorcerers sought to slay others, their attacks were met by an invisible shield.

The strong wind summoned by the druid pushed away the horrendous downpour, but the damage had already been done. The defenders' lines faltered.

Then, the Infernals began dropping.

The initial wave did not reach the earth. Two exploded and several more suddenly bounced against empty air, soaring in random directions away from the night elves. A bolt of blue lightning cut through one, two, three demons in rapid succession.

But despite the efforts of the sorcerers, the wizards, and the druid, too many of the Infernals descended. One struck the center of the already-ravaged line with catastrophic results. A dozen catapults filled with explosive powders could have done only a fraction of the havoc the single demon did. Like leaves in the wind, the night elves were tossed about. The shock of the strike sent others tumbling to the ground, where the Fel Guard quickly and viciously dispatched them.

More Infernals struck in rapid succession. All order fled the defenders' front. Worse, each massive demon who landed then rose from the steaming craters that they had created and began barreling through the night elves.

The powerful roots that Malfurion had summoned proved ineffectual against the skull-faced Infernals, who ripped through them as if they were nothing. By the scores the fiery behemoths pounded the night elves, wreaking mayhem wherever they moved.

Then a lance lost by a fallen soldier rose into the air just before one Infernal. Blazing blue, it suddenly shot toward the demon at a speed that made even the Infernal appear sluggish. As it flew with unerring accuracy at the demon, the lance grew, its head transforming into a sharp, almost needle-like point.

It skewered the one Infernal with such ease that the demon did not at first realize he was dead. The behemoth gaped, then twitched madly. His forward momentum ceased as the lance, propelled by magic, continued to drive ahead.

As if no heavier than an infant, the huge Infernal was dragged backward. The lance continued to speed up, catching another Infernal just as he emerged from the crater. The demon had time only to stare wide-eyed before it, too, was impaled.

Its swiftness not in the least decreasing, the magical spear caught a third Infernal unaware. Only then did its momentum cease and the missile and its victims dropped among the dead.

From Malfurion's side, Rhonin, his brow furrowed, nodded his satisfaction. But just when it appeared that the defenders might turn the battle again, horns sounded from the north.

"The Legion!" Krasus shouted. "They come from the other side!"

The full, awful truth now lay revealed. As if rising from the earth itself, an immense horde emerged from the north and fell upon the soldiers there. Like those above, they had been hidden by a spell. Now they swarmed like ants. The night elves fought valiantly, but their already-damaged lines buckled under the new onslaught.

The demons had planned their trap well, relying much on the arrogance of the night elves. What Ravencrest had seen as a minor skirmish, an easy victory with which to stoke the courage of his troops, had been instead a costly, sinister trick.

"We've got to retreat!" Rhonin said. "It's the only way at this point!"

At first, it appeared that Lord Ravencrest would not do what needed to be done. No signal to retreat came even though the demons pressed hard. Infernals continued to drop upon the night elves and the Eredar, some protecting the others, cast one vile spell after another. Malfurion and his companions could no longer attack; they had to do everything they could simply to deflect most of the warlocks' assaults. Even the Moon Guard could do little but shield the battered host.

Finally, the horns called out for retreat. The Burning Legion gave no quarter, though, and each step back was bought with more blood.

"This attrition is too great!" Krasus hissed, joining the druid. "We must create a gap between us and them!"

"But how?" asked Malfurion.

The slim mage's expression grew darker yet. "We must cease trying to fight the Eredar and concentrate only on keeping the main force of the demons from us!"

"But the warlocks will strike hard while we do that! They'll slay countless soldiers—"

"And *more* will perish if we move at this snail's pace!"

Krasus spoke the truth, however much the druid did not wish to hear it. The Fel Guard whittled away at the night elves left and right, constantly cutting at whatever foe lay within reach. The Eredar, on the other hand, needed time to cast their spells, and while those also did terrible damage, overall they now did less than the blades of their comrades.

"You must tell your brother to do as we do," the mage instructed.

"He won't listen to me. Not for that." It had been trouble enough to make Illidan look up. To convince him to do as Krasus desired would take far too long, if it was even possible.

"*I'll* do it," Rhonin offered. "He may listen to me better."

In truth, Illidan looked up to the human. Rhonin knew

how to cast spells even Malfurion's twin could not yet handle. Illidan almost saw him as a *shan'do*.

"Do what you can, then," Krasus said to Rhonin.

As the fire-tressed wizard rode off, Malfurion asked, "What do we do?"

"Anything that separates them from us."

The druid had hoped for more, but he understood that Krasus did not wish to overly guide him. They would work best if each did what they felt was most comfortable. The ways of the elder mage were not necessarily those of Malfurion.

Without waiting to see what the night elf would attempt, Krasus gestured toward the battle. At first Malfurion could not tell what he did, but then he noticed the foremost demons seem to shrink a foot or two. Only after a moment more did he see that they struggled with a sudden bog that had opened up beneath their feet. Those behind them clustered together, trying to battle through to the other side.

Rather than trying to attack again, the night elves wisely continued their retreat. But Krasus had only managed to aid *one* area of the battle; in others, Malfurion saw that the demons continued to cut down the defenders. He immediately reached down and spoke to the plants again, asking that they give of themselves their roots once more. They knew the dire developments and were aware that once the night elves left, they and all other life would be purged by the Legion. Nevertheless, they freely offered what they could.

Tears rolling down his eyes at this sacrifice, Malfurion carefully crafted his spell. The roots came up in even greater clusters than previously, becoming a veritable forest in reverse. The demons hacked away at the strong tendrils. Even the Infernals were finally slowed. The druid felt each cut into the roots, but his spell had the effect that he had intended. More and more, the night elves pulled away from their devious foe.

An unexpected reprieve came in the south in the form of night saber riders. Malfurion had forgotten about the force sent earlier by Ravencrest. Their numbers were smaller than he recalled, though they fought with no less fury. Several of the panthers had wounds already and more than one rider looked battered, but still they cut into the Burning Legion, buying precious seconds for those comrades on foot.

"The north!" Krasus shouted. "Focus on the north!"

Although they could not physically see the struggle in the north, both Malfurion and the mage had other methods by which to observe it. Reaching out, the druid sought birds or winged insects. He found none of the former, but still a few of the latter. Even the smallest fauna understood that to stay near the demons was to invite death. Yet the beetles he came across, already in the process of fleeing, agreed to be his eyes.

Through their peculiar field of vision, the druid soon viewed the other end of the struggle. What he saw made his heart sink. In even more vast numbers than he had ever seen them, the Burning Legion poured over the soldiers. The dead lay scattered everywhere. Faces too much like his own stared sightlessly in horror at what had slain them. Felbeasts tossed the dead around while other demons eagerly sought to add to the piles.

Malfurion looked for some creature or plant that he could use, but only the beetles seemed present. A breeze blew one of the insects about, finally giving the druid an idea. Speaking with the wind through the beetle, he first told it how much he admired its forceful gale, then convinced it to show him more.

The wind responded obligingly, creating a dust devil. With more urging by Malfurion, the dust devil grew larger and larger, soon dwarfing the huge demons. As it swelled in size, its intensity also increased a hundredfold.

When it had grown powerful enough, the druid directed its force against the demons in the forefront.

The Burning Legion ignored the fierce wind at first . . . that is, until it engulfed the first few and threw them to their deaths. Those nearest then scattered, but now they were pursued by a full-fledged tornado. Malfurion felt no pity for the demons, and hoped that they would soon be joined by many of their comrades.

"Do not grow overconfident," came Krasus's voice. "Our tactics have bought the army time, but nothing more."

The druid did not have to be told that, but he said nothing. The night elves were in no state to turn events around. All that Malfurion and the other spellcasters had done simply enabled the soldiers to survive.

Not satisfied that he had done enough, Malfurion sought through the beetles' eyes anything else that might be of use against the demons. The insects fluttered bravely over the Burning Legion, giving him five views simultaneously. Surely there had to be *something* that—

The druid screamed as something seized one of the beetles and crushed the life from it. Two of the survivors immediately fluttered away, but the remaining pair turned, giving the shaking night elf a glimpse at what had killed the hapless insect.

In the midst of the demons stood a dark-skinned figure who towered over the rest of the Burning Legion. He strode like a giant among his children, calmly directing the fearsome warriors in their monstrous efforts. Vaguely he reminded Malfurion of the Eredar, but was as much above them as they were above the Infernals. He wore elaborate shoulder armor and surveyed the violent battlefield with analytical indifference. From his right hand, the massive demon dropped the bits of shell that were all that remained of the beetle . . . then stared directly at one of those still being used by Malfurion.

And into the druid's mind.

So . . . you are the one.

An intense pressure filled Malfurion's head. He felt as if his brain was expanding, pressing against his skull.

Malfurion tried to call out for help, but his mouth would not work. In desperation, he sought the aid of anything near the demon, something that would distract the druid's attacker before it was too late.

Deep within the earth, something stirred. The rocks themselves, the eldest and hardiest of living forms, woke from their eternal slumber. They touched Malfurion with anger at first, for few things mattered to them more than their sleep. But the druid quickly focused their attention on what lay in the wake of the Burning Legion's rampage, pointing especially to the landscape itself.

Few there were who understood that rock lived, much less had any sense of the world. Now those he had awakened discovered the awful truth about the demons—that even the earth itself could not escape death at their hands. The foul magic that was an inherent part of the demons killed *everything*. Nothing, no matter how deeply buried, ever escaped.

And that fate included even the rocks. Those that lay buried behind the Burning Legion lacked any sentience whatsoever. Their life essences had been destroyed as readily as the blades of the Fel Guard killed night elves.

Malfurion fell to one knee as the demon's attack squeezed

his skull tight. It became impossible to think. The druid started to black out . . .

The ground rumbled. Malfurion dropped to both knees. Oddly, the pressure in his head now decreased.

Through the eyes of the beetles, he watched with astonishment as crevices opened up all around the monstrous figure who had attacked him. A smaller demon nearby tumbled into one fissure, which promptly shut on him. Other demons scattered from the area, leaving their gigantic leader to his own defenses.

The indifferent look never left the face of Malfurion's foe, but it was clearly all he could do to keep from falling into one of the many increasingly-vast chasms surrounding him. The sinister colossus reached out toward one of the beetles, but Malfurion immediately ordered both remaining creatures away.

As they retreated, the druid saw the demon draw a circle around himself. An immense green sphere formed, protecting its occupant from the savage quake. It hovered above the chaos even as other, lesser demons spilled into the new ravines.

The deep, monstrous orbs watched in turn the retreating forms.

I will know you, insect . . .

He did not refer to the beetles, but rather Malfurion. As his foe dwindled from sight, the druid realized that he, too, would recognize the demon when next they met. Already Malfurion suspected he knew by what name to call him, for surely this could only be one of the horrific commanders of the monstrous horde.

Surely this could only be *Archimonde*.

Hands seized him by the shoulder, breaking his link to the beetles. Instinctively, Malfurion expected to be torn apart by some other demon, but the hands were gentle, and the voice soft and caring.

"I have you, Malfurion," Tyrande whispered in his ears.

He could only nod. Vaguely noticing that he was no longer seated atop his night saber, Malfurion wondered what had become of the animal. Tyrande gently drew him up onto her own mount. Showing surprising strength, she hefted him in front of her, then urged the massive feline on.

Heart still pounding, Malfurion caught bits and pieces of the catastrophe as the priestess of Elune carried him off. Hundreds of soldiers trudged quickly over the rolling landscape as, far in the background, demons pursued them. In several places, flames rose between the forces, and here and there an explosion caused by some spell was punctuated by screams—whether night elf or demon, he could not say. Once, Malfurion witnessed the personal banner of Lord Ravencrest flutter by, but he saw no sign of the noble himself.

Faces passed across his vision as the night saber brought Tyrande and him to safety. Gone from the soldiers was the look of expectant triumph. In its place a terrible truth could now be witnessed; it was very possible that the night elves might *lose* this struggle.

He must have moaned upon seeing this, for Tyrande leaned close to his ear, whispering, "Never fear, Malfurion . . . I'll attend to your wounds the moment we can pause."

The druid managed to twist around and see her face. Much of it was hidden behind the war helmet of the sisterhood. The rest was covered in grime—and blood. From the determination with which Tyrande moved, Malfurion gathered the blood was not hers. It startled him to think that she had likely gotten closer to the heart of the battle than he had. He had always thought her calling a more gentle one, even with the armor.

"T-tyrande," the druid finally managed. "The others?"

"I've seen Broxigar, the wizards, and your brother all. Even the erstwhile Captain Shadowsong, who guides them like a protective herder." She said the last with an all-too-brief smile.

"Ravencrest?"

"He is still master of Black Rook Hold."

So, even after many losses, the core strength behind the host remained intact. Still, neither Ravencrest nor his many spellcasters had been able to prevent the disaster.

"Tyrande—"

"Hush, Malfurion. It amazes me that you can still speak, considering all that has happened to you."

He understood the intensity of the mental assault Archimonde had thrust at him, but did not know how she could have sensed it.

The priestess suddenly held him close. While Malfurion welcomed her touch gladly, he did not like the anxiousness he felt.

"Elune must have truly watched over you! So many ripped apart around you, even your own mount stripped bare, a horrific tangle of flesh and bone—and you barely marked."

Ripped apart . . . his own night saber torn to pieces . . . what had happened around him? Why had he not noticed the butchery? How had he survived all that in addition to the mental attack? The very notion of the terrible spectacle that had taken place unnoticed around him made him shiver.

Malfurion had no answers to his questions, but he did understand one thing. He had survived what had been thrown at him by one of the archdemons. On the one hand, he could be grateful for the miracle; on the other, he was aware that he had now been marked by Archimonde. They would meet again, that was almost assured.

And when they did, Malfurion knew the demon lord would do his best to make certain that next time, there would be no escape.

SEVEN

Peroth'arn struggled wearily into his personal chamber, finally free to recuperate a little of the strength that his constant work on the portal had drained from him. Before leaving to take personal command of the demonic horde, Archimonde had laid in place a concise plan by which the portal would gradually be adapted to withstand the entrance of the great Sargeras. Unlike Mannoroth, who flung the Highborne sorcerers into their work with no regard for their flagging power, Archimonde recognized that the night elves would not survive long enough to fulfill their duty if they did not have a chance to sleep or eat. He worked them hard, yes, but the respites he gave them actually had enabled the work to advance as never before, even under the guidance of Lord Xavius.

Thinking of his former master, Peroth'arn could not help but look over his shoulder. The room—a small chamber with but a wooden bed, a table, and a brass oil lamp—was filled with shadows, each of them reminding the sorcerer of the thing that had emerged after the glorious Archimonde. That the beast who walked on two legs had once been Xavius unnerved most of the Highborne. They had all lived in fear of the queen's advisor when he had been one of them, but now he radiated an unsettling presence that of late even haunted Peroth'arn's dreams.

Trying to shake off such concerns, the night elf distastefully inspected the bed. He was as dedicated to the work as they all were, but as one of the Highborne he was used to far better accommodations. He longed for his villa and his mate, neither of whom he had seen in days. Mannoroth had permitted no one to leave the palace, and in that, he and Archimonde were in full agreement. Therefore, the sorcerers had to sleep wherever they could—in this case, chambers once used by the officers of the guard. Captain Varo'then had willingly offered them up to the spellcasters, but Peroth'arn could have sworn that the scarred soldier had done so with a slight wry smile. Varo'then and his underlings were used to a more spartan existence and Peroth'arn suspected that they enjoyed the discomfort the sorcerers now had to endure for the sake of the cause.

But all would be worth it when the lord of the Legion made his entrance. The world would be expunged of the unclean, the undeserving. Only the Highborne, the most perfect of Azshara's subjects, would survive. Peroth'arn and others like him would populate a fresh, remade land, creating a paradise as none had ever before dreamed.

There would be much work after, of course. As had been explained to them by the queen, the Burning Legion had to raze what already existed out of necessity. The world would have to begin from scratch. Much would be expected from the Highborne, but boundless were the rewards their efforts would reap.

With a martyr's sigh, Peroth'arn sat down on the hard bed. Once paradise was created, a softer, more lush place to sleep would be among his first requests.

He had barely put his head to the gray lump that acted as his pillow when a voice whispered in his ear.

"So much sacrifice . . . so much hardship undeserved . . ."

Peroth'arn bolted to a sitting position. Again he peered around the chamber, but saw nothing save the horribly-unadorned walls and meager, undecorated furniture.

"Forced to take such squalor . . . you are to be admired, dear Peroth'arn . . ."

A sharp intake of breath was the Highborne's only response as a piece of shadow detached itself from a corner. Onyx eyes with streaks of ruby coursing across them fixed upon the startled sorcerer.

"Xavius . . ."

The satyr's hooves clattered ever so slightly as he moved closer to Peroth'arn. "I lived that name once," he murmured. "It doesn't mean as much to me as it did then."

"What are you doing here?"

Xavius chuckled, a sound much like the bleat of the creature he resembled. "I know your ambition, Peroth'arn. I know your dreams and how hard you've struggled for them."

Despite his distrust of the horned figure, the night elf felt a sense of appreciation. No one else seemed to understand all that he contributed. Not even the queen or Archimonde.

"I pushed you hard, you know, because I expected much from you, my friend."

Peroth'arn had not known and hearing it now from his former master made his chest swell with pride. Lord Xavius had been the bar by which the other Highborne had measured their skills. He had been the unparalleled master of his craft. Who else would willingly forfeit their own eyes to better understand the powers that they wielded? There was no sacrifice asked of the others that the advisor himself had not first suffered.

"I . . . I am honored."

Tilting his head, the horned satyr grinned. For some reason, Peroth'arn did not find that grin as frightening as he had earlier.

"No . . . 'tis *I* who am honored, good Peroth'arn . . . and I come now in the hope that I may be honored even more."

"I don't understand, my—I don't understand."

"A little wine?" The hooved figure produced a flask from the air and offered it to the night elf. Peroth'arn opened the flask and sniffed. The heady bouquet thrilled his senses. Surely this was rainbow flower wine, his personal favorite.

Xavius leaned near. "From her own cellar . . ." he said, leering. "But we can keep that secret between us, eh?"

The thought of so bold a transgression against Azshara initially stunned the sorcerer, but then thrilled him. Xavius had performed this act of betrayal against the queen just for Peroth'arn's sake. Azshara had executed loyal subjects for far less.

"Captain Varo'then would be aghast," Peroth'arn suggested.

"He is not one of us . . . and therefore not a concern."

"True." To the rest of the Highborne, the captain and his soldiers were a necessary evil. They were servants of the queen, to be certain, but they lacked the noble blood and flamboyant airs of the others. Most of the Highborne considered them no better than those who had once lived beyond the walls of the palace, but never let such notions show in their expressions. Captain Varo'then had ways of quietly dealing with those who showed him contempt.

"Drink," Xavius urged, pushing the flask up.

With the mouth of the bottle already near his lips, Peroth'arn saw no reason to hesitate anymore. He let the gentle liquid flow over his tongue and down his throat. His entire body tingled as he swallowed the rare vintage.

"A long-overdue reward," Xavius said. "One of many."

"Delicious."

His hooved companion nodded. The more he sat with the satyr, the less Peroth'arn feared Xavius. The former advisor gave him the respect he so richly deserved. That was truly an honor for the night elf, for was not Xavius now a much respected servant of the great Sargeras? Was he not now more to the lord of the Legion than all the Highborne combined?

"He watches you, too," the satyr commented quietly, as if passing a secret to a trusted comrade.

" 'He'? You mean—"

"*All* are under his wise gaze, even from so far away." A tapering finger thrust at the sorcerer. "But some are observed more than others . . . in the hopes that they may be groomed for further greatness."

Peroth'arn was speechless. *Sargeras* had marked him so? He quickly downed another huge gulp of wine, his eyes wide and calculating. How the others would have envied him.

"To his enemies, Sargeras is death incarnate, but to those who serve him well, he is benevolence unbridled." Xavius guided the flask to Peroth'arn's lips again. "He took me from beyond. He drew me back and granted me not only life again, but a special place at his side."

Stretching to his full length, the satyr displayed his form for Peroth'arn. Seeing it now as a precious gift of the great god, the night elf admired it. In truth, Xavius was now much more than he had been in his previous life. His features were broader, more imposing. Xavius looked stronger, more agile despite the hooves. It was also evident that he had an even greater mastery of the arts. Peroth'arn could sense the power radiating from his former master and suddenly felt pangs of jealousy. This was power such as he, too, deserved.

Perhaps the wine had made Peroth'arn not so cautious in guarding his emotions, for suddenly Xavius pulled away from him as if struck. The satyr nearly melted back into the shadows. Peroth'arn clutched the flask tightly, fearing that he had offended one blessed by the god.

But as quickly as he had retreated, Xavius returned to him. The satyr loomed over the seated night elf, staring deep into Peroth'arn's eyes. The sorcerer could not look away.

"No . . ." whispered Xavius half to himself. "It is too soon . . . but . . . he said that I must find those worthy . . . perhaps I could . . . yes . . . but to take on such a mantle, one would need the strength and resolve . . . dare I hope that *you* have such resolve, friend Peroth'arn?"

Leaping from the bed, Peroth'arn gasped, "I have whatever strength and resolve you need! I would do anything to be more worthy of my queen and Sargeras! Grant me the chance to be one of the worthy, I beg you!"

"It is a fearsome path you would take, dear Peroth'arn . . . but you would rise above the other Highborne! You would be under my guidance! All who beheld you would know you for one blessed by the lord of the Legion! Your power would grow tenfold and more! You would be the envy of all others, the first to join me!"

"Yes!" roared the night elf. "I will do whatever I must, Lord Xavius! Do not forsake me! I am worthy, I swear! Grant me this gift!"

The horned figure grinned, a sight that now filled his companion not with anxiousness, but rather with hope. "Yes, my dear Peroth'arn . . . I believe you. I believe that you are indeed worthy to take on the aspect of one of his most trusted, just as I have."

"I am."

"Your world will never be the same . . . it will be far better."

Peroth'arn set the flask on the bed, then went down on one knee. "If I can be accepted here and now, I ask that it be so. Please say it is possible!"

The grin grew wider. "Oh, it can be done now."

"Then I plead with you, Xavius—make me as you are! Give me the blessing of the god so that I may be a more perfect servant! I am worthy!"

"As you wish." Taking a step back, Xavius seemed to grow. He filled Peroth'arn's view completely. The ruby streaks in the satyr's eyes flared wildly.

"It may cause you some pain at first," he murmured to his convert, "but you will have no choice other than to endure it."

Xavius raised his clawed hands high . . .

But as the spell struck him, Peroth'arn shrieked. He felt as if his body were being stripped to the bone bit by bit. The agony was like none he could have ever imagined. Tears filled his eyes and, unable to articulate words, he pleaded by moans for the pain to end. This was not what he wanted.

"No," responded the satyr, ignoring his pleas. "We must finish now."

And the screams rose to new, horrific levels. That which had once been Peroth'arn would hardly have been recognizable to his fellow Highborne. His body constantly mutated, pushed slowly and deliberately by Xavius's power to what he desired. The screams became sobs, but even they did not disturb the satyr's dark work, no matter how loud they, too, eventually became.

"Yes . . ." Xavius said with a gleam in his unholy orbs. "Unleash the pain. Unleash the fury. No one beyond this chamber will hear. You may scream as much as you like . . . just as *I* did." His grin grew savage, animalistic. "It is little enough to suffer for the glory of Sargeras . . ."

The night elves had thought that the demons would pause somewhere along the way. They had expected that when they returned to Suramar they would at least be able to regroup and hold the enemy. And they had been certain that, if all else failed, Black Rook Hold would become their sanctuary.

They were wrong on all counts. Rhonin and Krasus understood why before Lord Ravencrest or any of the other night elves did. They had seen foremost the work of Archimonde, the sinister giant who, for a very good reason, commanded the Legion with the foul blessing of his master.

"He will give us no respite," the dragon mage said, putting to voice what both had long thought. He absently touched his chest where he had adhered the scale, recalling Archimonde's unholy relentlessness.

"He'll run the demons into the ground before he lets that happen," Rhonin agreed. "But we'll all collapse long before they ever do."

The night elves tried in vain to stop the rout at Suramar, if only so that the Hold could be readied for their entrance. It was hardly large enough to contain the population of the area, much less the huge force Ravencrest had gathered, but the noble had hoped that securing it would steel the hearts of his followers again. That, however, was not to be. There was not even time to enter the edifice. The soldiers held long enough for the civilians to flee behind them, but that was it. There was no chance to make Black Rook Hold ready and, to his credit, Ravencrest did not seek shelter there while the Burning Legion crushed all else.

"Never would I have thought the Hold so useless!" he snarled at Illidan. "But our host is too great despite our losses and if we sit here, the demons will chop away at those left outside, then starve those within."

"Surely we can survive a siege!" Malfurion's twin insisted.

"Against others, aye, but these will not tire and leave! They will destroy all around us, then wait for the inevitable!" The bearded night elf shook his head. "I will not let our end be so ignoble!"

After less than a day, they abandoned Suramar to the enemy, aware that nothing would be left to rebuild should the Burning Legion eventually be defeated. Wherever the demons marched, nothing remained but ruin. Even before the last glimpse of the city dwindled in the distance, the defenders could see the massive trees toppling, the walls collapsing under the relentless onslaught.

But even though so much of the Burning Legion had to be taking part in Suramar's demise, those stalking the army continued after as if undrained of even a single warrior. So far there had been only one slim benefit to the lengthy retreat and that being the fading airborne threats. The Eredar still cast what spells they could to harass the night elves, but their demanding efforts had clearly exhausted them. The Infernals' attacks had also lessened, at least from above. However, they still barreled ahead of the other demons, striking the defenders' lines whenever the opportunity arose.

Day faded into night, then night into day, and still Ravencrest's force was pushed back. More than one night saber rider lay asleep atop their mounts, and many a foot soldier eyed them with envy. Those who were stronger aided the ones beginning to falter. Worse, the population of refugees ahead of the soldiers grew with each hour, and they lacked the coordination and stamina of the fighters.

Generations of peace had left them unprepared for such a catastrophe, and soon the army found itself merging unwillingly with the weary civilians.

"Get along there!" shouted Jarod Shadowsong to a number of slow-moving figures in front of him and his charges. "You can't stop in the middle of this! Keep going!"

Krasus frowned. "This will only worsen. Ravencrest will be unable to maintain order even over his soldiers if they and the refugees become too entangled. This is exactly what Archimonde desires."

"But what can we do?" Rhonin's eyes had deep shadows. Like the others, he had not truly rested since before the trap had been sprung. Of all of them, only Brox looked at all fit. Having grown up in wartime, the orc had been forced many times to survive days without sleep. Still, even he appeared ready to nap if given the chance.

In fact, it was Brox who answered Rhonin's question, but not in words. With their own party becoming as trapped by the flow of refugees as the rest of the armed force, the orc began taking action. Pushing ahead of Jarod and the bodyguard, Brox roared at the nearest of the mob and swung his ax around his head. He was such a sight to behold that the night elves fearfully started to open the way for him.

"No!" he rumbled. "Ahead! No going that way! Ahead only! Help others!"

And as his companions watched, the grotesque figure began herding the refugees as if he had been doing the same with cattle or sheep all his life. None of the night elves sought his fury and they obeyed his commands to the letter.

Jarod quickly took up his example, spreading the guard unit wide and using them to sweep forward the civilians before his party. Order was soon reestablished there and as more officers became aware of what was happening, a true line started to form. With careful deliberation, the armed host herded their charges on. The night elves' pace as a whole picked up.

Yet still the Burning Legion drove them on. Krasus noticed a mountain in the distance, one that struck a vague recollection. He looked to Jarod and asked, "Captain Shadowsong, is there a name to that dire peak?"

"Aye, Master Krasus. It's Mount Hyjal."

"Mount Hyjal . . ." The mage pursed his lips. "Are we driven back so far as that?"

Rhonin noted his expression. Speaking only for Krasus's ears, he asked, "You recall that name?"

"Yes . . . and it means that the night elves' situation is most dire."

The human snorted. "Something we already knew."

Krasus's eyes took on a darker cast. "We cannot permit this retreat to go on much farther. The host must make a stand, Rhonin. If we fall back beyond Mount Hyjal, then surely all is lost."

"Memories stirring?"

"Or simply common sense. Whichever the case, I remain resolved that we can go no farther than the mountain. Despite what history says, I cannot see the night elves triumphing if we fail to make a halt."

"But Lord Ravencrest is already doing all he can and we've worn ourselves out just buying time."

"Then we must do more." The dragon mage raised himself up as much as riding a night saber would permit. "Would that I could find Malfurion. His skill would be one needed now."

"I last saw him with the priestess, Tyrande. He looked as pale as one of his kind could get. He battled something out there that nearly destroyed him."

"Yes, I think it was Archimonde."

"Then Malfurion would be dead."

Krasus shook his head. "No . . . and that is why I wish he were here. Nonetheless, with or without him, we must begin our assault anew."

"Begin *what* anew?"

Rhonin's former mentor turned back toward the direction of the demons. "Yes, we must take the offensive again."

The greatest of the dragons gathered in the Chamber of the Aspects, led there by Alexstrasza and Neltharion. The four Aspects present guided the proceedings, attended only by their consorts and those of the absent Nozdormu. All other dragons had given of themselves already; but for those of such power as now awaited their turn, the process required more delicacy.

The Earth Warder's three mates remained all but hidden behind him. They were larger than Korialstrasz, but were still dwarfed by the black male. As he studied them, Alexstrasza's youngest consort noted that they seemed but shadows of the Earth Warder, their every movement based upon what Neltharion did or said. The red dragon found this disturbing, but no one else seemed to notice.

The emerald males attending Ysera were slim, almost ghosts in comparison to the other great leviathans. More unsettling, they, like their mistress, moved about with their eyes constantly closed. Yet, beneath those lids, one could see the eyes shift back and forth. The greens constantly existed in two planes, more often than not in the Emerald Dream. They were silent and still, but Korialstrasz felt their magical senses monitoring the situation closely.

Malygos and his mates were a distinct contrast. They were constantly in motion, nudging one another and looking here and there and everywhere. Their blue-white scales glittered in merry little displays of magic and occasionally small details concerning one or the other would alter as the whim struck. Korialstrasz found them more refreshing than the blacks and greens.

Almost as solemn as Ysera and her mates were the four consorts of Nozdormu. They had the same sandy bronze texture as the Aspect, but were more solid than the almost-fluid monarch of Time. Korialstrasz wondered exactly where Nozdormu had gone that he would miss such events. From what little he had gleaned from his queen, it seemed that even the Aspect's mates did not know with certainty what had happened.

Yet, the Timeless One was still here in essence and that was a vital point. In the paws of the eldest of the females stood an hourglass made of what appeared to be pure golden sunlight. Within it, glittering bronze sands flowed not down but up. When the top filled, they then descended, only to begin their upward march once more.

The sands were a part of Nozdormu, set separate by him for urgent need by his flight. All the Aspects supposedly had some part of their essence put aside, for they were more than huge, reptilian beasts. They represented the most powerful forces of the world, the very fabric of its being, created by those who had molded the world itself. True, they were bound by its earthly laws, but they were as much above the other dragons as dragons were the younger races.

The various flights had alternated their offerings, one at a time. Now only two remained, the last, ironically, being Korialstrasz.

For some reason, he did not feel very much honored.

But before Korialstrasz presented himself, the essence of the Timeless One had to be brought forth. Saridormi, the

Aspect's prime mate, carried the hourglass gently in her left forepaw as she stepped up to the Dragon Soul.

Neltharion's creation floated in the very midst of the chamber, its simplistic form radiating a fearsome yet majestic glow. All were bathed in a rainbow of colors that, not coincidentally, matched the shadings of the dragons.

"I come bearing representation of He Who Is Without End, He Who Sees Past, Present, and Future!" Saridormi intoned. She raised the glittering timepiece above the shimmering disk. "In his name I add his strength, his power, his *self*, to this weapon that we will use against the fiends attacking our realm!"

With a single squeeze of her powerful paw, the gargantuan dragon broke the hourglass.

The sand that was the essence of Nozdormu did not fall in a heap, as Korialstrasz had expected. Instead, it swirled out—as if itself a live, sentient thing—and began to spin above the Dragon Soul. As it spun, a light sprinkle of bronze rained down upon the disk. Each particle struck with a brilliant flash, then vanished within.

A bright radiance filled the chamber as the last grain sank inside, a luminous sunburst that momentarily blinded Korialstrasz. He turned his eyes away and did not look again until the light had faded. The red leviathan saw that the rest, even the greens, had been forced to shield their view. Only Neltharion appeared to have watched it all, his wide, avid gaze drinking in everything.

"My love," came Alexstrasza's whisper.

Still ill at ease for reasons he could not explain, Korialstrasz strode forward. By himself, he would have chosen to deny the Dragon Soul his essence, but his queen had asked this boon of him as she had all the others; how could *he* be the only one to say no? Nevertheless, he stared at the talisman as if seeing not the salvation of the world, but something that tainted it.

That was foolish, though, he thought. *For what reason would the Earth Warder do such a heinous thing?*

Then, the Dragon Soul loomed before him. So close, Korialstrasz found nothing insignificant about it. Here was power such as many in the past had dreamt of, and others would do so again for centuries on. Here was the joined essences of all the dragons, the most powerful of the world's children.

"It is waiting for you."

The red dragon looked up into the huge visage of the black. Neltharion never blinked. His breathing came in rapid gasps, as if he grew more and more frenzied with each second that Korialstrasz hesitated.

There is something not right in this . . . Alexstrasza's mate thought. But then he recalled how willingly she, Malygos, and Ysera had given of themselves. Malygos, in fact, had been determined to be the first among them to sacrifice a bit of himself, his way of championing his friend's cause. If the Master of Magic trusted the work of Neltharion, who was mere Korialstrasz to say otherwise?

And with that thought still hanging over him, the red opened himself up to the Dragon Soul.

The disk flared, bathing him in its daunting illumination. Korialstrasz bared his chest to it and willed away all the natural magical defenses dragons kept about themselves. He felt the Dragon Soul reach into him as he had seen it do to the others, reach in as if his armored hide were nothing but illusion . . .

Seconds later, the unsettling force reemerged from his chest—but with it the Dragon Soul drew something else. It was an intangible, squirming thing—not exactly light, not exactly substance. A faint crimson aura surrounded it, and as the last bit separated from Korialstrasz, he felt a loss that saddened him.

Steeling himself, the red watched as the illumination of the Dragon Soul pulled the offering toward it. Slowly, the light sank back into the disk.

As that which the Dragon Soul had taken from him followed suit, Korialstrasz gasped. He wanted to reach out and take back what was his, but to do so would destroy the effort and, worse, shame him before his beloved Alexstrasza.

And so Korialstrasz watched helplessly as the Dragon Soul absorbed his essence, added it to the others. He watched helplessly as Neltharion snatched the disk almost covetously and held it before the other leviathans.

"It is done . . ." the Earth Warder declared. "All have given that which must be given. I now seal the Dragon Soul forever so that what has been attained will never be lost."

Neltharion shut his eyes. His body took on a black, ominous aura, one that flowed from him to the tiny but mighty talisman in his forepaw.

The other great dragons started. For a moment, a very brief but telling moment, the Dragon Soul burned as black as its creator.

"Should that be?" asked Ysera quietly.

"For it to be as it must, yes," Neltharion replied almost defiantly.

"It is a weapon like no other. It must be like no other," added the knowledgeable Malygos.

The Earth Warder nodded his appreciation for the blue dragon's words. Neltharion gazed around the chamber, seeing if anyone had further questions. A few came to Korialstrasz's mind, but he felt unworthy to ask them in the face of his queen's satisfaction with events.

"The final casting will take time," the black leviathan informed the others. "It has to be taken from here to a place of silence and privacy, where the most delicate castings will be made."

"How long?" asked Alexstrasza. "It must not be too late."

"It will be ready when it needs be ready." And with that, Neltharion spread his wings and rose into the air. His mates followed suit almost perfectly, like puppets whose strings were attached to the Earth Warder.

The other dragons watched as he vanished through what seemed the solid wall of the chamber, then also began taking off. Alexstrasza remained where she was, and so Korialstrasz did likewise.

But as his gaze followed the departing behemoths, his thoughts continued to reflect upon what they had wrought this day. He could never deny the incredible power of the tiny, golden disk. Truly, Neltharion had crafted a weapon the likes of which even the endless hordes of the demons could not stand against.

Nor, for that matter, he realized belatedly, even *dragons*.

EIGHT

Malfurion dreamed. He dreamed that he and Tyrande lived in a beautiful tree home in the midst of grand Suramar. It was the high time of the year and all was in bloom. Lush plant life covered the region like a beautiful carpet. The immense tree cooled them with its thick, shading foliage, and flowers of all colors and patterns surrounded the trunk's base.

Tyrande, clad in a glorious gown of yellow, green, and orange, played a silver lyre while their children, a boy and a girl, darted around the tree, giggling and laughing as they ran. Malfurion sat near the window of his proud abode, breathing in the fresh air and savoring the life he had attained. The world was at peace, and his family knew nothing but happiness . . .

Then, a violent tremor shook the tree. Malfurion clutched the window and saw with horror the homes and towers of Suramar quickly tumble over. Other structures collapsed. People screamed, and massive fires burst to life in every direction.

He looked for his children, but they were nowhere to be found. As for his mate, Tyrande continued to sit on one of the thick branches just outside, her fingers strumming a tune on the lyre.

Daring to lean out, Malfurion shouted, "Tyrande! Come inside! Quickly!"

But she ignored him, blithely caught up in her music despite the growing catastrophe and her own precarious position.

The tree house abruptly tipped. Malfurion tried using his druidic powers to keep it from collapsing, but nothing happened. The tree—all the flora—felt dead to his senses.

The house's fall finally awoke Tyrande. Dropping the lyre, she screamed and reached for Malfurion, but the distance was too great. Malfurion's mate lost her balance and slipped off the branch—

But a figure in black swiftly rose into the air, readily catching her. Illidan smiled magnanimously at Tyrande, then nodded congenially to his brother. However, instead of coming to Malfurion's aid, the other twin began to fly off with his catch.

"Illidan!" Malfurion shouted, trying to maintain his hold. "Come back!"

His sibling paused in midair. Still holding Tyrande tight, he turned and laughed at Malfurion.

And as he laughed, Illidan transformed, growing larger, more horrific. His garments tore as armor hidden underneath burst through. His skin color darkened and a savage, jagged tail sprouted from behind him. A clawed hand held out the druid's mate over the ruined city, shaking her like a rag doll.

And Malfurion stared in horror as Archimonde dangled Tyrande before him—

"Nooo!"

He bolted upright, then nearly tumbled off the night

saber upon which he had been half-sitting. Strong but slim fingers kept him from losing what remained of his balance and pulled him tight against an armored torso. Recalling Archimonde, the druid instinctively sought to pull away from that armor.

"Hush, Malfurion! Be careful!"

Tyrande's voice brought him completely back to consciousness. He gazed up into her concerned face. She had the helmet back so that he could fully see her features, a most welcome sight.

"I dreamt—" he began, then stopped. There were parts of his dream that were too personal to tell one who was not promised to him. "I . . . dreamt," Malfurion concluded apologetically.

"I know. I heard you speak. I thought I heard my name, and Illidan's."

"Yes." He dared not say more.

The priestess touched his cheek. "It must've been a terrible dream, Malfurion . . . but at least you finally slept."

Suddenly aware of his close proximity to her, the druid straightened. He looked around, noting for the first time the sea of figures surrounding them. Most were civilians, many of whom looked confused and completely out of their element. Few night elves had ever suffered much. This displacement surely had to have pushed many to the brink.

"Where are we?"

"Near Mount Hyjal."

He gaped at the peak. "So far? This can't be!"

"I'm afraid it is."

Malfurion hung his head. So, after all their efforts, his people were still doomed. If the demons had already driven the defenders this far back, how could the night elves possibly hope to recover?

"Elune watches over us," Tyrande whispered, reading his expression. "I pray to her for guidance. She'll give us some reprieve, I'm certain."

"I hope so. Where are the others?"

"Your brother is with the Moon Guard, over there." She pointed north. "I've not seen Krasus or the others."

It was not Illidan to whom Malfurion desired to speak. After his confrontation with Archimonde, the druid wanted desperately to find the wizards. They had to be warned that the powerful demon led the forces pursuing them.

That assumed, of course, that Krasus and the rest still lived. Had Archimonde hunted them down after dealing with Malfurion?

"Tyrande, I've got to find the outsiders. I believe they are still the key to our survival."

"You'll never make it on foot. You're still weak. Take my night saber."

He felt ashamed that she would sacrifice her own mount for his possibly-futile search. "Tyrande, I—"

But she gave him a look that he had never seen before, a steadfast, determined expression such as Malfurion had noticed only on the most senior, most dedicated priestesses of Elune. "It is important, Malfurion. I know that."

She slipped off the huge cat before he could argue again. Taking only her pack and her weapons, Tyrande looked up at the druid and insisted, "Go."

Unable to do anything but nod his thanks, Malfurion shifted his position, then urged the night saber through the throng. He was determined that he would not fail Tyrande's trust; if the others lived, Malfurion would find them.

The cat battled its way through soldiers and civilians, snarling but never striking despite its obvious discomfort of being surrounded by so many bodies. The druid was pleased to see that the soldiers had kept order for the most part. The majority of the civilians were being politely but firmly herded on, their pace consistent. The demons had no doubt counted on the chaos caused by mixing the two diverse groups together. At least that danger had so far been avoided.

But with so many more bodies added to the host, finding even three such unique figures as the orc, the human, and Krasus proved daunting. Only after letting his gaze sweep over the crowds for the dozenth time did Malfurion finally think to make use of his arts.

He refused to enter the Emerald Dream just yet, as there were other means by which he believed he might sense them. Reining the night saber to a halt, the druid shut his eyes and reached out around him. Throughout the region, he touched the minds of the other night sabers that he could see, speaking to them as he had the beasts of the forest during his lessons. Malfurion even touched the mind of Tyrande's mount so as not to miss the slightest chance of a sighting. The cats, well-familiar with their masters, surely would notice the differing scents of the three strangers.

But the first animals did not recognize those the druid sought. Bracing himself, Malfurion stretched his senses farther, reaching to creatures far beyond his sight. Some of the refugees carried with them pets, and even those Malfurion asked. The more minds he contacted, the better his odds.

At last, one of the dark panthers responded. The answer came not in words, but rather smells and images. It took the druid a moment to digest them, but in the end he realized that this creature had recently seen the orc. Brox was the most distinctive of the trio, and so it was small wonder that the night saber would recall him best. To the cat, the warrior was a mix of heady, thick smells reminiscent of the deeply-buried wild side of the mount. In Brox, the night saber sensed a kindred spirit. In fact, the animal's image of the tusked warrior made the orc resemble a night saber on its hind legs, one arm ending in a huge pair of claws that had to be Brox's ax.

Finding out exactly when and where the cat had seen Brox proved a bit trickier. Animals did not measure time and distance as night elves did. Yet, with some effort, the druid finally determined that the panther had seen Brox only an hour or two earlier, near the center part of the great exodus.

Veering his own mount in that direction, Malfurion continued to ask other night sabers of any sightings. More and more, he came upon those who recalled not only Brox, but also Rhonin and Krasus. Something about the elder mage now took prominence in the creatures' minds; they looked to him with a respect that such able predators reserved only for far superior ones. However, they did not fear Krasus as they might have another beast, almost as if they understood that he was something much, much more. In truth, Malfurion soon discovered that the night sabers would have been more likely to obey a command by Krasus than they would the handlers who had raised them.

Marking this as yet another of the many mysteries surrounding the not-quite-night-elven mage, Malfurion spurred his cat to greater speed. The going was difficult, for they rode against the living tide, but with the druid's guidance, the night saber made headway without injuring any of those in its path.

The general situation worsened as he approached where the outsiders had to be. The sounds of battle rose in the distance and unsettling flashes of crimson and dank green light rose from the horizon. Here the soldiers were more wary and exhausted. These were clearly those who had been most recently up on the front line holding the demons back. The scars and terrible wounds Malfurion passed gave testament to the unabated fury of the Burning Legion.

"What are you doing here?" demanded an officer with blood and ichor on his once-immaculate armor. His eyes teared. "All noncombatants to the head of the flow! Begone with you!"

Before the druid could explain, someone behind Malfurion called, "He's *supposed* to be up here, captain! That should be plain with just a look at his face!"

"Illidan?" Glancing over his shoulder, Malfurion saw his brother, virtually unscathed, riding up. Illidan wore the first grin that his twin had seen in his journey; it looked so out of place in the situation that Malfurion feared his sibling had gone mad.

"I had thought you lost!" the sorcerer said, slapping Malfurion hard on the shoulder. Failing to notice his brother wince, Illidan turned to the officer. "Any more questions?"

"No, Master Illidan!" The soldier saluted quickly and moved on.

"What happened to you, brother?" the black-clad twin asked. "Someone said that they saw you struck down, your mount torn to pieces . . ."

"I was saved . . . Tyrande brought me to safety." The instant he mentioned her name, Malfurion regretted it.

The grin remained, but the good humor behind it fled. "*Did* she? I'm glad that she was so close to you."

"Illidan—"

"It's good that you're here at this time," the druid's sibling went on, cutting off any further discussion of the priestess. "The old wizard's been trying to organize something and he seems to think *you're* important."

"Krasus? Where is he?"

The sorcerer's grin grew almost macabre. "Why, just where you're heading, brother. Up at the very edge of the fight . . ."

The wind howled. An oppressive heat tore at the night elves who had been chosen to be the defending line. Now and then, a cry would come from somewhere in the ranks, and the triumphant roars of a demon would immediately follow.

"Where is Illidan?" Krasus asked, even his tremendous patience wearing thin. "The Moon Guard refuses to act without him save to shield themselves!"

"He said he was coming," Rhonin interjected. "He needed to speak with Ravencrest first."

"He will receive credit enough if we succeed, and no one will blame him if we fail, for we'll all be dead . . ."

Rhonin could not argue with his former mentor. Illidan wanted nothing more than to please his patron. Malfurion's brother was the opposite of the druid—ambitious, wild, and oblivious of the risks to others. The two wizards had already discovered that three of the Moon Guard they had hoped in part to rely on were no longer available. The demons had not slain them; they were simply crippled with exhaustion from feeding Illidan their power.

Yet, despite his reckless use of the other night elves, they appeared to have bound themselves to him. When it came to casting spells of any substance, Illidan could do what they could not. He also had the political backing of Lord Ravencrest, and night elves were nothing if not status-conscious, even in the face of annihilation.

Rhonin suddenly straightened. "Beware!"

What resembled most a floating mushroom made of mist descended upon the line. Before the spellcasters could act, the edges touched where the soldiers stood.

Several of the fighters screamed as their faces suddenly swelled with dozens of red, burning pustules. One after another, the pustules burst, regrew, and burst again, spreading rapidly over any unprotected part of the victim's body.

"*Jekar iryn!*" Krasus hissed, gesturing at the cloud.

A blast of rich, blue light ate away at the foul mushroom with such swiftness that scores more were saved from the horrendous plague. Unfortunately, there was no saving those already affected. They dropped one after another, their ravaged flesh reminiscent of a field of erupting volcanoes.

Rhonin stared in disgust. "Horrible! Damn them!"

"Would that we could! We can wait no longer! If the Moon Guard will not follow our lead, then we must hope we can do something by ourselves!"

But as the wizards prepared to do just that, Rhonin spotted a pair of riders approaching. "Illidan comes—and he's got Malfurion with him!"

"Praise the Aspects!" Krasus turned to meet the duo. As they rode up, he set himself before Malfurion's brother. "You are late! Gather the Moon Guard! You must be ready to follow my lead!"

From most others, Illidan likely would have not taken such a brusque command, but he had a healthy respect for both wizards, especially Rhonin. Peering over Krasus and seeing Rhonin's dark expression, the sorcerer nodded, then hurried to obey.

"What do you hope to do?" asked Malfurion, dismounting.

"The demons must be stopped here," Krasus answered. "It is vital that we not be pushed back beyond Mount Hyjal and that we turn this rout into an aggressive attack on our part!"

The druid nodded, then said, "Archimonde is out there. I barely escaped him."

"I had suspected that he was." Krasus considered the night elf. "And the fact that you lived through a confrontation with him says I was correct in desiring your presence at this moment."

"But—what can *I* do?"

"What you have been trained to do, naturally."

With that, Krasus turned back to Rhonin, who had already set himself to face the distant demons. The elder mage stood next to his former pupil, with Malfurion imitating him a moment later.

Krasus glanced at the human. "Rhonin, in matters of magic, Illidan looks to you more than anyone. I leave it to you to establish a link with him."

"As you wish." The fiery-tressed figure blinked once. "It's done."

The mage returned his attention to the druid. "Malfurion, imagine the most powerful spell you think you can cast. But by all means, do *not* tell me what it is! Use whatever method, whatever contact with the powers of the world you require, but do not complete your casting until I say so. We must be relentless against our foes."

"I . . . I understand."

"Good! Then, we begin. Follow my lead. Rhonin?"

"I'm ready," the younger wizard replied. "I know just what I want to do."

Krasus's eyes widened. "Ah! One other detail, Malfurion; be prepared to randomly shift the focus of your attack. Move your spell to wherever it seems there is a gap in our effort. Do you understand?"

"I believe so."

"May the powers of light be with us, then."

That said, Krasus abruptly froze. His eyes stared unblinking across the gap separating the night elves from the demons.

Rhonin quickly leaned toward Malfurion. "Use everything. Leave no defenses. This is all or nothing."

"They are approaching the point." Krasus informed his companions. "Would that Archimonde be among the first ranks."

They could all sense the approaching horde. The evil permeated the very air, sending a foul radiation their way. Even Krasus shuddered, but from disgust, not fear.

"Rhonin, I have Jarod Shadowsong prepared. Are the Moon Guard ready?"

"Yes."

"Almost . . . " The pale visage tightened. Krasus's eyelids flickered. "Now."

They had no knowledge of one another's attack, exactly how Krasus intended it. He desired true random effort, the better to foul up whatever defense Archimonde and the others might devise. His plan had as much potential for disaster—if not *more* even—than success, but that very fact was what the dragon mage counted on.

From the clouds suddenly dropped glittering spears of ice that fixed on the enemy horde. To the north, the ground shook, and demons suddenly scattered as the earth swelled. Elsewhere, huge, black birds appeared from nowhere, heading toward the airborne elements of the Legion.

All along the front, one spell after another assaulted the enemy. Some were concentrated in specific areas while others seemed to act everywhere. No two were alike and although a few appeared to be in conflict with one another, they did far worse damage to the oncoming horde.

Demons died pierced by ice, burned by crimson flame, or

buried by molten earth. Those in the sky fell beaten and torn by hundreds of claws or tumbled to their deaths after winds tossed them against one another.

The Eredar attempted to counter, but Krasus suddenly commanded, "Shift your focus!"

Immediately, Malfurion, Rhonin, and—to the north—the Moon Guard and Illidan altered the direction in which they focused their spells. Krasus sensed the warlocks grow confused, uncertain as to where to first apply their counter-assaults. On the ground, the Fel Guard and other demon warriors tried in vain to defend against something that their weapons could not cut in two or impale.

The relentless advance finally came to a halt.

"They are stalled!" shouted Krasus. "Shift focus again and push harder! We must begin to retake ground!"

Again they adjusted the locations of their attacks. A few areas quieted, but just as the Burning Legion sought to take advantage of those lulls, someone among the spellcasters filled the gaps. Nowhere could the demons now stand their positions, much less press forward.

"They're giving way!" Malfurion called.

"Do not let up!" Krasus gritted his teeth. "Rhonin, I am alerting the captain!"

The druid dared to look at the human for a moment. "What does he mean?"

"It took some convincing, but Shadowsong rode to Ravencrest! He's been waiting for our signal!"

"For what?"

In answer, the battle horns sounded. A sudden electricity filled the night elves. Gone was the dying hope, the resignation. Once more the soldiers responded to the horns' cries with vigor, and the host advanced.

The spellcasters adjusted as they, too, slowly moved forward on foot. Their trained cats following close behind, they marched with the soldiers toward the enemy.

And finally the Burning Legion began to retreat full.

First the night elves crossed the ruined gap that the Moon Guard and wizards had earlier wrought to buy them time. Then they started to climb their way over the first of the demon dead. They also passed many of their own, lost hours earlier, but more and more, it was the demons who lay as corpses before the soldiers. The Burning Legion, softened by the unpredictable attacks of the spellcasters, fell away easily as the night elves cut into them.

Another set of horns blew. A lengthy, well-savored roar of anticipation unexpectedly erupted throughout the host. The night elves surged forward, more than doubling their pace.

"Ravencrest must follow the plan!" Krasus snapped. "They cannot chase the Legion too far or too fast!"

A flight of arrows fell upon the demons, slaying scores more. Panther riders charged the remaining fragments of the opposing line, the great cats eagerly tearing into their prey.

Malfurion's heart beat swifter. "We're doing it!"

"Do not let up!" stressed the mage.

They did not. Fueled by their success, the druid and the others continued adding to the support of the troops. Exhausted though they might be, they understood well that this was a most critical juncture. Mount Hyjal still loomed behind them, but now it receded slightly.

Then, another welcome surprise—chanting came from the center of the advance. The Sisterhood of Elune, resplendent in their battle armor, strengthened the fighters further. Day might have held precedence at the moment, but the priestesses' rhythmic singing literally fed the nocturnal warriors. It was as if the moon herself suddenly hung over the host.

Yard by yard they struggled, demons falling with each step. Krasus looked to the shrouded sky and said, "Now! Strike the Eredar at will!"

Every spellcaster focused his efforts on the airborne warlocks. Thunder ravaged the sky. Lightning flashed in a jarring display of colors. Winds howled.

They could not see the results of their attacks, but they could sense them in other ways. The Eredar tried to regroup, but they had to also protect their bearers. That left them strained, weaker. Whenever a spell slew one of the demon mages, the defenders felt a sudden lessening of the evil forces arrayed against them. And the more that happened, the harder Krasus's group attacked the survivors.

At last, the warlocks pulled completely back. Their retreat left the monstrous warriors on the ground bereft of any shield against the wizards and the Moon Guard.

"They're fleeing!" Malfurion whispered, awed by the success of his party.

"They are too valuable. Archimonde will need them again," Krasus replied more dourly. "And he *will* need them again. The war is not won, but the battle is saved."

"Should we not keep after them until we push them through the portal and back into their hellish domain?"

Krasus chuckled, so unusual a sound from him that even Rhonin started. "You sound more like your brother than you, Malfurion. Let not the euphoria of the moment take you too far. This host will never survive a pitched battle all the way back to Zin-Azshari. They are running on will alone right now."

"Then . . . what is the point?"

"Look around you, young night elf. Your people *survive*.

That is more than they thought they could do only an hour before."

"Will Ravencrest follow your instructions, though?" asked Rhonin, peering back to look for the noble's banner.

"I believe he will. Look there, to the north."

The advance had slowed there and now the soldiers seemed more interested in securing the ground that they had gained rather than taking more. Mounted officers went about waving other soldiers back to the main group. Some seemed a bit disappointed, but others looked more than happy to rest, even if they still had to stand to do it.

Within minutes, the entire front line had completely halted. Night elves soon began clearing the carnage and creating a strong front line, with solemn but determined warriors positioning themselves to repel anyone who might seek to undo the miracle that they had accomplished.

And only then did Krasus exhale. "He listened. Praise the Aspects. He listened."

Ahead of them they could see only the vague shapes of the horde. The Burning Legion had moved far beyond the range of the arrows, even beyond the efforts of the weary spellcasters at the moment.

"We've done it," Rhonin uttered, his voice almost a croak. "We kept them from pushing us back beyond Mount Hyjal."

"Yes," murmured Krasus, eyes not on the demons, but rather the haggard defenders. "Yes, we did. Now the most difficult part begins."

NINE

Mannoroth bent before the black portal, his stocky front legs in a kneeling position and his wide, leathery wings folded tight behind him. The tusked demon tried to make himself as small as possible, for he now communed with Sargeras, who seemed not at all in a pleasant mood.

The way is not yet open to me . . . I had expected better . . .

"We struggle," Mannoroth admitted, "but the task . . . it's almost as if the world itself seeks to prevent your coming, Great One."

I will not be denied . . .

"N-no, Great One."

There was silence for a time, then the voice in Mannoroth's head said, *There is a disruption, a wrongness . . . there are those who should not be but are, and those who seek to awake what should not be awoken.*

The massive demon did not pretend to understand, but he still replied, "Yes, Sargeras."

They are the key. They must be hunted.

"Archimonde is in the field and the Houndmaster is long on the trail. The transgressors will be brought to ground."

The sinister-looking gap fluctuated, squirming as if alive. Mannoroth could feel the lord of the Legion's desire to make his way into this rich world. The frustration Sargeras radiated chilled even his hardened lieutenant.

One must be brought whole . . . so that I may have the pleasure of tearing him asunder slowly and delicately.

An image materialized full-blown in Mannoroth's mind. An insignificant creature of the same race as the Highborne. He was younger, though, and wore, in comparison to his fellows, rather drab garments of green and brown. The vision the demon had of him showed the night elf in the palace itself. Mannoroth recognized the chamber where the original portal had been created . . . a place now only a windswept ruin.

Mark him well.

"I have already, Great One. Archimonde, Hakkar, and I all watch for his presence. One of us will snare him."

Alive, commanded the presence from beyond, now beginning to recede from Mannoroth's head. *Alive . . . so that I might have my pleasure with his torture . . .*

And as Sargeras vanished, Mannoroth shuddered, knowing full well what fate this Malfurion would face once the Great One had him in his grasp.

The monumental task of reorganizing the host was made more so by the countless refugees accompanying them, but to his credit, Lord Ravencrest did as best as possible. He took an accounting of all supplies, especially food and water, and distributed accordingly. Some of the high-ranking among the refugees protested at not receiving what they thought their rightful—and more *bountiful*—shares, but one black glare from the bearded commander silenced all.

Tyrande and the sisters also did what they could for the

soldiers and civilians. Her helmet pushed back, the priestess of Elune led along a night saber she had borrowed earlier as she stopped to speak with one person after another. All, whether old or young, of high caste or low, welcomed her presence. Perhaps it was just the moment, but they appeared to her especially comforted after she was through. Tyrande did not mark this as the result of any special gift she had, merely assuming that her gentle demeanor was an extreme relief in contrast to all else the others had faced of late.

A small figure crouched by herself seized the priestess's attention. A young female, two or three years away from being able to enter into the service of Elune, sat in miserable silence, staring at nothing.

Kneeling at her side, Tyrande touched her shoulder. The girl started, turning to glare at her like a wild beast.

"Be at peace . . ." Tyrande said soothingly, handing her a water sack. She waited until the girl had finished, then added, "I am from the temple. What's your name?"

After a moment's hesitation, the child answered, "Sh-Shandris Feathermoon."

"Where is your family?"

"I-I don't know."

"Are you from Suramar?" The priestess could not recall her, but that did not mean that Shandris was not from the same city.

"No . . . Ara-Hinam."

Tyrande tried to hide her concern. Shandris was one of the refugees that the demons had been pursuing when they had set their trap. Based on what the priestess had gathered from other survivors, many people had perished before the Burning Legion had allowed the rest to escape. The child's family might still live . . . but then again might not.

"When did you last see them?"

Shandris's eyes grew huge. "I was with a friend . . . when the monsters came. I tried to run home, but someone grabbed me . . . told me I had to run the other way. I did." She put her hands to her face, the tears spilling over them. "I should have gone home! I should have gone home!"

The tragic tale was not what Tyrande had wanted to hear. The priestess would make inquiries wherever she could, but she was near-certain that no one in Shandris's immediate family had survived and that the girl was now all by herself in the world.

"Has anyone taken care of you since your flight?"

"No."

The refugees from Ara-Hinam, a smaller settlement, had been on the run for two days prior to meeting up with the host. It was remarkable to think that Shandris had survived on her own even for that period. Many older night elves had fallen to the side; the priestess's people were not, in general, up to such strife. Night elves, while hardly weak, were very ill-prepared for life outside their cushioned world—a failing only now becoming evident. Tyrande gave thanks to Elune that she, Malfurion, and Illidan had been raised differently, but they were in the minority.

There were so many in the same situation Shandris suffered, but something about the child especially touched the priestess. Perhaps it was that she somewhat resembled Tyrande in face and form at that age. Whatever the case, the sister bade the child to rise.

"I want you to climb atop the night saber. You're going to come with me." It went against her orders, but the priestess did not care. Though she could not save everyone, she would do what she could for Shandris.

Her face drawn but her eyes for the first time clear,

Shandris mounted the cat. Tyrande made certain that she was secure, then led the night saber on.

"Where are we going?" the child asked.

"I've more work to do. You'll find some dried fruit in the pouch hanging on the left side."

Shandris eagerly twisted to the pouch, rummaging through it until she discovered the simple fare. Tyrande made no mention of the fact that the girl was also devouring her ration. The sisterhood trained its members to learn to survive at times with minimal sustenance. There were even four periods of ritual fasting each year, done in general as a sign of dedication to the goddess. Now, it paid off in time of war.

Moving on to the next refugees, Tyrande continued her ministrations. Most were simply exhausted beyond belief, but some had injuries. The latter she always tried to help as much as possible, praying to the Mother Moon for the strength and guidance necessary. To her joy, the goddess saw fit this day to grant success in all her efforts.

But then she came upon one infected injury that shocked her. Whether an intentional wound or an accident, it was at first difficult to say. Tyrande studied the unsettling greenish pus around it and wondered at the peculiar cuts. The victim, an older male, lay pale and unconscious, his breath coming in rapid gasps. His mate, her hair bound back with what remained of a ruby- and emerald-encrusted broach, cradled his head.

"How did he do this?" asked Tyrande, not certain if she could even slow the course of the infection. There was something disquieting about it.

"He did not. It was done to him."

"I don't understand."

The elder female's expression tightened as she fought to

maintain her calm long enough to explain. "This thing . . . he said it looked like . . . like a wolf or hound . . . but twisted, as if out of a horrible dream . . ."

Tyrande shivered. She knew that the other female spoke of a felbeast. The four-legged demons had nearly slain Malfurion more than once. They especially desired those who wielded any sort of magic, draining it from the bodies and leaving only a dry husk.

"And he made it all the way from Ara-Hinam like this?" The priestess marveled that anyone could survive so long with so hideous a wound.

"No . . . from there we escaped whole." Bitterness tinged her words. "This he got but two days ago, while sneaking off to find us food."

Two days? That would have put them with the mass of bodies flowing toward Mount Hyjal. But none of the demons had managed to break ahead of the horde, of that Tyrande was certain.

"You swear that it was only two days? It happened near here?"

"Back in the wooded lands now again to our south, I swear it."

The priestess bit her lip; woods that were behind the night elven lines.

Leaning over the wound, Tyrande said, "Let me see what can be done."

She forced herself to touch it, hoping that she could at least prevent it from spreading. From behind her she heard Shandris gasp. The girl feared for her, and rightly so. One never knew what a demon-caused wound might do. The Burning Legion would not be averse to spreading plague.

The moon was not present in the sky, but that did not concern Tyrande. While the priestesses were strongest when it was visible, they were fully aware that it was never far away. Their link to Elune was powerful no matter what time of day or night or even cycle.

"Mother Moon, hear my entreaties," she whispered. "Grant this humble one the cool, soothing powers of your touch. Guide my hands to the source of this abomination, and let me remove the taint so that this innocent might recover . . ."

Tyrande began humming under her breath, a way of focusing her will into her work. The injuries that she had healed for Broxigar paled in comparison to what she attempted now. It took all her control just to keep from feeling that she would fail.

Without warning, a pale, silvery light shone around her fingers. The victim's mate stared wide-eyed, and again Shandris gasped. Tyrande's hopes rose; once again, Elune was responding to her. Truly the goddess was with her this day!

The healer traced her fingers around the wound, taking special care where the foulness was worst. Tyrande could not help but grimace as she touched the pus-ridden areas. What sort of evil were the demons that their very bite or scratch left such horror in its wake?

As her fingertips went past the ravaged areas, the injury grew less horrific in appearance. The pustules shriveled, finally disappearing. The bloody crevice narrowed at each end, as if slowly sealing itself.

Encouraged, Tyrande continued praying to Elune. The infection shrank to a small, oval patch, while the wound itself became a scar, first fresh, then nearly gone.

The male suddenly groaned, as if awaking from a deep sleep, but Tyrande did not stop. She could not presume that the disappearance of outer signs meant that the wound had completely healed *inside*. There would be poisons from the infection in the victim's blood.

Several tense seconds later, when the male's chest finally rose and sank at a more sedate rate and his eyes fluttered open, the priestess knew that she had defeated the demon's work. With a long exhalation, Tyrande leaned back and gave thanks to Elune. The goddess had granted her a miracle.

The female reached forward and took one of Tyrande's hands. "Thank you, sister! Thank you!"

"I am merely the vessel for the work of the Mother Moon. If there is one to thank, it is Elune."

Nevertheless, both the stricken male—Karius—and his mate continued to express their gratitude for what they saw as the priestess's heroic effort. Tyrande nearly had to fend them off, so thankful were they.

"You can repay me by telling me in more detail what occurred," she finally told the former victim.

Nodding, Karius related the story as much as he could recall. In the midst of their troubles, the two had realized that they needed food. However, the chaos at the time prevented them from finding anyone among the refugees who had enough to share. Most had fled with only as much as they could carry in their arms.

Spotting an area of forest he thought might contain berries and fresh water, Karius had left his mate with the promise that he would return shortly. Desperation made him attempt the foolhardy hunt at all, for surely others had stripped the forest of anything edible long before.

Karius had been forced to go deeper into the woods than he had intended. He began to worry that he might never find his mate again, although she had told him that she would stay behind if he was gone too long. When at last he discovered a bush with ripe, purple berries, Karius had quickly tried to fill the pouch on his belt, allowing himself an occasional berry to eat immediately so as to preserve his strength.

But just as he had filled the pouch, he heard something huge rummaging through the forest. His first thought was that it might be a tauren or bear. He had started back, his gaze constantly over his shoulder so that whatever emerged would not catch him by surprise.

And so it was that he was looking in the wrong direction when the beast charged him from the front.

Having once served Black Rook Hold, Karius still had some swiftness left to him despite the debilitating journey. He twisted around just as the monster—some sort of demonic hound with two horrific tentacles sprouting from its upper back—had tried to fall upon him. The beast did not seize his throat as it had intended, but instead clamped down on the leg.

Somehow, Karius had managed not to scream, although every fiber of his being had demanded it. Instead, the night elf grabbed for something, anything, with which to defend himself. His groping hand found a thick, pointed rock, and he swung it with all his might against the creature's nose.

He had heard something crack. A harsh whine filled his ears and the beast released his leg. Even then, Karius doubted that he would have escaped the demon, but from somewhere in the distance, a sharp sound had suddenly echoed.

The hideous hound's reaction to it had been both instantaneous and astonishing. It cringed first, then immediately leapt toward the source of the noise. Self-preservation urged Karius to immediately drag himself in the opposite direction. He had not even paused to bind the wound, which at that time had only been bloody. The mauled night elf had struggled all the way back to his waiting mate, each harsh step of the journey expecting the creature to return to finish him.

Tyrande digested his tale with a great sense of foreboding. Karius had indeed been very fortunate to survive an encounter with a felbeast. What that abomination had been doing behind the lines, however, worried her. Of course, one such beast, while dangerous, could be readily dealt with by Malfurion or the wizards. But what if there were more?

That in mind, she asked, "You mentioned a sound that drew it away. What sort of sound?"

Karius thought for a moment before responding, "It was a sharp, cracking sound."

"Like thunder?"

"Nay . . . it reminded me of . . . of the crack of a whip, I'd say."

The priestess rose to her feet. "I thank you for your patience. If you'll forgive me, I must be on my way."

"Nay!" protested the female. " 'Tis *we* who thank you again, sister! I thought to lose him!"

Tyrande did not have time to argue any more. She gave both the blessing of the temple, then quickly went to where Shandris watched her with eyes as wide as plates.

"You healed him completely! I-I thought he would be dead before you could start!"

"As did I," Tyrande returned, mounting behind the child. "The Mother Moon was generous to me."

"I've never seen a priestess heal a wound so horrible . . . and that monster that made it—"

"Hush, Shandris. I must think." The priestess took command of the night saber, turning the cat toward where last she recalled seeing the spellcasters. In her role as cleric, Tyrande often obtained information that even Lord Ravencrest's strategists never picked up. Now, once again, she had heard something that Malfurion and Krasus needed to know.

The Legion's assassins were closing in on them.

The black dragons returned under cover of night to their vast lair. Neltharion had been eager to come home, for there was much to be done. His plan was so near to fruition that he could taste it.

A smaller male atop a peak resembling an upraised talon dipped his head in homage. The Earth Warder paid him no mind, his thoughts too caught up in the moment. He landed in the mouth of the flight's main cavern and immediately turned to his consorts, who dropped behind him. Deeper within the cavern, the roars of other dragons could be heard.

"I go below. I must not be disturbed."

The females nodded, having heard this command from him oft before. They did not ask what the Aspect did down there. Like all in the black flight, they existed to obey. Every creature in the mountain was touched to some degree by the same madness that affected Neltharion most of all.

The huge black maneuvered through tunnels that barely allowed his immense form passage. As he descended deeper, the sounds of dragon life vanished and a new, odd noise echoed over and over. To any who listened, it most resembled what one might note in a blacksmith's shop, for there could be heard repeated hammering on metal. The hammering went on without end, and as it increased in tempo, Neltharion's savage smile grew wider, more satisfied. Yes, everything was coming to pass.

But the dragon did not head to the source of the hammering. Instead he turned at a side passage and continued his descent. After a time, the hammering faded away, leaving only Neltharion's heavy breathing to echo in the dark corridors. No one but he was allowed to walk these lower chambers.

At last, the Earth Warder reached the vast chamber where he had cast his spell upon the Eredar. Yet, as he entered, the dragon's head picked up, for he sensed that, despite appearances, he was not alone.

And the voices in his mind, the voices that had remained but steady murmurs while he had been among the other dragons, suddenly rose in a frenzy of excitement.

Soon . . .

Soon . . .

The world will be set to right . . .

All those who have betrayed you will know their place . . .

Order will be restored . . .

You will take your rightful rule . . .

This and more they repeated over and over to the Earth Warder. His chest swelled with pride and his eyes glittered with anticipation. Soon his world would be as *he* desired it!

"They have all given of themselves," he told the empty air. "Even absent Nozdormu."

The voices did not reply, but the dragon seemed to accept that they were pleased. He nodded to himself, then closed his eyes and concentrated.

And at his summoning, the Dragon Soul materialized.

"Behold its beauty," he rumbled as it floated level with his admiring gaze. "Behold its perfection, its power."

The golden aura surrounded his creation, glowing with an intensity never before achieved. As Neltharion fixed his will upon it, the Dragon Soul began to quietly vibrate. Throughout the chamber, the stalactites and stalagmites began to shake as if stirring to life.

The disk's vibration increased with each eager breath by

the Earth Warder. The entire chamber now trembled. Fragments of rock broke free from the ceiling, and several huge stalactites quivered ominously.

"Yes . . ." the dragon hissed eagerly. Neltharion's eyes burned with anticipation. "Yes . . ."

Now the very mountain rumbled as if some huge volcanic eruption or great tremor took place. The ceiling began to break in earnest. Huge stones dropped everywhere, striking the floor with ear-shattering booms. Many bounded off the massive dragon's hard hide, but he cared not at all.

Then, from the Dragon Soul ethereal shapes arose. They were shadows of light, vague images that darted around. Most had wings and their outlines were akin to that of Neltharion. Some were black, some bronze, others blue or red. They began to swarm above the disk, rapidly growing in number.

There were other shapes as well, smaller but more grotesque ones. They glowed a sickly green and many had horns and deep pits for eyes. Their numbers were far smaller, but there was an intensity, an evil, that made them as arresting as the intermingling ghosts above them.

They were the essences of all those who had contributed to the Dragon Soul's creation, willingly or not. Tied to the disk, they represented, together, power that dwarfed even that of an Aspect such as Neltharion. Their simple appearance was enough to cause cracks and fissures in the solid mountain as the entire region now shook with vehemence.

A gargantuan stalactite suddenly broke free. Caught up in his reverie, the Earth Warder did not notice it until it was too late.

Only a formation of this magnitude could have injured the black dragon. It struck Neltharion on the left side of his jaw, ripping away even the hard, scaled flesh. One piece of bloody scale went flying, its hard edge hitting the Dragon Soul at the center.

Neltharion roared with horror, not for himself but rather at what had happened to his precious creation. The scale gouged the disk deep, ruining its perfection. The shapes above and below spun in an uncontrolled frenzy.

The dragon acted quickly, ending the spell. The ghostly figures sank back into the disk, but slower, more hesitantly than he desired. As they vanished, the tremor ceased, leaving only drifting dust to mark its brief but terrible passage.

When it was safe to do so, Neltharion seized the Dragon Soul and held it close. The gouge was not as deep as he had thought, but that it existed at all nearly threw him into a new fit. He had not expected anything, much less *himself*, to be a danger to the disk.

"You will be healed," he whispered, cradling the tiny piece in his paw as a mother might cradle her child in her arms. "You will be my perfection again . . ."

Clutching the disk tightly, he departed the chamber as quickly as he could on three limbs, heading back up in a swift, half-hopping motion. Neltharion radiated a pensiveness that would have unnerved even his consorts. The Earth Warder's breathing turned ragged, as if he feared that all he had wrought would now be for nothing.

Rather than return to where his own kind dwelled, however, the dragon veered to another series of tunnels. The hammering echoed louder as Neltharion moved his tremendous bulk through the narrow corridors, soon becoming distinct sounds of hard work. Peculiar voices chittered away, but their exact words were drowned out by the hammers.

Neltharion thrust himself into the new chamber. The fiery illumination forced him to let his eyes adjust for a moment. When they had, they revealed scores of tiny, limber goblins busy in various stages of metalwork. There were huge ovens everywhere, all fueled by the raging, molten earth far below. Half a dozen of the green-skinned creatures struggled to remove from one huge casing what seemed an oval shield fit for a giant. The metal inside blazed a bright orange. The goblins quickly turned the casing over, letting its contents drop into a vat of water. Steam rose in a tremendous burst, nearly boiling one slow worker.

Other goblins hammered away at various pieces. A few wearing smocks wandered among the rest, making certain that everyone did his task properly.

Not finding what he searched for around the chamber, Neltharion roared, "Meklo! Meklo, attend me!"

The leviathan's cry overwhelmed all other sounds. Startled, the goblins halted in their work. Two almost poured molten iron on a comrade.

"To work, to work!" snapped a high-pitched, irritated voice. "Want to ruin all?"

The laborers immediately obeyed. From a walkway above, a spindly goblin of elder years, with a tuft of gray fur atop his otherwise bald head, scampered down to the impatient dragon. The chief goblin muttered to himself all the way, but his words held no anger against his master. Instead, he appeared to be constantly calculating things.

"Density of eight inches with a surface area of a hundred twenty square feet, which means approximately adding forty-two more pounds to the mix and—" His foot bounced against the center toe of the remaining forepaw. The goblin glanced up, acting almost surprised to see the leviathan. "My Lord Neltharion?"

"Meklo! See this!"

The Earth Warder brought his huge paw close so that the

goblin could study the disk. Meklo squinted, making a *tsk*ing sound.

"Such craftwork, and now marred! The design was flawless!"

"A scale of mine fell upon it, goblin! Explain why that should damage the invulnerable!"

"Blood, too, I see." Meklo looked up, surveying Neltharion's injury for a moment before tsking again. "Of course, this makes perfect sense! My Lord Neltharion, you were integral in the formation of the disk itself, yes?"

"You were there, goblin. You know."

"Yes. You created the matrix of its construction." The head goblin thought a moment more, than asked, "The others, they've given their essences? They're tied into the disk's matrix?"

"Of course."

"Aaah, but *you* are not. You created the Dragon Soul matrix, formed it with your power and blood, but you are the only dragon not directly bound to it." The goblin grinned, showing pointed yellow teeth. "That makes you its *only* weakness, my lord. The scale, your blood . . . any part of you has the capability of destroying the Dragon Soul. You could crush the disk with ease, I imagine." Meklo made a squashing gesture with his index finger and thumb.

The Earth Warder's eyes grew monstrous to behold, even for the goblin. "I would never do such a thing!"

"Of course not, of course not!" babbled Meklo, groveling for Neltharion. "Which means that *nothing* can ever destroy it, eh?"

The fury smoldering within the dragon lessened. Neltharion's lip stretched back, revealing teeth larger than the goblin. "Yes, *nothing*. So, my Dragon Soul is . . . is invulnerable!"

"So long as you take no part in its destruction," the spindly figure dared remind him.

"Which shall never happen!" Neltharion gazed down at the damage wrought on the Dragon Soul. "But this must be repaired! The disk must be perfect again!"

"It'll require what it did last time."

The dragon scoffed. "You will have all of my blood that you need! It will be whole!"

"Naturally, naturally." Meklo peered back at the other goblins. "It will slow completion of your other plans. We need your blood and magic for those, as well."

"All else can wait! The disk cannot!"

"Then we shall begin now, my lord. Permit me a moment to shut down work. I will return with the necessary assistance, then."

As the goblin retreated, Neltharion breathed easier. His precious creation would be healed. Like him, it would be perfect once more.

And together, they would rule all . . .

TEN

"**T**his is insufferable!" Lord Stareye said, removing a pinch of powder from his pouch and sniffing into one nostril. "A perfect opportunity wasted, Kur'talos!"

"Perhaps, Desdel. Perhaps not. Still, it's done and must be looked past now."

The two nobles stood in Lord Ravencrest's tent with several other aristocratic officers, discussing a plan of action now that the rout had been stopped. Desdel Stareye, however, was convinced that Krasus had been premature in deciding that the host had to come to a halt just when they had their enemy on the run. Stareye felt certain that the night elves could have advanced all the way to Suramar unhindered if they had just listened to him—an opinion he had voiced more than once since Krasus and the others had joined the group.

"The soldiers have fought valiantly," the mage replied politely, "but they are of flesh and blood and are flagging. They must have this rest."

"Food, too," grunted Brox, who had accompanied the spellcasters. The night elves had clearly not desired the orc's company, but as Ravencrest had not commanded him to be put out, no one, not even Stareye, would make an objection to his presence.

"Yes, there is that," the master of Black Rook Hold agreed. "The soldiers and refugees are eating and bedding down and that's the end of it. Now, then, we move on to what must happen next."

"Zin-Azshari, certainly!" piped up Lord Stareye. "Queen Azshara must be saved!"

The other nobles echoed his sentiments. Krasus frowned, but said nothing. He and the others had discussed the matter before their arrival, and all had agreed that the night elves would cling to the belief that their monarch was a prisoner of the demons. Since Zin-Azshari was also the access point by which the Burning Legion entered Kalimdor, it seemed futile to argue for any other course of action. For one reason or another, the capital had to be taken.

Krasus did not think, however, that Malfurion's people could do it alone.

Ignoring protocol, he stepped up and demanded, "My Lord Ravencrest! I must speak again on a subject I know you wish not to hear, but that cannot be avoided!"

Ravencrest accepted a goblet of wine poured by Lord Stareye. Even in the midst of crisis, the hierarchy of the night elves insisted on some benefits. "You'd be referring to communications with dwarves and such."

Next to him, Stareye scoffed. Similar expressions graced the features of most of the other nobles.

Despite that it was clear that this would be a repeat of all his previous defeats, the mage persisted. "At this moment, the dwarves, tauren, and other races are surely fighting their own struggles against the Burning Legion. Separately, there is some small chance that you will survive, but a concerted effort by all *could* see Zin-Azshari taken with a loss of far fewer lives!"

"Tauren in Zin-Azshari?" blurted one noble. "How barbaric!"

"They'd rather have the *demons* there?" muttered Rhonin to Malfurion.

"You wouldn't understand," the druid replied morosely.

"No, I wouldn't."

The bearded commander downed his wine, then handed the goblet back to Lord Stareye. He eyed the mage as one would a respected, albeit misguided, elder. "Master Krasus, your contributions to our strategy have been well appreciated. Your knowledge of your craft exceeds that of any of our sorcerers. In the guidance of the arts, I heartily turn to you for suggestions." Ravencrest's frown deepened. "However, when it comes to *other* matters, I must remind you that you aren't one of us. You don't understand basic truths. Even if I did something as mad as summon the dwarves and tauren to our aid, do you think honestly they would come? They distrust us as much as we do them! For that matter, even if they would join us, do you expect our soldiers to fight alongside?"

"The dwarves are more likely to turn on us," interjected Stareye. "Their avarice is well-documented. They would rob us and then scurry back to their holes."

Another officer added, "And the tauren would spend as much time fighting with one another. They are beasts more than intelligent creatures! Their chaos would spill over into *our* fighters, cause such disarray that we would be easily wiped out by the demons!"

Lord Ravencrest agreed. "You see, Master Krasus? We would be inviting not only bedlam into our midst, but certain destruction."

"We may yet face that by going on alone."

"This particular discussion is at an end, good wizard, and I must respectfully order that you do not bring it up again."

The two stared at each other for several seconds . . . and it was Ravencrest who glanced away first. Despite that small victory, though, Krasus acquiesced.

"Forgive me for overstepping my bounds," he said.

"We are about to discuss supplies and logistics, Master Krasus. There really is no need for the presence of any spell-caster during this session, save Illidan, who serves me directly. I would suggest that you and the others get some much needed rest yourselves. Your skills will be welcome when we advance again."

Krasus bowed politely, saying nothing more. With the others following, he calmly glided out of the tent.

But once out of earshot of those within, the pale mage commented bitterly, "Their shortsightedness will put a tragic end to this struggle. Alliance with the other races is the key to victory . . ."

"They won't accept them," Malfurion insisted. "My people will never fight alongside such."

"They accepted Korialstrasz readily enough," countered Rhonin.

"There are few who can deny a dragon, Master Rhonin."

"Too true," muttered Krasus, looking thoughtful. "Rhonin, I must go find them."

"Find who?"

"My—the dragons, of course."

Brox snorted and Malfurion looked startled. The druid knew that Krasus had a link with Korialstrasz, but even now he did not understand the full truth.

"The dragons, Master Krasus? But they're a force unto themselves! How can you possibly think to do so?"

"I have my methods . . . but to accomplish the fact also requires swift transportation. The night sabers will never do for that. I need something that can fly."

"Like a dragon?" Rhonin asked wryly.

"Something smaller will suffice, my friend."

To the surprise of the others, it was Malfurion who suddenly came up with a suggestion. "There are woods not far from here. Perhaps . . . perhaps I can contact Cenarius. He may have a solution."

From Krasus's expression, this was not entirely satisfying, but no one could come up with anything better. He finally nodded, saying, "We shall have to depart as soon as possible, then. Captain Shadowsong will otherwise either seek to detain us or, even worse, follow with his troops behind us. I fear that will draw both the Burning Legion and the night elves to our mission."

Jarod and the rest of the bodyguard had been given time to recuperate. No one thought the wizards in physical danger amidst the host, and the soldiers could hardly defend against any magical assault better than their charges. Come the march, the bodyguard would immediately resume its duties, of course.

But by then, Krasus hoped to be on his way.

"Do you really think this necessary?" asked the red-tressed wizard.

"I go for two reasons, Rhonin. The first is that of which we speak. The dragons can turn the tide. As for the second reason, that is more personal. I go to see why I sense only silence from them. That should not be so, as you understand. I need to discover the truth."

He received no more objections. Lord Ravencrest intended for the night elves to march at first dark, and Krasus had to be far from here before he was discovered missing.

Rhonin nodded. "What about Brox and me?"

"If our druid friend here can gain me transportation as he says, he will be able to return well before nightfall. In the meantime, you and Brox must try to stay from the sight of Lord Ravencrest. He may ask about us. He will be furious enough when he discovers I have left."

"Maybe, maybe not. At least no one will be questioning his decisions out loud."

Ignoring the human's jest, Krasus turned to Malfurion. "We must go. If we take a pair of night sabers toward the area of the refugees, the soldiers will not bother with us much. We can then come around and head toward the woods." He let out a slight hiss. "And then we must pray that your patron will come to our aid."

They quickly left the others, following the elder mage's suggestion as to their course. Soldiers eyed them with some suspicion and curiosity, but as the pair were not heading toward the front, the looks did not last long.

Malfurion was still uncomfortable with Krasus's mission, but did not question the conjurer. He respected the latter's wisdom and knew that Krasus understood the dragons better than anyone he had ever met. Often, he even seemed almost one of them. Surely somewhere in his past, Krasus had enjoyed the unique experience of having dwelled among the ancient creatures for some period of time. What other explanation could there be for his link to the leviathans?

It took nearly three hours, but they finally entered the woods. The comfort Malfurion felt the last time he had entered such a place did not touch him now. This forest had experienced the taint of the Legion and the marks remained. If not for the sudden turnaround by the defenders, it very well would have been reduced to ruin already.

Despite the imminent threat, life still abounded here. Birds sang, and the druid could sense the trees sending ahead word of the new intruders. The rustling grew particularly fierce whenever Krasus neared, almost as if the forest, too, could sense his differences. They did, of course, also welcome the night elf, clearly noting his aura and the obvious blessing of Cenarius.

But of the demigod, the druid sensed nothing. Cenarius had many tasks at hand, foremost trying to stir his counterparts to an active and organized defense of their world. How, then, could Malfurion hope that the woodland deity would have time to respond to his call?

"This land has suffered much already," his companion uttered. "I can taste the evil that has been here."

"So do I, Krasus, I don't know if Cenarius will hear me here after all."

"I can but ask you to attempt to reach him, Malfurion. If you fail, I will not hold it against you. I will then have to make do with the night saber, although that will slow my journey greatly."

They reached a spot deep in the woods where the druid sensed a bit more tranquillity. He informed Krasus of this and the pair dismounted.

"Shall I leave you alone?" asked the mage.

"If Cenarius chooses to come, he will do so even if you are with me, Master Krasus."

Malfurion found a seat among the soft, wild grass. Krasus stepped respectfully to one side so as not to disturb the druid.

Closing his eyes, Malfurion focused. He reached out first to the trees, the plants, and other life, seeking from them any hint of the demigod's recent presence. If Cenarius had been here, he would soon know.

But the forest offered no hints of the deity. Frustrated, the druid considered his other options. Unfortunately, only the Emerald Dream truly offered him a certain way of immediately contacting his *shan'do*.

It was as he had feared. Exhaling, Malfurion concentrated on the ethereal realm. He did not have to enter it completely, only touch upon its edges. Then he could send out his thoughts to Cenarius. Even interacting that much with it bothered Malfurion, but it had to be done.

He felt himself beginning to separate from his mortal shell. However, instead of allowing the transition to complete, the druid held himself midway. Doing so proved more of a strain than he had thought, but Malfurion did not plan to stay in such a state long. He imagined Cenarius as he knew him, using that to help create a link . . .

His concentration was suddenly jarred by a voice in his ear.

"Malfurion! We are not alone!"

The rapid retreat back into his body shook the druid. Momentarily stunned, he could do nothing else save open his eyes . . . in time to see a felbeast charging toward him.

Someone muttered words of power, and the hideous hound shriveled within itself. The beast curled and twisted, swiftly becoming a grotesque, mangled pile of bone and sinew.

Krasus grabbed Malfurion by the arms, lifting him with startling strength. The elder mage asked, "Can you defend yourself yet?"

The druid had no time to respond, for suddenly the woods came alive with not only the demonic hounds, but horned, bestial Fel Guard. The two spellcasters were outnumbered at least ten to one. Their mounts, bound to one tree, snarled and pulled at their tethers, but could not free themselves. The demons, however, ignored the panthers, their targets clearly being the mage and the druid.

Drawing an invisible line around them, Krasus uttered another short spell. Crystalline spikes thrust up from the ground, growing to the height of a night elf.

Three Fel Guard became impaled on the spikes. A felbeast howled as another spike tore off part of its muzzle.

Krasus's swift action gave Malfurion time to think. He looked to the trees nearest the oncoming demons and asked of them their aid.

Thick, foliage-covered branches stretched down and snagged four of the monstrous warriors. They pulled the demons high, dragging them from sight. Malfurion could not see what happened to the victims, but he noted well that they did not reappear.

Other trees merely stuck their branches out, timing their appearance to the Legion's charge. One felbeast tumbled helplessly as it fell over a branch; another was even less fortunate, its neck cracking when it collided with the unexpected obstruction.

Yet still the demons swarmed them, especially the hounds. They seemed to leer as they approached, the notion of two trapped spellcasters no doubt stirring their hunger.

Despite the effectiveness of Malfurion's attack, the demons seemed to fear Krasus more, and with good reason. Possessing knowledge of his craft far greater than the night elf's of his own, the mage cast with both speed and extreme ruthlessness. It was a far cry from the sickly figure he had been when first they had met. True, Krasus appeared under immense strain even now, but he in no way faltered because of it.

A crack like thunder echoed throughout the forest. Krasus grasped at his throat, where a thin, blazing tentacle now wrapped around it, tightening like a noose. The mage was pulled back off his feet and dragged toward the very spikes he had created.

Daring a glance over his shoulder, the night elf beheld a sight nearly as frightening as Archimonde—a huge, skeletal knight, his head a horned skull with flames for eyes, using a fearsome whip to drag Krasus to his doom. The newcomer stood taller than the other demons, and from the way they parted for him, Malfurion guessed that this was the leader.

Seizing a few blades of grass, the druid tossed them toward the sinister lash. The grass blades spun swiftly as they flew, then sliced away at the whip like well-honed knives until at last one cut completely through.

Krasus gasped as the end of the lash separated. He fell to his knees, trying to unbind what remained. The demon stumbled a few steps back but managed to sustain his balance. He drew back the whip and prepared to use its still-formidable length against the druid.

Surrounded by demons, his companion incapacitated, Malfurion did not hold much hope for his chances of survival. He and Krasus had not only left themselves open to the demonic assassins ever trailing them, but this time their leader had come to ensure there would be no escape. No Jarod would come to their aid. Only Rhonin and Brox knew of their departure, and both assumed that the pair would be all right. How misguided they had all been.

To his surprise, though, the demon did not immediately strike again. Instead, he hissed to Malfurion, "Sssurrender, creature, and you will be ssspared! I promissse thisss in the name of my mossst honored massster, Sssargerasss! It isss your only hope of sssurvival . . ."

Krasus coughed, trying to clear his throat. "S-surrendering to the Burning Legion i-is a fate far worse than the most terrible death! We must fight even if we are destined to lose, Malfurion!"

Grim memories of his brief encounter with Archimonde made the night elf think the very same thing. He could just imagine what the demons would do with prisoners, especially those who had been instrumental in foiling their plans so far. "We'll never surrender!"

His fiery orbs flickered angrily, and the demon snapped his whip four times. Lightning flashed as the lash struck the earth. Huge shapes suddenly formed before the demon. With each snap, a fiendish hound materialized.

"Then my petsss will feed well upon you, ssspellcast-ersss!"

Krasus steadied himself, then turned to gaze at the lead demon. His eyes narrowed dangerously.

But the skeletal knight was prepared for his attack. He swung the whip around and around, creating a haze. The haze sparkled suddenly, as if something exploded against it.

The night elf bit back an epithet. Their adversary had easily dealt with what should have been a powerful spell.

"It is as I feared," Krasus muttered. "It is the Hound-master. *Hakkar!*"

Malfurion would have liked to ask him what he knew of the demon, but at that moment the other monsters resumed their charge. The spikes provided some defense, but the demons now began tearing, clawing, and chopping them apart. In the background, their leader laughed, a sound like a hundred angry serpents.

Yet, just as the first of the Fel Guard tore through and started for the pair, warriors astride night sabers charged into the battle from all sides, their beasts mauling some of the demons before the latter realized they were under assault. As the newcomers attacked, they sang.

Malfurion gaped at them, only belatedly realizing that they were not the soldiers of Jarod Shadowsong. Their armor was more silver and—he looked twice—shaped for more feminine figures. The song he heard was in praise of the Night Warrior, the fearsome battle incarnation of the Mother Moon.

The Sisterhood of Elune had come to their rescue.

For the first time, Malfurion saw the quiet, gentle priestesses in their wartime roles. Many carried long, curved swords, while others wielded short lances with points on both ends. A few even had bows no longer than their forearms, from which they swiftly shot dart after dart.

The effect on the demons was immediate. Felbeasts dropped, riddled. A priestess swung her blade with the ease of a soldier, decapitating a horned warrior. Two night sabers dropped upon another hound, slashing it repeatedly from both sides until all that remained was a bloody carcass.

And among the fearsome figures now wreaking havoc on the Burning Legion, he saw Tyrande.

Before he could call to her, a demon thrust at him. The towering Fel Guard would have cut through the druid if not for his swift reflexes. The night elf rolled out of range, then cast a spell.

The ground beneath his adversary's feet turned into a wet, sandy mixture. The Fel Guard sank in up to his waist, but managed to keep from dropping any farther. He clawed at the edge with his free hand, trying to pull himself free.

Malfurion gave him no such opportunity. He kicked the blade out of the demon's hand, then ran after it. The monstrous warrior twisted about, trying to snare his legs. Malfurion slipped, one foot caught by his foe. He seized the hilt of the sword just as the demon dragged him to the quicksand.

Swinging with all his might, the druid buried the blade in the Fel Guard's head.

As the demon sank slowly into the mire, Malfurion saw that not all was going well. The sisterhood had the upper hand, but more than one of them faced imminent threat. Even as he straightened, one priestess was torn from the saddle by a felbeast, who bit through her neck as easily as through silk. Another sister tumbled to the ground as a demon drove his weapon through the open jaws of a night saber, the other end of the blade bursting out between the cat's shoulder blades. A second warrior dispatched the priestess a moment later.

But what terrified Malfurion most was when his gaze fixed upon Tyrande once more. Locked in combat with one of the Fel Guard, she failed to notice the Houndmaster and his whip.

The lash should have wrapped around her throat, but a chance shift by her mount instead had it bind her arms to the sides. The skeletal knight tugged hard, pulling Tyrande off her panther as if her armored form weighed nothing.

"No!" cried Malfurion, starting after her.

Krasus, in the midst of casting a spell, tried to grab his arm. "Druid, you are safer here—"

But the night elf cared only about Tyrande. His training all but forgotten, he angled his way through the battle. When he got near enough, he leapt—but not for his childhood friend.

The immense form of the Houndmaster resisted Malfurion's weight as he struck the demon, but it did cause the hideous figure to lose his concentration. The whip loosened its grip on the priestess, letting her land softly on the earth.

"Fool!" spat the Houndmaster, grabbing the druid by his shoulder. "I am Hakkar . . . and you are nothing."

He did not see the dagger that Malfurion pulled from his belt. The small blade sank into the demon's arm at the place where the elbow joint offered some vulnerability.

With a howl, Hakkar dropped his quarry. He pulled the dagger free, the sharp blade covered in the thick ooze that was the demon's blood. However, instead of using the dagger on Malfurion, the Houndmaster tossed it aside and retrieved his fallen whip. He stalked toward the rising druid, arm already raised.

"Hisss ordersss are to keep you alive if posssible . . . I think it will *not* be posssible, though . . ."

Hakkar struck. Malfurion clamored in pain as lightning flared all over his body. He felt as if he were being burned alive.

However, a part of him remained calm throughout his agony. It drew upon Cenarius's teachings, pulling Malfurion away from his pain. The anguish of the whip faded into nothing. The Houndmaster struck him a second and third time, but it might as well have been a slight breeze for all the druid felt it.

Malfurion understood that the punishment would eventually ravage his body regardless of the lack of pain. His *shan'do*'s teachings but gave him the chance to do what he could to defend himself . . . if at all possible.

"I will keep you jussst barely alive, perhapsss," mocked Hakkar, hitting him again. "All he ssseeksss isss enough life to torture! There will be jussst that . . . "

The fearsome giant raised his whip again.

Malfurion's gaze twisted up to the heavens. The cloud cover offered him his best hope, and the Houndmaster, ironically, had aided in that choice.

The wind assisted him first, stirring the clouds to motion. They disliked being so disturbed and in their anger quickly grew black. Although it went against his nature, Malfurion fed their rage, then played on their vanity. There was one here who commanded lightning of his own and flaunted it.

Hakkar took his stillness for surrender. Eyes blazing, the Houndmaster pulled his arm back. "One more ssstroke, I think! One more ssstroke . . ."

The clouds rumbled, shook.

Lightning shot down, not one but *two* bolts that hit the huge demon dead on.

Hakkar let out a roar of pain that made every bone in Malfurion's body shiver. The Houndmaster stood bathed in brilliant light, his arms outstretched as if he sought to embrace that which destroyed him. The whip, already burnt black, fell from his trembling grasp.

All around the scene of the battle, the felbeasts abruptly paused in their struggles and howled mournfully.

At last, the heavenly illumination faded away . . . and the ashy corpse of the demon lord dropped limply to the grass.

The monstrous hounds howled once more, then their bodies glowed as they had when first summoned. As one, the felbeasts *vanished,* their cries still resounding.

Bereft of both Hakkar and his pets, the few remaining demons put up little resistance against the priestesses and Krasus. As the last fell slain, Malfurion staggered over to Tyrande.

She sat on the ground, still half-stunned. When she saw him, however, Tyrande's face broke out into a wonderful smile that made Malfurion forget his own pain.

"Tyrande! This miracle is yours . . ."

"No miracle, Malfurion. One who I healed told me of a felbeast behind our lines. He also described hearing what I believed was the demon commanding them." She gazed briefly at what remained of Hakkar. "I went to warn you and the others, only to find that Krasus and you had departed for here. Perhaps it was Elune speaking to me, but I felt certain that you were at risk."

"So you turned to the sisterhood. I've seen few soldiers who fight better."

She gave him another smile, this one tired but pleased. "There is much about the temple that outsiders do not understand." Her expression grew more serious. "Are you all right?"

"I am . . . but I fear that Krasus and I came here for no good reason. I'd hoped to contact Cenarius so that the wizard might be able to gain some sort of mount that could carry him to the land of the dragons."

"Rhonin and Brox hinted as much, but I could scarcely believe—does he truly dream that he can meet with them?"

The druid glanced over at Krasus, who had been aided in rising by two of the sisters. Like so many others, they treated him with reverence even though they were not quite certain why. The mage strode toward where the Houndmaster lay, his expression perturbed. "You see him. You sense something within him, Tyrande. I think he can do it, if somehow he reaches their realm."

"But unless a dragon itself carries him there, how else can he make the journey in good time?"

"I don't know. I—" A sudden shadow covered the pair. Malfurion looked up, and his hopeless expression changed to one of wonder.

They circled the party thrice before finally ascending in an area away from the nearest night saber. The cats hissed, but did not otherwise attempt to attack the new arrivals, perhaps because they themselves were not sure what to make of them.

With their vast, feathered wings and ravenlike heads, they

resembled jet-black gryphons at first sight. Even the fore-limbs were scaled and taloned like those of the aforementioned creature. Beyond that, however, they were entirely different animals. Instead of leonine torsos and hindquarters, these two had equine forms, even down to the thick tails.

"*Hippogriffs,*" declared the knowledgeable Krasus, his disturbed expression shifting to one of intense satisfaction. "Swift and certain fliers. He could not have chosen better, your Cenarius."

Tyrande did not look so thrilled. "But there are *two* of them."

The mage and Malfurion studied each other, both recognizing why Cenarius would send more than one mount.

"I'm to go with Krasus, it seems," answered the druid.

Seizing him by the arm, Tyrande snapped, "No, Malfurion! Not there!"

"I see the sense of the forest lord's decision," Krasus interjected. "The druid will be better able to guide the hippogriffs, and his link to Cenarius will give him good standing with the queen of the reds, Alexstrasza . . . She Who Is Life."

The priestess's eyes pleaded with him, but Malfurion had to agree. "He's right. I have to go with him. Forgive me, Tyrande." On impulse, the druid hugged her. Tyrande hesitated, then returned the brief hug. Malfurion gazed down at her and added, "I fear you might have to help Rhonin and Brox explain our absence. Will you do that for me?"

She finally surrendered to the inevitable. "Of course I will. You should know me that well."

The hippogriffs squawked, as if impatient to be on their way. Krasus obliged them by quickly mounting. Malfurion climbed aboard the second one, eyes still on Tyrande.

Seizing his wrist, she suddenly started whispering. It took

a moment for the two riders to realize that Tyrande was giving Malfurion a blessing from Elune.

"Go safely," she finished quietly. "And return the same way . . . for me."

The druid swallowed, unable to say anything. Krasus ended the awkwardness of the situation by gently prodding his hippogriff in the ribs with his heels. The beast squawked again, then turned in preparation for flight. Malfurion's mount instinctively followed suit.

"Farewell and thank you, Tyrande," he called. "I'll be back soon enough."

"I will hold you to that, Mal."

He smiled at her use of his childhood nickname, then had to cling on tight as the hippogriff charged into the air after its mate.

"The journey will be long," shouted Krasus, "but not nearly so long, thanks to the demigod's gift!"

Malfurion nodded, not entirely paying attention. His gaze remained on the shrinking figure below. He watched her watch him in turn, until finally he could no longer see her at all.

And even then he watched more, at that instant knowing in his heart that Tyrande did exactly the same.

ELEVEN

The demons did not regroup and attack, which the night elves took as a promising sign even if Rhonin and Brox felt otherwise. Ravencrest dared use another evening to let his troops rest more and although both outsiders agreed with the need for that, they also knew that the Burning Legion would be in no way idle during that period. Archimonde would be plotting, planning, each second his adversaries delayed.

The discovery of the disappearance of Krasus and Malfurion did not sit well with the night elves. Jarod looked as if he were heading to the gallows, and not without good reason. It had been his responsibility to see that nothing happened to the desperately-needed spellcasters, and now some of them had abandoned the host under his very nose.

"Lord Ravencrest will have my hide for this!" the former Guard officer uttered more than once as he and the others headed to the noble's tent. That Tyrande, who had just returned after seeing Malfurion and Krasus off, had insisted on coming to help explain matters did not comfort Jarod in the least. He was certain that he would receive the most terrible punishment for having let such valuable members of the host simply leave.

And, indeed, it initially appeared that the bearded elder might do as he said. Upon hearing the news, Lord Ravencrest let out a furious roar and struck aside the small table that he had been using for his various charts and notes.

"I gave no permission for such foolish activities!" yelled the master of Black Rook Hold. "By perpetrating this outrage, they threaten the stability of our forces! If word should leak out that two of our spellcasters have abandoned us at this integral moment—"

"They didn't abandon anyone," protested Rhonin. "They went for help."

"From the dragons? Those two might as well walk directly into the jaws of the first one they see, for all the aid we can expect from those creatures! The wizard's pet was good enough assistance under his guidance, but wild dragons . . ."

"The dragons are the oldest, most intelligent race of our world. They know more than we will ever learn."

"And they're likely to *eat* most of us before we even get the chance to!" Ravencrest retorted. He glanced at Tyrande, and his tone grew a bit more respectful. "And what part does a Sister of Elune have in all this?"

"We have met before, my lord."

He peered closer. "Aaah, yes! We have! Your female friend, Illidan!"

The sorcerer, who had been silently standing to the side, nodded. Illidan's expression revealed nothing.

Ravencrest crossed his arms. "I had hopes that *either* of you might have some influence over young Malfurion at least. I know that no one can command Master Krasus, no one, indeed."

"Malfurion meant to come back," the priestess countered, "but his patron gave indication that he should travel with the wizard."

"Patron? You refer to that nonsense about the demigod, Cenarius?"

Tyrande pursed her lips. "Illidan can attest to the existence of the forest lord."

His mask crumbling, Malfurion's twin muttered, " 'Tis true. Cenarius is real. I've seen him."

"Hmmph! Dragons and now demigods! All this might and magic abounding around us, yet we are *losing* strength, not gaining! I suppose this Cenarius also has reasons for not siding with us!"

"He and his kind battle the demons in their own manner," she answered.

"And speaking of the demons, did not either of these fools consider that they're constantly at risk from assassins? What if they were attacked before they ever—" Ravencrest paused as he noted the shifting gazes of the party. "*Were* they attacked?"

The priestess bowed her head. "Yes, my lord. I and my sisters were there. We aided them in defeating the demons. Both left uninjured."

Next to her, Jarod grimaced and Illidan shook his head in exasperation. Ravencrest exhaled, then fell back onto the short bench he had been utilizing for a chair. Grasping an open flask of wine, he downed a good portion and rasped, "Tell me about *that*."

Tyrande did, briefly recapping her discovery of assassins nearby, then her horror when she found out that Malfurion and Krasus had already ridden off to the woods. She and her sisters had raced like the proverbial wind after the pair, and had come upon them in the midst of a titanic struggle. The priestesses had charged in fully aware that they risked their own lives and a few had perished, but all had felt that Krasus and the druid were essential to the overall victory. No sacrifice was too great to keep them alive.

At this point, a slight snort escaped Illidan, but Ravencrest appeared most interested. He listened carefully to the details of the battle, and when Tyrande spoke of the demon with the whip, his eyes lit up.

"One of their commanders, surely, the leader of their assassins," he noted.

"It seemed so. He was powerful, but Malfurion summoned the lightning from the heavens and slew him."

"Well struck!" The noble seemed caught between admiration and frustration. "And exactly the reason why at least the druid should've returned to us! We need his power!"

"The Moon Guard and I will make up for his unpermitted absence," Illidan insisted.

"It'll have to, sorcerer. It'll have to." He put the flask aside and stared at the party, especially Rhonin. "Do I have the word of *you*, wizard, that you'll not follow the path of your compatriot?"

"I want to see the Burning Legion defeated, Lord Ravencrest."

"Hmmph! Not at all a satisfactory answer, but one I expected from one of your ilk. Captain Shadowsong . . ."

Swallowing, the younger night elf stepped forward and saluted. "Yes, my lord!"

"I at first considered having you punished severely for your failure to keep this band under control. However, the more I know of them, the less I can imagine *anyone* managing to do that. That you've kept them alive and intact this long speaks of your merits. Continue your task—so long as you still have anyone to watch, that is."

It took a few seconds for the words to register with Jarod.

When he realized that the noble had actually *complimented* him for surviving his time with the spellcasters, the officer quickly saluted again. "Yes, my lord! My thanks, my lord!"

"No . . . *my* sympathies to you." Ravencrest leaned forward, reaching for one of the charts. "You are dismissed, all of you. You, too, Illidan." He shook his head as he eyed the sheet and muttered, "Mother Moon, spare me from all spellcasters . . ."

Malfurion's brother took his expulsion as if his patron had struck him full across the face with his gauntlet. Dipping his head in an aborted bow, the sorcerer followed the rest out of the commander's tent.

Brox and Rhonin strode side by side, both silent. Tyrande walked with the captain, who still looked awed that he had departed with his head attached to his neck.

A hand touched the priestess's shoulder. "Tyrande . . ."

The others moved on while she turned to face Illidan. Gone was his brief anger at being dismissed by his lord. Now he wore an intense expression akin to the last time that the pair had talked.

"Illidan? What—"

"I can't stay quiet any longer! Malfurion's terrible naïveté brings this on! This is the final straw! He's grown reckless, undeserving of you!"

She tried to politely step away. "Illidan, it's been a long, difficult—"

"Hear me out! I accepted his desire to learn this 'druidism' because I understood his hopes to be different! *I*, of all people, understood my brother's ambitions!"

"Malfurion is not—"

But again he would not let her finish. Amber eyes almost glowing, the sorcerer added, "This path he follows is erratic, dangerous! It is no saving grace! I know! He should've followed my path! The Well is the answer! See what I've accomplished in such a short time! The Moon Guard are mine to command and through them I've sent many a demon to death! Malfurion's path leads only to his own destruction—and possibly yours, as well!"

"What could you mean by that?"

"I know you care for both of us, Tyrande, and we, in turn, feel much for you. One of us will be your intended, we all know that, but where once I was willing to stand aside and let you choose without influence, I can't anymore!" He clutched her arm tightly. "I've got to protect you from Malfurion's insanity! I say again that the Well of Eternity is the only true source of power that can save us! Even the priestesses of Elune cannot cast the spells that I do! Be mine, and I can protect you properly! Better yet, I can *teach* you as your temple never could, make you understand the might the Well can offer you! Together, we could be a force more formidable than all the Moon Guard combined, for we'd be one in spirit and body! We'd—"

"Illidan!" she suddenly snapped. "Recall yourself!"

He immediately released her, looking as if stabbed in the heart. "Tyrande—"

"You shame yourself with your words concerning your brother, Illidan, and make assumptions with no basis in fact! Malfurion has done everything he could to save all our lives and the path he's chosen is a valued one! He may be the true survival of our kind, Illidan! The Well's becoming tainted! The demons draw from it in just the same manner as you. What does that say?"

"Don't be ridiculous! You compare the demons with my work?"

"Malfurion would—"

"Malfurion!" he shouted, his countenance increasingly

grim. "I see it now! What a bungler, what a buffoon I must seem to you!" He clenched his fist and raw energy flashed around it. "You've already chosen, Tyrande, even if you haven't said so."

"I've done nothing of the sort!"

"Malfurion . . ." Illidan repeated, teeth clenched tightly. "May the two of you be very happy . . . if we survive."

He spun around and headed to where the Moon Guard had stationed themselves. Tyrande watched him stride away. A tear fell unbidden from her eye.

"Shaman?" came a voice from behind.

The priestess jumped. "Broxigar?"

The orc nodded solemnly. "He's hurt you, shaman?"

"N-no . . . just a misunderstanding."

Brox eyed Illidan's receding backside. A low growl escaped the bestial warrior. "That one misunderstands much . . . and underestimates more."

"I'm all right. Did you wish something?"

Shrugging, the orc answered, "Nothing."

"You came back because I was with Illidan, didn't you?"

"This unworthy one owes you much, shaman . . . and owes that one something more."

The priestess's brow furrowed. "I don't understand."

Brox flexed his fingers, the same fingers that had been burned once by Illidan. "Is nothing, shaman. Is nothing."

"Thank you for coming to my aid, Broxigar. I'll be all right . . . and so will Malfurion. I know it."

The orc grunted. "This humble one hopes so."

But his eyes continued to watch Illidan closely.

Rhonin paused, watching the orc and the priestess talk. He understood perfectly why Brox had suddenly turned back to speak with Tyrande. Illidan's affections for her had begun to border on obsession. The sorcerer had not seemed all that fearful for his brother's life, and—from what the wizard could see—had been attempting to use Malfurion's absence to further his own cause with Tyrande.

But the triangle among the three night elves was the least of Rhonin's concerns. He was more preoccupied with what he had learned of the attack in the forest. While Rhonin was relieved that both Krasus and the druid had survived, their victory had, without meaning to, unnerved the human more than anything else since his arrival here.

They had battled Hakkar, the Houndmaster. Rhonin recalled that name with dread, for with his whip the foul demon could summon an endless pack of felbeasts, the scourge of any spellcaster. How many wizards from Dalaran had perished horribly because of the demon's pets during the Legion's second coming?

Yes, Rhonin had good reason to despair even hearing the Houndmaster's name, but he feared something else even more.

He feared Hakkar's death, here in the past.

The Houndmaster had perished in the *future*. The demon had survived the war against the night elves.

But not this time. This time, Hakkar had been slain . . . which now meant the future was certain to be different.

Which now meant that this first war, despite the slaying of a most powerful demon, could definitely be lost.

The hippogriffs soared over the landscape, cutting away the miles with each heavy beat of their vast wings. Though they could not fly as swiftly as a dragon, few other creatures could match them. The animals lived for flying, and Krasus felt their excitement as they raced each other over hills, rivers, and forest.

Born to the sky, the dragon mage lifted his face to the wind, savoring the sensation now forbidden him because of his transformation. He smiled as an unbidden memory of his first flight with Alexstrasza returned to him. That day, he had only just become her consort, and the pair had finally begun the ritual before their initial mating.

During that ritual, Krasus—or Korialstrasz in his true form—had circled the much larger female over and over, displaying for her his strength and agility. She, in turn, flew in a vast circle around the realm of dragons. The female had kept her speed constant, neither too fast nor too slow. Her new mate was supposed to show his prowess in all things, but he also had to have the energy needed afterward to breed with her.

Korialstrasz had performed all manner of aerial maneuvers to impress his mate. He flew on his back. He darted between tightly-packed peaks. He even let himself drop toward one of the most jagged ones, missing impalement by a few bare yards. Reckless he had been at times, but that was part of the game, part of the ritual.

"My Alexstrasza . . ." Krasus whispered to the wind as the memory faded away. It may have been that a tear briefly graced one eye or perhaps it was only a drop of moisture in the sky. Either way, the wind quickly carried it off and he concentrated again on the journey ahead.

The landscape had just begun to turn more rocky and hilly. They had almost reached the midway point. Krasus was pleased but still impatient. Something was amiss and he had a fairly good idea as to the cause.

Neltharion.

The Earth Warder.

Known in Krasus's true time period as the monster *Deathwing*.

Although he had lost much of his memory during his fall through history, there was no way by which Krasus could ever forget the black beast. In the future, Deathwing was evil itself, ever working to bring the world to ruin so that he might have dominion over the wreckage. Already Neltharion had crossed the threshold of madness, and Krasus had suffered for it. When last he had traveled to his home—brought there by his younger self—Krasus had run afoul of the Earth Warder's paranoia. Fearing that the dragon mage would warn the others of his coming treachery—a reasonable assumption, in fact—the black leviathan had crafted a subtle spell that prevented his foe from speaking out about him. Most of the other dragons now thought Krasus half-mad himself because of that spell.

The silence noted first by young Korialstrasz and now detected by his elder self as well could only mean that Neltharion had pressed on with his intentions. What exactly they were, Krasus could not yet recall and it pained him that of all things this should be lost. If there was one thing the mage would change in the past without fear of repercussions in the future, it would be the Earth Warder's betrayal. That, more than anything, had been the final spiral down for the dragon race.

Krasus suddenly realized that Malfurion was calling his name. Shaking his head, he looked to the druid.

"Krasus! Are you ill?"

"In a manner in which I can never be cured!" returned the elder spellcaster. He frowned at his own carelessness. Centuries of learning to keep his emotions masked had all vanished with his return to this turbulent time. Now Krasus had little more self-control than Rhonin or even the orc.

Nodding even though he did not understand, the druid looked away. Krasus continued to silently berate himself. He had to maintain control. It was essential if he hoped to keep everything from collapsing into chaos.

Malfurion did not understand what the death of Hakkar meant, but how could he? He did not know that the Houndmaster had been among the demons who perished in the future. Rhonin would understand when he heard. The implications were staggering. Now Krasus had no idea what the future held.

If there still *was* a future.

On and on their journey continued. The hippogriffs descended once to satisfy their thirst at a river, and the duo took the opportunity to do the same. After sharing some rations, they mounted their beasts and took to the air again. The next time they landed, Krasus hoped it would be in the domain of his kind.

The landscape grew more mountainous. Huge peaks jutted up to the heavens. In the distance, a pair of large black birds flew toward them from the opposite direction. The dragon mage became tense. Soon, very soon, he would be home.

Krasus only prayed that he would find everything intact.

Malfurion's hippogriff squawked. The mage belatedly noticed that the two birds continued to fly toward them . . . and that they were much larger than he had first calculated.

Too large, in fact, to be birds at all.

He leaned forward, squinting.

Dragons . . . *black* dragons.

Krasus prodded his mount on one side, at the same time shouting to Malfurion, "To the southern edge of the mountain chain! Hurry!"

The druid, too, now recognized the threat and obeyed. As the two hippogriffs veered away, the dragons did not adjust.

Despite their keen eyesight, the behemoths had not yet noticed the smaller creatures.

Aware that at any moment that might change, Krasus urged his beast to as swift a pace as it could set. Perhaps it was simply coincidence that these two giants were out here, but the mage suspected otherwise. Understanding Neltharion's growing paranoia, Krasus believed it more likely that the Earth Warder had sent these two guardians out to watch for any intruders entering the dragon lands. Ironic that his madness would now prove him correct.

The hippogriffs descended at a breathtaking rate, soaring toward the lower mountains. Once there, Krasus could relax; the blacks would surely fly right past them.

Yet, one of the dragons glanced their way just when it seemed that they would evade notice. He roared, and his comrade twisted his sinewy neck around to see what had garnered the first's attention. When he noted the two riders, he, too, bellowed his outrage.

With the perfection of creatures born to fly, the dragons banked and raced after their prey.

"What can we do?" called Malfurion.

"Fly lower! We can skirt the mountains better than they! They must follow or risk losing us, and they will not wish to displease their lord!"

It was as much as he could say about Neltharion without the Earth Warder's spell taking hold. He thanked the Aspects that the druid had not tried to ply him with foolish questions such as why they were fleeing from dragons when dragons were what they had come to find. Malfurion clearly recognized Krasus's knowledge in this circumstance and understood that if the mage wanted them to flee, they needed to flee.

The larger of the two beasts—and, therefore, the older—

began to push ahead of his companion. He roared again, and a burst of what at first seemed like flame shot from his savage maw.

It came within only a few scant yards of the wizard, causing his mount to squawk loud and heating the air around the fleeing figures several degrees. The "flames" began falling earthward, revealing themselves to have actually been a column of molten lava, a breath spell inherent to the black flight.

Before the dragon could send forth another shot, the hippogriffs darted into the mountain chain. Their pursuers were right behind, dipping to the side to avoid colliding with the hard peaks.

Krasus scowled. He knew how talented his kind was at maneuvering through mountains. Dragons played at such games from the moment they could fly. He had his doubts that even here he and the druid could escape, but they had to do what they could.

Then the mage thought of those games again, and his hopes rose.

He caught Malfurion's attention and made several gestures to try to explain what he wanted, the last a quick jab with his finger toward a peak to the northeast. Fortunately, the druid was quick to read him. From Malfurion's expression, the night elf also had his doubts, but like Krasus, he understood that they had little other hope. Casting a spell sufficient to drive back not one but two dragons would be very difficult even for the most trained mage.

As they dove toward one particular peak, the druid abruptly steered his hippogriff to the right. Krasus did the opposite. The mage quickly glanced over his shoulder and saw the dragons do the same, the larger one pursuing him.

"Alexstrasza guide me . . . this must work . . ." he muttered.

He could see neither Malfurion nor the other dragon, but that was to be expected. Krasus no longer concerned himself with the druid; there were two ways that his plan might succeed, but both depended upon him keeping ahead of his pursuer.

That was proving far from simple. The huge black was a skilled flyer, rolling and banking as the narrow gaps his prey sought necessitated. The hippogriff, too, excelled in flying, but had to beat its wings much, much more just to keep pace with the monster behind it. Even with those efforts, however, the dragon slowly inched closer.

A roar warned Krasus moments before another column of lava flew past where he had just been. Only his knowledge of a black dragon's tactics had saved him that time. Even still, several places on his robe smoked from where tiny splatters had caught him, while his mount squirmed from ash that had landed on one hind leg.

Krasus rode under a massive beaklike projection on the side of one mountain, then soared through a crack that made two peaks out of one. Each time, the dragon managed to avoid crashing despite the incredible speed with which he raced.

The mountain that the dragon mage had pointed out to Malfurion was fast approaching. In spite of the danger to him, Krasus took the time to peer south, where the druid should have been. He neither heard nor saw anything, but continued on as he planned, hoping that somehow matters would work out.

Again the dragon roared. A blast shot past Krasus, who frowned at his pursuer's sudden lack of aim.

Only when the mountainside ahead on his right shattered, spilling toward him, did Krasus know that he had been outmaneuvered.

He had the hippogriff pull up swiftly and away. Even still, both were pelted by a storm of earth and rock. A chunk the size of Krasus's head bounded off the flank of the animal, causing it to squeal and nearly toss its passenger to his doom. Only Krasus's deathlike grip kept him from slipping.

A great stench washed over rider and steed. The black was right behind them. Krasus raised his hand and uttered the quickest spell he could command.

A random series of light bursts exploded in front of the leviathan. They were relatively harmless, but they startled the dragon, even blinded him momentarily. He twisted, roaring his anger. One wing struck a mountain, tearing away tons of stone.

Krasus's quick thinking had bought him a few scant seconds, nothing more. He hoped that the druid had managed to outpace the other dragon, but Krasus knew his kind's tenacity. If Malfurion still lived, he likely held no greater a lead on his hunter than the mage did with his own.

Then, just as the mountain he had chosen for the rendezvous arose before him, Krasus caught a glimpse of the other rider. The hippogriff looked frantic, and Malfurion had his head buried in its neck. Right behind them came the second behemoth.

Krasus guided his own mount toward Malfurion's, trying to keep just a little ahead of where the druid would be when they crossed paths. His animal called out, alerting not only its mate, but the druid, too. Malfurion lifted his head, the only sign that he had noticed his companion.

As they met at the southern face of the mountain, Krasus urged his hippogriff around it. Malfurion cut in the opposite direction. A moment later, the larger black, ignoring the other tiny figure, followed after Krasus. His comrade continued his chase of the druid.

If there was one advantage that Krasus had over the black dragons, it was that they did not know he was one of their kind. Nor, for that matter, did they realize that he had flown this region so often in his long life that he likely knew its myriad paths better than anyone or anything.

Again the giant behind him roared, and this time the blast struck so close that it left a seared edge on the mountain. making Krasus choke. Still the hippogriff raced along, trusting in its swiftness and its rider's guidance. Krasus had it drop slightly, then forced it to slow. The animal fought the second command, but the mage used his considerable will to overcome any resistance.

And just as the hippogriff obeyed, Malfurion materialized around the mountain's edge.

Krasus had his beast rise slightly to compensate for the oncoming druid. He and Malfurion rode nearly level; any closer and they would have collided.

The mage caught sight of the edge of a leathery wing behind his companion.

He forced the hippogriff down again.

Malfurion had the second animal drive up into the sky with such speed and abruptness that the druid almost slid off its back.

Krasus's pursuer had no time to register the change in direction. Nor, for that matter, did the druid's. So caught up in their own hunts, the dragons could not stop their momentum.

With a thundering boom, the two giants collided head on.

The dragons roared in pain and shock. Tangled together, they rolled to the side, crashing into the very peak that Krasus had earlier chosen.

The entire region shook as they battered against it. From

his high seat, Krasus thought he heard the crack of bone, but he did not wait around to find out. As the two dragons fell from sight, Krasus waved Malfurion on. By the time the two leviathans recovered, the mage and the druid would be long gone.

Krasus eyed the peaks rising ahead. He was very near his goal now . . . and more than ever, he needed to know just what was happening.

TWELVE

Illidan should have been going over strategy with the Moon Guard, but at that moment he couldn't have cared less about the war. All he could think about was that he had made an abysmal fool out of himself in front of Tyrande. He had bared his soul to her, only to discover that his brother had already staked his territory. Tyrande had chosen Malfurion.

The worst of it was, his twin was probably too caught up in his craft to notice.

Lord Ravencrest's personal sorcerer stalked past a picket. The guard stationed there raised his weapon and, in a slightly anxious voice, declared, "All are to stay within the bounds of the camp, Master Illidan! By order of—"

"I know whose order it is."

"But—"

Illidan's amber eyes stared deep. The soldier swallowed and stepped aside.

The area beyond was still slightly wooded, the Burning Legion having lost the opportunity during their brief hold to destroy everything. While many took heart from this fact, Illidan would not have cared if the entire area had been scorched. He raised one hand slightly and even considered starting the conflagration himself, then dropped the idea.

Even though Malfurion had run afoul of demons in the lands south, his brother had no fear of doing likewise here. In the first place, Illidan walked only a short distance from the camp, stepping barely out of sight. In the second place, any demon who tried to attack him now would have been reduced to ash in the blink of an eye. Illidan's inner rage was such that he dreamed of fighting something, *anything*, in order to drain himself of the jealousy he felt now against Malfurion.

But no felbeast sought to drain him dry, no Infernal attempted to barrel him over. No Eredar, no Doomguard, not even one of the laughable Fel Guard. The whole of the Burning Legion feared to face Illidan alone, for they knew he was an unbeatable force.

Save where it concerned the love of one person.

Finding a huge rock upon which to sit, Illidan thought over all his wonderful plans. Lord Ravencrest's adoption of him as one of his most trusted servants had been a coup; it had enabled the twin to at last seriously consider what had been formulating in his mind for the previous three seasons. He had long looked past Tyrande as a child, and saw her as the beauteous female that she was. While Malfurion had talked to birds, he had planned on how to ask Tyrande to be his mate.

In his head, everything had fallen into place perfectly. One could not but help admire his position, and he knew that many other females had indicated their desire for him. Over a short period of time, Illidan had gained control of those Moon Guard left alive, and his hand had saved many night elves from destruction. He was powerful, handsome, and a hero. Tyrande should have fallen over herself to be his.

And she *would* have, if not for Malfurion.

With a snarl, the sorcerer gestured at another rock nearby. It transformed instantly into a recreation of his brother's face, so much his own and yet not.

Illidan clenched his fist.

The face shattered, fragments crumbling into a loose pile.

"She should've been mine!"

His words echoed through the woods. Malfurion's sibling snarled at his own voice, each repetition reminding him how much he had lost.

"She would've been mine . . ." he corrected himself, lost in pity. "If not for you, brother Malfurion, she would've been mine."

He is always taking precedence, came the sudden thought into his head, *when clearly it should be you.*

"Me? Because I have these eyes?" Illidan laughed at himself. "My miraculous amber eyes?"

A sign of greatness . . . an omen of legend . . .

"A jest played upon me by the gods!" The sorcerer rose, heading deeper into the woods. Even on the move, however, he could not escape the voice, the thoughts . . . and some part of him did not truly wish to.

Malfurion does not even know she wants him. What if he would never know?

"What am I supposed to do? Keep them apart? I might as well try to keep the moon from rising!"

But if Malfurion would perish in the war before he could ever know the truth, it would be as if her choice never happened! She would surely come to you if there was no more Malfurion . . .

The sorcerer paused. He cupped his hands, and in the palms he created an image of Tyrande dancing. She was slightly younger and wearing a flowing skirt. The image was her as Illidan recalled from a festival a few seasons back. That had been the first time he had considered her more than a play friend.

If there was no more Malfurion . . .

Illidan suddenly clapped his hands shut, dissipating the vision. "No! That'd be barbaric!"

And yet Illidan paused immediately after, perversely fascinated by the thought.

Many things could happen to one in the midst of battle. Not death, perhaps, but the demons must know about Malfurion, especially. He destroyed the first portal, slew the queen's advisor, and now one of the Legion's commanders . . . they would want him alive . . . very much alive . . .

"Turn him over . . . to them? I—"

Battles become confused, some are left behind. No one is ever to blame . . .

"No one is ever to blame . . ." murmured Illidan. He opened his hands, and once again Tyrande's image danced for him. He watched it for a time, considering.

But once more, the sorcerer clapped his palms tight. Then, as if sickened by his dark thoughts, he brushed his hands against his garments and quickly headed back to camp. "Never!" he growled under his breath. "Not my brother! Never!"

The sorcerer continued muttering to himself as he walked. He therefore did not notice when the figure separated itself from the trees, watching him from a distance and chuckling at the night elf's momentary lapse of honor and brotherhood.

"The groundwork is laid," it whispered in amusement, "and you yourself will build upon it, twin of the druid."

With that, it snuck off in the opposite direction . . . moving along on two furred limbs ending in hooves.

Unwilling to wait any longer for the druid and the mage to return, Lord Ravencrest ordered the night elves to move out the next day. It was clear that most of his followers would have preferred to march at night, but the noble would not let the demons see him as too predictable. His fighters were gradually becoming as accustomed to the sun as much as they could, even though it meant that their strength was not at its peak. Ravencrest now relied on the determination of his people, their understanding that, if they failed, this would be their end.

The Burning Legion, in turn, awaited them not all that far away. The night elves marched knowing that bloodshed lurked just beyond the horizon, but they marched nonetheless.

And so, once more the struggle for Kalimdor went on.

While the night elves battled to survive and Illidan sought to come to grips with his foul thoughts, Krasus struggled with an entirely different matter, one that Malfurion suspected he had not planned for.

"It goes on for as far as I can detect," the mage hissed in frustration.

"It" was invisible to the eye, but not to the touch. "It" was a vast, unseen shield that held them but a day—by Krasus's measurement—from their goal.

They had discovered it the hard way. Krasus's hippogriff had collided with *nothing*, the crash so violent that the mage had been thrown from the injured animal's back. Malfurion, aware that his own hippogriff could never reach Krasus in time, sought out the aid of the wind. A powerful mountain blast threw his companion *up* again, close enough for the druid to grasp the mage's arm. They had then landed to study this new obstacle.

And after several hours of study, Krasus appeared no closer to the answer . . . and the sight of him looking so baffled unnerved the druid more than he let on.

At last, Krasus uttered the unthinkable. "I am defeated."

"You find no method by which to pierce it?"

"Worse, druid, I cannot even contact anyone within. Even my thoughts are barred."

Malfurion had come to deeply respect Krasus. The mysterious mage had helped save him when Lord Xavius had captured his spirit. Krasus had also been instrumental in enabling the night elf to vanquish the queen's advisor and destroy the first portal. To see him thus . . .

"So close," continued the mage. "So very close! This is his work to be sure!"

"Whose work?"

His eyes narrowing, Krasus looked just enough like a pale night elf to make his expression that much more unsettling. He appeared to be measuring his companion and Malfurion suddenly found himself hoping to be found worthy.

"Yes . . . you should know. You deserve to know."

The druid held his breath. Whatever Krasus desired to reveal, it surely had to be of monumental importance.

"Look directly into my eyes, Malfurion." When the night elf had obeyed, Krasus said, "There are three of us that you and yours term 'outsiders.' There is Rhonin, who calls himself a human, and there is Brox, the orc. You know not their races, but they are as you see them—a human and an orc."

The elder figure paused. Thinking he had to respond, Malfurion nodded. "A human and an orc."

"Have I ever said what it is *I* am? Have either of the others specified?"

Thinking back, the night elf could not recall anyone giving name to Krasus's race. "You're of night elven blood. You look enough like us to be kin, if—"

"I might look like one of your kind if he were dead a year or more, but that is as close to a resemblance as we can admit, yes? What you see is only a guise; there are no blood ties between your race and mine . . . nor, for that matter, mine with humans, orcs, dwarves, or tauren."

Malfurion looked confused. "Then . . . what are you?"

Krasus's gaze drew him in further. All he could see were those alien eyes. "Look deep, druid. Look deep and think of what you know of me already."

As he stared into his companion's eyes, Malfurion recalled everything he knew, which was not much at all—a spellcaster of remarkable knowledge, and talent. Even at his most ill, Krasus had carried about him an aura of incredible age and ability. The sisterhood had sensed it, although none of them seemed to understand exactly what it meant, as did the Moon Guard. Even the night sabers treated him better than they did the masters who had raised them.

And for a time, the mage had even commanded the friendship of a dragon . . .

. . . A dragon . . .

Without the behemoth near, Krasus had suffered as if on his deathbed. The dragon, too, had shown signs of weariness beyond the ordinary. Together, however, they had been as one, their strength magnified.

But there had been more to it than that. Korialstrasz had spoken with Krasus like none other—as an equal, almost a brother.

Seeing the growing realization on the druid's face, Krasus whispered, "You are at the threshold of understanding. Cross it now."

He opened himself up for Malfurion to see. In the night elf's mind, Krasus transformed. His robes ripped to shreds as his body grew and twisted. His legs bent in reverse and his feet and hands became long, clawed appendages. Wings sprouted from his back, expanding until they were great enough to blot out the moon.

Krasus's face stretched. His nose and mouth became one, growing into a savage maw. His hair solidified, turning into a scaled crest that ran down the length of his back all the way to the tip of the tail that had formed at the same time as the wings.

And as crimson scales covered every inch of the other's body, Malfurion blurted the name by which all knew such huge, fearsome leviathans.

"Dragon!"

Then, as quickly as the incredible image had appeared before him it now vanished. Malfurion shook his head and eyed the figure before him.

"Yes, Malfurion Stormrage, I am a dragon. A red dragon, to be precise. Long have I worn the form of one mortal creature or another, however, for it has been my choice to walk among you, teaching and learning as I strive for peace among all of us."

"A dragon . . ." Malfurion shook his head. It explained so much in retrospect . . . and raised many more questions in turn.

"Among those in the host, only Rhonin fully knows who and what I am, although the orc may understand and the sisterhood likely has its suspicions."

"Are humans allied to dragons?"

"Nay! But in my guise as you see me, Rhonin was my student, an exceptional mage even for one of his versatile race! I trust him in some ways more than I do many of my own people."

As if to emphasize that fact, Krasus—Malfurion could not yet accept terming him a dragon—slapped one hand against the invisible barrier. "And *this* only adds credence to why that is so. This should not be here."

"A dragon . . . but why didn't you transform in order to fly here? Why have me summon the hippogriffs?" More curious incidents occurred to the night elf. "You could've been slain more than once, including when last we fought the demons!"

"Some things must remain hidden, Malfurion, but I tell you this much; I do not transform because I *cannot*. That ability has been stripped from me for the time being."

"I . . . I see."

Krasus turned his gaze back to the concealed wall, again seeking some entrance through it. "You perceive why I felt so certain that I would be able to confront the dragons. They will listen to one of their own. They will also tell one of their own why they are acting so mysteriously." He hissed savagely, startling the night elf. "If I can contact them first."

"Who would do this?"

It almost appeared that Krasus intended to answer, but then he clamped his mouth tight. After several seconds of obvious inner turmoil, he glumly responded, "It does not matter. What does is that I have failed. The one hope I had for ensuring the outcome of the war is beyond my reach."

There was much that the dragon mage had not told Malfurion, and the night elf knew it. However, the druid also respected Krasus enough not to pursue the matter any further. All Malfurion wanted to do now was help, especially with his new understanding of the situation. If Krasus could convince his kind to join with the defenders, then surely that would spell a quick end to the Burning Legion.

But their spells could not open the wall, and neither of the two could simply walk through it like a ghost or—

Swallowing hard, the druid said, "I may know of a way through, at least for me."

"What do you mean?"

"I-I could walk the Emerald Dream."

The mage's visage darkened, then grew thoughtful. Malfurion wanted him to reject the idea out of hand, but instead Krasus nodded. "Yes . . . yes, that may be the one way."

"But will it help? I don't even know whether or not they'll be able to hear or see me . . . and if they do, will they listen?"

"One may be able to do all. You must seek her specifically. Her name is Ysera."

Ysera. Cenarius had spoken her name when offering to teach his student how to walk the dream realm. Ysera was one of the five great Aspects. She ruled the Emerald Dream. Certainly, Ysera would be able to both hear and see the druid's spirit form . . . but would she bother to listen to his words?

Reading the night elf's obvious reluctance, Krasus added, "If you can convince her to bring you to the attention of Alexstrasza, the red dragon, then perhaps she, in turn, can question Korialstrasz, who knows us both. Alexstrasza will listen to him."

From the way the inflection of his voice changed whenever he spoke the other name, Malfurion understood that this other dragon was very, very important to Krasus on a personal level. He knew of Alexstrasza as another of the

Aspects and wondered how Krasus could speak of her so easily. His companion was more than simply a dragon who spied on the younger races; he held some status among even his own kind.

The knowledge strengthened Malfurion. "I'll do what I can."

"Should Ysera show reluctance," Krasus further advised, "it would be good to mention Cenarius to her. More than once, if necessary."

Not certain why that should make a difference but trusting to Krasus's wisdom, the night elf nodded, then sat down right where he was. Krasus watched him in silence as he positioned his body. Satisfied with the arrangement, Malfurion shut his eyes and focused.

At first he meditated, calming his body. As he relaxed, the night elf felt the first hints of slumber touch him. He welcomed them, encouraged them. More and more, the mortal world retreated from the druid. Peace draped over Malfurion like a blanket. He knew that Krasus watched over him, so there was no fear of letting go. The mage would protect his defenseless form.

And before he knew it, Malfurion slept. Yet, at the same time, he felt more awake than ever. The night elf concentrated now on departing from the mortal plane. He did as Cenarius had bid him, working to separate his spirit from his body.

It proved so simple to do both that and locate the way into the Emerald Dream that Malfurion felt ashamed about his earlier hesitation. So long as he remained fixed on his quest, surely it would be safe to traverse the other realm.

A hint of green immediately shaded everything. Krasus faded away as Malfurion's surroundings changed. The mountainous region looked surprisingly similar in both dimensions, but the peaks in the Emerald Dream were sharper, less weathered. Here was how they appeared when the creators had first raised them up from the primal soil. Despite the urgency of his mission, Malfurion paused to admire the celestials' handiwork. The sheer majesty of all he saw astounded him.

But nothing would remain in the true world if the Burning Legion was not stopped, and so the druid finally moved on. He reached out to the barrier, expecting resistance, yet nothing slowed his hand. Sure enough, in the Emerald Dream, the spell did not exist. The dragons expected any intruders to be of the more earthly kind and, therefore, subject to the world's natural laws.

Drifting on past where the wall had been, Malfurion headed toward the tallest peaks in the distance. Prior to his collision with the barrier, Krasus had indicated them as where his kind could be found. Since the elder mage had said nothing contrary before the druid had acted, Malfurion took it for granted that he should continue on in that direction.

He flew over the silent land, the huge mountains making him feel most insignificant. The green hue coloring everything, coupled with the lack of any animal life, added to the surreal feel of his surroundings.

As he neared what he believed his destination, Malfurion concentrated. The green coloring faded somewhat, and he began to notice details of weathering. The druid's spirit still "walked" the Emerald Dream, but he now saw into the present-day world as well.

And his first view was that of the overwhelming, ferocious countenance of a crimson dragon.

Startled, Malfurion pulled back. He expected the behemoth's head to dart forward and snap him up, but the sentinel continued to stare through him. It took the druid a few seconds to realize that the dragon could not see him.

The presence of the guardian, who perched atop a high, pointed peak, verified that the night elf had to be near where the dragons gathered. However, Malfurion did not feel he had the time to go searching one mountain after another for their location. Instead, he thought of what he knew. Ysera was mistress of the Emerald Dream. This near to her, surely she would hear his mental summons.

Whether Ysera would answer, however, was another question.

Knowing he could only try, the druid faded back into the Emerald Dream and imagined the green dragon. He knew that his perception of her was far from fact, but it gave his thoughts something upon which to concentrate.

Ysera, mistress of the dream land, great Aspect, I humbly seek communion with you . . . I bring the word of one who knows She Who Is Life, your sister, Alexstrasza . . .

Malfurion waited. When it became clear that he would not be receiving an answer, he tried again.

Ysera, She of the Dreaming, in the name of Cenarius, Lord of the Wood, I ask this boon of you. I call upon you to—

He broke off as he sensed the sudden presence of another. The druid twisted his head to the right and beheld a thin female of his race, clad in a translucent robe that fluttered even though there was no wind. The hood of the robe covered all but her face, a beautiful yet calm face whose only offsetting feature was the eyes . . . or rather, the closed lids that covered them.

The figure might have looked like a night elf, but in addition to the bright emerald hair she had—more arresting than the green of any true night elf—her skin, garments . . . all were tinted one shade or another of the same color.

There could be no doubt that this was Ysera.

"I have come," she responded, quiet but firm, her eyes never opening, "if only to put an end to your shouting. Your thoughts reverberated through my mind like an unceasing drumbeat."

Malfurion sought to kneel. "My lady—"

She waved a slim hand. "I need not be flattered by such gestures. You have called. I have come. Have your say and be-gone."

His success still amazed the night elf. Here, in this other form, stood one of the great Aspects. That she had deigned to respond, he could scarcely believe. "Forgive me. I would never seek to disturb you—"

"And yet, here you are."

"I've come with one who knows of you well—a dragon called Krasus."

"His name is known, even if his mind is suspect. What of him?"

"He seeks an audience with Alexstrasza. He can't break through the barrier that surrounds this place."

As he spoke, Malfurion had to focus hard on the Aspect. Ysera constantly shimmered in and out, almost as if she were a figment of his imagination. Her expression did not change, save that beneath the eyelids there was constant movement. That she saw, Malfurion did not doubt, but *how* she did made him most curious.

"The barrier has been set because the planning we do is of the most delicate nature," spoke the Aspect. "No word of what we do must be revealed until the time is ripe . . . so says the Earth Warder."

"But he must enter—"

"And he will not. I have no say over the matter. Is that all?"

Malfurion mulled over Krasus's words. "Then, if he can speak to Alexstrasza through you . . ."

Ysera laughed, such a startling shift that the night elf stood as if stricken. "You are audacious, mortal creature! I am to be your conduit as he interrupts my sister during a most pressing time! Is there anything *else* you would like while you are asking?"

"By my *shan'do*, Cenarius, this is all I seek, and I wouldn't do it if it wasn't necessary."

A peculiar thing happened when he mentioned the demigod by name. Ysera's image grew especially hazy, and the eyes beneath her lids seemed to look down. The reaction, although very brief, was so very noticeable.

"I see no reason to continue this irritation. Return to your companion, night elf, and—"

"Please, mistress of the Emerald Dream! Cenarius will vouch for me. He—"

"There is no reason to bring him up!" she suddenly snapped. For just the briefest of moments, Ysera almost looked ready to open her eyes. Her expression had become one that Malfurion recognized all too well from his childhood. Earlier, he had thought that Cenarius and Ysera had been lovers. But that was not the case, from what he could read in her expression.

Ysera—She of the Dreaming, one of the five great Aspects—had reacted to the demigod's name as might a loving *mother*.

Somewhat ashamed, the druid retreated from her. Ysera, clearly caught up in some memory, paid him no mind. For the first time since he had met Krasus, Malfurion was angry with him. This was ill knowledge and his companion should have known that.

He started to depart the dream realm, but Ysera turned her sightless gaze toward him and suddenly announced, "I will be the bridge you need to reach Alexstrasza."

"My lady . . ."

"You will speak no more about this situation, night elf, or I will cast you out of my domain forever."

Shutting his mouth tight, Malfurion acquiesced. Whatever her relationship with the forest lord, it had been very, very deep and long in term.

"I will guide your spirit to where we now meet, and you will wait until I indicate that your time to converse with my sister has come. Then and only then will I transmit your words to her—your words and *his*."

The acidic tone by which she said the last word spoke of her fury toward Krasus. Praying that his companion's rash suggestion would not get them both killed, the druid voicelessly agreed.

She stretched forth her hand. "Take it."

With the utmost respect, Malfurion obeyed. He had never touched another spirit in the Emerald Dream, and had no idea what to expect. To his surprise, though, Ysera's hand felt like a mortal one. It had no ethereal quality. He might have been holding his mother's hand.

"Remember my warning," the Aspect said.

Before he could respond, they entered the mortal plane. The transition was so immediate, yet so smooth, that the night elf had to adjust to his change in surroundings. Then he had to adjust to Ysera's sudden disappearance.

No, she had not disappeared. She stood but a few yards from where he floated, the mistress of the Emerald Dream now revealed in her full glory. A massive dragon with glittering green scales, she dwarfed Korialstrasz, the only other dragon that the druid had ever met.

And she was not the only one. As his surroundings registered on him, the night elf discovered the two of them were far from alone. Three other gargantuan dragons stood near the center of the huge chamber. The red one surely had to be Alexstrasza, the one Krasus sought. She had a beauty and dignity akin to Ysera, but more animation, more life. Next to her was a male nearly as large whose scales constantly shifted—from silver to blue to a combination of both— seemingly at whim. He had, for one of his kind, an almost bemused expression.

In utter contrast to blue, the huge black beast that Malfurion eyed next sent shivers through even his spirit form. Here was raw power, the strength of the earth . . . but something more. Malfurion had to look away from the ebony giant, for each time he attempted to study him, a sense of unease touched the night elf. It was not simply because two of the same color had pursued the druid and his companion. No, it was something more . . . something dread.

But if he thought to find more peace looking elsewhere, Malfurion had chosen the wrong direction, for now he stared at what so intrigued the giants.

It was tiny, tiny enough to fit into his own palm. In the paw of the huge black, it was almost a speck.

"You see?" rumbled its wielder. "All is in readiness. It is but the moment that we wait for."

"And when will that moment come?" asked Alexstrasza. "Each passing day, the demons ravage the lands. If not for the fact that their commanders have drawn more of their forces to take on the night elves, the other directions would be all but lost by now."

"I understand your concern . . . but the Dragon Soul will be best applied when the heavens are in alignment. It must be that way."

The red Aspect gazed at the golden disk. "Let us pray then that when it is utilized, it is all you say, Neltharion. Let us pray it is the deliverance of our world."

The black only nodded. Malfurion, still awaiting Ysera's signal to talk with Alexstrasza, peered closely at the simple-looking creation, his hopes rising. The dragons were acting. They had come up with a solution, a talisman of some sort that would rid Kalimdor of the Burning Legion.

His curiosity got the better of him. He weakened his end of the link with Ysera so that with all else going on she might not notice what he attempted. With his mind, he probed the shining disk—so insignificant in appearance, and yet, apparently filled with such power that even dragons paid it homage. Truly, the demons would stand no chance against something like this . . .

Not at all to his surprise, a protective spell surrounded the Dragon Soul. The druid studied it and in its elements, he detected a peculiarity. Each of the great dragons had their own distinct auras—as all creatures did—and Malfurion sensed some of those auras now. He felt Ysera's—most known to him—plus those of Alexstrasza and the blue. The black dragon's was also present, but not in the same manner. His seemed entwined around the rest, as if it held them at bay. It almost seemed to the druid that the spell had been designed to keep the others from sensing something within.

More curious than ever, Malfurion used Cenarius's teachings to infiltrate the spell. He slipped through with far more ease than he had expected, perhaps because the disk's creator had never thought one such as he would even make an attempt. The druid pushed deeper, finally touching on the forces within.

What he discovered within made him reel. He pulled out, stunned. Even in his present form, he shivered, unable to come to grips with what he had sensed. Malfurion looked again at the black dragon, astounded by what the leviathan had wrought.

The Dragon Soul . . . that which was to save Kalimdor . . . held within it an evil as great as the Burning Legion itself.

THIRTEEN

The demons had a tendency to slaughter anything and anyone in their path. That made it difficult to gather prisoners for questioning, something Captain Varo'then felt a necessity. He had finally convinced Archimonde to send him a few, but the ones that arrived proved more a tangle of broken body parts than living creatures.

The scarred night elf spent a few minutes on the last of the lot, then did the ruined figure a favor by slicing open his throat. The interrogations had been a debacle, but not through any fault on his part. The Legion's commanders did not seem to understand the basic need for questioning.

Varo'then would have preferred to be out in the field, but he did not want to leave the palace, especially not of late. The thing that had been Lord Xavius had not been seen for days, but in that time several of the Highborne had utterly vanished. Mannoroth took it in stride, and so the captain suspected that he knew the reason. The officer disliked being left out of the information loop in any way.

"Dispose of that rubbish," he ordered the two guards. As they moved to obey, Captain Varo'then cleaned his dagger and replaced it. He gazed around the interrogation chamber, a blocky six-by-six room with only a single blue glow-crystal to illuminate it. Shadows filled the corner. An iron door three inches thick was the only exit.

Centuries of blood stained the floor. The queen never visited the lowest depths of her residence, and Varo'then did not encourage her. Such work was not for one of her acute sensibilities.

The soldiers dragged the unfortunate's corpse out, leaving the captain to his thoughts. There had been no news from the Houndmaster. Mannoroth had not revealed any concern, but the night elf wondered if something had befallen the powerful demon. If so, then it behooved someone to take the lead in hunting down the spellcasters. The demons had failed so far, and Varo'then itched for a chance to redeem himself in that regard after having lost two of them to an enchanted and hostile forest.

But that would mean leaving the palace . . .

He reached down with both hands to adjust the sword at his side—and suddenly brought the blade out, thrusting it into the shadows to his left.

The keen edge came within an inch of a figure unseen in those shadows until now. Rather than be startled, however, the other simply leered at the captain.

"A sharp sword, a sharp wit, Captain Varo'then . . ."

At first the soldier thought that he was dealing with Xavius again, but a closer study showed differences in the face. Varo'then ran through his analytical mind the faces of all the Highborne and matched this hooved creature's visage with one.

"Master Paroth'arn . . . we'd wondered where you'd gone."

The former sorcerer edged out of the shadows as

Varo'then sheathed his weapon. "I have been . . . relearning."

With barely-concealed distaste, the night elf eyed the transformation. To him, the satyrs were an abomination. "And have others been 'relearning' also?"

"A select few."

At last the captain had an explanation as to where the missing Highborne had gone. They were still here, merely changed into these grotesque parodies. Xavius's new form had been one of the few decisions by Sargeras that Varo'then questioned. More powerful he supposedly might be, but the former advisor's mind had clearly been altered, too. There was something animalistic about him that went beyond his outer appearance, something animalistic and devious.

And from what little he had seen of Peroth'arn so far, the rest of the missing Highborne were likely as unstable as their leader.

"Where is Xavius?" he asked of the satyr.

"Wherever he must be, good captain," replied the horned figure. "Performing that which will make sooner come true our glorious god's desire . . ."

"He's no longer in the palace?"

Peroth'arn chuckled. "A sharp sword, a sharp wit . . ."

Captain Varo'then felt tempted to draw that sword again and impale the mocking creature, perhaps even mount Peroth'arn's head over a fireplace afterward. The satyr grinned back, as if daring the soldier to react.

Restraining himself, the scarred night elf asked, "And what, then, are you doing down here? You've some interest in the interrogations?"

"Amusement, you might say."

"I've no time to waste on your antics and silly wordplay." Varo'then pushed past Peroth'arn, reaching for the door handle. "Nor, for that matter, those of the one who leads you."

"You served him once. You'll serve him again."

"I serve the great Sargeras and my queen and no other!" retorted the officer. "And if he thinks—"

As he spoke, the captain glanced back to where the satyr had stood. However, when he sought Peroth'arn, he found only shadow.

With a snarl, the night elf barged out of the chamber. The queen would have to be told more about these accursed satyrs. He did not trust them. He certainly did not trust Lord Xavius anymore.

If only he knew where the former advisor had gone . . .

Malfurion could not believe the utter evil he sensed within the Dragon Soul. How could a thing created to be the *savior* of the world radiate such *malevolence*? What had the dragon Neltharion wrought?

Bracing himself, the druid cautiously probed the disk again. So simple, so innocent in appearance. Only by seeking within could anyone understand the awful truth.

It amazed him that Ysera could not sense it. Surely the mistress of the Emerald Dream would have understood. Yet, like the others, the disk was shielded from her in such a subtle fashion that even if she held it, he doubted the Aspect would have noted a thing.

Perhaps . . . perhaps if Malfurion dismantled the protective spell, then the others would realize the truth before it was too late.

Putting aside his disgust, he pushed deeper into the disk. Through his highly-trained senses, he located the spell's nexus. The druid began trying to unravel it—

A jolt like a thousand bolts of lightning instantly ravaged his ethereal form, almost tearing it to insubstantial shreds. Malfurion silently screamed. He looked for aid from Ysera, but to his horror she did not seem to note his agony.

But another did.

He did not look directly at the night elf, but his thoughts practically barreled over the stricken druid. In an instant, the madness of the Dragon Soul's creator became all too clear.

So! Neltharion roared even though on the mortal plane he continued speaking so politely and amiably with the others. *You try to steal my glorious Dragon Soul!*

A monstrous, invisible force compressed Malfurion from all sides. At first he stared in fear as his body contorted. Then he realized that the image he had of himself in his present state was just that—an image. Neltharion could have stretched him into a thin string and it would not have much affected the druid's health. That was not what the Earth Warder intended; he sought to crush Malfurion into a magical prison, preventing the intruder from giving any warning or touching the disk again.

Stirred on by dread memories of his confinement at the hands of Lord Xavius, Malfurion managed to break free of the spell before it sealed. He immediately turned his focus to Ysera, hoping she would yet sense his danger.

No! They will not interfere! Neltharion's mental presence was staggering. *You will not betray all I have done! None of you will!*

With Ysera still ignorant of his danger, the druid did the only thing he could think of—he abandoned the chamber and the mortal plane, retreating into the solitude of the Emerald Dream.

A calmness immediately surrounded him. He floated

over the indistinct vision of the mountains where he had first contacted She of the Dreaming. Relieved, Malfurion tried to collect his thoughts.

With a roar, a huge shadowy form sought to swallow him whole.

Pulling back at the very last moment, the druid could not believe what had now happened; Neltharion had followed him into the dream realm! The dragon was even more terrible to behold here than in the mortal plane. His face was a distorted, diabolical caricature of its true self, every element of the evil with which the black had imbued the Dragon Soul evident in his jagged, disfigured countenance. Neltharion was twice as huge as in true life and his sharp claws spread for miles. His wings alone shadowed the entire mountain chain.

I will not surrender what is mine by right! Only I am fit to rule! You will tell no one!

Neltharion exhaled. Green flames filled the Emerald Dream.

Malfurion screamed as the fire engulfed his form. What the behemoth was doing should have been impossible; not only had he invaded Ysera's domain without her evidently knowing, but now he sought to burn away the druid's intangible essence.

Something that Cenarius had once taught him suddenly came to mind. *Perception is deceptive, my student,* his *shan'do* had told him. *What you think must be is not always the truth. In the world of which you are now part as a druid, perception can become whatever you think it.*

Not certain that he understood, but already nearly consumed, Malfurion denied the flames killing him. They could not exist as such here. They were, like his body and Neltharion's huge form, what he *expected* to be real, yet they were not. They were images, illusions.

And so the fire could not burn so much as one false hair on his imaginary head.

Both the agony and the flames vanished. Neltharion still remained, his face and form more distorted than ever. He eyed the tiny figure with some repugnance, as if he wondered how the druid had dared not to perish.

Not certain how lucky he might be against whatever next the Aspect might throw at him, Malfurion took the only route of escape remaining to him. He concentrated on his body, willing himself to return to it.

The green-tinted mountains suddenly flew away from him. Neltharion, too, dwindled swiftly in the distance. The druid felt the closeness of his own body—

No! came Neltharion's fearsome voice again. *I will have you!*

Just as the night elf felt himself re-entering his mortal form, something struck him hard. With a grunt, Malfurion, still half-asleep, fell back, his head hitting the hard, rocky ground. The last vestiges of the Emerald Dream disappeared, and with their going ceased the angry roar of the black dragon.

"Druid!" called another. "Malfurion Stormrage! Can you hear me? Are you whole again?"

He tried to focus on the new speaker. "K-Krasus?"

But when Malfurion first glanced at the mage's visage, he instantly tried to pull away. A dragon's monstrous face filled his view, the jaws opening to swallow him—

"Malfurion!"

The sharp cut of Krasus's voice sliced cleanly through his fear. The night elf's vision cleared, revealing not a dragon but the determined, pale countenance he had come to know well.

Concern colored Krasus's expression. He helped Malfurion

to a sitting position, handing him a water sack from which to drink. Only after the druid had satiated his thirst did Krasus ask him what had happened.

"Did you reach She of the Dreaming?"

"Yes, and I had to mention Cenarius more than once . . . as you hinted."

The dragon mage allowed himself a brief one-sided smile. "I had recalled some bit of knowledge Alexstrasza had once passed on to me. I thought that this far in the past, the feelings would be stronger yet."

"So I was right to think that she and my *shan'do*—"

"Does it surprise you? Their spheres of influence cross in many ways. Kindred spirits are often drawn together, regardless of their differing backgrounds."

Malfurion did not press. "She agreed to bring me to where they were meeting."

Krasus's eyes widened. "All five of the Aspects?"

"I saw only four. Ysera, your Alexstrasza, a silver-blue dragon with a mirthful expression—"

"Malygos . . . how that one will change."

"And—and—" Suddenly, the night elf could not speak. The words teetered on the tip of his tongue, but they would not fall. The harder he tried, the more infantile the druid sounded. Sounds that made no sense whatsoever escaped him.

Putting a hand on Malfurion's shoulder, Krasus nodded sadly. "I understand, I think. You cannot say more. There was another there."

"Yes . . . another."

It was all Malfurion could add, but he saw that Krasus did indeed understand. The night elf eyed his comrade in shock, realizing that the mage could no more speak of Neltharion than he could. At some point in the past, Krasus, too, had fallen afoul of the black behemoth.

Which meant that Krasus likely also knew of the Dragon Soul.

They stared into each other's eyes, the silence communicating much of what their mouths could not. Small wonder that the dragon mage had been so adamant about reaching his people and discovering the truth. The ancients themselves had been betrayed by one of their own, and the only two who knew could say nothing about it, not even to each other.

"We must leave," muttered Krasus, helping him to his feet. "You may well imagine why."

Malfurion could. Neltharion would not rest with leaving him alive. The spell had been a last effort before the druid had escaped the Emerald Dream, but the black dragon would not be satisfied. He was too near his goal. Likely only circumstance had saved Krasus earlier, but from what Malfurion had witnessed of the black's madness, neither would be safe long. And although Neltharion would not dare act directly . . .

"The sentinels!" he managed to gasp.

"Aye. We may see them again. It would be good if we returned to the hippogriffs and departed."

So the idiosyncrasies of the spell allowed them that indirect communication. A small and fairly useless gift. They could hint to each other about their doom.

Still weary, he had to rely on Krasus to help him walk. With effort, they made their way to where the animals waited impatiently. One of the hippogriffs squawked when he noticed the pair, causing the other to flap its wings in startlement.

"Will they carry us the entire way back?" the mage asked Malfurion.

"Yes. Cenarius would—"

The ground shook violently. The night elf and Krasus

toppled over. Nearby, the hippogriffs fluttered a few feet upward.

From beneath where the mounts had waited, a monstrous worm thrust its sightless head into the air. A wide crack at the tip of its head opened incredibly wide, revealing a round mouth with teeth lining the edges. With a savage rumble, the worm swallowed the slower of the two hippogriffs whole.

"Run!" commanded Krasus.

The duo scurried across the harsh landscape. Despite the meal it had just eaten, the worm turned in their direction. Again it rumbled, then burrowed back into the earth.

"Separate, Malfurion! Separate!"

No sooner had they gone in opposite directions than again the ground exploded and the horrific creature burst up. It snapped at the area around it, seeming frustrated that it found nothing to add to its earlier course.

Although the worm had no visible eyes, it somehow sensed where Malfurion had gone. Its mammoth, segmented body twisted toward him, the rounded mouth opening and closing hungrily.

This could be no coincidence. Neltharion had surely sent this burrowing monstrosity after them. The dragon's paranoia had grown so terrible that now nothing was allowed to risk his dark desires.

The worm darted forward. The smell of decay emanating from within its mouth nearly overwhelmed the druid. Malfurion ran as fast as he could, even knowing that it would not be fast enough.

But just before the worm reached him, something flew in its path. With a savage squawk, the surviving hippogriff ripped at the fleshy head with its talons. Its beak tore into the hide as it likely sought to avenge its mate.

Rumbling ominously, the worm tried to bite its flying adversary. The hippogriff darted out of range, then dropped again in order to cut at the head.

"*Kylis Fortua!*" shouted Krasus.

Huge chunks of hard earth and rock, dug free by the worm's arrival, rose up into the sky and began battering the creature. The worm swung back and forth, trying to avoid the onslaught. Most of the rocks did little true damage, but Krasus's spell had clearly frustrated the beast.

Taking a breath, the druid tried to aid in his own way. There were few plants in this mountainous region, but one nearby caught his attention. Apologizing to it, Malfurion plucked several barbs from its branches, then threw them at the huge predator.

The wind carried the barbs along for him, thrusting them faster and faster toward their target. Malfurion concentrated, touching upon that which controlled the barbs' growth.

And just before they struck, the thorny pieces swelled. They tripled in size, then tripled again. By the time they hit the worm, many were nearly as large as the druid himself.

More important, they were also harder of hide. Each of the needles facing the worm impacted with the force of a steel lance. Scores of thorns more than a yard long buried themselves in the monster's body.

This time, the creature let out a roar. Green, sizzling pus flowed from its wounds, spilling onto the ground where it continued to burn. The barbs stuck wherever they had hit. The worm shook back and forth, but none would release.

"Well done!" exclaimed Krasus, seizing Malfurion by the arm and pulling him along. "Try to summon the remaining hippogriff!"

Malfurion reached out to the animal, trying to get it to come to them, but the hippogriff's fury overrode his summons. The worm had devoured its mate and it wanted vengeance.

"It won't listen!" yelled the druid, panic creeping into his voice.

"Then we must continue to run!"

Still trying to shake off the savage barbs, the worm followed after them. It did not move quite as fast as before, but still fast enough to force the pair to their limits.

The segmented giant slammed into the ground again, burrowing deep. The earth below vibrated so violently that Malfurion stumbled. Krasus kept on his feet, but made little progress.

"I must attempt something!" he shouted. "I have feared to try it since coming to your land, but without the hippogriff, it seems our only hope!"

"What?"

Krasus did not respond, the dragon mage already casting. Malfurion felt unsettling forces arise near his companion, who drew an arc with his right arm and muttered words in a language the night elf had never before heard. As Krasus's hand cut the air, the latter literally sliced away, creating a gap in reality.

No, not *a gap*, Malfurion mentally corrected himself. A portal.

As the wizard completed the huge circle, the earth quaked. Turning to the druid, Krasus cried, "Through the gate, Malfurion! Through the—"

The worm again broke through to the surface. Krasus tumbled backward. The night elf, just starting to obey, turned back to aid his companion.

"You should have gone on!" snapped Krasus.

Its maw wide open, the monstrous burrower closed on the pair. Malfurion pulled the mage up, then threw both of them toward the portal. He could feel the worm closing on them, smell its deathly odor. Escape seemed so far away—

And as they entered the portal, the worm lunged . . .

FOURTEEN

The demons met them in earnest just west of Suramar. The new advance halted completely and a deadlock began. The night elves could not push the Burning Legion any farther, but neither could their foe regain ground.

The warriors of the Burning Legion fought relentlessly, but there was one thing in the night elves' favor. They were far more familiar with the landscape than the demons. The region around Suramar was one of rolling hills and rivers. Forest, too, had marked much of the region, but now most of that was scorched or torn asunder. Still, many dead trunks and ruined dwellings dotted the area, and they acted not only as additional landmarks, but also protection.

Scouting parties were sent out to discover the exact extent of the demons' lines. One such group consisted of Brox, Rhonin, and several members of Jarod Shadowsong's company, including the captain himself. The orc and the human had volunteered themselves for this mission, well aware that they understood the ways of the Burning Legion better than anyone. However, Ravencrest had made them swear that, like the rest of the scouts, they would return at an appointed hour and no later. Otherwise, he could not promise that they would be safe should he decide it opportune to strike one flank or another quickly, based on whatever the other outriders reported.

Night had fallen, but that by itself did not make the going so slow. Simple darkness alone had no effect on any of the party and, in fact, would have aided their search. However, a thick, foul mist with a dank, greenish tinge covered *everything*. The mist seemed to spread wherever the demons went, and left open the threat that monstrous warriors could be lurking only yards away unnoticed.

Slowly the group, numbering a dozen, crossed the ruined land. Withered and blackened trees cast eerie shapes in the mist. No amount of squinting could much penetrate the haze.

It was perhaps fortunate in one way. So near Suramar, the scouting party crossed through an area where once there had been a settlement. Now and then, the remnants of a treehouse could be spotted sprawled on its side, the entire structure ripped out at the roots, then chopped to pieces. All knew that the inhabitants themselves had likely suffered a similar fate.

"Barbaric . . ." muttered Jarod.

Brox grunted. The night elves had been very quickly forced to harden themselves to the butchery, but they could scarcely learn to accept it the way the orc could. Brox had grown up around brutality. First the end of the war against the Alliance, then the violent march to the reservations, and lastly the struggle against the Burning Legion and the Scourge. He mourned the dead, yes, but there was little he saw that twisted his gut anymore. In the end, death was death.

To the orc's right, Rhonin quietly cursed. The spellcaster clamped his hand tight, then thrust his palm into a pouch attached to his belt. He had tried using a scrying stone to survey the area for any hint of demons, but the mist apparently befouled the sensitive magics involved.

Brox had his own method for seeking out the enemy. Every few yards, he lifted his nose up and sniffed. The smells that mostly assailed his nostrils were pungent and spoke quite succinctly of death. So far, the only demons he noted were foul corpses covered in the ichor that had once flowed through their veins.

There were, of course, many other bodies. The mangled remains of night elves littered the settlement—some of them soldiers from the retreat, others hapless civilians who had moved too slow. No victim had been left whole; arms, legs, even heads had been lopped off. Several corpses appeared to have been cut up *afterward,* which strengthened the expressions of disgust and bitterness worn by the soldiers in the party.

"Stay spread out, but within sight," Jarod commanded, tightening the reins of his own night saber. "And keep your beasts under control."

The last order he had repeated more than once already. The huge panthers seemed particularly distressed about their situation, as if they knew something that their riders did not. It made the scouting party even more tense.

A nightmarish shadow rose up before them . . . the outer edge of Suramar. The Burning Legion had not had sufficient time to ravage the entire city, and so part of its skeleton still stood as a grim reminder of all that had been lost . . . and all that still could be.

"By the Mother Moon . . ." whispered one soldier.

Brox glanced at Jarod. The captain stared at his home with eyes that barely blinked. His hands crumpled the reins. The vein in his neck throbbed.

"Hard to have no home," the orc commented to him, thinking of his own life.

"I *have* a home," Jarod growled. "Suramar is still my home."

The orc said nothing more, understanding the night elf's pain.

Through the fallen gates they entered the city. Utter silence surrounded them. Even their breathing seemed far too raucous a noise for this still place.

Once inside, they paused. Jarod looked to the wizard for a suggestion as to their next move. Ahead of them the path split in three directions. Safety demanded that they all stay together, but the time limit set to them made inspecting Suramar that way impossible.

Rhonin frowned, finally saying, "No one goes wandering off in this. There's a magic in the mist. I don't care if we can't search everything, captain."

"I'm inclined to agree," Jarod returned with some relief. "I never thought to be so distrusting of a place in which I grew up."

"This is no longer Suramar, Shadowsong. You must remember that. Whatever the Burning Legion touches, it taints. Even if the city is empty of demons, it could be very, very dangerous."

Brox nodded. He recalled all too well the things that had come out at him from the mist during his people's fight against the demons. What the night elves had battled so far proved pale by comparison.

Just enough of the city remained intact to give the ruins a semblance of their former self. Now and then, a building would materialize that had not been touched. Jarod had soldiers check these structures out, thinking that anyone who had survived the carnage might have taken refuge inside.

Not once did they find a living soul, though.

In spite of their intention to stay together, the devastation eventually demanded otherwise of them. The path became too confused and debris-filled to allow the scouting party to ride together without vastly slowing the search down. With great reluctance, Jarod had three soldiers on each end head off toward side streets.

"Go around the wreckage and meet up with us as soon as your route allows," he told the six. As the two groups rode off, the captain quickly added, "And keep together!"

With Shadowsong and his remaining three fighters creating an escort for Rhonin—and Brox by association—the main group moved on. The night sabers had to pick their way up and over the rubble. Three huge tree homes had been torn down and in the process collided with one another over the path. One leaned atop the other two, the former residence dangling menacingly over the orc and his companions.

Brox's night saber hissed as it stepped on something. Rhonin leaned over, then informed the orc, "The owner never left."

They found more corpses as the cats reached the highest point. Again they were residents of the city, but these had evidently tried to flee when they were caught by the Burning Legion. Other than the grotesque wounds left by their slayers, the victims were oddly untouched. Neither decay nor carrion eaters had disturbed them.

"They had to have perished in the initial destruction," the wizard noted. "You'd think they'd look even worse."

" 'Tis a foul enough sight for me already," Jarod Shadowsong gasped.

With the panthers moving as gingerly as possible, they finally began descending to the original path. As he held on tight, Brox again raised his nose to the air and sniffed.

For a brief moment, the orc thought he sensed something, but the scent was faint and old. He looked around and discovered the body of a felbeast that some soldier had speared. Brox grunted in satisfaction and resumed clinging on for dear life.

Finally, the six reached level ground. Jarod pointed ahead, saying, "I recall an avenue just out of sight. We should be able to join up with the others, Master Rhonin."

"I'll be glad of that."

Only a short distance later, the captain's chosen avenue materialized. The party paused when it reached the intersection and Jarod looked around.

"We must've gotten ahead of them," he noted.

Brox straightened. Rhonin shifted uneasily in the saddle, his fingers flexing in what the orc knew was a preamble to spellcasting.

"Aah!" Jarod looked relieved. "Here comes one party now!"

From the orc's left rode three of the soldiers. They looked very pleased to see their comrades again. Even the cats moved with much eagerness.

"What did you find?" Shadowsong asked the new arrivals.

"Nothing, captain," responded the most senior in rank. "More ruins, more corpses. As many of our people as those monsters."

"Damn . . ."

"Are several of those you knew not among the refugees with us, Shadowsong?" asked Rhonin.

"Far too many. And the more we find here, the less chance that I've just missed them in the crowds."

It was an old tale to Brox. How many of those with whom he had grown up had died in one battle or another?

Small wonder that he had once regretted outlasting his com-rades in the war; by then, the orc had already survived most of his blood brothers. He realized that part of his desire to die had also been due to loneliness.

Jarod eyed the opposite direction. "The others should be here at any moment."

But that moment and a hundred others came and went, and still the missing soldiers did not reappear. The riders grew tense. Their darkening mood spread to the night sabers, who hissed and spat more and more as the minutes passed.

Brox could finally wait no longer. Even as Captain Shadowsong began to raise his hand in order to suggest that they move out and look for the vanished soldiers, the orc rode past him, toward where last the trio should have been.

He steered his mount down the other pathway, searching warily for any sign. Far behind him, Rhonin and the night elves hurried to catch up.

Rubble filled the street. Torn cloth and old bloodstains added the only color to the scene. The orc readied his ax and forced his mount to continue on.

Then a peculiarity about his present surroundings struck Brox. He twisted in the saddle, carefully looking around for one hint that his suspicions were correct.

But nowhere did he see any sign of even a single body. No night elves, no demons. Even the likely corpses of the three missing soldiers and their mounts could not be found.

What had happened to them? Brox wondered. How had this street remained unsullied by the deaths of innocents?

The slight sliding of rocks caused the green-skinned war-rior to jerk to his right. A figure slowly coalesced in the mist—a soldier, but on foot, with his weapon drawn.

"Where's your mount?" the orc rumbled.

The soldier trod awkwardly toward him. There were splotches on his armor, and his mouth hung open.

As his face came into better view, Brox saw with consternation that part of it had been ripped open. One eye was completely gone, and the jagged gap descended all the way to the center of the throat . . . or what remained of it.

And as he neared the orc, the macabre figure raised his weapon. Behind him, Brox suddenly noted other shapes following the soldier.

Although no coward, the green-skinned fighter pulled hard on the reins, turning the night saber about. As it moved, the cat swung one clawed paw at the oncoming soldier, batting him away like a toy.

The others rode up just as he started back. Jarod glanced beyond him, to where the soldier had fallen. "What did you do to him? You made your beast strike him dead—"

"Already dead before! Hurry! More coming!"

The night elf started to argue, but Rhonin put a hand across his chest. "Look into the mist, Shadowsong! Look!"

Jarod did—and shook his head in horror. The soldier arose, his face and chest now even more terrible to behold. Still wobbling, he gripped his sword and headed toward the party. Behind him, the first of the other shapes grew distinct—night elves, but in even more monstrous shape than the soldier. Several were ripped open from head to toe and others missed limbs. All wore the same empty expressions, and moved with the same deathly determination.

"Ride!" the captain shouted. "Back through the city gates! Follow me!"

With Jarod and the wizard in the lead, the party pulled away just before the first of the ghoulish figures could reach them. They sped up the way that they had just come, but when they reached the intersection, Jarod had everyone turn in the opposite direction.

"Why this way?" shouted Rhonin.

"A shorter and smoother path to our goal . . . I hope!"

But as they rode, other figures began to emerge from the ruins. Brox growled as what had once been an elder female in the blood-encrusted remains of a once-glittering silver, turquoise, and red gown snatched almost hungrily at his leg. He kicked her back, and for good measure severed her head with one mighty swing of the enchanted ax. Even after that, her body grabbed wildly for anything it could reach, but, fortunately, by then the orc had ridden away.

Rhonin suddenly pulled up short. "Watch out!"

His warning came too late for one of the soldiers nearest him. A mass of clawing, tearing hands pulled the night elf off his mount. He slashed one with his sword, but he might as well have been stabbing the air for all the good it did.

Jarod started to come to his aid, but before he could reach his comrade, the hapless victim vanished beneath the shambling corpses. His scream cut off almost immediately.

"It's too late for him!" the wizard insisted despite Jarod's clear intention of still trying to retrieve the soldier. "The rest of you, keep riding! I've some notion what to do here!"

"We can't leave you!" argued the captain.

Brox steered his mount next to Rhonin. "I stay with him!"

"We'll only be a few moments behind, Shadowsong! The way looks clear a little after this! You should be able to get out of the city!"

The night elf did not want to leave, but to stay would risk more lives. Of them all, Rhonin had the best chance for survival.

"This way!" the captain called to the rest of his command.

As they pushed off, the riderless night saber behind, Rhonin turned to face the oncoming mob. "Brox! I need a few seconds!"

Nodding, the orc pushed forward. With a battle cry, he slashed back and forth, his ax sweeping out before his mount with deadly accuracy. Grasping hands, gore-encrusted chests, torn throats . . . all he chopped at with every iota of strength that he could muster.

Just as Brox began to flag, Rhonin called, "Enough! Pull back!"

No sooner had the orc done so than the wizard tossed a small vial at the encroaching horde. As it flew, it somehow managed to arc along the front row, splattering each of the undead.

And the moment the spilling liquid touched its targets, the ghouls burst into blue flame.

An inferno quickly blossomed. The corpses behind the first row walked mindlessly into the flames, igniting themselves. Some of those already ablaze teetered into others, spreading the fire to them.

"Something I once used against the Scourge," the human remarked with grim satisfaction. "Come on! We've got to—"

A fiery figure rushed forward and collapsed into Brox's mount, setting it, too, ablaze. The orc struggled as the night saber abruptly turned and raced madly away from the source of its agony . . . in the process dragging its rider deeper into Suramar.

Rhonin called out after him, but Brox could not stop his animal. Crazed by the smoldering flames, the panther charged wildly through the streets.

The orc tried to smother the fire, but only made his situation worse. His night saber suddenly slowed, then threw itself on the side that burned. Brox barely had time to fling himself to safety lest his leg be crushed under the beast's immense weight.

The night saber rolled over on the affected area, then, seeming unsatisfied with its attempts, ran off before the orc could stop it. Brox whirled around, expecting to be attacked on all sides by the horrific mob. Breath coming out in heavy pants, he swung his ax again and again, only gradually realizing that he was not in any imminent danger.

Of course, he was also without either a mount or the presence of the wizard.

Eyes wary, Brox started back the way from which he thought the night saber had come. Yet, as the brawny fighter proceeded through the ruins, he saw nothing that gave any hint as to whether his path was the right one. The injured cat had run with such manic swiftness that it had clearly dragged its rider farther than first imagined.

The orc smelled the air, but caught no scent of either the human or the night elves. Worse, his usually infallible sense of direction failed him here. The mist had a headiness to it that played with all of his senses.

Growing more confused as to his whereabouts, Brox turned down what seemed a vaguely familiar avenue. Ruined trees, scorched landscape, and the crumbling remains of dwellings appeared out of the haze, but none did he recognize with any certainty.

Then, something momentarily assailed his nose. The hulking orc hesitated, sniffing the air again. His heavy brow crushed together and he ground his yellowed teeth.

With new resolve he headed to his right, every other step smelling the air again. His new path demanded that he climb over the tangling roots of an upturned giant oak and across the crushed shell of a night elven home, but Brox would not be deterred. He climbed cautiously, trying not to make the slightest sound—a difficult task considering that he also refused to free his other hand by putting away his ax.

As he reached the top of the shattered domicile, Brox caught a fresh scent. It made his nostrils wrinkle in disgust, but urged him forward.

And when he peered over, it was to see the demons at work.

There were four of the Fel Guard and one Doomguard soldier, as well. However, they were not so much of a threat in Brox's eyes as the two standing in the forefront. The orc snarled as he recognized from his own time the horrific, winged figures in midnight blue armor. They gestured with fingers that ended in savage, bladelike nails, a pale green aura covering their hands as they worked.

Nathrezim, also called *Dreadlords.*

They stood taller than the other demons, and their aspects were more terrible to behold. Huge, dark, curled horns thrust high from their heads. They had dead, gray skin like a corpse, and no hair whatsoever on their monstrous heads. Two sharp canines jutted down, reminding Brox of the tales he had heard of the Dreadlords' vampiric traits. In point of fact, the Nathrezim were psychic vampires, feeding on the weak-minded and often using their victims as slaves.

The pair stood on thick, powerful legs like those of goats, their feet cloven hooves. While cunning and extremely skilled at magic—even more so than the Eredar—they were also deadly fighters. Yet, it seemed that in this particular incidence, it was their dark spells that the orc and his companion had to fear most.

Brox had found the necromancers.

The two Nathrezim had done the abominable, successfully raising the dead they and their comrades had so brutally slaughtered. The orc recalled what he had heard of the

Undead Scourge and their own ghoulish spells. To one of his kind, what these creatures did now was far more monstrous than any death caused by the weapons of the Fel Guard of Doomguard.

In his mind, Brox imagined what he would have felt like if the bloody bodies of his comrades had risen up to join the enemy against the orcs. This was sacrilege, a dishonoring of spirits. His heart pounded, and Brox felt an uncontrollable rage filling him.

He suddenly thought of Rhonin and the night elves. It was possible that they had escaped, but with so many dead under the control of the Nathrezim, it was also possible that they fought dearly for their lives . . . provided they had not already been slain.

And if slain . . . they would likely join those the Dreadlords had raised.

Brox could hold back no longer. He rose from his hiding place and, with a war cry akin to the one he had uttered with his comrades back at the pass, leapt upon the group.

His shout echoed through the stillness. To his immense pleasure, the demons actually jumped at the sound, so unexpected in this place. Their surprise slowed their reflexes, exactly as the warrior had planned.

The ax Malfurion and the demigod had created for him cut smoothly through the armored chest of the first Fel Guard, spilling the demon's foul innards. As his first foe collapsed, Brox brought the ax up, slicing through the forearm of another creature.

The Dreadlords did not cease their work, relying on their comrades to deal with one attacker. However, they had not fought orcs—not yet—and that lack of understanding worked well for Brox. He slammed into the next nearest Fel Guard, bowling over the huge demon with his own considerable mass, then rolled away as the Doomguard soldier attempted to run him through.

Brox traded blows with the winged warrior, then whirled just in time to deflect a strike by another opponent. He cleaved the second demon in half at the waist, then for good measure used the back end of his war ax to crush in the skull of the fighter that he had maimed earlier.

Now one of the spellcasters at last took notice. Leaving his comrade to continue their foul work, he turned and pointed at the orc.

In desperation, Brox threw himself between the spellcaster and the Doomguard. Yet, no sooner had he done that than the winged figure shrieked and twisted. He contorted as if something sought to burrow out of him—and then his chest exploded.

Something struck the orc from behind. Brox fell dazed. The last of the Fel Guard loomed over him, the Nathrezim coming up next to the monstrous warrior. The fiendish spellcaster stared down at their adversary, demonic eyes gleeful.

"You will fight well for us . . ." he hissed. "Kill many of your friends . . ."

The vision of himself shambling toward Tyrande and the others sickened Brox; he had been willing to accept death, but this was a terrible parody of it.

"No!" Brox pushed himself up, knowing full well that he would never beat either the Fel Guard's weapon or the Nathrezim's unholy spell.

Then, the other Nathrezim unexpectedly howled. The agonizing cry barely escaped his mouth before he burst into blue flames.

The two demons turned, giving Brox his chance. He immediately went for the remaining spellcaster, thrusting up the ax. The sharp blade not only cut through the

Nathrezim's throat, but also completely severed the head.

A blade came at his side, cutting a streak along the orc's torso. Brox grunted with pain, then turned to face his adversary. His ax met the demon's blade, shattering the other weapon. The Fel Guard tried to retreat, but the orc cut him down.

Breathing heavily, the veteran warrior looked around. From the wreckage of another downed tree, Rhonin led his own night saber forward.

"I thought you might be able to handle the situation if I provided a little diversion." The wizard studied the bodies. "If I needn't have bothered at all, please tell me."

With a snort, Brox replied, "A good warrior welcomes all allies, human. This one thanks you."

"I should thank *you*. You found the ones animating the dead. It was like the horror of the Scourge all over again."

Thinking of the shambling corpses, Brox quickly surveyed the area again, but saw nothing.

"Rest easy, Brox," Rhonin assured him. "When the Nathrezim perished, I sensed their work cease. The dead are at rest again."

"Good."

"You're wounded."

The orc gave a noncommittal grunt. "Had many wounds."

Rhonin grinned. "Well, for now you'll be riding. Jarod and the others should be just outside the gate. I doubt the erstwhile captain will go far without us. He's already lost Krasus and Malfurion. He doesn't want to go back to Ravencrest empty-handed."

Most other times, Brox would have argued about accepting a ride. To show anything but the utmost strength to another was considered shameful in the eyes of his people.

Still, he felt weak in the legs and decided that a good warrior also did not unnecessarily risk those who had come to his aid. The orc mounted the night saber and allowed Rhonin to guide it.

"It's beginning . . ." muttered the human. "They're starting to experiment with creating an army of the unliving. This is probably not the only place that they've been attempting this."

The thick mist made their going slow. Brox, peering about, saw the body of a dead night elf, one of the original inhabitants by the look of the garments. That it lay unmoving gave the orc a conflicting feeling of relief and distaste.

"You understand what I'm saying, don't you, Brox?"

The orc did. Anyone who had survived the final war against the Burning Legion and lived through the awful aftermath would have understood. No one in their time period had not at the very least heard the horror stories, the tales of the Plaguelands and the ghoulish hordes wandering it. Too many more had experienced their own loved ones rising up from the dead and trying to add the living to their grisly ranks.

The Scourge now stalked the world, spreading terror as they attempted to make of it one vast Plagueland. Quel'Thalas was all but gone. Most of Lordaeron, too. The undead haunted nearly every realm.

Here, in the far past, Brox and Rhonin had just come across the first inklings of the Scourge's creation . . . and both knew that, despite this small victory, there was nothing that they could do to change *that* terrifying part of the future.

FIFTEEN

The voice was constantly in Illidan's head, whispering what at first were unthinkable things. Yes, he was jealous of his brother, but the sorcerer could never see himself causing Malfurion any harm. That would have been like cutting off his own left arm.

And yet . . . he could not help finding such thoughts also a slightly bit *comforting*, a way in which his misery over losing Tyrande could be somewhat assuaged. Deep down, Illidan still harbored some slight hope that she would see things differently, that the priestess would realize how superior he was to his brother.

The foul mist that had spread all the way from Zin-Azshari did nothing to lighten his mood. As he strode up to Lord Ravencrest, he saw that the bearded noble looked none too pleased, either. Despite their renewed progress, now not only were Malfurion and Krasus gone, but Rhonin had yet to return from the mission upon which he had insisted on going. Illidan was certain that the night elves could survive without the other spellcasters, but he at least would have preferred the human to return. Rhonin was the only one capable of teaching him anything concerning his craft.

Going down on one knee before his master, Illidan bowed his head. "My lord."

"Rise, sorcerer. I summon you to prepare yourself and the others for departure."

"But Master Rhonin—"

"Has but minutes ago returned and reported. What he tells me urges our immediate march. We must crush the demons and take the capital as soon as possible."

That Illidan had not sensed the wizard's return surprised the younger night elf. As he stood, he said, "We shall be ready to ride."

The sorcerer turned to depart, but Ravencrest shook his head. "That isn't the only reason I've summoned you, lad. It's to tell you what the wizard discovered, and it is for your ears only."

Illidan's chest swelled with pride. "I will tell no one, not even the Moon Guard."

"Not until I tell you to do so, yes, lad. Hear what Master Rhonin discovered and digest it well . . . if you can."

Then, the master of Black Rook Hold related the horrific tale of what had happened to Rhonin's party. The sorcerer listened first with disbelief, then astonishment. He did not, however, react with the disgust, the dread, with which Lord Ravencrest did. Instead, for the first time, Illidan found himself *admiring* the audacity of the demons.

"I didn't think such possible!" he said once the noble had finished. "What command they have of their spellwork!"

"Yes," returned Ravencrest, not noting Illidan's morbid fascination. "Too dark and lethal a command. We now face a greater threat than even I believed. How abominable a thing to consider, even by them!"

Illidan did not see the matter in the same light. The demon's spellcasters allowed no limits to their imagination. They worked to create whatever their abilities allowed, the better to gain their ultimate goal. While the goal itself was not to be admired, the efforts of the warlocks surely were.

"I wish that we could capture one of the Eredar," he murmured. The sorcerer imagined conversing with the demon, learning how its manner of spellcasting differed from his own.

"Capture one? Don't be silly, lad! I expect them to be slain on sight, especially now! Every dead warlock means less chance for a repeat of this horror that Master Rhonin and the others confronted!"

Quickly smothering any hint of his esteem for the warlocks, Malfurion's brother quickly nodded. "O-of course, my lord! That remains one of our highest priorities!"

"I should hope so. That's all, sorcerer."

Illidan bowed, then immediately retreated. His mind was awhirl with thoughts concerning what he had just learned. *To raise the dead!* What other fantastic feats could the Eredar perform? Even the two wizards had never hinted of such abilities, or surely they would have seen the good sense in calling up the battlefield casualties of both sides to use against the Burning Legion!

Lord Ravencrest was making a terrible mistake. How better to defeat an enemy than to learn their strengths and add them to your own arsenal? With such skills added to those which he had already picked up, Illidan believed he would be nearly capable of crushing the demons by himself.

Surely *then* Tyrande would see that he was the superior choice.

"If only I could learn from them . . ." he whispered.

Almost as soon as he said it, Illidan glanced around anxiously, certain that there was someone nearby who had heard. However, the sorcerer found his immediate surroundings empty, the nearest soldier many yards away.

More confident again, Illidan marched off to rejoin the Moon Guard. He had much thinking to do. Much thinking.

The shadow moved away from Illidan's retreating back, skirting the tent of Lord Desdel Stareye. Even with his hooves, the figure walked silently across the harsh ground. Guards making their rounds somehow missed seeing him despite being very near at some points. Only those he chose to hear or see him ever did so.

Xavius leered, quite pleased with his efforts. The satyr had not only served his glorious master, but set well into motion his own vengeance. He had marked the druid's brother immediately, and now the process of corruption had begun. The questions, the desires, were there, and Illidan Stormrage himself would now fan the flames. It was only a matter of time.

The satyr slipped out of the camp to where the others awaited him. Even Archimonde did not realize everything Xavius plotted, for the former night elf answered now to Sargeras alone. Neither Archimonde nor Mannoroth had any sway over him.

Yes, Xavius thought, if all went as planned, when Sargeras entered the world, it would be *he* who stood at the right hand of the demon lord . . . and Archimonde and Mannoroth who would be forced to kneel before him.

Pain woke Krasus, pain that wracked every fiber of his being. Even trying to breathe hurt so very much.

"Hush, hush," twittered a feminine voice. "You are not yet fit to rise."

He tried opening his eyes, but that also proved too much of a strain. "Wh-who . . ."

"Sleep, sleep . . ." Her voice was pure music, but had in it something that told the stricken wizard that she was more than a human or a night elf.

Krasus fought against the suggestion, but his strength abandoned him and he drifted off. Dreams of flight filled his slumber. He was a dragon again, but this time he had a proud plumage like a great bird. The mage thought little of this, simply thrilled to be aloft once more.

The dream went on and on, never ceasing to tantalize him. When someone shook Krasus and finally tore him from it, he almost cursed the intruder.

"Krasus! It's Malfurion! Awaken!"

The dragon mage grudgingly returned to consciousness. "I . . . I am with you, druid."

"Praise Elune! I thought you would sleep forever."

Now that he was awake, Krasus realized that the night elf had quite possibly done him a tremendous favor. "I believe I was supposed to sleep . . . at least until our host returned." The slim spellcaster looked around at their surroundings. "And perhaps I am still sleeping."

The room around them, while spacious, was of such odd construction that Krasus had to inspect it. It was formed from many, many branches, vines, and other material packed together with dirt and more. The room was rounded at the ceiling, and the only entrance appeared to be a hole far to his right. He looked down and noticed that his own bedding was of similar material, made soft by a draping of fresh leaves artfully woven together. On a small table made from the stump of a tree, a bowl carved from an impossibly-huge nut held water, which he assumed was for him.

Sipping from it, the dragon mage continued his inspection. His eyes narrowed as he realized that what he had taken for an inner wall was, in point of fact, a passage. The curve of the room and the way the walls had been created made it almost impossible to see the corridor without standing directly in front of it.

"It goes for a very long distance," Malfurion offered. "I found another, much larger chamber, and from that I went on to two more. Then I ran across more corridors and decided I had better return to you."

"A wise thing." Krasus frowned. His sharp ears had picked up a sound from without that he had finally been able to identify. Birds. Not just one type, however; the wizard heard at least a dozen different calls, some of them extraordinarily unique.

"What is outside?"

"I'd rather not say, Master Krasus. You should see it yourself."

His curiosity stirred, the slim figure rose and walked to the opening. As he neared it, the calls grew more intense, more varied. It was as if every type of bird nested outside . . .

Krasus hesitated, surveying the room again. *That* was what his surroundings reminded him of . . . a huge bird's nest.

Already suspecting he knew what he would see, the dragon mage stuck his head through the entrance.

It seemed that every species of bird *did* nest around them. Certainly they had the room. Everywhere Krasus looked, he saw huge, outstretched branches filled with foliage. In each of the branches, some avian had made its home. At a quick glance, he saw doves, robins, cardinals, mockingbirds, and more. There were birds from temperate zones and others from more exotic climes. They intermingled. They sang together. There were berry feeders, fish catchers, and even those who preyed on other birds—although the last seemed quite content with the rabbits and lizards they now brought for their young.

Gazing above, Krasus discovered more nests. The foliage of this incredibly huge tree was filled to the brim with all the birds of the world.

It was also filled with the astounding structure of which his chamber was one of only hundreds.

Like the myriad tunnels of a giant ant colony, the "nest" spread throughout the branches. A quick estimate by the wizard measured it large enough to house the entire night elven army—mounts included—plus the refugees with more than ample room to spare. Despite its outwardly weak appearance, Krasus was also quick to see that the edifice was more durable than it seemed. As the wind rocked the foliage, the "nest" waved and adjusted accordingly. The dragon mage touched one edge of the entrance and realized that it was held together better than the stones of a mighty fortress.

Then . . . he finally looked down.

To imagine that a dragon could suffer from vertigo would once have been impossible for Krasus to even consider. Yet now he teetered at the entrance, unable to come to grips with what he saw.

"Master Krasus!" Malfurion pulled him away from the entrance. "You almost fell! I'm sorry! I should've told you what to expect!"

Krasus exhaled, regaining his senses. "I am all right, my friend. You can release me. I know full what to expect now."

"I had to throw myself back when I first looked," the druid told him. "I was afraid that I'd be blown outside by the wind."

Now better prepared, Krasus returned to the opening. He gripped the sides, then peered down again.

The tree extended down for as far as he could see, branches jutting out everywhere. As elsewhere, birds perched or nested in them. Krasus stared as best he could, but of the base of the tree he could still make out no sign. Clouds drifted past, huge ones that signified just how high up they were.

The night elf came up beside him. "You can't see the ground, either, can you?"

"No, I cannot."

"I've never heard of a tree so vast, so *huge*, that one could not see the ground beneath it!"

"I have," Krasus replied, dredging up ancient memories from his ravaged mind. "It is . . . it is G'hanir. The Mother Tree. It is the place of all winged creatures, separate from but a part of the mortal world in a manner akin to the Emerald Dream. G'hanir is the tallest tree atop the tallest peak. The fruit it bears carries the seeds of all earthly trees." He thought further. "It is the home of our host . . . the demigoddess, Aviana."

"Aviana . . . ?"

"Yes." A fleet, white form flying toward their general direction caught his attention. "And I believe she is on her way to us even now."

The winged figure grew rapidly in size as it approached, finally coalescing into a massive white peregrine falcon larger than either of them. Krasus urged the druid back, leaving the entrance completely open.

The gigantic falcon fluttered through. A transformation then overtook it. The legs grew, thickened. The wings shrank, turning into slim, feathered hands. The body re-shaped, becoming more like that of a female night elf or human, and the tail shifted into the trailing end of a gos-samer white gown.

A slim, wide-eyed woman almost human in features eyed the pair. Her nose was sharp, but very elegant. She had a pale, beautiful face the color of ivory, and for hair she wore a wondrous mane of downy feathers. Her gown fluttered as she walked—on two delicate but still sharply-taloned feet.

"Awake, awake you are," she said with a slight frown. "You should rest, rest."

Krasus bowed to her. "I am grateful for your hospitality, mistress, but I am well enough to continue on now."

She cocked her head as a bird might, giving the mage a reproving look. "No, no . . . too soon, too soon. Please, sit."

The duo looked around and discovered that two chairs, made in the same fashion as the nest, waited behind them. Malfurion waited for Krasus, who finally nodded and sat.

"You are the Mother of Flight, the Lady of the Birds, are you not?" asked the dragon mage.

"Aviana I am, if that is what you mean." Her wide eyes inspected Krasus. "And you are one of mine, one of mine, I think."

"The thrill of the sky is known to me, yes, mistress. I owe my soul to Alexstrasza . . ."

"Aaah . . ." The demigoddess smiled in a motherly fashion. "Dear, dear Alexstrasza . . . it is long since we spoke. We must do so."

"Yes." Krasus did not push the point that now was hardly the time for visits. He did not doubt that Aviana knew exactly what was going on in the world and that despite her pleasant visage, she conferred with the other demigods and spirits on how to deal with the Burning Legion.

The sky deity looked to the night elf. "You, you, on the other wing, are one of Cenarius's . . ."

"I am Malfurion."

Aviana twittered, a sound like a songbird. "Of course, of course, you are! Cenarius speaks well of you, youngling."

The druid's cheeks darkened.

A question burned in Krasus's mouth, and he finally had to blurt, "Mistress . . . how do we come to be here?"

For the first time, she looked surprised. "Why, you chose to come here, of course, of course!"

The last thing Krasus could recall was the worm closing in on them as they reached the gate. He looked to Malfurion for clarification, but the night elf obviously knew less than him. "You say I chose to send us here?"

Aviana raised one delicately-boned hand. A multicolored songbird with a sweeping tail flew through the entrance and alighted onto the back of the hand. The demigoddess cooed at the small creature, which rubbed its head against hers. "Only those who truly desire to come here do. This one found you and your friend lying among the branches, the branches. There was also much scattered flesh of a very large and tasty worm. The children will feast for some time on it . . ."

Malfurion looked sick. The mage nodded. When he had blacked out, the portal had collapsed, cutting the huge worm in two.

Ignoring his own distaste, Krasus said, "I am afraid that this is the sole time that it was in complete error, mistress. I did not mean for us to come here. I cast a spell that went awry."

Her petite mouth formed another smile. "So you do not wish to fly again, to fly again?"

Krasus grimaced. "I would like nothing more."

"Then that, then that, is in part why you ended up here."

The dragon mage mulled over her words. His continual longing to be what he was had evidently influenced his spell-casting and Aviana had sensed it. "But there's nothing you can do for me."

"So sad, so sad." The demigoddess let the songbird fly out

again. "But perhaps I can, perhaps I can . . . if you truly insist on departing."

"I do."

"Very well, very well." From within the inner plumage of her left wing, Aviana plucked one feather. As she held it up, a silver sheen covered it. The sky deity handed the feather to Krasus, who took the gift with reverence and studied it. Certainly Aviana's feather had power, but how would it enable him to fly?

"Place it upon your chest."

After some hesitation, Krasus pulled open the top of his robe, revealing his chest. He heard Malfurion gasp and even Aviana stared at him with wider eyes.

"So, so, you are indeed one of mine."

He had forgotten about the scale. Taken from his younger self, it felt so comforting that he had forgotten it. Briefly he pondered whether he could have used it to somehow penetrate the barrier, but quickly realized that by the time they had reached the area, Neltharion had sealed off the dragons' domain from all but his own sentinels. The Earth Warder had wanted no one disturbing his final spellwork. "Will your plan still work?" he asked.

"But of course, but of course! More so now, more so!"

Placing the feather against a part of his chest that was not covered by the dragon scale, Krasus waited.

The downy piece adhered much as the scale had. The silky tendrils of the feather spread flat, and as Krasus watched, the tendrils suddenly grew. They reached along his torso, snaking over it in every direction.

Malfurion looked distraught, but Krasus shook his head. He understood what Aviana intended and welcomed it. The dragon mage's heart pulsated at twice its normal rate, and he felt the urge to go leaping out of the nest.

"Not yet, not yet," warned the demigoddess. "You will know when its work is done, when its work is done."

A peculiar sensation spread across his upper back, near the shoulder blades. Krasus felt his garments shift and heard slight rips.

"There's something coming out of the back of your robes!" the druid gasped.

Even before they began to stretch, to define themselves, Krasus knew what they would be—huge, expansive white wings identical to the ones that Aviana had worn when transformed into a bird. Thick, white feathers covered them. Krasus instinctively flexed the wings and found them as responsive as his own.

"They are yours for this journey, for this journey."

The dragon mage indicated his companion. "What about him?"

"He is not born to the sky, to the sky. With learning, yes, with learning. Too long, too long, though. You must carry him, carry him."

In his present form, Krasus doubted that he had the strength for such a lengthy trek and said so. His concerns did not seem to bother their host, though.

This time, Aviana plucked a single strand from another feather. She brought it to her lips and gently blew it toward Malfurion. The druid looked uncertain, but stood his ground as the tiny bit of feather drifted over to him.

It touched his shoulder, adhering there. Malfurion shook once, then found great satisfaction with his hands, his legs, his entire body.

"I feel—" He jumped up and nearly struck the ceiling. Landing, Malfurion grinned like a child.

The birdlike deity smiled at both, her gaze returning to Krasus. "You will find him no burden at all, no burden at all."

"I—" Krasus choked up. He had not realized until now how great his distress had been over losing his ability to soar among the clouds. A tear slipped from one eye as he went down on his knee before Aviana and said, "Thank you . . ."

"No need for gratitude, no need." She bid him to rise, then led both toward the entrance. "Away you will fly, you will fly. To that high branch, then the right, the right. Through the clouds, through the clouds and descend. Well on your way you will be, you will be."

"The feather. How will I—"

She put a gentle finger to the mage's lips. "Hush, hush. It will know, it will know." As Malfurion joined Krasus, Aviana grew more solemn and said to the druid, "Your *shan'do* wishes you to know that he is with you, with you. We do not ignore the danger, the danger. Our will, our will, is strong . . ."

"Thank you. That gives me hope."

"Gives all of us hope," added Krasus. "If only we could do something about the dragons."

She agreed. "Yes . . . even we do not understand what goes on there, what goes on there."

Her two visitors eyed each other, Krasus saying, "They have a plan, but there is a threat to—"

Suddenly, his mouth felt as if full of cotton. His tongue seemed to twist. Aviana waited for more, but Krasus could give her nothing.

Seeing his silence as some hesitation of his own, the demigoddess gave him a respectful nod, then bid the dragon mage to step through the hole.

Krasus did so immediately, almost leaping into the sky. The wings instantly reacted, carrying him aloft. Around the area, birds twittered and sang out in recognition of a fellow flying creature.

The heady experience made him momentarily forget

Malfurion and his mission. The sensation of having his own wings was so spectacular that Krasus had to fly up among the branches, then dive around them before rational thought returned.

Somewhat chagrined, the mage finally dropped down to where the druid and Aviana awaited him. The night elf had an awestruck expression and the demigoddess smiled like a proud parent. She indicated to Malfurion that he should step out and, after a cautious glance down, the druid obeyed.

Coming up over the night elf, Krasus took him under the shoulders. He felt as if he carried nothing.

"Are you comfortable?" the mage asked his companion.

"Not until my feet touch the ground," Malfurion muttered, "but I'll be good enough until then, Master Krasus."

"Go then, go then," Aviana said to the pair. To Krasus in particular, she added, "And when the end of your days comes, youngling, I will have your nest here ready, your nest here ready."

Krasus blanched. He looked around at the endless number and variety of birds; so many species living together, even though they should not be.

And the reason that they could live together here . . . was that they did not live at all. These were their spirits, brought up here by the demigoddess. Somewhere there would be larger flying creatures, perhaps the hippogriff that had been slain and . . . and, of course, those dragons who had seen the end of their days.

"Go now, go now," the white figure cooed. "You shall return soon enough, soon enough . . ."

Put off guard as he had never been before, Krasus swallowed. "Yes, mistress . . . thank you again."

She smiled, which in no way eased his mind.

Rising up several yards, Krasus studied the direction in

which she had told him to fly. He adjusted his grip on an anxious Malfurion, then started off.

As they flew, the night elf asked, "What did she mean by that? What did she mean that you would return?"

"We must all die someday, Malfurion."

"We—" The druid shivered, the truth finally dawning on him. "You mean . . . all of this—?"

"All of it." Krasus refused to say more, but, his curiosity aroused, he dared look back at the nest. His eyes widened as the mage realized that he had seen only a tiny bit. For the first time Krasus saw the structure in all its immensity. It ran everywhere and at each turn a huge, rounded chamber stood. The dragon mage studied the entire edifice, then the towering tree that dwarfed it. High up, he noticed winged creatures that even he could not identify.

And then, while he was still caught up in the sight . . . they entered the clouds.

SIXTEEN

The night elven host met the demons again just beyond Suramar. The Burning Legion held them there for a short time, then fell back toward Zin-Azshari. Midway through the next evening, the battle intensified, and once more no ground was gained or lost. Night elves and demons perished horribly, either through the blade or the magic arts.

Ravencrest could not stand this repeated stalemate, and so he had summoned Rhonin and Illidan again.

"Magic looks to be the deciding factor in this!" he said to the human in particular. "Can you do anything?"

Rhonin considered. "There is something that may be possible, but I'll need the full cooperation of the Moon Guard to put it into effect. It may backfire, too."

"I doubt it can make anything worse. Well, Illidan?"

"I eagerly await to aid Master Rhonin in whatever spell he crafts, my lord," Malfurion's twin said with a bow to the wizard.

Rhonin kept his expression neutral. He hoped that Illidan would maintain control and not try to build on what the red-haired spellcaster planned. If he did, chaos might ensue.

And chaos meant defeat.

"We're going to draw upon the Well as deeply as we can," Rhonin informed Illidan as they made their way to the Moon Guard. "I want to try something that the wizards of Dal— that the wizards of my homeland discussed doing, but were unable to try before things fell apart."

"Will it be that complicated, Master Rhonin?"

"No. They spent weeks preparing it, but I have in here—" He tapped his head. "—all that they completed. It may take us a few hours, but we should be successful."

Illidan grinned. "I have the utmost faith in you, Master Rhonin!"

Again, the human wondered if the night elf would be able to follow orders without attempting to turn the spell into something of his own rash design. More and more, Illidan appeared unable to *not* be the center of any casting. He lived for his sorcery, and cared not that much of his prowess had to do with the forces fed into him by the Moon Guard.

By the gods! Rhonin thought suddenly. *He almost sounds like a demon that way . . .*

But in so many other ways, the amber-eyed night elf was a potentially more terrible threat. An Illidan who sought to dominate . . . there, indeed, was a path to destruction.

I'll keep him under control. I have to with Krasus gone. He could only hope that his former mentor had succeeded in reaching the dragons. If not, Rhonin did not know what might happen. He had not planned on utilizing such a very dangerous spell, but with the knowledge that the outcome of this war was anything but set, there seemed no other choice.

Not wanting to leave the soldiers defenseless against the warlocks' dark magic, Rhonin had Illidan pick out a dozen of the best from the sorcerers' ranks, and left the rest to see to the battle. He would only need them once he had the spell ready to cast. The Moon Guard would amplify it, spread it where he needed it to go.

But only if Rhonin succeeded with his part.

"Illidan . . . I need you to guide me," the wizard said when everything else was prepared. "I need you to bring me to the Well itself."

"Yes, Master Rhonin!" The night elf eagerly stood next to him as they prepared to reach out with their minds to the source of all night elven magic. Up until this point, Rhonin had been touching peripherally on the power of the Well. Unlike Illidan's people, he had not needed to rely on direct use, which gave him a very distinct advantage. Illidan and a few others had learned from the human how to do this, but not to the same degree. Now, however, Rhonin needed to draw as much as he could so that he could be guaranteed of the results he desired.

Far away, a horn sounded. Lord Ravencrest was setting up everything in preparation for Rhonin's grand spell . . . or grand catastrophe.

Standing side by side, the two spellcasters reached out with their thoughts and linked. Rhonin felt Illidan's wild nature and tried to keep it in check. The night elf's zealousness was a definite threat to the stability of the spell.

Illidan's mind drew the wizard forward. Through his inner eye, Rhonin watched the landscape rip past as he and his companion sought to touch the Well. Endless rows of demons followed by miles of ravaged landscape passed within a single second. Briefly, the ruined city of Zin-Azshari rose up, then filled his gaze. The grand palace of Queen Azshara dominated next . . . and finally the black waters of the Well of Eternity greeted the human.

Its power staggered him. Rhonin had always assumed that he had sensed the Well enough simply by drawing upon that part of it which permeated all Kalimdor. Now he realized he had been mistaken, that the Well itself was such a fount of pure energy that if he could command it all, he felt it would make of him a god.

A *god* . . .

Everything that Rhonin had dreamed of when first he had taken up the robes of wizardry now seemed so simple. He could raise up entire cities, or tear them down with the blink of an eye. He could call up the power of the earth, then send it crashing down on any who opposed him. He could—

With tremendous effort, Rhonin freed himself of his dark ambitions. A sudden anxiety filled him as he recognized the Well. He had known what it was all along, and yet his mind had denied the evil.

It had the same taint as the demons. Pure magic it might be, but in its way it corrupted as much as Sargeras did.

But it was too late to turn back. Rhonin had to delve into the Well this once, then never touch it in such a manner again. Even drawing upon it as he had in the past now repulsed him, but to give it up completely meant that he would have to give up all magic . . . and Rhonin knew he was too weak of soul to ever do that much.

Sensing Illidan's impatience and curiosity, the wizard quickly took up the power he needed from the dark depths. The temptation to let it all engulf his mind proved daunting, but with effort he retreated from the cursed waters.

Within moments, the minds of the night elf and him had returned to their bodies. The link to the Well remained as strong as ever. Rhonin prepared to cast, knowing that the sooner he did, the sooner he could be rid of the foul sensation in his soul.

It begins now, he told Illidan.

Instantly, he felt Malfurion's twin prepare the Moon Guard for the task. What the wizard fed them they would send out toward the enemy, multiplying its intensity more than a hundredfold.

With ease, Rhonin constructed the spell matrix that his masters in Dalaran had died working on. He briefly thanked their departed souls, regardless of the fact that none of the wizards would be born for centuries to come. Then, when Rhonin was satisfied that the matrix would remain stable—the wizard unleashed the spell.

Illidan and the others mentally shook as it reverberated through their systems. To his credit the young sorcerer kept the much more practiced spellcasters from buckling. The very ambition that Rhonin feared now kept his plans together.

And so, they struck at the demons' lines.

A ripple of ear-shattering sound hit the Burning Legion without even touching the soldiers who frantically battled them. Massive demons shrieked and dropped their weapons as they tried to shut the sound out. The vibrations shattered their insides, tore apart their minds. As the wave raced over their forces, the demons fell as if swept by some giant broom.

All across the front, they perished. The soldiers stood frozen, shaken up by what they witnessed.

"Now, Ravencrest," Rhonin whispered. "Now."

The horns sounded, urging a rapid advance.

The night elves shouted. Panther riders led the way. They charged across the field, seeking the enemy . . . but ahead of them lay only the dead. The sound wave continued to race on, cutting a swath of swift but violent death. No demon caught in its path lived. Hundreds perished.

Rhonin suddenly felt his body give up on him. He wobbled, his head feeling as if it, like the demons', would explode.

The wizard fell.

"I have you, Master Rhonin . . ."

Illidan eased him to the ground, the night elf none the worse for the wear. He was, in fact, the only one. The rest of the Moon Guard involved in the grand spell looked as terrible as the wizard felt. Most of them sat or even fell down, not at all caring that the soldiers now advanced from them.

"Did you see it? Did you see what we did?" demanded Illidan eagerly. "This proves it! There's no power like the Well!" He glanced at something or someone whom Rhonin himself could not see. "The Well is the way, brother! You see? Nothing else compares!"

He continued shouting to an absent Malfurion. Rhonin, still seeking to regain his strength, could only stare. Illidan's avarice, his jealousy, was so apparent that it almost bordered on hatred for the druid.

Rhonin's spell had sent the demons into flight, possibly turned the tide of the war forever . . . but as he watched Illidan's intense expression and thought of his own near seduction by the Well, the wizard wondered if he had just unleashed something more terrible on the night elf race.

Korialstrasz brooded, his patience growing very thin. The dragons had all been ordered to await the word of the Aspects. When that came, every flight would take to the air as if of one mind, one soul. The plan was to descend upon the demons as a terrifying force, the Dragon Soul ripping apart the demon lines before the leviathans themselves struck.

A simple, workable plan. A faultless plan.

A plan that, for reasons he could not express even to himself, Korialstrasz did not trust.

But the male red was loyal to his queen, his mate, and so

he did nothing. Alexstrasza trusted in Neltharion's creation. More to the point, she trusted in the Earth Warder himself. Whatever uncertainties Korialstrasz had, they had to remain unspoken.

"Ever the thinker, my love. Ever the worrier."

He raised his head in surprise as the gigantic female entered his lair. "Alexstrasza," he rumbled. "You are to be with the other Aspects . . ."

"I have made excuses for my momentary absence. Neltharion is not pleased, but he will have to control himself."

Korialstrasz lowered his head in homage to her. "How may I be of service to you, my queen?"

A hint of indecision glinted in her eyes. In a voice so very quiet for a dragon, she replied, "I need you to disobey me."

Her consort was perplexed. "My love?"

"All save the sentinels that each of us posted are supposed to remain in this, the vastest of the cavern systems, until the moment of the launch. I wish you to ignore my earlier command and leave."

He was stunned. Clearly the other Aspects were not to know of this departure. "And where am I to go?"

"I don't know precisely, but I hope that you'll be able to sense exactly where once you're beyond the barrier. I want you to find Krasus."

Krasus. The mysterious mage had been much on the mind of Korialstrasz, too. Krasus likely knew things that would have cleared up much that disturbed the consort. "He should still be with the night elves—"

"No . . . he was near us only a short time ago. Ysera told me that a night elf called Malfurion sought to act as his messenger through her. However, she distrusted such an action, and so made the night elf wait until the moment was right."

"And?"

"When Ysera sought for Malfurion again, he had vanished. She told me all this while Neltharion and Malygos discussed the spellwork of the Soul."

"But why would Krasus come here?" The anxieties felt by the male red multiplied. The journey from the lands of the night elves was quite a distance for one who could not fly several miles in the space of a few minutes.

"That is what I want to know."

"I'll do my best to find him, but it may prove harder than you imagine."

The queen snorted. She shut her eyes in thought for a moment, then nodded. "Yes, you must know now."

"Know what?"

"My love, you've felt the closeness between you and Krasus. You would almost describe him as a clutch brother, wouldn't you?"

He had not thought so before, but now that Alexstrasza said it, Korialstrasz realized that, yes, Krasus did hold such an esteemed place in his heart. It had nothing to do with the scales they had shared to overcome their weakness; something about the mysterious figure had made the consort come to trust him as much as he did his glorious mate.

And, at times, even more so.

Alexstrasza read his face. "Know this, my love. The reason you and Krasus are so close is that he and you are one and the same."

The male red blinked. Surely he had heard wrong. Surely Alexstrasza meant something else.

But she shook her massive head, stating, "Krasus is *you*, Korialstrasz. He is you much older, much more learned, much wiser. He is you countless centuries forward."

"That is impossible—" A sudden thought occurred to

him. "Is this some trick of Nozdormu? His absence has been very questionable . . ."

"Nozdormu has some part in this, yes, but I can't tell you exactly how. Just understand that Krasus is here because he must be."

"Then, the outcome of the war is assured. The Dragon Soul will help us triumph over the demons. My concerns were for naught."

"Your concerns are valid. We don't know anything about the outcome. Krasus fears that Nozdormu has sent him here because the timeline has shifted. There was a point where I had to consider eliminating him and his companion in order to preserve it, but it soon became evident that matters had gone beyond such."

Korialstrasz gazed at her with wide, wondering orbs. "You would have slain . . . me?"

"At his insistence, my love."

He mulled that over and saw her reasoning. "Forgive me. Yes, my queen, I'll go searching for him."

"I thank you. His memories were much damaged by the journey to our time, perhaps because he already existed here as you. Still, he is sharp of wit in most ways, and if there is something he urgently needed to discuss, then it behooves us to find him."

"I go immediately."

Alexstrasza dipped her head in gratitude. "I must pretend that you do this by your own leave, Korialstrasz."

"Of course. I won't fail you, my queen."

She gave him a most loving look, then departed his lair. The male waited just long enough for her to be nowhere near, then left, too.

To his relief, it proved not at all difficult to leave the mountain itself, for most of the dragons now sat poised, awaiting the command to fly. The few others were like himself or Tyran, consorts with positions of leadership who had to be near if the Aspects needed them.

Evading the sentinels beyond was slightly more troublesome. The first—of his own flight—he managed to evade by being aware of the other's personality traits. Horakastrasz was a young, eagle-eyed male, but he had a tendency to become distracted. As Korialstrasz came upon him, the bored guardian had begun batting large rocks into the air with his tail, then watching them plummet to the ground far below. As he hit the next, Korialstrasz soared over him, flying high enough that the other red would not sense the shift in the air currents.

By one means or another, he passed the rest undiscovered. As he flew toward the barrier, Korialstrasz prepared himself for contact. He struck the invisible wall head-on, feeling as if he pushed through molasses. Wings flapping as hard as possible, the dragon burst through the other side, soaring miles beyond before he managed to regain proper control.

Perching on a squat mountain, Korialstrasz quickly imagined Krasus. For good measure, he touched with one claw the scale that his older self had traded to him. So much made more sense now; he had wondered why the exchange should aid the pair so well. By doing so, the two halves of himself had become more complete. Korialstrasz still suffered some pain and weariness, but nowhere near what he had before that event.

He put all his concentration into finding Krasus, seeking that link that only two who were one could possibly have. The dragon doubted that his other half was still near, for if it had been him—and it was—Korialstrasz would have continued seeking some way to enter. He would not have gone into hiding. Therefore, circumstances had demanded that Krasus flee.

Trying not to think of just what might have forced his elder form to abandon the area of the barrier, the red reached out. Only a dragon's will could encompass the expanse that Korialstrasz's did now. Over countless lands his mind stretched, hunting that which was him.

But his patience soon frayed as nowhere did he sense himself. It should have been a relatively simple task. Had some dire fate befallen Krasus? The very thought sent shivers through Korialstrasz. No creature yearned to discover his ultimate fate.

But then, as if abruptly reborn, the dragon sensed the familiar presence. He could not detect the exact location, but knew which direction he should at least fly.

Korialstrasz immediately launched into the air, flapping as hard as he could. The sooner he retrieved his other self, the sooner he could feel secure once more.

Krasus became his utter focus. His surroundings blurred. With his huge wings, he ate away at the miles, but, even still, he felt it much too slow.

So obsessed, Korialstrasz did not know that he was under attack until the claws tore into his back.

With a startled roar, he rolled in the air, taking his attacker by surprise. The monstrous visage of a black dragon filled his gaze.

"Stop!" the red shouted. "By the glory of the Aspects, I demand that you—"

In response, the other dragon opened his mouth.

Korialstrasz ceased flapping, his huge body immediately dropping like a rock. It was the only thing that saved him from a fearsome burst of molten flame. The searing heat shot just past his head, making his eyes tear.

Pain wracked Korialstrasz where the other's claws had torn through scale. Although slightly larger than the black, Korialstrasz's inherent weakness more than evened the battle.

"Leave me be!" he said, trying again to use reason. "There is no need for confrontation between us!"

"You will not interfere!" the black retorted, eyes wide and surely mad.

Alexstrasza's consort had no idea what his adversary meant by that, but it strengthened the fear that something had happened to Krasus.

The ebony behemoth dropped down on Korialstrasz, forcing him, in turn, to descend further. Korialstrasz allowed it to happen, intending to spin out from under his foe at the last moment.

But as he neared the mountain tops, he discovered that he had been played for a fool.

Korialstrasz's adversary suddenly released his hold. As he did, another black dragon leapt from behind a nearby peak. It collided with the red, sending both spinning out of control. The jagged earth below rushed up toward the pair.

"You'll slay us both!" shouted Korialstrasz.

"For the glory of my master!"

The rushing wind forced back the black's wings. Only then did Alexstrasza's consort see that one had been broken and torn. This dragon could no longer fly properly; he intended to sacrifice himself in order to send his foe to his death.

Korialstrasz, however, had no intention of perishing so. Beating his wings hard, he did what the other was incapable of doing, using the leathery appendages to direct their fall. Suddenly, instead of the red being on the bottom, the sinister black found himself there.

The injured giant roared and tried to flip them back around. Farther up, an answering cry warned Korialstrasz that his other foe had realized what was happening.

Pulling in all four legs but keeping his grip, the red calculated the seconds remaining. He watched the harsh landscape near, his attention in particular on the short, sharp hills mixed among the mountains.

And as he and the black reached them, Korialstrasz stretched his legs, thrusting his adversary down even as he beat his wings hard to lift his own considerable mass.

With a painful howl that echoed throughout the region, the injured black collided with the ground. His bones shattered, and he briefly flailed like a leaf caught in a breeze. Blood spilled over the immediate area.

A final gasp escaped the stricken leviathan . . . and then his head rolled to the side, his tongue lolling free.

The second attack nearly caught Korialstrasz as he struggled to keep from joining the dead dragon. Again the claws raked the red's back, forcing a cry from him. The strain of the battle began to tell on Korialstrasz. His breathing grew weary, and it took increasing effort to keep aloft. Neither he nor Alexstrasza had expected this betrayal by Neltharion's flight.

"You must die!" roared the black wildly, as if by telling his prey this Korialstrasz would understand.

The red dragon managed to avoid the deadly talons again, but his foe pressed him hard. The other behemoth was not only swift, but driven by a manic desire to please the Earth Warder. Like the first black, he appeared ready to sacrifice himself if it would serve the cause.

But what cause? Why be so furious that one dragon was not among the rest? Why had fear of that very fact caused Neltharion to command these to die for him?

Whatever the reason, Korialstrasz could no longer worry about it. A fierce column of molten fire caught him full in the chest. He spun around madly, unable to focus.

Claws dug into his chest. The fetid breath of the black nearly caused him to gag.

"I have you!" roared the insane creature. The dark giant inhaled for another blast, one certain to slay his opponent at such close range.

Desperate, Korialstrasz thrust his head forward. His huge jaws clamped tight on the black's neck, squeezing so hard that it cut off the air passage.

The other dragon shook violently as the forces it sought to unleash could not find an exit. He clawed frantically at Korialstrasz, leaving scars in the face and body.

The black literally exploded.

Releasing the neck, Korialstrasz roared in agony as burning ichor poured over him from the ruined corpse. It was too much. His strength gone, he and his dead adversary dropped to the earth.

And as he blacked out, the red dragon could only wonder how his death would affect his future self.

SEVENTEEN

Archimonde watched his legions retreat from the spell and the oncoming night elves. He watched as the landscape before him filled with the forest-green armor of the foe. The demon commander could feel their sense of triumph, hear their roars of imminent victory.

How easy these creatures are to deceive, he thought. *They think that they will win now.*

With that, the gigantic demon turned and slowly, confidently, walked after his fleeing minions.

"Unngh!"

Malfurion started at the sound from Krasus. A moment later, he felt the mage struggle with his grip. Looking down, the druid saw that they were much too high up for him to drop safely even with the magical feather.

Clutching onto Krasus's arms as best he could, Malfurion shouted, "What is it?"

"I do not—I feel as if my beating heart has been torn from my chest! I—I must land quickly!"

The night elf quickly scanned the area. There were woods and grassy plains below, more of the latter fortunately. He saw one area that looked softer than the rest and pointed at it. "Can you make it to there?"

"I—will—try!"

But Krasus flew haphazardly, and the spot that Malfurion had chosen began to disappear to the right. Instead, they headed for a copse of trees that might break their fall, but would also likely break their necks and skulls.

Krasus grunted hard, lifting them into the air a bit higher. The trees passed and again open plain welcomed them. They started to descend, slowly at first, then much too fast for the druid's taste.

"I think—I think you must be prepared to save yourself, Malf—"

Suddenly, the mage released him.

Precious seconds passed before Malfurion realized what he could do. He reached out with his thoughts to the grass below . . .

That area of the field rapidly grew taller and thicker. The grass bunched so tight it created a padding of sorts. As the night elf dropped on it, it gave slightly, then reshaped. Every bone in his body shook, but Malfurion survived intact.

He felt his shoulder, only to find the gift from Aviana missing. Still, Malfurion gave thanks that he had acted swiftly and avoided disaster.

Krasus fluttered several yards farther, moving like a hawk fatally shot by an archer. Malfurion could not react quickly enough to aid the dragon mage, who finally crashed into the tall grass beyond.

The instant that he hit, Krasus's wings dissipated like dust in the wind. The limp figure fell forward, vanishing from the druid's sight.

"Master Krasus! Krasus!" Pushing himself to his feet, the

night elf struggled through the field toward where he had last seen his companion.

But of his companion, there was no sign. Malfurion gazed at the grass, certain that he had the correct location.

Then, some distance to the south, he heard a brief moan. Shoving aside the grass, Malfurion hunted for the source.

Moments later, the still form of Krasus greeted his fearful eyes.

He knelt by the mage, cautiously looking for any outward injury. Finding none, Malfurion slowly turned him over. As he did, he noticed something slip from his companion's body.

Krasus's feather. It looked withered, brown. Touching it with one finger, the druid gasped as the feather crumbled, vanishing in the dirt and grass.

Another moan escaped Krasus. Adjusting him so that he lay perfectly on his back, Malfurion checked for broken bones. However, despite his much harder fall, Krasus appeared untouched. Apparently, the only thing affecting him had been whatever ailment had stricken him in flight.

The pale figure's eyes flickered open. "I . . . I am tired . . . of waking in s-such a condition . . ."

"Careful, Krasus. You shouldn't move yet."

"I will soon not be moving at all . . . Malfurion, I . . . believe I am dying."

"What do you mean? How? What happened to you?"

"Not me . . . another. I am tied to Korialstrasz . . . and he to me. I think—I think he has been attacked. He is . . . nearly dead, and . . . if he goes, there is no hope for me."

Malfurion looked Krasus over again, trying to find something he could do to help. "Is there no hope?"

"Perhaps if you could—could heal him . . . but he is far

from here, and . . . as he is a dragon . . . it would be most d-difficult. I—"

He grew silent. Malfurion thought quickly, but nothing else came to mind. All the skills that Cenarius had taught him could be applied, but not when the true victim lay countless miles away.

Then he saw—half-revealed by the wizard's crumpled robe—the scale. "Krasus. This piece—"

"Wh-what I thought would . . . save us earlier. A bit of him . . . for a b-bit of me. It did—did work for a time."

"This is *his* scale," Malfurion said to himself. "*His* scale."

It was an audacious, impossible plan—and the only one he had. He ran his finger across the scale, marveling at its texture and sensing the power of it. The druid's intention borrowed from differing aspects of his learning, things that Cenarius had never linked together. Still . . . certain basics surely applied . . .

"I may have an idea, Krasus."

But the mage did not answer; his eyes once again had closed. At first the night elf feared that he had already passed away. Only when he leaned close and listened to Krasus's quiet but still steady breathing did Malfurion's tensions ease slightly.

He could not hesitate any longer. Krasus had only minutes remaining.

Placing both hands on the scale, the druid opened his mind back up to his surroundings. Already the grass knew him and it reacted to his call. The wind tousled his hair and the earth stirred to waking, curious about his plea.

But before he could ask of them anything, he also needed to see if he could truly link with the dragon, Korialstrasz. Eyes shut, the druid let himself flow into the scale, seek of it the bond to its original wearer.

At first there was some confusion, Krasus and Korialstrasz so bound together that he almost mistook the former for the latter. Finally realizing his mistake, Malfurion steered his thoughts toward the red dragon, hoping that a tenuous link remained between the scale and Korialstrasz.

To his surprise, that part proved quite easy. Immediately his senses threw him across miles, across lands, to a harsher, mountainous region. Both the landscape and the journey reminded him of his attempt to reach the dragons hidden behind the barrier, only this time he did not travel quite so far, nor had he, thankfully, had to make use of the Emerald Dream.

Then, a horrible sense of loss hit Malfurion. He nearly blacked out. Fearful, however, of accidentally joining Krasus's and Korialstrasz's death experience, the night elf steeled himself. His senses stabilized, and he discovered that he now felt the dragon's dying emotions.

There had been a battle, a terrible battle. Malfurion thought at first that the Burning Legion had attacked, but then he sensed from the red's splintered thoughts that the foe had been other dragons—black ones.

Recalling the sinister pair who had pursued Krasus and him, Malfurion suspected that he knew which beasts had attacked. He gathered that they were dead, which made him marvel that Korialstrasz had even survived to this point. Truly a powerful, magnificent creature this dragon had been . . .

No! He was thinking of Korialstrasz as already dead. That condemned not only the dragon, but Krasus as well. Malfurion had to stop such speculation if he hoped to save them.

One of the first true lessons that Cenarius had taught him had been the health and healing of woodland creatures. In the past, Malfurion had saved the lives of foxes, rabbits, birds, and more. He could apply that work now, just amplifying the effect.

Or so the druid hoped.

Malfurion called to his surroundings. He needed their sacrifice; only life could give life. The earth, the flora, they had the capability of regenerating in a manner no animal could. The night elf still asked much from them, however, for now he sought to save a *dragon*. If his plea was rejected, he could lay no blame.

Trying to relay the importance of saving Korialstrasz— and by doing so, Krasus—Malfurion reached out to the grass, the trees, anything that would give to him. In the back of his mind, he noted the dragon's life force ebbing. There was barely any time left.

Then, to his relief, Malfurion felt the land give of itself for his efforts. The life force flowed into him, exhilarating the night elf so much that he almost forgot for what purpose he had requested it. Recalling himself, he positioned his fingertips on the scale, then fed the energy through.

Krasus's body shook once, then calmed. Through the link, Malfurion sensed the life force pouring into the dragon. The night elf's heart raced, sweat dripping down his face, as he struggled to maintain the bond.

So much flowed through, and yet, Malfurion felt no change in Korialstrasz. The dragon continued to hang on the edge of death. Gritting his teeth, the druid drew more and more, sending it to the stricken giant as quickly as he could.

At last, he noted a slight change. Korialstrasz's soul pulled back from the abyss. The tenuous link to life solidified.

"Please . . ." the harried night elf gasped. "More . . ."

And more came. The land around him gave as he needed,

understanding that the dire situation affected not just the two ill figures, but also so many others.

Slowly, ever so slowly, the tide turned in life's favor. Korialstrasz grew stronger. The druid felt the leviathan's consciousness return and knew that the dragon wondered at this miracle.

Krasus's body again shook. The elder mage moaned. His eyes slowly opened.

At that point, Malfurion finally knew that he had done enough. Pulling his fingertips from the scale, the night elf leaned back and exhaled.

Only then did he see that the grass for yards around him was black.

All life had been drained from the tendrils. Peering around, Malfurion saw that the field for as far as he could see was dry and black. A pair of trees stood leafless in the distance.

Fear at what he had done made the druid shiver until he felt the stirring of life beneath the earth. The roots of the grass still lived and, with the earth's help, they would soon grow new, mighty stalks. The trees had also survived and, if given the opportunity, would create for themselves healthy new leaves.

The night elf sighed in relief. For a few desperate seconds, he had imagined himself no better than the Burning Legion.

"What . . . what have you done?" managed Krasus.

"I had to save you. I did the only thing I could think of."

The mage shook his head as he pushed himself up to a sitting position. "That is not what I meant. Malfurion . . . do you have even the slightest concept of what you have accomplished? Do you understand all that your effort entailed?"

"It was needed," Malfurion explained. "I regret that I had to ask so much of the land, but it was willing to give it."

For the first time, Krasus noted the blackened grass. His eyes narrowed as he surveyed the evidence of the night elf's tremendous work. "Malfurion, this is not possible."

"It was based off of my *shan'do's* teachings. I merely modified it to suit the situation."

"And managed a result that should have been *beyond* you—beyond almost any spellcaster." With some doing, the dragon mage rose. He frowned as he discovered the true extent of the blackened grass. "Astounding."

Still not understanding just what so disturbed Krasus about his spell, Malfurion asked, "Can you sense Korialstrasz? Is he well?"

Krasus concentrated. "The link is fading to what it was before your spell, but I can still sense him for the moment. He is . . . fit . . . but his mind is confused. He recalls the battle some and that he was supposed to find me, but there are gaps." This, for some reason, caused Krasus to let loose with a very uncustomary chuckle. "Now we are more alike than ever, he and I. Truly, the fates mock me."

"Do we wait for him?"

"We do, but not for the reason for which I suspect he wanted to find me. Knowing him as I do, he likely planned to bring me back to Alexstrasza, but there is no more time. I have this terrible feeling that we need to return to the host now. You may call it a hunch or perhaps much too much experience. Whichever, when Korialstrasz reaches us, we head back there."

Malfurion immediately thought of Tyrande . . . and then, belatedly, his brother. "How long will it take him to do that?"

"He is a dragon . . . and now a very healthy one," Krasus remarked with a brief but satisfied smile. "Not too long at all if I know him . . ."

• • •

Tyrande had become very unique among the Sisters of Elune. She was the only one of them who had two shadows, the second even named.

It was called Shandris Feathermoon.

Wherever the priestess went, the orphan followed. Shandris watched everything that her savior did with the eyes of one who wanted desperately to learn. When Tyrande prayed over an injured or wounded night elf, the young female repeated those words, trying at the same time to match the former's gestures.

Tyrande felt conflicted about Shandris. With no parents, Shandris had no one to turn to. True, there were others in similar straits, but something about this one orphan still struck her. Her dedication to Tyrande's work marked her as a possible novice, and the temple always welcomed new sisters. How would it look, then, to fling her back among the refugees and forget her? The priestess had to keep her nearby; she could not live with herself otherwise.

Unfortunately, not every situation was one where an untried, unblooded female was safe. The sisterhood continued to take their turn fighting on the front line, each group switching off as the high priestess commanded. Tyrande did not want Shandris wandering up near the demons, who would have no compunction about cutting up an innocent. Shandris, however, had already once almost frightened her to death by sneaking along behind the sisters when they had ridden out to warn Malfurion and Krasus. Only belatedly had the priestess discovered that, when the orphan let slip a comment about the event that could have only been spoken by one who had witnessed it.

"No more!" Tyrande commanded her. "Please stay behind when we go to battle! I can't worry about you and fight!"

Looking crestfallen, Shandris nodded, but Tyrande doubted that this was the end of the discussion. She could only pray to Elune that the young one would see sense.

But as she contemplated her predicament, Tyrande noticed one of the sisters in charge of a neighboring group approach her. The other priestess, taller and senior by several years, wore an expression of deep thought as she joined Tyrande.

"Hail, Sister Marinda! What brings you to this humble one?"

"Hail, Sister Tyrande," Marinda returned dourly. "I come from the high priestess."

"Oh? Has she news for us?"

"She . . . she is dead, sister."

Tyrande felt as if her entire world had just been shattered at its foundations. The venerable mother of the temple—dead? She had grown up watching and listening to the woman, as had nearly all other worshippers. It was because of her that Tyrande had taken up the robes of the novice.

"H-how?"

Tears streaked down Marinda's cheeks. "It was kept secret from us. She insisted that only her attendants would know. During the push back toward Suramar, a demon lanced her in the stomach. She might have survived that, her skills for healing strong, but a felbeast caught her first. She was apparently almost dead when some of the others slew it. They brought her back to her tent, where she's been since . . . until she died but an hour ago."

"Horrible!" Tyrande fell to her knees and started praying to the Mother Moon. Marinda joined her and, without coaxing, Shandris imitated them.

When the two priestesses had finished their farewell to their superior, Marinda rose. "There is more, sister."

"More! What could there be?"

"Before her death, she named a successor."

Tyrande nodded. This was to be expected. The new high priestess had, of course, immediately sent out messengers like Marinda to spread the word of her ascension.

"Who is it?" There were several worthy candidates.

"She named you, Tyrande."

Tyrande could not believe her own ears. "She—Mother Moon! You jest!"

Shandris squealed and clapped. Tyrande turned and gave her a severe look. The orphan quieted, but her eyes gleamed with pride.

Marinda did not appear to be at all jesting, and that put fear into Tyrande. How could she, barely into the role of priestess, take over the *entire sisterhood*—and in time of war yet?

"Forgive me for saying so, Sister Marinda, but she . . . she must have been stressed of mind because of her injuries! How could she with all sincerity choose me?"

"She was of clear mind, sister. And you should understand, she had made mention of you before this. The senior sisters all understood that you were the one . . . and no one among them argued the decision."

"It's . . . it's impossible! How could *I* lead? How could I, with so little experience, take on the mantle? There are so many more who know the temple better!"

"But none so attuned to Elune herself. We've all seen it, all felt it. There are already tales of you spreading among the refugees and soldiers. Miracles. People healed by you when others have failed them utterly—"

This was something that Tyrande had not heard. "What do you mean?"

And Sister Marinda explained. All the priestesses spent

part of their rest period doing anything but resting, with so many in need, none of the sisters felt right *not* helping. But desiring to help and actually doing so were two different things. Yes, they succeeded in healing many, but countless others their skills could not touch.

Tyrande, on the other hand, had left behind her an unbroken string of successes. Anyone and everyone she attempted to heal had recovered. Without realizing it, Tyrande had even aided several whom other sisters had failed to heal. If that had not surprised the rest of the priestesses enough, she had then gone on without rest to aid others.

"You shouldn't even be able to stand, yet you fight, too, Sister Tyrande."

It had never occurred to the young priestess that she had done anything other than fulfill her duty. She would pray to Elune and Elune would answer. Tyrande would feel grateful, then move on in the hopes of healing someone else.

But according to the others, she had done much, much more.

"I—this can't be right."

"It is. You must accept it." Marinda took a deep breath. "You know that, normally, there would be a ceremony, a long entailed one that as many worshippers as possible would be invited to see."

Lost in thought, Tyrande vaguely replied, "Yes . . ."

"We'll do our best to prepare something, obviously. With your permission, I'll pull the other sisters from the battle and have them—"

"What?" In addition to all else, they planned to do *that*— and because of *her*? Drawing herself together, Tyrande declared, "No! I'll not have that!"

"Sister—"

Using her newfound, if undesired authority, she gave

Marinda a look that would brook no argument, then added, "It seems that I've no choice in accepting this, but I can't do it if it means setting up a ceremony that distracts us from the danger! I'll become high priestess—at least until this war is over—but I will keep my present garments—"

"But the robes of state—"

"I will *keep* my present garments and there will be *no* ceremony! We can't afford to take such a risk with our people. Let them see us continuing to heal and fight in the name of the Mother Moon. Is that understood?"

"I—" Marinda went down on her knees, bending her head forward. "I obey, mistress."

"Rise up! I want none of that, either! We are all sisters, *equal* in heart! All of us give homage to Elune! I want no one doing so for me."

"As you wish." But the elder sister did not rise and, in fact, seemed to expect something of Tyrande. After a moment's confusion, she finally understood just what.

Forcing her hand not to shake, Tyrande reached out and touched the top of Marinda's head. "In the name of the Mother Moon, great Elune who watches over all, I give the blessing."

She heard the other priestess sigh in relief. Marinda rose, her expression now akin to those that had been worn by the other sisters—Tyrande included—when in the presence of their venerable mistress. "I'll convey your will to the others. If I may be permitted?"

"Yes . . . thank you."

As Marinda departed, Tyrande nearly collapsed. This could not be possible! In some ways, it was almost as terrible a nightmare as facing the Burning Legion. *She* the head of the order! Truly, Kalimdor faced destruction.

"How wonderful!" Shandris exclaimed, clapping again.

She ran up to Tyrande, nearly hugged her, then tried instead to look very serious. As Marinda had done, the orphan knelt before the new high priestess and awaited a blessing.

Defeated, Tyrande gave her one. Shandris's expression changed to awe. "I'll follow you for the rest of my life, my lady!"

"Don't call me that. I'm still Tyrande."

"Yes, my lady."

Unleashing an exasperated sigh, the new head of the temple considered what she had to do next. There were probably endless details and rituals that the high priestess had to perform. Tyrande recalled her predecessor leading this chant and that. The temple also held a blessing each evening for the rising of the moon and the good will of the gods. In addition, the leading nobles always had to have some sort of recognition ceremony for various anniversaries and other events . . .

She stared bleakly at her future, feeling trapped, not honored.

Her contemplations were jarred by a sudden moan from somewhere among the refugees. Tyrande recognized that sound, having heard it so often before. Someone was in terrible agony.

The ceremonies could wait. The rituals could wait. Tyrande had joined the order for one thing most of all—to help others through the gifts of Elune.

Following the sound of the moan, the new high priestess continued her work.

EIGHTEEN

The queen had decided to go riding, and when Azshara set her mind on something, not all the demons in the world could convince her otherwise . . . which meant that Captain Varo'then had no chance whatsoever.

It had been quite some time since she had left the confines of the palace. Surrounded on foot by her hulking bodyguards and an additional unit of the captain's crack troop, Azshara and her retinue of handmaidens rode serenely through the gates and out into Zin-Azshari.

The *ruins* of Zin-Azshari.

It was the first time since its destruction that the ruler of the night elves had seen it up close. Her lidded eyes studied the crushed domiciles, the littered streets, and the occasional corpse still left untouched due to a lack of enough carrion eaters. Azshara's lips pursed, and on occasion she sniffed at something not to her liking.

Varo'then glowered at the outside world. He wanted nothing to disturb his queen. Had he been able to take a sword to the destruction as he would a foe, the officer would have done it.

A felbeast rose from behind a crumpled tower, its savage jaws filled with something. It chewed loudly as the queen's column passed, then darted back into hiding.

They rode for some distance, Azshara not speaking once and so no one else daring to do so. Her Fel Guard kept close despite a lack of threat, the demons now as adamant in their loyalty to her as any of the soldiers. Had she demanded of them to attack their own kind, they likely would have obeyed without hesitation. Of course, Azshara would have never done that, for there was only one other than herself whom she did not wish to displease and that was the lord of the Burning Legion, Sargeras.

"Will it be soon, do you think, my dear captain?" she asked.

The officer was confused. "Light of Lights?"

"His coming, captain. *His* coming."

Varo'then nodded immediately. "Oh, yes, my queen, very soon! Mannoroth claims that each night sees the portal stronger than the previous."

"He must truly be a god among gods for it needing to be so powerful simply to allow him entrance."

"As you say, my queen."

"He must be . . . *glorious*," Azshara uttered in a tone she generally reserved only for herself.

The scarred night elf nodded again, trying to hide his envy. No one could compete with a god.

The same green mist that now covered so much of Kalimdor continued to drape over the city. To Azshara, it added a wonderfully mysterious look to her capital, while at the same time keeping from her eyes many things which might have offended her sensibilities. When the world was rebuilt, she would ask Sargeras to remove the haze; until then, it suited her well.

As they came to what had once been an open square, Azshara looked around. She reined her night saber to a halt, patting its head afterward to keep it calm. Like all else in the palace, even the animals had been touched by the presence of Sargeras. The huge cats of the party had eyes that were crimson and fierce. They would have attacked any of their own kind who was not a part of the royal stables, lustily tearing and biting their foes to bloody shreds.

"The captain and I will continue on alone for a few minutes."

Neither the night elves nor the demons looked pleased with this . . . save Varo'then, of course. He looked back at his men and growled, "By the order of the queen!"

Unable to argue with such a fact, the retinue held its place while the pair slowly rode on.

Azshara did not speak until they were far out of earshot from the rest. Smiling at Varo'then, she said, "Does it all go well?"

"All what?"

The queen glanced to the horizon. "The cleansing of my realm. I thought it would be done by now."

"Archimonde will see to it that it comes to pass, my queen."

"But I would like it done *before* Sargeras comes! Wouldn't that make for a tremendous gift . . . for my intended?"

It was all Varo'then could do to hold back. Swallowing his jealousy, he managed to say, "A tremendous gift, yes. It'll all come to pass."

"Then what delays it?"

"There are many things. Logistics, chance—"

She leaned toward him, granting the veteran fighter with a striking view of her form. "My dear, dear Varo'then! Do *I*, in any manner of the imagination, look like a hardy, muscular soldier such as yourself?"

His cheeks darkened. "Nay! Nay, Vision of Perfection!"

"Then please . . . do not use such military terms. I would prefer you simply show me." Azshara raised her hand palm up; in it appeared a small crystal sphere the size of a pea. However, as Varo'then watched, it grew to the dimensions of a large piece of fruit. Even despite the dimness, it glowed as he recalled the full moon once had.

"Will you do me the pleasure, dear captain?"

Taking the globe, the scarred soldier concentrated. While hardly at the level of a Highborne sorcerer, he had his skills with the arts. The view globe immediately reacted to him, turning his thoughts into visions.

"You ask me what delays matters, my queen? I would say that these are some of the reasons."

From his memory, he first dredged up the image of a red-haired creature like nothing Azshara had ever seen. She peered closely, eyes glittering.

"Handsome in his . . . foreign ways. *Definitely* male."

"A wizard. Powerful." The face twisted like putty, altering in shading and shape. An older, wise figure appeared.

"Gracious! Is this a corpse you show me?"

"Nay. Despite his coloring—or lack of it—this creature lives. He was little danger to us when we encountered him, but I suspected then that he suffered some malady . . . and since that time, my spies have reported that he was seen in the company of a dragon—"

Now this impressed the queen. "A *dragon*?"

"Aye, and between him and the beast, they caused no end of trouble for Archimonde's warriors. Both've vanished, though I suspect this one'll be back."

"Perhaps not so ghastly after all," Azshara commented, eyeing the pale figure so akin to a night elf. "And it's only these who keep my world from perfection?"

Captain Varo'then scowled. "There are some of our own, of course, my lady. Misbegotten or misguided. I've learned of two Your Glory might find of interest. You will forgive me if the images are indistinct, but they are from the minds of others passed on to me."

Azshara gazed at the new figures. One had his hair tied back and wore black, the other let it hang loose and seemed to be in drab-colored garments. Both faces were so akin to each other that she at first thought them one and the same.

"Twins, my queen," he clarified. "Brothers."

"Twins . . . how delectable." She ran her fingers over the shifting images. "But so young . . . surely not leaders."

"Powerful of magic, it seems, but, nay, neither they nor the others lead the resistance. That falls, of course, to the esteemed Lord Ravencrest."

"Dear Kur'talos . . . I always thought him my most cherished servant, and this is how he rewards me."

Captain Varo'then dismissed the queen's globe. Eyes overshadowed by his dark brow, he said to her, "Black Rook Hold has ever envied the palace, Light of Lights."

She pouted briefly. "I've decided that Lord Ravencrest has displeased me, Varo'then," Azshara finally declared. "Can you remedy that?"

He showed no sign of surprise. "The cost will be great . . . but it can be done, if that is your wish."

"My fondest one, darling captain."

Azshara stroked his cheek ever so slightly, then abruptly turned her mount around and headed back to the waiting guards. Her long, translucent gown fluttered behind her.

Pulling himself together, the officer contemplated the desires of his mistress. Kur'talos Ravencrest had displeased her, and there was no greater crime in all Kalimdor.

"It will be done, my queen," he muttered. "It *will* be done."

• • •

They left Suramar far behind and pressed the demons in the direction of Zin-Azshari. Rhonin's master spell had begun the push, but now Illidan's Moon Guard and the soldiers on the line took over in earnest, crushing the demons wherever they attempted to make a stand.

Rhonin did not let up despite his success. Although he gave himself moments to recuperate, he, too, took advantage of the situation to wreak new havoc on the Burning Legion. Every demon who fell the human imagined as the one who might harm his family if he failed. Rhonin no longer cared what effect his presence in the war had; if the Burning Legion was utterly destroyed here, then neither they nor the Undead Scourge would ever scar the world in the future.

Brox, too, had long gone past any hesitation. He was an orc warrior and orc warriors fought. Brox let others worry about repercussions. He only knew that he and his ax thirsted for the blood of demons.

The night elven host drove a wedge deeper into the center of the demon lines. On the flanks, the Moon Guard chopped away at the enemy. The Eredar and Dreadlords still struck back on occasion, but with nothing that Illidan's forces could not handle.

"We're pushing them up into the hills of Urae!" Jarod called to Rhonin. "Beyond that lies only Zin-Azshari herself!"

"A good thing that we've whittled them down so much!" the wizard returned grimly. "If they had enough reinforcements or organization, this would be a foul place to have to fight them! They'd have the upper ground!"

"Once we reach the other side, though, the hills will be ours to take advantage of!"

"Then the sooner we reach them, the better . . ."

The demons continued to back into the hills in chaotic masses with little direction. Of Archimonde, Rhonin saw no sign. If the demon lord had been in control, then surely the Burning Legion would have fought better than this. Unless . . .

Could it be? he wondered, startled by the mere possibility.

"Jarod! Brox! I need to find Ravencrest!"

"Go!" growled the orc as his ax cut through the armor of a Fel Guard, then the demon himself.

Feeling guilty about leaving his comrades at such a time, Rhonin nonetheless felt certain that he had to find the commander and quickly. A horrible notion had occurred to him, but only the noble could verify or repudiate it.

But locating Lord Ravencrest was no simple task. His night saber pushing slowly through the advancing soldiers, the wizard surveyed the area left and right with no success. His quarry could be in a thousand places, possibly even under Rhonin's very nose.

Anxiety growing, he finally managed to locate someone who might know Ravencrest's whereabouts. Lord Desdel Stareye's armor looked absolutely spotless and his own cat was still well-groomed. Rhonin wondered if he had even gotten close to the battle, much less participated in it. Still, Stareye had the ear of Lord Ravencrest, and that was all that mattered for the moment.

"My lord! My lord!" shouted the red-haired wizard.

The night elf gazed at him as if seeing something unsettling. Stareye reached into his pouch and took a bit of powder, which he sniffed. His sword remained sheathed.

"This is a most inopportune time, spellcaster!" he chided. "What is it you want?"

"Lord Ravencrest! Where is he? I need to speak with him!"

"Kur'talos is quite busy enough right now. Shouldn't you be back up front casting something?"

Rhonin had met this night elf's type often in his own time. Leaders like Desdel Stareye were not only ineffective, but they were dangerous if put in command. Born to leisure, they had no true concept of war, treating it like a game.

"This is highly important, my lord—"

"Concerning what?"

The wizard had no time for this, but saw that he would get nowhere unless he convinced Stareye of the seriousness of the situation. "I have to find out if Ravencrest's had any outriders return of late! I want to know if anyone's been beyond the hills!"

The night elf snorted. "You'll be able to see beyond the hills yourself in a few short hours."

Rhonin regretted that he had not forged some sort of magical link to the commander, but Ravencrest had forbidden such communication with him. It was the night elf's belief that, despite their powers, the spellcasters were more susceptible to invasion of their thoughts. He did not wish to risk his own plans, in turn, being read.

The notion was a laughable one to the human, but he had long given up arguing for such a link. Now that surrender had come back to haunt him.

"Lord Stareye . . . *where* is he?"

A brief look of contemplation crossed the noble's haughty countenance. Finally, he answered, "Follow me, then, wizard. I'll lead you to where I last saw him."

Exhaling in relief, Rhonin rode up behind Stareye. To his surprise, however, the night elf began steering away from the battle. Rhonin almost objected, then saw that by doing so they would make better time crossing from one end of the host to the other. Here there were less soldiers causing a living barrier.

But even with this maneuver, precious time slipped away as they wended their way to where Stareye said that he had most recently recalled Ravencrest. Meanwhile, the night elves pushed further up to the hills, the demons now forced through ever-narrowing passes.

Maybe Stareye was right, the wizard thought dourly. *By the time we do find Ravencrest, the elves'll be over the hills and almost on the path to Zin-Azshari . . .*

"There!" his companion finally shouted. "You see his banner?"

Rhonin did not. "Where?"

"*There,* you fool! It—" Stareye shook his head. "Gone from sight now! Come! I'll lead you to it, then!"

But if Stareye thought to soon rid himself of the wizard, he was sorely mistaken. Rhonin watched carefully as he and the night elf now forced their way through the tightly-packed throng, but not once did he make out Lord Ravencrest's banner. With the host moving so swiftly, the bearded commander had to constantly shift position, and that made Rhonin's task all the more daunting.

"Blast!" uttered the night elf after a time, wiping a bit of mud from his immaculate armor. "He was there! I saw him!"

They cut across the advancing lines, yet still there was no sign of Ravencrest. Rhonin peered at the hills, so close now. They loomed like savage teeth. He could make out demons moving among them, their retreat much slowed by the climb. In some places, the Burning Legion had even ground to a halt.

Or *had* they?

Stareye raised a gloved hand to point ahead, but just at that moment a speck of dirt got into the wizard's eye.

Rhonin turned his head from the direction it had come and sought to blink it out.

The banner of Black Rook Hold greeted his startled eyes.

"There he is!" the human yelled.

"No, I think this—" Stareye cut off as he followed Rhonin's gaze. "Yes, of course! There!"

Not bothering to wait for the noble to follow, Rhonin urged his mount toward Ravencrest's position. Riding against the human tide proved harder than any part of the long trek so far, but Rhonin would not be denied. There was still a chance. All he had to do was reach—

An uproar rose from the front. Horns sounded. Drums beat. Faces around the wizard looked aghast.

"What is it?" he shouted at a soldier. When the soldier did not answer, Rhonin looked back.

"No . . ." he uttered in horror.

The hills now swarmed with demons heading *toward* the night elves. That alone would not have stopped Rhonin dead, but there were also demons pouring around the edge of the hills—a veritable flood of fiery, monstrous figures. Worse, in the hazy sky above, he saw a shower of huge rocks dropping toward the defenders. They were not rocks, of course, but another deadly rain of Infernals.

The portal could not have supplied Archimonde's force this well. As Rhonin watched the monstrous warriors swell to numbers greater than during any previous part of the struggle, he realized why the demon commander had let such a rout take place. He could only have been drawing fighters from other areas of Kalimdor, rightly seeing the night elves as the main opposition to the Burning Legion's triumph.

And now Archimonde had his adversaries exactly where he wanted them.

• • •

The voices in Neltharion's head whispered eagerly. The black dragon listened to each of them with the same rapt attention even though they all said the same thing.

It is time . . .

It is time . . .

It is time . . .

He clutched the Dragon Soul tight and held it high in his forepaw. Gaze sweeping across those of the other Aspects, he thundered, "It is *time*."

Bowing their heads in acknowledgment, they departed one by one from the cavern. Only when he was alone—save for the voices, of course—did Neltharion say anything more.

"*My* time . . ."

Mere minutes later, from every chasm, every cave mouth, they began to emerge. Some crawled out from beneath the ground while others leapt off the high mountain peak. Wherever there was an exit to the outside world, the dragons issued forth.

It was time to act.

Never before in the history of the world had there been so many assembled in one place. Now, as they took to the air, their combined magnificence awed even most of them. Red flew beside bronze who flew beside green. Blue and black darted up in the air, the five great flights now one.

There were dragons whose wings seemed to spread across the heavens, others who in comparison were but like gnats. Whether ages old or new to the air, all had been included. The word of the Aspects had demanded it be so.

The first dragons to leap into the heavens did not immediately head toward the realm of the night elves, however. Instead, they circled high above the mountains, gliding on thermals and waiting for their brethren. They filled the sky, many flying under or over one another to avoid collision.

And the legendary behemoths continued to emerge from the mountains. To any who saw them, it looked as if the end of the world had come . . . and perhaps it had. The dragons understood the evil of the demons and that no one could stand idle in the face of such a threat. Dragon after dragon roared lustily as they stirred their blood in preparation for battle.

Then the Aspects themselves appeared. Alexstrasza the Red, the Mother of Life. Malygos the Blue, the Spellweaver. Green Ysera, She of the Dreaming. In the absence of Nozdormu, the Timeless One, the eldest of his consorts took upon herself his part.

Only when they were assembled did Neltharion the Black, the Earth Warder, present himself.

The tiny disk gleamed so very bright, dazzling the dragons despite its otherwise plain exterior. Neltharion roared as he launched into the air, his cry echoing over and over throughout the chain.

As Neltharion soared off, the other dragons followed. The time of reckoning was at hand. They had given of themselves to create the mightiest of weapons for use against the mightiest of foes, and if that proved not enough, they had claws, teeth, and more with which to still assail the demons.

And if all *that* would not prove enough . . . then surely nothing would.

Tyrande heard the cries, heard the horns. She knew immediately in her heart what they meant. Again the struggle had taken one of its mercurial shifts. The demons had struck back, and clearly hard.

With a blurted apology to the unfortunate whom she had

been healing, the new head of the order leapt atop her night saber. Shandris, already astride, made quick room for her, and the two rode off to find the other sisters.

Most were already waiting for her. They included not only those who had originally been assigned to Tyrande, but many of the elder priestesses as well. All knelt or bowed their heads as she neared.

"Please! Stop that!" Tyrande begged, clearly uncomfortable. "It's not necessary!"

"We await your orders," Marinda respectfully said.

Tyrande had been dreading this moment. It was one thing to organize aid for the refugees and wounded soldiers, another to fling the entire sisterhood into the heat of battle.

"We must—" She stopped, silently prayed to the Mother Moon for guidance, and continued. "We must divide up evenly and support those areas weakest along the front lines . . . but not all of us! I want . . . I want a third of us to keep to the back and do what can be done for any of the injured or wounded."

Some of the sisters looked disturbed, clearly desiring to be up front alongside the fighters. Tyrande understood that, but also recognized that just because the battle was desperate, this was not the time to put aside the other skills the temple taught.

"We need healers among the soldiers. Any soldier able to come back to fight aids our cause. Consider this also: There must always be a Sisterhood of Elune. Should we all stand and fight—and perhaps die—who will be left to spread her word and her love among our people?" Tyrande tried not to think about the possibility that there would be no people to teach about Elune if the demons won here.

"We hear and obey," one of the senior priestesses said. The rest nodded.

"Marinda, I leave those caring for the wounded in your hands."

"Aye, mistress."

Tyrande considered further. "And if I should perish, I wish you to take over."

The other night elf looked aghast. "Tyrande—"

"The chain must be unbroken. I understand that. I hope you do, too."

"I—" Marinda frowned. "Yes, I do." Her eyes briefly measured some of the other sisters. As Tyrande had done, she already considered who would be best to lead if she fell.

The new high priestess exhaled. Perhaps her decisions had been rash ones, but she could not be concerned about that now. They were needed. Elune was needed.

"That's all I have to say . . . except, may the serene light of the Mother Moon illuminate your paths."

The ancient farewell said, Tyrande watched as many of the sisters left. Those who would follow her began mounting.

One of them glanced toward Tyrande. "Mistress . . . what about her?"

"Her?" She blinked. Having grown so accustomed to Shandris riding with her, Tyrande had forgotten that the younger female could not possibly come with her now.

Likely knowing what was to come, Shandris tightened her grip. "I'm going with you!"

"That is not possible."

"I'm good with a bow! My father taught me well! I'm probably as good as any of these!"

In spite of the looming situation, her defiance caused many of the sisters to smile.

"That good?" one gently mocked.

Tyrande took Shandris's hand. "No. You stay here."

"But—"

"Dismount, Shandris."

Her eyes tearing, the orphan climbed down. She stared up at Tyrande with huge, silver orbs that made the high priestess feel guilty.

"I'll be back soon, Shandris. You know where to wait."

"Y-yes . . . mistress."

"Come," Tyrande ordered the others. If Elune had thrust her into this role, she had to accept it and do her best to live up to her calling. That included keeping as many of her sisters alive as the Mother Moon allowed.

Even if she had to sacrifice *herself* to do it.

Shandris watched them vanish. The orphan's face was tear-stained, and her hands were balled into fists. Her heart pounded in time to the beating of the war drums and the cries of the dying.

When she could stand it no longer, Shandris ran after the priestesses.

NINETEEN

Although he had told Malfurion that Korialstrasz would arrive before long, Krasus insisted that he and the elf begin heading in the general direction of the battle. He did not do it because he felt that it would cut down the trek. Hardly that. The distance they covered could be flown by an aged, ill dragon in barely a few minutes. Healed by the druid's miraculous spell, Korialstrasz would take only one.

No, they walked because the dragon mage needed to walk in order to keep his impatience in check. He wanted so much to do something to hasten their journey, but he dared not create another portal to reach their destination, not after the last disaster. That left it to waiting for his younger self, but even with a fleet dragon coming to pluck them up, Krasus felt as if he had no more time remaining. Events were coming to a head, and he was out of options.

If Korialstrasz could get them to the struggle swiftly, then things could still be salvaged. If not—

"Master Krasus! I think I spy something behind us!"

Praying that it was not another of Neltharion's hunters, he peered back. A single huge shape moved determinedly toward them. There could be no mistaking that it had seen them.

Krasus suddenly felt a tingling in his head. He allowed himself a smile. "It is Korialstrasz . . ."

"Praise be!"

The red leviathan's wings beat hard, each stroke seeming to eat away another mile. Korialstrasz grew rapidly, his expression finally visible. Krasus thought his younger self looked extremely relieved.

"There you are!" thundered the behemoth, landing a short distance behind them. "Each second of flight felt like an hour even though I flew my fastest!"

"You are a welcome sight," the mage told him.

Korialstrasz lowered his head and eyed Krasus most curiously, as if puzzled by something concerning him. "Is it truly so?"

The way he asked made Krasus start. Korialstrasz knew exactly who and what the spellcaster actually was.

"Yes," he replied to his other self, "it is."

"And you," the dragon said, turning to Malfurion. "I am forever in your debt, night elf."

"There's no need for that."

The behemoth snorted. "So *you* say. You were not the one dying."

Krasus's eyes narrowed. "You were attacked, were you not?"

"Aye, two of the Earth Warder's own! They were filled with a horrid madness! I slew one, but the other caught me. He, too, is dead now, though."

"It is as I feared." The mage could say no more, the spell preventing him. Frustrated, he turned to a subject he could discuss. "We must return to Rhonin and the others. Are you prepared to take us there?"

"Climb aboard and we will be on our way."

The two did as the dragon bade. Once they had settled at his shoulders, Korialstrasz stretched his wings, then gently took off. He circled the field twice before heading toward the direction of the battle.

As they flew, Krasus constantly glanced behind them. He was certain that they were fast approaching the point when the dragons would be coming, but so far he noted nothing. That gave him hope that he could devise a plan to deal with Neltharion's betrayal before it took place. If the evil of his creation could be stopped or, better yet, wielded by one not tainted, then the demons could be defeated, and his own kind saved from their slide to near-extinction.

"We must be getting near," Malfurion called. "The sky is growing hazy!"

Sure enough, the foul mist that pervaded wherever the demons had marched soon met them. Korialstrasz tried to keep low, but in order to avoid flying blind, he had to practically let his torso scrape the ground. When that effort finally proved unmanageable, he said, "I must fly higher! Perhaps there we will find a limit to this murk!"

Through the mist the trio rose. Krasus squinted, but saw nothing beyond his younger self's nose and sometimes not even that far. With visibility so poor, he knew that Korialstrasz had to rely on smell and other senses to make headway.

"There *must* be an end to it!" the red dragon snapped. "I will find it even if it takes me—"

A winged figure suddenly appeared in their path. The Doomguard darted back into the mist the moment he saw the dragon.

Korialstrasz immediately gave chase, forcing Krasus and Malfurion to hold on tight.

"Leave him!" the mage shouted. "We must get to the battle!"

But the fierce wind created by Korialstrasz's swift flight carried away his words. Krasus beat on the dragon's neck, but the heavy scales prevented the other from noticing.

"What about a spell?" Malfurion cried. "Just something to attract his attention!"

Krasus had wanted to do that, but knew better. "If we startle him at all, he may jolt and drop one or both of us! In this thick mist, it would be impossible for him to catch us before we hit the ground below!"

Forced to let Korialstrasz continue his pursuit, the two could only lean low and hope that the dragon either caught the demon quickly or gave up. However, recalling exactly how determined he had been when younger, Krasus knew that Korialstrasz would not turn back so soon. His own stubbornness now worked against all of them.

Again the demon flickered into sight. The fearsome, horned warrior flew as fast as his fiery wings could carry him. Even he understood that he could not stand against such a giant.

The mage frowned. The Doomguard had their share of cunning, and could see through this mist far better than their foes. The demon should have been able to figure out a way to lose Korialstrasz, who was clearly having trouble locating him. If not for the almost straight line the demon flew—

The truth suddenly dawned on Krasus. "Malfurion! Prepare yourself! We are about to be attacked!"

The druid looked around, seeking a foe in the fog.

A second later, he and Krasus were greeted by many.

The winged warriors came at the trio from all angles. At least half a dozen rose up under Korialstrasz, striking at the dragon's chest and stomach. Others dropped down, seeking to either slay or knock off the two riders. Several more fluttered about in front of and behind the leviathan.

Korialstrasz roared, sending out a flood of fire at those in front of him. Most of the demons scattered, but one he caught dead center, reducing the horned warrior to ash.

The red's massive tail swung like a mace, battering three of the Doomguard away. The others darted in, slashing with their horrific blades and even managing a few cuts in the scales.

Atop him, Krasus and Malfurion were harried. The dragon mage managed to cast a quick spell that created a glowing orange shield above them, but the demons battered relentlessly at it, quickly weakening his work.

The night elf reached into a pouch at his side. He took from it some small particles, then cast them at those demons most immediate. As they touched each of their targets, the particles blossomed into huge tendrils—creeper vines. Malfurion muttered under his breath, and the vines expanded in every direction.

The demons began tearing and slashing at the plants overwhelming them, but the vines grew at a swifter pace than they could cut.

Several encircled and tightened around one demon's throat. There was a crackling sound, and the horned warrior slumped . . . then plummeted from sight.

Other demons found their limbs and, most important, their wings, entangled. Two fell screaming to their deaths.

Krasus cried out as a Doomguard who had gotten under the shield cut him on the shoulder. Eyes blazing, the mage took out much of his frustration with a single word of power. The demon howled as his flesh melted like wax, dripping over and through his fiery armor. That which passed for bones clattered in a heap before spilling groundward.

Yet still there seemed Doomguard everywhere. Krasus could not help but feel that they had been set there to await either the return of the one dragon that had aided the night elves or any other of the great beasts. The irony that the demons might have delayed Neltharion's betrayal long enough for Krasus to do something about it did not escape the mage.

Hindered by the fact that he carried riders, Korialstrasz could not dive about as he normally would have, but the dragon nonetheless made good use of his other skills. One demon came too close. With a snap of his jaws, Korialstrasz crushed the attacker, then spat out the remains.

Shaking his head, he uttered, "Horrible taste! Horrible!"

Krasus continued to look around. The Burning Legion never came in one assault. They always had another attack waiting for the proper moment.

He spotted four Doomguard flying side by side. After a moment, he realized that they all held onto what at first seemed a long, thick rope. As they neared, however, he saw that it was not a rope, but rather some sort of flexible metal line.

He jerked his gaze in the opposite direction. Sure enough, four more demons carried a similar object, and both groups appeared headed for Korialstrasz's wing area.

"Malfurion! Look there!"

The druid did, his expression turning perplexed. "What do they plan to do with that?"

"Tangle or bind his wings, likely! Korialstrasz is too distracted! We must do what we can to stop them!"

Even as he spoke, the elder mage sighted two more groups likewise armed. The demons wanted to ensure they accomplished their dire task.

As those carrying the lines neared, the other Doomguard

fought with more frenzy. Krasus and the night elf tried focusing on the true threat, but the Burning Legion would not permit them.

A huge gust of wind abruptly scattered many of the hellish warriors above. Malfurion exhaled, the spell—with all else—taking something out of him. However, he had bought Krasus time to act.

Borrowing from one of the druid's most potent attacks, the one that had slain Hakkar, Krasus eyed the first group. The demons nearly had the impossibly-long wire over a distracted Korialstrasz's left wing. If they succeeded in looping it around, the dragon would be forced to try to stay aloft with the right—an insurmountable task.

The bolt struck only one of the demons, but the very line they carried sent the shock through to the others. The monstrous attackers shook and screamed, then, as the lightning faded, their limp hands released the metal bond. The four plummeted into the mist.

Although he had stopped one set, Krasus now saw that there were at least five others. The other winged fighters closed again, bedeviling the three.

"I must ask of you the greatest of favors!" thundered the red dragon. "Cling to me as if your lives depended upon it, for they certainly will!"

The two smaller figures immediately obeyed. Krasus shouted, "Hook your feet under the scale, Malfurion! Quickly!"

Just as they both did what he suggested, Korialstrasz spun on his back.

The tactic took the Burning Legion by complete surprise. Korialstrasz's huge, leathery wings struck demon after demon. Two of the groups carrying the metal lines went floundering, their burdens vanishing into the mist below.

As he spun, the red behemoth also unleashed three quick but stunning bursts of flame. The first two utterly ravaged a pair of Doomguard. The last missed, but scattered several more attackers.

"Look out!" Malfurion cried.

A huge missile barreled into the dragon's chest. Krasus's footing slipped, and he suddenly dangled by his hands. The druid could do nothing to help him, barely holding on himself.

The fiery figure bounded away from its victim. The Infernal dropped into the mist unconcerned about the tremendous distance it would fall. Even from up here, the demon would survive a crash below unscathed.

The other attackers used the moment to close. Krasus kicked at the blade of one as he pulled himself back onto the red dragon's back. Malfurion threw some more particles from his pouch, but the now wiser Legion forces all but avoided them. Only one Doomguard fell prey to the vines, but with so many others around, the loss was negligible.

As Krasus seated himself again, one of the groups began winding the long line around Korialstrasz's right wing. Jabbing his fingers at the four, he spoke another word of power.

His fingernails snapped off, flying at the demons. As the nails flew, they stretched to more than a foot long each. In rapid succession, all four demons froze where they were as the sharp missiles bored through them. Krasus rubbed his fingers—where new nails were already growing—and watched as the demons dropped.

"Korialstrasz!" Krasus shouted. "We must break free! We cannot stay here and fight like this!"

This time, his younger self heard him, and, although clearly he did not like to leave the battle unfinished, he deferred to Krasus. "That may be more difficult than you think!"

Krasus understood exactly how difficult it would be. There were Doomguard everywhere and the dragon, mindful of his riders, had to move with care. That was what the Burning Legion now counted on.

But they had to leave. They had already delayed too long.

The leviathan paused to incinerate a careless Doomguard. "I have one notion! It worked before! Hold tight again!"

Neither Krasus nor the night elf had ceased holding tight since nearly being tossed earlier. Still, they both gripped the dragon by the scales as best they could.

And no sooner had they done it than Korialstrasz's wings ceased beating.

The dragon sank like a rock, leaving the startled demons hovering high above. By the time they started after, Korialstrasz was far, far out of reach.

Malfurion shouted. Krasus gritted his teeth and recalled too late that this had been a favorite strategy of his when younger. Most opponents, even other dragons, expected his kind to stay aloft. Vaguely Krasus remembered experiencing something like this when Korialstrasz had fought the two blacks.

Down and down they fell, the dragon using his wings only to keep from flipping over. It seemed impossible that his passengers would hold on, but somehow they did.

It occurred to Krasus that, with the mist so thick, his younger self might not see the ground soon enough, but then a strange thing happened—the mist simply *vanished*. It was as if some great being had cut a wedge out of the haze. A faint touch still remained, but visibility was so good that Krasus could see hills far, far away.

"Ha!" roared a triumphant Korialstrasz. He beat his wings, jostling his companions slightly. The dragon caught the wind and eased smoothly into flight again. Of the Burning Legion, there was no sign.

Korialstrasz did not wait for them to catch up. He flew on toward their original destination, moving at a speed that none of the demons could possibly match.

Behind Krasus, Malfurion gasped, "May I never have to do *that* again! Night elves were surely not meant to fly as much as I have!"

"After this journey, I would hardly blame you for such feelings . . ." Krasus suddenly eyed the path ahead. "Once again, I am having a sense of déjà vu. Most disturbing."

"What is it? What's wrong now? More demons?"

"That would be a simple situation, druid. This appears far more complex."

"What do you mean?"

"Look at this swath of clarity in what has been one continuous blanket of evil since the Burning Legion's arrival."

"Maybe my people are defeating them and this is the first sign."

Krasus wished that he could share Malfurion's optimism. He raised his head to the air and, as Brox often did, sniffed for a scent. What the mage sensed nearly overwhelmed him and confirmed his fear.

"Korialstrasz! Smell the air! Tell me what you detect!"

The dragon immediately obeyed. What Krasus could see of his expression turned startled. "I sense . . . I sense our own kind . . ."

"Only one?"

"No . . . there are so many, they overlap . . ."

"What does it mean?" Malfurion asked Krasus.

The dragon mage hissed. "It means that the demons we

fought have done us more harm than I could have imagined!"

"But . . . we escaped virtually unscathed . . ."

Krasus would have preferred a few new wounds to what they had instead suffered. Even the minutes used to fight their way free of the trap had been too much. The others would be far ahead by now.

There was so much that he wanted to relay, but the spell cast on him prevented it. To Malfurion, Krasus could only utter one thing, but it was enough.

"The other dragons are ahead of us, druid . . . and *he,* no doubt, is at the head of the flight."

Krasus saw that Malfurion had grasped the essence of his words immediately. The dragons were heading for the battle, certain that they wielded a power sufficient to destroy the Burning Legion.

They could not know that Neltharion, the one who led them to that battle, would there betray them . . .

Miles ahead and swiftly approaching their destination, the dragons flew ready for battle. Neltharion had led them along a route low to the ground, using the might of the Dragon Soul to eradicate the mist. That in itself had impressed the rest, including Alexstrasza and the other Aspects. No one doubted the amazing properties of his creation.

And as he soared toward his impending triumph, Neltharion's head filled with the whispering voices. *Nearly there, nearly there!* they said. *Soon, soon!* they promised.

Soon all would bow before his glory, and the world would be made right.

"What do you wish of us?" Alexstrasza called to him.

I wish you to bare your throat to me . . . the Earth Warder thought, but instead answered, "I have described the array! I need all set in the sky as I asked! The Dragon Soul will do the rest!"

"As simple as that?"

I want to make it easy for you to bow to me . . . "Yes, as simple as that."

She asked no more questions, for which Neltharion was grateful. His mind raged, and her nattering had nearly caused him to give himself away.

The Dragon Soul—*his* Dragon Soul—continued to clear the way for their eyes. As Neltharion peered ahead, he caught a glimpse of movement on the ground, movement like thousands of ants.

They had come upon the battle. He could scarcely contain his glee.

Patience . . . murmured the voices. *Patience* . . .

Yes, the black dragon could afford to be patient a little longer. He could be magnanimous. The prize was so great, a few more minutes would not matter.

Just a few more minutes . . .

Brox saw them first. Wiping the sweat from his brow after having dispatched a felbeast, the orc happened to glance up and see the first of the leviathans arrive over the battle scene. He gaped for a moment, almost losing his head to a Fel Guard for his stupidity. Brox traded blows with the demon, cut the creature into three pieces, then stepped back and looked around. Unfortunately, that one was not near.

The orc snorted. Rhonin might not know of the dragons yet, but surely it would not be long before *everyone* became aware of their presence.

The struggle, Brox decided, had just grown a lot more interesting.

• • •

Rhonin had never reached Lord Ravencrest. The noble stood within sight of him, but the sudden shift in the fight had forced the wizard to concentrate instead on keeping the front line from collapsing before him. Several quick spells of short duration had helped stabilize it, but he could not save the situation all by himself. Unfortunately, the Moon Guard was already stretched thin in some places and in others Illidan had them focusing on him so that he could cast his grand spells.

Malfurion's brother had grown more and more reckless, and not simply because of the circumstances. He flung spells left and right as if they were pebbles, not caring that he came precariously close to hitting his own people.

Another area threatened to buckle. Prodded on by the Doomguard, three Infernals collided with the soldiers there, tossing them everywhere. Fel Guard poured through, chopping and thrusting at anything that still showed life.

The red-haired wizard gestured, but just as he finished the last bit of his spell, an explosion rocked the region in question. The Infernals shattered and the monstrous warriors behind them fell, their armor and most of their flesh torn away.

Had that been the only result, Rhonin would have cheered. However, among the demon dead were many night elves who had suffered the same horrible fate. Survivors cried out for aid. Blood splattered everything.

Rhonin cursed, but not because the fault had been his. His spell remained uncast.

His furious gaze fell upon Illidan. The sorcerer had finally done it. He had killed his own, and the most horrific part was that he had either not noticed or not cared.

The Burning Legion forgotten, Rhonin began shoving his way toward Malfurion's twin. Illidan had to be taken to account; this could not happen again.

The subject of his righteous ire turned and saw him approaching. Illidan gave him a smile of triumph, which did nothing to alleviate the wizard's anger.

But then Illidan looked up past Rhonin. Both his eyes and his smile widened as he pointed.

Despite wanting nothing to distract him, Rhonin had to look.

His eyes, too, widened . . . and a curse escaped his lips.

There were dragons in a suddenly-clearing sky. *Hundreds* of dragons.

"No . . ." Rhonin growled at the high-flying figures. He made out one at the forefront, a black so large that he could be only one dragon. That, in turn, meant that this could be only one particular event in history . . . the very worst of events, as far as the defenders could be concerned. "No . . . not now . . . not now . . ."

TWENTY

There was little that could dismay Archimonde. He attacked every situation with an analytical mind—night elves, magic, even dragons.

But now his composure had been shaken. He had not expected the dragons to come in such numbers. All he had learned of them indicated that they remained out of worldly matters, so aloof that they could not see the end of their world coming. A few, of course, had been expected to act as mavericks, rogues. Archimonde had planned for those, countless Doomguard hiding in the mists and ready to take them on.

But not only had he been outmaneuvered by the beasts . . . they had *all* come.

The demon commander quickly composed himself. Sargeras permitted no failure at this point. Archimonde reached out with his thoughts, touched the minds of every Eredar and Dreadlord, and ordered them to turn their magics on the approaching flights.

Confident that the sorcerous might of the Burning Legion would deal with these interlopers, Archimonde returned his attention to the battle. The Nathrezim and warlocks would eliminate the dragons. The latter were only creatures of *this* world, after all, their power limited to its laws. The Legion was so, so much more.

Yes, there was definitely nothing even the dragons could do to prevent his glorious victory.

Tyrande's sisters had been pushed toward a hilly region upon which stood a few gnarled and dead oaks. The surprise swarming of the demons had left all night elves stunned, and regardless of the sisterhood's attempts to rally those around them, even they had a hard time keeping hopeful under such a crushing blow.

The new high priestess now fought on foot, her night saber having sacrificed itself against blades meant for its mistress. Tyrande had slain the demons who had killed it, and now went to help another sister wounded badly in the same assault. Tyrande pulled the bloody figure up to the trees, where she hoped that the priestess could be left without being noticed by the attackers.

From her higher vantage point, the struggle took on an even more ominous tone. Everywhere Tyrande looked, she saw a sea of fiery figures pressing her people. Night elves fell left and right, mercilessly slaughtered.

"Elune, Mother Moon," she suddenly muttered. "Is there nothing more you can do for your children? The world will end here if something cannot be done!"

But it seemed the goddess had given all that she could, for death continued to come to the night elves. Tyrande leaned down, hoping to at least aid her fellow sister, while at the same time wondering if she should even bother.

Then, the odd sensation that someone watched her made the high priestess pause in her healing. She looked over her shoulder, certain that she had glimpsed a shadow.

However, when she peered close, Tyrande saw only the dead trees.

She almost returned to her work, but then something else caught her attention. Tyrande looked up to the sky and her crestfallen expression changed to one of hope.

Dragons filled the air, dragons of every flight.

"Praise Elune!" she gasped.

Her determination renewed, Tyrande focused on healing the other priestess. The Mother Moon had answered her prayers again. She had sent a force with which even the Burning Legion could not reckon.

Surely now there was nothing more to fear . . .

The dragons spread through the sky as Neltharion had dictated, alternating by their various colors so as to spread the particular talents and traits of each flight as evenly as possible. Near the Earth Warder, Alexstrasza, Ysera, Malygos, and the bronze female poised. Had Neltharion glanced at the red dragon, he might have noticed that Alexstrasza's eyes darted here and there, as if seeking someone. In his madness, the black had not even registered the absence of her youngest consort.

Far below, the tiny figures had begun to notice the dragons' overwhelming presence. A great, toothy smile spread across Neltharion's reptilian features. His audience was ready.

"Now," he rumbled, "let the Dragon Soul be revealed to our enemies below!"

The tiny disk flared so bright that every behemoth save the Earth Warder had to turn their eyes from it. Neltharion ignored the burning sensation in his orbs, so captivated was he.

The Dragon Soul struck.

Its attack came as a flash of the purest golden light, purer than the sun and stars, purer than the moon. It swept down across the demon horde and utterly vaporized the Burning Legion wherever it touched.

The demons howled. The demons shrieked. They spilled away from the killing light, fleeing as they had done before no foe, not even the night elves. Fear was a thing little known to their kind, but they felt it now.

The defenders at first watched in abject awe, so silent that one might have mistaken them for stone. Even the haughtiest among the nobles could not but gape at such power unleashed, power that made their command of the Well's energy laughable at best.

Among the night elves, Rhonin shook his head, repeating, "No . . . no . . . no . . ."

Farther away, Illidan watched the epic destruction with the utmost envy, realizing that all he had learned was nothing compared to what the dragons wielded.

And on the other side of the battle, Archimonde frowned as his monstrous force collapsed like straw before a single power. Already he could sense Sargeras's displeasure and knew that *he*, not Mannoroth or the Highborne, would suffer the brunt of his master's wrath.

The Burning Legion did fight back, however ineffectively. The Eredar and Nathrezim focused their dark magic on the disk and its creator, casting spells that should have melted the Dragon Soul and stripped Neltharion of hide, flesh, and bone. They assailed all the dragons, seeking a swift end to this attempt to crush them.

"It is time!" roared the Earth Warder, barely able to suppress his madness. "Let the matrix be set!"

The other leviathans linked themselves by mind and power. Already tied into the disk by their earlier contributions, they had little difficulty in feeding the Dragon Soul yet more of their strength.

With a mocking cry, Neltharion unleashed the disk's energies on the attacking spellcasters.

Eredar by the scores crumbled to dust, their screams short but telling. Dreadlords fluttering in the sky fell as light burned through them, reducing the fearsome demons to skeletal pieces. In other places, warlocks perished by a hundred different and horrific manners as the disk turned their very spells back upon them.

In the end, even the most cruel of them fled in panic. This was no power with which they could deal. Even their fear of Sargeras could not keep them from routing.

And when the Fel Guard, Doomguard, and others saw how their brethren fell to the power of the dragons, the last of their courage melted away almost as literally as many of their comrades had. Archimonde found himself a commander without anyone to command. His threats went unheeded, even when he slaughtered several of those around him to prove how much he meant them.

Astride his night saber, Lord Ravencrest gave out a bellow and pointed at the retreating horde. "The moment is at hand! For Kalimdor and Azshara!"

His call was taken up by the soldiers. The host pressed forward. At last, the war would be won.

Only Rhonin hesitated. Only he knew the truth. Yet, how could he argue with all that the others had witnessed? The dragons' creation had done the task for which it had supposedly been created.

He looked around desperately for the one other who would have realized the threat, who could have told him what they might do.

But still there was no sign of Krasus.

• • •

Neltharion roared in triumph, watching as the puny demons scattered. He had proven to all the might of his Dragon Soul and, therefore, his own superiority.

Then, one of those he knew would betray him dared interrupt his moment of glory.

"Neltharion!" called Alexstrasza, her voice strained. "The demons are on the run! The Soul has done its work magnificently! Now is the time for us to break the matrix and assault them from all sides—"

"No!" He glared at her, no longer able to or desiring to hide the madness within. "No! I will say what will be done from here on! I, not you, Alexstrasza!"

The other Aspects suddenly stared at the Earth Warder as if seeing him for the first time. Malygos, in particular, appeared troubled as he tried reasoning with the black leviathan. "Good friend Neltharion! She meant no disrespect! It's just that we can now be more effective if—"

"Be silent!"

The disk flared.

As one, the assembled flights stiffened, their wings caught in mid-flap. They did not plummet, however; the monstrous power of the Dragon Soul instead kept them frozen in the air. Their eyes were the only sign that they still had any consciousness, and all save those of the blacks held horror at the revelation that one of their most powerful had turned upon them.

"There will be no betrayal of me! I will do what is my right! My destiny is at hand! This land, *all* lands, will bow before my might! I will remake the world as it *should* be!"

His terrible gaze fell upon the battle, but not at the Burning Legion. The black behemoth held out the golden disk and hissed at the advancing night elves. "Let all see that they live by *my* choosing!"

And the power of the Dragon Soul was cast upon the defenders.

Caught up in what should have been their moment of victory, the night elves had even less of a chance to defend themselves against the disk's power, not that it was likely they could have done anything. The brilliant light flashed across the foremost ranks . . . and they vanished, only their brief shrieks marking their passing. Riders atop night sabers perished in mid-run, their mounts dying with them. Scores of foot soldiers fell in the blink of an eye.

The grand assault splintered as the horror registered. Night elves now fled away from their retreating enemy, leaving a vast area of baked earth and a few gory fragments.

Chaos reigned. Neither the night elves nor the demons knew what to expect. All eyes turned to the fearsome black shape that wielded such death.

The Earth Warder's voice overwhelmed all other sounds as he spoke to the tiny figures beneath him. "Know me, vermin! Know me and pray! I am Neltharion! I am your god!"

The voices in his head had risen to a crescendo, urging him to more mayhem. However, for once Neltharion ignored them. He now wished to savor his triumph, make the puny creatures bow to his magnificence, and acknowledge his supreme power. He could, after all, decimate them whenever he pleased.

Which he would do as soon as he had tired of them.

"All must kneel before me! Now!"

Many did, while others stood in confusion and uncertainty.

The Dragon Soul eradicated that reluctance, its deadly light flowing once over the demons, then over the night elves. The lesson was a powerful one, and the rest fell to their knees in rapid succession.

"I have watched," the insane leviathan snarled. "I have seen my world *ruined* by you pitiful insects! There must be order! I will have my world perfect again! Those who are not fit to serve me will be slain!"

A slight hiss from behind him made Neltharion whirl. Despite being unable to move save at his command, Alexstrasza had managed to give one hint of her anger and contempt.

"And *you* . . ." the black uttered, those below momentarily forgotten. "You, the rest of these traitorous 'friends' of mine, you will live by my sufferance alone! For your conniving, your plotting, you deserve nothing better!"

Alexstrasza struggled to speak. Deciding to be magnanimous, Neltharion granted her that ability.

"What have you wrought, Neltharion? What evil have you perpetrated? You call us traitors, but I see only one for whom that title is deserved!"

"I give you permission to speak, dear Alexstrasza, but you should use it to plead for mercy for your crimes! *You* dare condemn *me*?"

She snorted at such words. "There is no one here among us who has committed more horrendous crimes than you!" Alexstrasza hesitated, then her tone abruptly softened. "Neltharion . . . this is not you! You always sought to make the world one of peace, of harmony . . ."

"And I *will*! When all obey my dictates, there will be no more chaos, no more war!"

"And no more death? How many must die to create your 'peace,' my old friend?"

"I—" The voices grew insistent, demanding that he put an end to her words, and to her. The black dragon shook his head, trying to clear his thoughts. "Alexstrasza . . . I . . ."

"*Fight* what madness has overwhelmed you, Neltharion!

You are strong! Recall what you once were . . . and destroy that abomination before it's too late for all of us!"

She had said the wrong thing. The Earth Warder's crimson orbs hardened again and he clutched the disk protectively. "No! So, your betrayal worsens! You would take what is mine, what I've created, for yourself! I knew it! I knew that none of you could be trusted!"

"Neltharion—"

"Be silent again!"

Alexstrasza's jaws froze. She clearly struggled to speak, but the power of the Dragon Soul was too much.

Dismissing her as of no more consequence, the dark giant again stared down at the throngs held still by utter fear of him.

"I have decided!" he told them. "I have decided that this place is best with none such as you befouling it!"

He held out the Dragon Soul.

The disk flared—

And a crimson juggernaut suddenly crashed into him.

They had arrived to find a scene of utmost horror—wholesale destruction below and, above, the dragons snared in a trap set by one of their own.

Krasus swore. "It is too late! Neltharion has committed his betrayal!"

No sooner did he say it than the mage realized the geas the Earth Warder had placed on him no longer existed. Why should it? Neltharion himself had revealed his treachery; there was no point to the spell anymore.

"This is monstrous!" roared Korialstrasz. "He has Alexstrasza prisoner! How dare he? I will slay him for that—"

"You must calm yourself!" Krasus interjected. "Neltharion is too powerful now that he has unleashed the Demon Soul!"

" 'Demon Soul'? Aye, a better name than that which he called it! Truly it is a demonic creation, more befitting the foul creatures of the Burning Legion!"

Krasus had not meant to say the name by which the disk would become known later in time, but it was too late. Perhaps this had even been the way the name had changed. The mage no longer knew what was a part of the original history and what had been altered by his interference. At this point, it hardly seemed to matter anymore. What *did* matter was that Kalimdor was in danger from a threat that made even the demons seem insignificant by comparison.

"What can we do?" asked Malfurion.

"The Dra—Demon Soul is not invulnerable! Neltharion is the key! He is its creator, and its weakness!"

"Do you mean to destroy it? We could use it to save my people!"

Krasus grew grim. "Druid, any other path to survival would be better than wielding that abomination! It is a corrupting influence! Surely you can sense that even from here!"

The night elf nodded. Anyone but apparently Neltharion could likely sense the evil within when the disk was in use.

Korialstrasz shook his head. "I can stand this no longer!"

Without warning, the red dragon descended toward a hilly region behind the defenders' lines and out of sight of the insane black. He dropped down with such swiftness that neither rider could protest.

Only when Korialstrasz had landed and his two riders dismounted did Krasus have the chance to say anything. "What is it you intend?"

"You know me as well as anyone. You know what I intend."

Krasus did and vaguely recalled that decision now. Yet,

what had once been set in stone no longer was. Korialstrasz had all but died once; a second time might prove permanently fatal.

Yet, even knowing that, he could no longer argue against the dragon's action. The love Korialstrasz had for his queen and mate was one that Krasus also felt.

"Strike low and to the back, then," he told his other self. "And do your utmost to break his grip on the disk."

The behemoth dipped his head in appreciation. "I take your wisdom to heart."

With that, Korialstrasz took to the air once more, wings beating rapidly as he sought to quickly gain speed before attacking. The two watched the dragon depart, Krasus particularly keeping his eyes on the red until the latter had flown off.

The moment it became evident to him that the die had been cast, the mage turned, saying, "Come, Malfurion! We must make with all haste for your people!"

Krasus raced along the landscape, all sense of dignity forgotten. Dignity was for those with both time and patience, commodities not available to him and his companion. All that mattered was reaching Rhonin and the others.

Of course, then the question would be . . . exactly what could they do?

On and on they ran, but to the mage it seemed that the night elves were as far away as ever. "This goes much too slow!" Krasus snapped. "By the time we make it there, it will be too late!"

"I could try to summon something! Perhaps Cenarius will be able to send hippogriffs again!"

"I doubt very much that we shall be so fortunate as previous! Perhaps . . . perhaps if I can reach Rhonin . . ."

He paused. Taking a deep breath, Krasus tried to reach out

to his former protégé. But although he sensed the human, there was too much turmoil going on. Krasus doubted that Rhonin even noticed his touch.

"I have failed," he finally said. "It seems that we must keep running."

"Let me try. Surely it can't hurt at this point."

Krasus eyed the druid. "Who do you think to contact?"

"My brother, of course."

The slim spellcaster considered the choice, then said, "May I suggest another? Tyrande, perhaps?"

"Tyrande?" Malfurion's cheeks darkened.

Trying not to embarrass the night elf more, Krasus added, "When we sought you in the palace, it was through *her* that the link became quickly established. I think, with my aid, you can do it again. Besides, she is more likely to have transportation for us."

Malfurion nodded, accepting the logic. "Very well."

Still facing each other, the two seated themselves. Krasus stared into the night elf's eyes as both concentrated.

"Tyrande . . ." Malfurion whispered.

Krasus felt him reach out to her. The druid and the priestess touched minds almost instantly, verifying his assumptions. They might not yet realize it themselves, but he could sense the deep feelings between the two as Malfurion again called to her. *Tyrande . . .*

Malfurion? She sounded both startled and relieved. *Where—*

Listen carefully! I can't explain much, he replied, stressing the urgency as best he could. *Krasus and I need mounts! Can one of your sisters head toward the southern hills?* He envisioned them as best as he could for her and felt her acknowledgment of the location.

I will come myself! the priestess said.

Krasus broke in before Malfurion could protest. *She will*

be able to follow the link directly to us. Another might ride around this area too long and still miss where we are.

The dragon mage sensed her agreement and, finally, Malfurion's submission.

I must find mounts first, but I'll be there quickly! With that, Tyrande receded from the link. She remained bound to Malfurion, but in a manner that would permit her to act on the situation without being distracted by his thoughts.

"Praise the Aspects!" Krasus announced as he severed himself from their connection. Helping Malfurion up, he declared, "We have a chance now."

"But how much of one? First the demons and now this! Surely Kalimdor is doomed!"

"Perhaps, perhaps not. We do what we can do." The mage suddenly looked up to where Korialstrasz had flown. The hills prevented the pair from seeing the upcoming struggle. "As do others," Krasus added bleakly. "As do others . . ."

TWENTY-ONE

Korialstrasz collided with Neltharion as hard as he could, aiming for the areas least protected by scales. At the same time, the red unleashed a burst of flame toward the insane Aspect's eyes.

He succeeded in startling the Earth Warder, but Neltharion did not lose the disk as Korialstrasz had hoped. The black dragon had a death grip on it. Even as Neltharion went rolling through the air, he kept enough presence of mind to prevent the loss of his cherished creation.

Korialstrasz hissed at his failure. Alone, he stood no chance against the much larger dragon. Worse, the red felt the pull of what Krasus had more rightly dubbed the Demon Soul and knew that, as he had done with the rest, the Earth Warder would be able to make Korialstrasz, too, a slave.

But still Alexstrasza's consort refused to back away. He had committed himself and he would fight until he died, if only to perhaps save his mate.

Before Neltharion could recover, Korialstrasz slammed into him again, this time driving his head into the black's torso. The Aspect gasped as the air was driven from him. His paw jerked open, and this time the disk slipped free.

"Nooo!" thundered Neltharion. With a frenzied show of force, he shoved back the other dragon, sending Korialstrasz hurtling. The Earth Warder dove quickly after the piece. Wings pressed behind him, Neltharion dropped so quickly that he managed to grab the Demon Soul before it had fallen very far.

Pulling up, the black behemoth roared in rage at the smaller beast. "How . . . *dare* . . . you?"

Korialstrasz tried righting himself, but moved too slowly. To his horror, he saw Neltharion hold the disk toward him.

"You will bare your neck to me!"

The flash of light overwhelmed Korialstrasz. It burned as nothing he had ever before experienced. It felt as if his scales melted, his bones seared. He cried out in agony.

But still the red forced himself *forward*, not back. He fought against the pain, closing in on Neltharion. The Earth Warder bellowed his frustration. In his madness, Neltharion had sought to destroy, not enslave, and that now worked against him.

They clashed. So close, the Soul did not prove as useful as Neltharion might have imagined. Both dragons were momentarily reduced to claws and teeth, and Korialstrasz held his own.

Neltharion snapped at his throat. The red inhaled, sending a full blast of heat into the Earth Warder's face. This time, the attack proved more successful. The black dragon spun back, his head smoking.

But Korialstrasz's victory proved short-lived. Fluttering just beyond his reach, Neltharion pressed the Demon Soul to his heaving chest and grinned madly at his opponent.

"You are no longer amusing, young Korialstrasz! You are a gnat to me, an insect which must be squashed! Enslavement is too good for you . . ."

As he spoke, the disk glowed bright. Its golden aura spread out, encompassing Neltharion. His laughter held no more sanity. The Earth Warder's eyes blazed, and he seemed to swell out of proportion.

"An insect!" he repeated almost merrily. "All of you, nothing but insects to me!"

The black dragon now shook as if almost ready to explode. He held out his free paw and pointed at the distant ground.

The earth buckled. Demons and night elves scattered further from one another as volcanic eruptions began. Magma and fire shot high in the sky, raining down on those unfortunates not swift enough to escape. The very power of the earth that he had sworn to wield wisely, Neltharion now used to kill indiscriminately. Before Korialstrasz's eyes, the Earth Warder perverted his role, transforming himself from an Aspect of the world to its antithesis.

As he committed his latest atrocities, Neltharion changed further. A rip appeared in his torso, scales torn apart as if made of paper. Yet, blood did not flow from the wound, but rather pure fire. Another tear formed on his chest, and a third on the opposite side of the first.

As if the unleashing of a plague, horrific rips materialized all over Neltharion. The high scales on his back tore into pieces. Even to see all this caused Korialstrasz pain, but the huge black seemed not to notice. If anything, Neltharion appeared to revel in what was happening to him. His eyes burned bright with power reflecting that of the disk, and he continued to laugh as he unleashed devastation.

Steeling himself, Korialstrasz tried one more time to stop the hideous leviathan. He soared toward Neltharion, already preparing for his own death. Korialstrasz silently apologized to an absent Krasus, who would surely die the moment that he did.

Although caught up in his murderous work, Neltharion still managed to notice his adversary's return. With as close to a sneer as his reptilian visage could produce, the black dragon pointed the Demon Soul at Korialstrasz.

Its power hammered the red, thrusting him down toward the ground. Korialstrasz tried to slow his descent, but the disk's power proved relentless.

With an ear-shattering thud, he crashed. Even then, Neltharion would not let up; he was determined to crush the other giant into the earth.

Then a crackling field of blue energy surrounded Neltharion, causing him to hiss and draw the Soul back to his chest. The black behemoth roared angrily as he sought the source of his captivity.

Through watery orbs, Korialstrasz saw a wave of motion heading toward Neltharion.

The other dragons were free. Between his battle with Alexstrasza's consort and the havoc he had unleashed on the night elves and demons, Neltharion had not focused enough attention on the spell holding the rest as slaves. Now that mistake gave Kalimdor hope.

One group quickly detached itself from the rest. A flight of blue furies circled wildly around the caged Aspect, at their head one who had, until the betrayal, championed the Earth Warder's cause more than any other.

"Neltharion!" roared Malygos. "Friend Neltharion! Look what you become! The thing that you've created will destroy you! Give it to me so that I can put an end to its corruption!"

"No!" Neltharion shouted back. "You want it! You all want it! You know how powerful it can make you! It can create a god!"

"Neltharion—"

But Malygos got no farther. The black dragon hissed and his body grew more fiery. The golden aura spread from both him and the disk, burning away the cage the blue had cast.

"You leave us no choice, old friend!" Malygos hissed as he dove for the other Aspect. Around them, the other blues positioned themselves to strike Neltharion from all sides with their power. Of all flights, the blues knew the intricacies of magic as none of the others. Here at last, a weak Korialstrasz thought, Neltharion would fall to defeat.

Like a pack of wolves closing in on the kill, the blue dragons swarmed around their foe. An aura of deep cobalt surrounded Malygos.

"That obscenity should never have become reality," the spellweaver informed his counterpart. "And as I've become instrumental in encouraging its creation, 'tis only fair, old friend, that I *erase* it!"

What seemed an arc of pure white flew at the disk. As it neared, it revealed that Malygos had spoken the literal truth when he had said he intended to "erase" the Demon Soul. Wherever it touched, an emptiness existed. No mist. No *sky*. A pure white emptiness remained. The effect on the heavens proved momentary, of course, but for the sinister disk the fate would certainly be permanent.

Or rather . . . *should* have been permanent. Neither the watching Korialstrasz nor any of the others would ever know whether Malygos's spell would have destroyed the Soul. Before it could touch the disk, Neltharion spat. His spit became a black, blazing sphere that met the arc but seconds before the latter would have touched his creation. A blinding series of sparks marked their collision . . . and then there was nothing.

With a savage cry, Malygos signaled for his flight to attack.

But Neltharion acted more quickly. Even before the white arc vanished, he held forth the Demon Soul. Instead of the golden light that had decimated so much of the land below, a gray one shot forth in every direction.

Malygos created a shield of smoke, but plain smoke it might as well have been. The gray light caught him, threw him back hard. He sailed over the hills, over the horizon, roaring in agony all the way.

For his consorts and followers, however, the fate that Neltharion had in mind was much more horrific.

As one, the dragons *shriveled*. They deflated like draining water sacks. Their cries were terrible to behold. Though they struggled, none could escape the grasping gray illumination.

The other dragons sought to come to their rescue, but it was already too late. Reduced to dry husks, their magic and their life force drained by the Demon Soul, the dying blue dragons faded at last to dust that scattered in the wind.

"No . . ." gasped Korialstrasz, trying to rise up. His head spun and he collapsed again, shattering what was left of the hillside he had landed upon. "No . . ."

"Fools!" rumbled the Earth Warder without the least bit of regret for what he had just done. "You have been warned time and time again! I am supreme! All that *is* belongs to me! All that lives, lives because I allow it!"

And with but a glance their direction, the fiery behemoth sent a hurricane wind that tossed about the other dragons as if they were nothing. Even Alexstrasza and Ysera could not stand against it, the two other Aspects blown back as easily as the rest. Along with the others, they tumbled far, far out of sight, all the while spinning haplessly. Not one dragon out of hundreds escaped Neltharion's spell.

His body swollen out of all proportion, blazing rips covering his torso, the monstrous dragon turned to again survey the night elves and their foes. "And you! You have not learned yet! You will! You will!"

He laughed again, his free forepaw clutching at one of the tears in his hide. For the first time he seemed to notice the terrible changes wrought upon his form, and his expression shifted momentarily to one of awe. Then, to the onlookers below, Neltharion shouted, "We will see who is worthy of my world! I leave you to your little war . . . you may *fight* to see who will be permitted to live and worship me!"

And with one last insane laugh, the black behemoth turned and flew away.

Korialstrasz gave thanks that the Earth Warder had not been able to continue on his mad path of destruction, but knew that the reprieve was only temporary. While he had gloried in the transformation wrought by the disk, Neltharion had finally realized that something had to be done about the forces ripping his body asunder. The weakened red had every confidence that the black would soon enough find a solution . . . and then Neltharion would no doubt return to claim his "world."

Again Korialstrasz tried to rise, but his body still would not obey him. He gazed up hopefully at the murky heavens, but of his people, of his Alexstrasza, the injured red saw no sign. A fear coursed through him, the fear that they had suffered a fate akin to that of Malygos's flight. Imagining his queen limp and lifeless atop some harsh mountain, a sizzling tear slipped from his eye. Yet, try as he might, even such images failed to enable Korialstrasz to rise.

Rest . . . I must rest . . . I will find Krasus, then . . . he will know what to do . . .

The red giant let his head fall back. All he needed was a few minutes. Then he could take to the air again.

But it was at that moment that a new and harsh sound assailed his sharp hearing. It took Korialstrasz only a second to recognize it.

The sound of battle.

The demons were attacking again.

A nightmare. Krasus found himself in the midst of a terrible nightmare. He and Malfurion had reached a point that, while it had not given them a view of the battle, it had at least allowed the pair to witness what took place up in the sky.

And so Krasus had watched as his kind fell to one insane creature.

He had seen his younger self bravely—if foolishly—attempting to confront an Aspect. The struggle had gone as the mage had expected, even though his memories of the time were all but gone. A chill had coursed through him when Korialstrasz had finally fallen, but although Krasus felt his pain, he also felt that the red lived . . . a minor victory at this point.

But worse to him, worse even than the knowledge that so many night elves had perished at Neltharion's hand, was what had happened to the other dragons. With Malygos's flight virtually decimated, now the spellweaver would begin to slip into his own madness as his kind became all but extinct. Gone would be the merry giant, and in his place would loom the ominous, reclusive beast.

And beyond that, the attack that had sent all the others tumbling far over the horizon rattled Krasus to his core. He kept telling himself that Alexstrasza would be all right, that most of the dragons would survive the epic winds that threw them half a world away. History told him so, but his heart kept insisting otherwise.

He tore ahead of Malfurion, trying in desperation to transform. He was older, wiser, and more skilled than his younger self; Krasus could have taken on Neltharion with better hope of success. The dragon mage struggled to change, to become what he should be . . .

In the end, however, he only succeeded in first stumbling, then falling. Krasus dropped face first into the earth, where he lay for a moment, all of his failures rising up to overwhelm him.

"Master Krasus?" Malfurion lifted him up.

Ashamed of his display, the mage buried his emotions under the mask he generally wore. "I am fine, druid."

The young night elf nodded. "I understand some of what you're going through."

Krasus almost snapped that the druid could not possibly understand, but realized almost immediately how harsh and stupid such a caustic remark would have been. Of course Malfurion understood; at this very moment, his people, possibly those he cared for, were dying.

Suddenly, his companion looked up. "Praise Cenarius! We're in luck!"

Luck? Following his gaze, Krasus spied a welcome sight. Tyrande rode toward them, two other sisters accompanying her. She also led along a pair of extra mounts, obviously for the two spellcasters.

Pulling up, she leapt from the night saber and hugged Malfurion without any sense of shame. The other sisters politely looked down; Krasus noted that they seemed very respectful of Tyrande despite clearly being elder.

"Thank the Mother Moon!" she gasped. "With all that

happened and Korialstrasz appearing like that, I feared that
you—"

"As did I, you," the druid replied.

Krasus felt a slight ache in his heart that had nothing to do
with either his or Korialstrasz's condition. In the place of the
two night elves, he imagined himself and another.

But that would never come to pass unless they stopped
both the Burning Legion and Neltharion.

"We must move on," he told them. "We must stop the
demons if we have even a hope of stopping the Earth
Warder."

With some reluctance, Malfurion and Tyrande separated.
When everyone had mounted, the band turned back, heading toward the site of the struggle.

They heard the cries and shouts long before they saw the
first bloodshed. The battle had shifted position entirely, even
surprising Tyrande and the sisters, who had just left it.

"It should not be this close!" blurted one of the latter.
"The lines are collapsing completely!"

The other nodded, then turned to Tyrande. "Mistress, we
need to find another path. The one we took is overrun."

Both Krasus and Malfurion noted the term used, but neither understood what it meant. Tyrande added to the mys-
tery by accepting the suggestion in a manner befitting one in
command: "Lead on where you think best."

They rode on, seeking another way to the host. A path
opened up before them, but it brought the group precariously near the fighting. Still, it seemed their only route left
unless they wanted to ride completely behind Ravencrest's
army, which would add wasted hours to their trek.

As the party rode, Krasus eyed the battle nearby. The
demons fought as if they still intended to take the world for
their lord when they were, in fact, as likely to be wiped out

by Neltharion as the night elves. Archimonde could only be assuming that he would somehow gain the upper hand quickly and then take on the black dragon. How he hoped to accomplish that, Krasus could not determine, but he put nothing past the demon commander. The future was no longer assured; anything could happen.

"Down this way!" called the priestess in the lead. She steered her mount around a descending trail, then vanished briefly around the edge of a hill that they had been skirting.

The others followed suit, aware that each second counted. But as they came around the hill, Malfurion shouted, "Look out!"

Coming seemingly out of nowhere, the battle flowed into them. Desperate soldiers fell back as grinning demons chopped into their weakening lines. The riders just barely missed colliding with the former. Worse, the fluidity of the line brought them face-to-face with the enemy.

The sister in the lead tried to deflect the burning blade of a demon, but she moved too slowly. The monstrous sword ripped through her shoulder and neck and she dropped like a stone. Her mount tore into the demon immediately after the attack, but there was nothing that could be done for its rider.

"Mistress!" the remaining sister shouted. "Get back!" She shared blows with a Fel Guard, beating him away from Tyrande.

Malfurion's childhood friend did not shirk from the battle, though. With a fierceness that reminded Krasus of one of his own, she came to her companion's aid, driving her blade under the demon's armor. The Fel Guard crumpled and briefly the defenders' line reformed.

"We need to reach Rhonin and Lord Ravencrest!" Krasus urged.

Yet, despite their best efforts, they found themselves

pushed back by the sea of bodies. Krasus cast a spell that sent the fallen weapons of other demons flying into those monstrous warriors in the forefront. Beset by both the night elves and the enchanted blades, many demons died.

The effort pushed Krasus more than he had expected. Again, Korialstrasz's weakness affected him, too. His younger self had expended himself against Neltharion, and the link between the two had evidently even let him draw from Krasus.

Malfurion proved more effective. He whipped up a dust storm that blinded only the Burning Legion, forcing the demons to swing recklessly in the hopes of finding some target. Soldiers picked off the confused warriors with ease.

Focused on the encroaching invaders, Krasus paid no attention to the sky; thanks to Neltharion, he saw no reason why anyone would need to look up anymore.

But when he heard the screaming sound and noted the growing shadow, Krasus finally did look up, just in time to curse his failing.

The two Infernals struck . . . and chaos overwhelmed all.

The hurtling demons hit the ground with devastating results. A tremendous quake overwhelmed everyone. Soldiers were sent flying. Others screamed as huge chunks of stone and earth—tossed up by the Infernals' landing—crushed them.

Tyrande's mount was struck by one such missile and fell, tossing the priestess into the fray. The other sister reached for her, but a fiery blade caught her through the heart. Malfurion, too, attempted to grab Tyrande, but one of the Infernals rose from the pit it created and barreled into his night saber.

He received no aid from Krasus. The dragon mage hung half-conscious in the saddle, the side of his head bruised by what must have been a huge rock. Worse, Krasus's mount, panicked by the tremors, ran off with the stricken figure.

The druid finally leapt from his night saber. The Infernal ran past him, the brutish demon interested only in general carnage.

Fighting through the mob of disheartened soldiers, Malfurion caught sight of Tyrande. One hand pressed against her head, she half-knelt in the mayhem. Her helmet lay at her feet, one part severely dented. The druid marveled that she was alive.

"Tyrande!" he cried, stretching a hand out to her. She stared blankly at it a moment before taking it. Malfurion dragged her back from the worst of the fighting.

With Tyrande leaning on him, the druid headed for somewhere to momentarily hide. All he cared about was getting her away from this area. Malfurion felt guilty for having asked her to come, even though there was likely no part of the battle where anyone could be considered safe.

He half-dragged her up the hillside. Even up here, it was not so safe, for night elves and demons already fought at the base. At the moment, however, it was the only possible choice.

A few green plants still hung to life on the hill. The druid touched one and begged of the plant its moisture. He brought the green leaves to Tyrande's lips, letting precious water drip into her mouth.

She moaned. He readjusted her position, letting her head rest in the crook of his arm. "Easy, Tyrande. Easy."

"M-Malfurion . . . the others . . ."

"They're all right," he lied. "Take a minute to clear your head. You struck it when you fell."

"Hel'jara! She—it went right through her!"

Malfurion quietly swore; if she recalled the one sister's

death, then she would soon recall too much more. "Try to relax."

But even as he asked that of her, Malfurion himself tensed. He felt certain that someone watched them.

Quickly peering behind him, the druid thought that he caught sight of a shadow. One hand immediately twisted into a fist. Had one of the attackers slipped through?

"Tyrande," he whispered. "I'm going to talk to Krasus. He's not far. You rest more."

She gazed at him with an expression that indicated she found something wrong with what he said, but could not identify just what. Hoping that her mind would not clear too quickly and make her remember that the mage had become separated from them, Malfurion gently let her rest against the hill, then slipped away.

As he cautiously wended his way toward where he thought he had seen the shadow, the druid focused on spells utilizing what existed around him. The land here would be only too eager to aid him if he sought to destroy a Fel Guard or other demon.

Someone or something had been here. He saw a slight depression in one area, but it was smaller than he would have imagined from one of the fearsome warriors. The print indicated either a very short figure or some animal, though he could not say which. There also seemed to have been more than one creature.

Pushing past a tree, he halted. Ahead came the sound of something scraping against rock. Malfurion rushed ahead, already prepared to attack.

However, as he came around another tree, he saw not a demon, but a slighter, more familiar figure. Another night elf.

She scrambled out of sight, slipping away too fast for him

to follow without leaving Tyrande dangerously alone. The young female had not been wearing armor or robes of the temple, but rather garments such as many of the refugees wore. In one hand, she had been carrying something long and wooden, but his brief glimpse had not given him enough of an image to guess just what.

It was not so surprising to find a refugee wandering about. The ordinary people were now likely scattering in fear. The host was being decisively beaten back, and nothing seemed capable of saving the night elves this time.

Malfurion turned and hurried back toward where he had left Tyrande. She was all that mattered to him now. He could do nothing for any young refugee who had gotten so far from the rest.

The druid scrambled among the trees, eyes already searching for Tyrande. Malfurion had wasted precious time chasing after the young figure; he had to get Tyrande and himself away from here quickly, before the fight rose to where she lay.

As he came around the last of the trees, Malfurion gave a sigh of relief. The sounds of combat were still some distance away. Tyrande would be safe—

He stopped dead as he came upon the prone figure of his childhood friend . . . and an ominous figure hovering over her.

It should have been impossible for the creature to hear him, but it turned to Malfurion nonetheless. Hooves kicked at the rocky earth as the goatlike figure confronted him. The upper half resembled one of his own kind, save for the wicked horns curling high above. The all-too-night-elven face leered at the druid as the newcomer's taloned fingers stretched in anticipation.

But what was most terrible, even more so than finding

this creature looming above his Tyrande, was the fiend's face.

Malfurion knew that face. He had told no one, but it haunted his dreams. Even though there were some changes in the features, he could never have forgotten the eyes . . . the black and crimson crystal eyes.

Lord Xavius had risen from the dead.

TWENTY-TWO

The lines of the night elves proved so fluid now that everyone's position shifted continuously. That notwithstanding, Lord Ravencrest did what he could to keep order, to keep morale. For all that he had argued with the noble in the past, Rhonin now felt thankful that the master of Black Rook Hold had the sway over his soldiers that he did. The wizard could not imagine someone like Desdel Stareye doing the same.

Ravencrest finally caught sight of the human. Riding toward him, he shouted, "Wizard! I need you up there, not back here!"

"One of us should remain near you, my lord!" In truth, Rhonin wanted to stay nearby to hear any reports that might come, but protecting the commander of the host had also become a priority with him.

"I'd rather you be up by the Moon Guard and Illidan!" For the first time, Ravencrest betrayed a secret. "I'd feel much better if you took the lead at this moment! The lad's good, but we need control now, not mayhem! If you'd please!"

Pointed out like that, Rhonin could hardly argue. Already he had sensed Illidan drawing ever more wildly from both his comrades and the Well itself. After witnessing the madness of the black dragon, Rhonin could easily imagine Illidan becoming likewise the more he freely immersed himself in his magic.

"As you say, my lord!" Urging his mount forward, the wizard looked for Illidan. It was not hard to locate the young sorcerer. Like a beacon of silver light, Illidan stood out among the defenders. The aura he wore about him nearly blinded those closest, but of course, Malfurion's twin was too blinded by his own might to realize how he affected the rest.

Even as Rhonin neared, the black-garbed figure unleashed a series of explosive bolts at the oncoming horde. Demons were tossed everywhere, scorched body parts even raining down near the wizard. Unfortunately, a few soldiers, also caught in the fringe of the spell, perished in the same horrible manner.

One of the Moon Guard collapsed. Illidan snarled at the rest and the much more experienced spellcasters sheepishly realigned themselves so as to remove the fallen one from their magical matrix.

What does he think he's doing? thought Rhonin to himself. *At this rate, they and everyone around him will be dead!*

Illidan started casting, then noticed the wizard. The night elf grinned at Rhonin, so pleased with his work that he failed to notice that the rest of the army was collapsing.

"Master Rhonin! Did you see—"

"I've seen everything! Illidan! Ravencrest wants me to take over! We need to coordinate our attack and bring back some semblance of order!"

"Take over?" A dangerous look flashed across the night elf's expression. "From me?"

"Yes!" Rhonin saw no reason to placate Malfurion's

brother; the fate of an entire people—an entire world—might very well hang in their hands.

With clear bitterness, Illidan acquiesced, then asked, "What do we do?"

The mage had already thought that out. For the time being, he wanted to remove Illidan from the matrix completely, giving the Moon Guard the opportunity to recuperate. With Rhonin at their head, they would be able to assist while still recovering.

"I've tried contacting Krasus, but to no avail! So much magic might be making it difficult! Your link to your twin should be stronger, more inherent! I need you to find the two of them for us! We need their aid in this, too!"

The sorcerer's eyes narrowed, a clear sign that he recognized what Rhonin was doing. Nonetheless, he nodded again. "I'll find my brother. We wouldn't want to be without *his* powers, would we?"

Illidan moved away before Rhonin could say anything. The wizard frowned, but knew that he could expect no better understanding from the hot-headed youth.

A few of the Moon Guard looked almost relieved when Rhonin joined their efforts. They no longer cared that he was an outsider; they just knew that he would lead them well.

"We need to sweep away their front line much the way we did once before," he informed the group. "Bind with me and we'll begin . . ."

As he prepared for his spellwork, Rhonin took one last glance at Illidan. The sorcerer still wore a look of aggravation, but appeared to be doing as told. Eventually, the wizard thought, Malfurion's brother would learn to appreciate what Rhonin had done.

At least, the fiery-tressed mage *hoped* so.

• • •

Illidan felt anything but appreciative after the clear dismissal. All his life he had been told that he was destined for greatness, for legend, and here he had thought that his time had come. His people were in panic, with nothing standing between them and genocide. Surely *now* was the moment when he became a part of epic history.

And perhaps he would have, if not for two of those he trusted most. Lord Ravencrest had taken him under his wing, raising Illidan up from nothing to a sorcerer of noble rank in the blink of an eye. His master had given him control of the remaining Moon Guard, and the twin believed that he had done well in the role of lead spellcaster.

Now, though, Ravencrest had removed him, replaced Illidan with one who was not even a night elf. For all the respect that Illidan had for Rhonin, this was too much. The wizard should have seen that, too; had Rhonin had any true confidence in him, the outsider would have refused the role.

His moment of greatness had been stolen from him . . . and in its place he was now reduced to calling for his so-admired brother.

The dark thoughts that had of late invaded his mind returned in full force. Although he worked to open the link that Rhonin had requested, Illidan half-hoped to discover that the reason Malfurion was still missing was that he had fallen victim to the Burning Legion. Illidan expected his twin to go down fighting heroically, of course, but beyond that he found that he was not at all that shaken by the image of a dead Malfurion. Tyrande would be upset, obviously, but the sorcerer would comfort her . . .

Thinking of Tyrande scattered away much of the darkness. Illidan felt regret for any pain that the actions he imagined would cause her. How could he *think* of putting her through that, even for him? She had chosen Malfurion, and that was that.

Forcing himself to focus on his twin, Illidan concentrated. First he would deal with this situation, then make a decision about his future. He had thought it lay with Ravencrest and Tyrande, and in both matters he had been wrong.

Now Illidan had to decide just *where* he belonged . . .

Brox swung hard, beheading the felbeast trying to break through the line. Near him, Jarod and what remained of the original bodyguard did the best they could to stem the tide. Most of them had long ago lost their mounts to the enemy, so now they fought side by side with the original defenders.

A half-torn banner carried by a mounted fighter fluttered past the orc's field of vision. Brox grunted in surprise, recognizing it as one generally positioned near Lord Ravencrest's. Had the defenders been shoved and pushed so to the brink that there was no more organization?

He looked to his left and had his fear verified; the black, avian banner of the Hold flew not all that far away. Brox could not even recall having moved so much, and yet here was absolute proof.

Ravencrest himself rode into sight. Unafraid to risk himself, he slashed at a Fel Guard, then kicked the wounded demon in the head. Flanked by his personal bodyguard, the lord of Black Rook Hold was impressive to behold even to the veteran warrior. Originally, Brox had had little respect for the night elves, but Ravencrest had proven a fighter born, one worthy of even being called an orc.

Other night elves swarmed around the noble, taking strength from his stalwart appearance. Ravencrest did what even the spellcasters could not—he literally strengthened his followers just by standing with them. The faces Brox saw were determined, proud. They expected to die, but they would do what they could to prevent the demons from winning.

With so many crowded around him, there were times when the night elven commander appeared almost in danger of being cut by his own soldiers. More than one blade came within inches of him, but he ignored them all, concerned only with the weapons of the enemy.

Then one mounted soldier drew much closer to Ravencrest's back than Brox thought necessary. The night elf had a grim look that did not quite fit with those of the others, and his gaze was on the commander, not the demons.

The orc suddenly found himself moving toward Ravencrest.

"Brox!" called Jarod. "Where do you go?"

"Hurry!" rumbled the green-skinned warrior. "Must be warned!"

The captain looked to where Brox pointed, and although he clearly did not see what the orc did, he nonetheless followed.

"Away! Away!" Brox roared at the night elves before him. He leapt up and saw the rider positioning himself. In one hand, the soldier held his sword and the reins of his mount. The other had slipped to his belt . . . where a dagger useless against the Legion hung. He drew it and leaned toward his commander.

"Beware!" shouted Brox, but Ravencrest did not hear him. The din of battle was too great for any warning.

The assassin's mount shifted, forcing him to readjust. Shoving several soldiers out of his path, Brox waved his huge ax high, hoping that Lord Ravencrest would notice it.

The noble did not . . . but the traitorous soldier did.

Eyes narrowing and the desperation in his face growing, the assassin lunged forward.

"*Look out!*" Brox called.

Ravencrest started to turn toward the orc. He frowned, as if annoyed at this untimely interruption.

The assassin drove the dagger into the back of his neck.

The night elven commander jerked in the saddle. He dropped his sword and reached for the smaller blade, but the soldier had already withdrawn it. Blood poured out of the wound, spilling onto the noble's regal cloak.

Most of those around Ravencrest had not yet registered what had happened. The assassin threw away the dagger and tried to ride off, but now the sea of bodies worked against him.

With a loud battle cry, Brox used the flat side of his ax to clear the way for him. Night elves gaped at what seemed a warrior gone insane. The orc no longer sought to tell them what had happened; all that mattered was reaching the betrayer.

Shuddering, Lord Ravencrest fell forward. His followers began to notice. Several reached up to grab hold of the commander before he could topple from his mount.

Brox finally managed to battle his way to where Ravencrest was. "There! There!"

A few of the night elves looked at him in confusion. Two finally followed after the orc.

The assassin could not maneuver his beast through the throng. He looked over his shoulder and saw the pursuit nearing. A fatalistic look crossed his dark features.

He shouted a command to his night saber. To Brox's dismay, the cat swatted a soldier who had been standing in the way. As the unfortunate fell, the night saber bit at another. Soldiers hurried to clear out of the path of what they perceived to be a maddened animal.

Calculating the distance, Brox leapt. He landed short, just behind the night saber. Reaching out, the orc swung wildly at the creature's flank.

The blow landed soft, barely scraping the fur, but it was enough to snare the giant cat's attention. Ignoring the commands of his rider, the animal turned to attack the newcomer.

Brox barely deflected its savage claws. The night saber spat, then lunged.

Bringing the ax up, the orc buried it under the cat's jaw. The sharp blade tore into the dark fur, and blood splattered Brox. He fought to keep the beast from falling on him as its own momentum drove it onto his weapon.

A sharp pain coursed along the orc's left arm. He glanced at the arm and saw a ribbon of open red flesh.

The assassin pulled back for another strike, but as he swung, another sword met his.

Jarod grunted as the downward force of the other's attack almost sent him to one knee. The traitorous soldier kicked at the captain, but Jarod stepped out of reach.

The captain did not count on the dying night saber. Flailing furiously, its life fluids spilling over the ground, the cat slashed out at anything near. It batted Jarod with the back of one paw, bowling him over.

Feeling its struggles ease, Brox quickly drew the ax from the cat. With a gurgling sound, the night saber stumbled forward. Its forelegs collapsed underneath and the animal fell in a heap.

The night elf leapt as his mount dropped, coming at Brox with his blade before him. The veteran warrior fell back as the two collided. Surprise on his side, the assassin landed on his feet while the orc fought valiantly to keep his balance.

"Stinking monster!" sneered the night elf. He thrust,

nearly cutting off Brox's ear. Brox kicked at the other's legs, but the soldier nimbly jumped.

The orc caught him with the ax while his feet were still off the ground.

Giving Brox a startled look as the ax cut through both his armor and torso, the betrayer tumbled back, still clutching his sword. Brox pushed himself up and met the wounded assassin head-on.

Gasping, Brox's adversary straightened. He held the sword ready and all but challenged the orc to take him.

Brox swung.

. . . And to his surprise, the assassin dropped his weapon and cried out, "For Azshara!"

Unhindered, the ax cut through its target at the chest. The night elf slumped forward, dead before his body collided with the blood-soaked earth.

Panting, Brox stepped toward the corpse. He nudged it with his foot, but the soldier did not stir.

Jarod came up to him, the captain holding his arm as if it were sore, but otherwise looking unharmed. One soldier who had followed them aided the officer. "You slew him!" Jarod called. "Excellent! Well done!"

But the accolades fell on deaf ears. The orc turned back and eyed the scene surrounding Lord Ravencrest. Several of the noble's followers held him up above the chaos as they carried him back from the battle. Ravencrest's eyes were closed, and he looked as if he slept, yet Brox could see that he did not. The night elf's jaw hung slack, and one arm that had escaped the hold of his loyal troops hung limply in a manner the aged fighter recognized all too well.

Brox had failed. The master of Black Rook Hold was dead.

The host was leaderless.

• • •

The hooved figure tilted his head in amusement. "Have you no lust for surprises, Malfurion Stormrage? Or have I become so much more that your limited mind cannot fathom who I once was?" He performed a mock bow. "Permit me to reintroduce myself! Lord Xavius of Zin-Azshari, late of her majesty's service . . . and late of life."

"I . . . I saw you die!" the druid snapped. "Torn apart—"

"You *killed* me, you mean!" Xavius said, the humor momentarily gone from his expression. "Scattered me to the sky!"

He took another step toward the druid, which was exactly as Malfurion had hoped. The farther the abomination that had once been Azshara's advisor moved from Tyrande, the better.

Malfurion vaguely recalled from legend the creature whose shape the dead night elf now wore. Satyrs, they had been termed, magical demons of cunning and deadly mischief.

"You killed me," Xavius continued, once more leering menacingly, "and condemned me to a worse fate! I had failed the exalted one, the great Sargeras . . . and as was his right as a god, he punished me most severely . . ."

Having seen the horrors perpetrated by the Burning Legion, Malfurion could well imagine that Xavius's punishment had been "severe." Mercy was a concept utterly foreign to the demons.

The monstrous artificial orbs flared as the satyr continued. "I had no mouth, yet I screamed. I had no body, yet I felt pain beyond comparison. I did not blame my lord and master, however, for he only did what had to be done." Despite saying that, the horned figure shivered briefly. "No, even throughout my ordeal, I kept in my mind one thing; I remembered over and over who it was that had led me to such terror."

"Hundreds *died* because of you," the druid argued, trying to draw the satyr even closer. If he wanted to attempt any spell at all against this more horrific Xavius, then he needed Tyrande at a safer distance. "Slaughtered innocents."

"The imperfect! The tainted! The world must be made pure for those who will worship Sargeras!"

"Sargeras will destroy Kalimdor! The Burning Legion will destroy *everything!*"

Xavius grinned. "Yes . . . he will."

His sudden declaration caught Malfurion off-guard. "But you just said—"

"What fools like to hear! What those like the good Captain Varo'then or the Highborne assume . . . what *I* once assumed! Sargeras will make the world pure for his worshippers . . . and then he will destroy it for the crime of having *life*. See how simple it all is?"

"How bloodthirsty, how insane it is, you mean!"

The satyr shrugged. "It all depends on your perspective . . ."

Malfurion had heard enough. His hand went to one of his pouches.

Without warning, strong arms wrapped around his, holding him tight. The druid struggled, but his captors were too powerful.

The other satyrs dragged him toward Xavius. The lead creature leered more, his terrible eyes mocking the night elf.

"When the great lord Sargeras cast me back onto this plane, he did so in order that I would bring to him the one who had caused the first portal to cease, and therefore delayed his glorious arrival."

Malfurion said nothing, but continued to fight against the two satyrs holding him.

Xavius leaned close, his breath washing over the night elf's face in stench-ridden waves. "But he left it to me as to *how* I would bring you back to him for punishment. I thought to myself, will it suffice simply to turn you over to the Great One?" He chuckled. " 'No,' I told myself! My Lord Sargeras wishes Malfurion Stormrage to suffer as much as possible, and it is my cherished duty to see that you do . . ."

To Malfurion's horror, the grotesque figure turned back to Tyrande, whose rest seemed oddly deep. The satyr bent low, his mouth coming so near to hers.

"Keep away from her!" the druid roared.

Xavius turned his head just enough to look at Malfurion. "Yes, I thought. He must suffer . . . but how? A resolute young male, no doubt willing to sacrifice himself . . . but what about *others*? What about those *dearest* to him?"

With one clawed hand, the satyr stroked the priestess's hair. Malfurion strained to reach him, wanting to throttle Xavius. He had never hated another creature—the demons not included—but right there and then, the druid would have happily crushed in the former advisor's throat.

His fury only amused Xavius. Still leaning close to Tyrande, the satyr added, "I discovered quickly that Malfurion Stormrage had two for whom he cared. One was like a brother to him—wait!—he *was* a brother, a twin! Close as youths, they now had grown separated by interests and yearnings. But, of course, Illidan was still beloved by his dear sibling, Malfurion . . . even if Illidan himself began to harbor envy for the one to whom *she* looked with favor . . ."

"You have me! Leave them be!"

"But where would be the punishment in *that*?" asked Xavius, rising. His aspect became cruel. "Where would the vengeance be? How greater your pain when you lose not just one, but both." He laughed. "Your brother is *already* lost to you, even if he doesn't know it, Malfurion Stormrage! This delectable one, on the other hand, was more trouble to seek out. I thank you for your assistance in drawing her to us . . ."

As the satyrs pinning his arms laughed with their master, Malfurion cursed himself for having asked Tyrande to help Krasus and him. By doing so, he had given her to these monstrosities.

"No! By Elune, I'll not let you!"

"Elune . . ." Xavius spoke the name with contempt. "There is only *one* god . . . and his name is Sargeras."

He snapped his fingers, and the others pushed the druid to his knees. Xavius walked toward him again, hooves clattering. Each step echoed in Malfurion's pounding head.

Then, a voice suddenly cut through the fog of his mind, a voice so much like and unlike his own. *Brother?*

"Illidan?" he blurted before he could stop himself.

"Yes," replied Xavius, taking the question for his captive's desperate need for more explanation as to what the satyr had done to the twin. "He was quite easy. He loves her as much as you, Malfurion Stormrage . . . and that she has chosen you over him he cannot accept . . ."

Illidan loves Tyrande? The druid was aware that his brother had cared for her, but not to that extent. *But she loves—me?*

Too late did he recall that his brother now sensed his thoughts. Illidan's fury and shame at this revelation suddenly enveloped Malfurion. He rocked backward from the force of his twin's emotions.

Again, Xavius misread what was happening. "Such surprise? How wonderful to hear that you've gained her love, and how terrible to know that because of it she will suffer as no one but you shall!"

Illidan! Malfurion called to his brother. *Illidan! Tyrande is in danger!*

Instead of concern, however, he felt only contempt from the sorcerer. *Then will she not turn to you, brother—the powerful, the magnificent master of nature? What help can she desire from a cursed buffoon, a misfit condemned by the color of his eyes to have false dreams, false hopes?*

Illidan! She will be tortured! She'll die a horrible death!

From his twin he received only silence. Illidan seemed to have receded from him. The link was still there, but just barely.

Illidan!

Malfurion was jarred from the inner conversation by the visage of Xavius filling his gaze. The unnatural eyes appeared to be boring through his own, as if wondering what was going on inside the druid.

"*This* is what condemned me to more than death?" the satyr hissed. "If you are my nemesis, then I see even more that I deserved everything the Great One did to me . . ."

He snapped his fingers, and from Malfurion's right came a half dozen more of the foul creatures. Xavius pointed at Tyrande's prone body, at the same time glancing in the direction of the battle. "They will soon be upon this place. Let us leave before it becomes . . . unruly."

Xavius returned to Tyrande while three of the satyrs—clearly also once Highborne—held high their hands and began casting. Malfurion recognized immediately what they planned. The creatures could not hope to escape by any other methods save a portal. Having created one that stretched beyond time and space, they could surely devise one for travel to Zin-Azshari.

And, once there, all hope for either Malfurion or Tyrande would be gone.

Illidan! Yet, even with the urgency he tried to convey, the druid felt no response from his twin. He was alone.

The raucous sounds of fighting crept closer. A blackness formed in the empty air among the three casting satyrs.

Xavius himself reached for Tyrande, his grin wider and more malicious than ever. "She will enjoy the Great One's company," he taunted, "before she dies . . ."

The portal stretched wide and tall, large enough to admit the demonic creatures and their captives. Xavius picked up the priestess as if she weighed nothing to him—

And a feathered bolt suddenly buried itself in the satyr's shoulder.

TWENTY-THREE

Black thoughts overwhelmed Illidan. He had done as Rhonin had asked and sought out his brother, only to be reminded again of his inadequacies and failures. Never mind that both his brother and the female that they loved had been caught in some terrible predicament; all that mattered was that Malfurion had lorded it over him that he had gained Tyrande's favor without even realizing there had ever been a contest. His innocuous brother had blundered into the greatest prize of all while Illidan, who had fought for her, had nothing to show for his efforts but an empty heart.

A small part of him nagged at the sorcerer to overlook that and help them. At the very least, he should have done something for Tyrande. Some dire force serving the Burning Legion had her in their clutches.

The Burning Legion. At times Illidan wondered how much better he might have fared if he had been one of those serving Queen Azshara and the Highborne. They now looked destined to reap the benefits of their alliance with the demons. Krasus and Rhonin claimed that the Legion would destroy all life, including the queen's people, but surely that was not the case. Why, then, would Azshara join with them?

All the Highborne had to do was close the portal and the threat was past. If they kept it open, it was because they knew better.

Illidan snarled. His head pounded from contradictory thoughts and notions that but a few days ago would have revolted him. He looked to the side, where Rhonin commanded the Moon Guard in their efforts. The wizard did not look like the type to give up such a position once he had gained it. Illidan swore. Now, in addition to his brother, both Rhonin and Lord Ravencrest had betrayed him . . .

Illidan! came Malfurion's voice again, this time more despairing.

The sorcerer shut his mind to the cry.

Tyrande slipped from the satyr's grip, but landed safely against the earth. She hardly stirred, which convinced Malfurion again that the priestess had at some point been bespelled by Xavius.

The former advisor clutched his shoulder where the shaft had buried itself deep. Blood poured from the wound, but Xavius was more angry than injured. He tugged at the shaft, but when it would not come out, he snapped off the end in frustration.

Even as the attack registered with the other satyrs, one of those holding Malfurion shook violently, then fell forward. An arrow identical to the first stuck out from between his shoulder blades.

Using his now free hand to grab from one of his pouches, the druid threw the contents in the face of his other guard. With a cry, the satyr clutched at his eyes, where one of the ground herbs that Malfurion had gathered under the guidance of Cenarius burned the soft tissue there. He stumbled to the side, no longer at all concerned about his captive.

Malfurion did not look back for his rescuer, instead drawing a dagger and slashing at the neck of the blinded creature. As the satyr slumped, the druid used the wind to guide his blade as he tossed it at Xavius.

Although wounded, the former Highborne dodged it with ease. Gaze shifting briefly to where the three others sought to solidify the portal, Xavius leered and grabbed for Tyrande again.

A third shaft sank into the ground inches from his hoof. Eyes blazing, Xavius waved at the satyrs not occupied by the spellcasting.

Two charged at Malfurion, the other after the unknown archer. The druid reached into his pouches again, then tossed a small, spherical seed toward one of the oncoming creatures.

The satyr drew back, letting the seed drop before him. However, as the grin started to stretch over his face, the pod opened and a burst of what appeared to be white dust engulfed him. The satyr began hacking and sneezing to such a degree that he finally fell to his knees. Even then, his suffering did not ease.

Malfurion threw another seed at the second, but the toss went wide. The abomination leapt upon him, clawed hands grasping for his throat. Behind his attacker, Malfurion saw Xavius try to lift Tyrande, but the wound had finally begun to tell; the satyr at last had to use only his good arm to start dragging her to the portal.

Fearful that Xavius would succeed despite his handicap, the night elf searched his mind quickly for some spell with which to remove his immediate threat. The satyr laughed mockingly as his nails scraped the skin under Malfurion's chin. Words spilled from the horned creature and the druid sensed a horrible heat rising around his neck, as if a suffocating collar had formed there.

And at that moment, the battle swept over the hill.

Night elves and demons locked in combat pushed up and into the area. Soldiers backing up collided with Xavius and his burden. The satyr growled, and with only his nails, beheaded one unfortunate fighter from behind.

But even Xavius could not stem such a tide by himself. Chaos swept over everything. The satyrs opening the portal struggled to keep it alive.

As for Malfurion, he was fast losing breath. The grinning satyr atop him raised a clawed hand with the obvious intention of ripping the druid's chest open. Fumbling for his pouch, Malfurion grabbed the first thing he found, then thrust it into his adversary's open mouth.

Eyes widening, expression turning fearful, the horned creature pulled away. As he did, the sensation of strangulation left the night elf. The satyr stumbled back, his eyes continuing to swell. Malfurion felt an intense heat radiate from the fiendish figure.

The struggling creature burst into flames that quickly and efficiently engulfed him. He shrieked as his body blackened and the fire ate away at his flesh.

Gagging, the druid covered his nose and mouth. During their last encounter, Cenarius had shown him how to harness the heat contained within the seeds and fruit of some plants, and magnify it a thousandfold. One of those prepared seeds had evidently been what Malfurion had thrust into the satyr's maw.

Mere seconds after swallowing the seed, the creature collapsed, his remains but a few charred bones. Malfurion had never truly appreciated some of the teachings of his *shan'do*, but now he saw that everything Cenarius showed him had power to it. Truly, there seemed no force stronger than that which nature itself wielded.

Looking past the dead satyr, he spotted Xavius again. One of the others had come to help their leader, and now the two carried Tyrande between them. However, when Xavius looked back and saw the druid racing toward him, he left the effort to his minion and turned on the night elf.

The satyr slammed one hoof against the ground, and a tremor sent Malfurion and several combatants falling. A crevice opened up, racing swiftly toward the druid. Malfurion barely had time to roll away before it would have swallowed him.

The path to his adversary cleared, Xavius approached. His bleating laughter, so monstrous in tone, shook the night elf to the core.

"To be the hero again, you must do something right," the fearsome figure mocked. "You should not be crawling around in the dirt, breathlessly awaiting your death."

Malfurion reached for his pouch, but Xavius acted first. He made a sweeping motion with his claws, and everything from the druid's belt went flying away.

"No more of that, if you please." Xavius seemed to grow as he neared, taking on a more animalistic appearance. "The great Sargeras desires you alive, but in this I think I will dare disobey him. He will find satisfaction in your brother and the female . . ."

Cenarius had taught Malfurion to care for all life, but only revulsion filled the druid now. He leapt at Xavius, snatching at the satyr and trying to bring him to the ground.

With his one good hand, Xavius readily caught his foe by the throat. He let Malfurion dangle above him, taking special delight in the night elf's frustrated grasping. "Maybe I will still leave just the hint of life in you, Malfurion Stormrage . . ." he teased, "if I can contain my full vengeance, that is."

Visions of Tyrande and Illidan in the clutches of the Burning Legion made Malfurion struggle harder. He kicked out as hard as he could.

His heel caught Xavius in the wounded shoulder, driving the broken bolt deeper.

This time, the lead satyr howled. His hand opened and the druid dropped. Malfurion rolled to the side, then managed to come up again.

"You've betrayed too many," the druid told Xavius. "You've hurt too many, lord advisor. I won't let you hurt anyone, anymore." He knew what he had to do. "From you, there'll only come *life* from now on, not death."

Xavius's black and crimson orbs flared. His smile held only malevolence. Dark power radiated around him—

But the druid struck first, the wooden shaft giving him an idea.

The broken piece suddenly healed, then sprouted *roots*. Whatever spell the satyr had intended, he now stopped as he again tried to remove the arrow from his shoulder. However, Malfurion's casting had done more than simply keep it embedded; roots also grew *within* the wound, the wood feeding from the satyr's very life fluids.

Xavius's body bloated like that of a dead fish. He cried out in fury, not pain, and his blazing hand touched the growing wood, seeking to burn it free. Instead, the satyr only screamed again, for the roots were now so much intertwined with his system that whatever *they* felt, so, too, did Xavius.

As the former Highborne stared, his claws turned gnarled, becoming tiny branches with burgeoning leaves. The satyr's horns spread out, growing into thick, higher branches from which foliage then sprouted. Xavius was not so much becoming a tree—rather, his body was providing

Malfurion's creation with the nutrients and building blocks to make itself.

"This will not end it between us, Malfurion Stormrage!" Xavius managed to cry. "This . . . will . . . not!"

But the druid refused to be shaken. He had to complete the spell despite the strong will of the satyr fighting it and the distractions of the battle around them.

"It will," he whispered, more for himself than Lord Xavius. "It *must*."

With one last bestial howl, all trace of the satyr vanished as the tree that the druid had created from the wooden shaft took full bloom. Xavius's skin mottled, then became thick bark. His mouth, still howling, turned into an open knot. Combatants around him scattered as the roots stretching down to his hooves burrowed deep into the ground and sealed his position.

And in the midst of so much devastation and death, a huge, proud oak spread a canopy of rich, green leaves over the hillside, the triumph of life over the mockery of it.

With a gasp, Malfurion dropped to his knees. He wanted to stand, but his legs would not permit him. He had drawn so much out of himself to force his spell against Xavius's powerful will. Despite the battle going on around him, all Malfurion wanted to do at that moment was curl up under the tree and sleep forever.

Then Tyrande's face filled his mind.

"Tyrande!" Struggling against what felt like a thousand iron chains wrapped around his body, the night elf pushed himself up. At first, Malfurion saw only soldiers and demons, but then finally caught sight of the three spellcasting satyrs. Mere feet away, the fourth carried Tyrande toward the ominous gateway.

"No!" He called on the wind to help him and it swirled

around the lone satyr, battering him as he tried to approach escape. Still far too exhausted, Malfurion struggled toward the priestess and her captor.

Then, yet another arrow caught the satyr in the chest. He teetered for a moment, finally falling toward his comrades. Tyrande slipped from his grasp, but the wind, mindful of the druid's desires, let her land gently on the ground.

Again giving thanks to both the wind and his unseen comrade, Malfurion gathered himself for one final run. He pushed his way toward Tyrande, each step a battle, but one whose reward kept him going.

As he neared her, however, one of the three satyrs broke away from the others. The portal shimmered, grew unstable.

The hooved figure scooped up Tyrande.

Letting out a wordless cry, the night elf lunged, but came up short. Something whistled past the satyr's head, nicking his ear and sending blood dropping on his shoulder. In spite of the wound, the monstrous creature held tight his prey as he leapt into the gateway—

He and Tyrande vanished.

The last two satyrs followed him even as the portal began its final collapse. As the third disappeared through, the black gap faded away as if it had never been.

And in doing so, it cut off any hope that Malfurion had of still rescuing Tyrande.

It was too much for him. The night elf collapsed where he was, ignoring the fearsome struggle closing in on him. He had defeated Xavius again, made certain that the one who had instigated the arrival of the Burning Legion would nevermore lend his nefarious hand to such vile causes . . . but all that meant nothing now. Tyrande was gone. Worse, she was the captive of the demons.

Tears rained down his cheeks. The sky darkened ominously, but the druid did not notice. All that mattered to Malfurion was that he had failed.

Failed.

Droplets fell from the heavens, matching his tears. They began to pour down at a more tremendous rate. Oddly, Malfurion remained the only one untouched by the sudden storm. Lightning flashed and thunder rumbled, mirroring his turbulent but darkening mood. Nothing was of importance without Tyrande. He knew that now . . . for what little good it did him.

The wind howled, mourning his loss. The new tree that perched atop the hill shook and swayed as tornado-strength gales battered everything but the distraught night elf . . .

Finally, a voice managed to cut through his despair. It came first as an irritation in the back of his mind, then an echoing sound in his ears. Malfurion put his hands to his ears, attempting to shut it out and return to the blackness overwhelming his thoughts. However, the voice would not be drowned out, growing more insistent with each call of his name.

"Malfurion! Malfurion! You must pull yourself free of this state! Hurry, lest you drown everything and everyone!"

He knew that voice, and although so much of him wanted to ignore its intrusion, just enough rallied. The warning in the tone forced the druid to at last look not within, but *without*.

Malfurion discovered himself amid an impending natural disaster.

The rain came down in such velocity and force that nothing much stood in it way. Curiously, other than him, only the new tree seemed somewhat immune to the raging storm.

"What—?" blurted Malfurion. But as soon as he spoke, the storm abruptly assailed him as well. He dropped to the muddy ground as he was hammered repeatedly by the hellish downpour.

Then, despite the incessant rain and shrieking wind, a huge form fluttered over him. Looking up, the night elf spotted a winged giant swooping down. He recalled the demigoddess Aviana, and wondered if this was her in the form of death. But he was no creature of hers, and the druid doubted that she would make an exception simply for him.

A booming voice identified the gargantuan figure. "Night elf! Stay exactly as you are! It is hard to focus in this chaos, and I do not wish to crush you by accident!"

Korialstrasz seized him in one gigantic paw and pulled Malfurion into the air. The dragon fought valiantly against the storm, but clearly every inch up took strenuous effort. The night elf sensed that the red was not at his best. In truth, it surprised him that Korialstrasz had even survived the encounter with Neltharion.

As they climbed, Malfurion made out some of the landscape below. Both armies were in flight, the demons heading back over the terrain that Neltharion had ravaged. The night elves scurried the opposite way. Both sides battled a new and deadly foe—the rain creating mudslides and treacherous trails. A high hill collapsed, pouring over a band of Fel Guard. A night saber slipped off a ridge as its claws sank uselessly into soft, wet soil. The cat and its rider tumbled to their deaths.

In the midst of the carnage, Malfurion located a small figure trying to make its way down the very hill from which he had been snatched. Mud poured around the young female night elf, half burying her. Higher up, a large portion of the hill looked ready to break loose, surely her doom.

In her hand she still clutched a bow.

"Wait! There!" he cried to Korialstrasz. "Help her!"

Without hesitation, the red dragon veered earthward,

heading for the stricken female. So caught up in her desperate struggles, she did not notice the leviathan until Korialstrasz's talons wrapped around her. She shrieked as the dragon pulled her from the life-threatening muck and carried her aloft.

"I will not hurt you!" Korialstrasz roared. The young female obviously did not believe him, but she quieted. Only when she saw Malfurion clutched in the other paw did the female finally speak.

"Mistress Tyrande! Where—?"

The druid shook his head. Her expression turned crestfallen and she leaned forward, weeping. Even then, she held the bow in a tight grip.

Returning his attention to the storm, Malfurion realized that it could not be natural. It had materialized too abruptly. Yet, it hardly appeared the work of the Burning Legion nor did it seem the efforts of his own people. Even Illidan would not have let something like this grow so out of control.

He peered up, expecting to find that the black dragon had returned. However, there was no sign of Neltharion or the dreaded disk. What, then, was the cause of the catastrophic tempest?

He broached the question to the dragon, but it was not Korialstrasz who answered. Instead, a figure grasping tight to the behemoth's neck and shielded somewhat from the elements by a shimmering golden glow, responded, "It is *you*, Malfurion! It is you who brings this down upon all!"

He stared up at Krasus, whom he had last seen taken away by a frightened mount. The mage did not look at all well, the welt on the side of his head still bright red, but he appeared as determined as ever to be a part of all things.

Still, his words sounded addled to the druid. "What do you mean?"

"This storm's birth is the result of your misery, druid! It radiates your despair! You must put an end to it and your hopelessness if anyone is to survive!"

"You're mad!"

Yet even as he said it, Malfurion could sense a familiarity about the storm. He reached out and touched it as Cenarius had taught him to touch all parts of nature and what he discovered repelled the druid. It was not the storm that so disgusted him, but that part of it which he knew was indeed himself. He had created this monstrosity, somehow utilizing his sadness and dismay. In turn, it had beset not only his enemies, but his comrades, too.

I am as terrible as the demons or the black dragon! the druid thought.

Krasus must have sensed some of his companion's thinking, for the dragon mage uttered, "Malfurion! You must not let such feeling drown your reason! This was accidental! You must transfer the power of your emotions to *aid*, not destroy!"

For what reason, though? Again, the druid thought of Tyrande, lost to the master of the Burning Legion. Without her, he saw no reason to go on.

It was, however, Tyrande who finally shook the blackness from his mind. *She* would not want this destruction. She had done everything she could to keep her people alive. Malfurion had failed her; if he let this storm continue, he would be failing her memory.

He glanced over at the young female who had clearly risked herself in order to save the priestess. Of too few seasons to be a novice, she nonetheless had used her skill with the bow to do anything she could regardless of satyrs and demons alike.

Thinking of that and watching her weep, Malfurion felt

all his emotions concerning Tyrande swell up again. Without hesitation, he stared into the storm, pressing his will on the wind, the clouds . . . every part of nature that combined to create such bedevilment.

The wind shifted. The rain still poured down, but it seemed to lessen where the night elves fled and worsen where the Burning Legion scrambled over Neltharion's ruined lands. Malfurion's head throbbed as he fought the weather's tendencies and made it focus all effort where the demons were.

The rain overhead ceased. The storm moved with obvious intent in the direction of Zin-Azshari.

Malfurion let out a gasp. He had done it.

The night elf slumped in the dragon's grasp. From above him, Krasus called out, "Well done, druid! Well done!"

He should have been astounded by what he had accomplished not once, but twice. Certainly, even Cenarius would have been. Yet, all Malfurion could think about was that he had failed to save Tyrande.

And that made all the difference.

The storm lasted three days and three nights. With the relentlessness with which it had been imbued by its creator, it drove the Burning Legion on and on. By the time it had dissipated, they were but two days from Zin-Azshari.

Unfortunately, the night elves could not rally enough to follow them far. On the other side of the volcanic region created by Neltharion, the defenders tried to mend their own wounds and regroup. To many, the destruction caused by the storm, the Demon Soul, and all else paled when compared to the death of Lord Kur'talos Ravencrest.

Unable to give him a proper burial ceremony, the night elven commanders did what they could. At Lord Stareye's demand, a wagon pulled by six night sabers was driven through much of the host. Atop it lay the dead noble, his arms crossed and the banner of his clan placed in his hands. Garlands of night lilies encircled the body. Ahead of the wagon, a contingent of soldiers from Black Rook Hold kept a path open. Behind, another group made certain that members of the weeping crowd did not seek to touch the body, lest it spill to the earth. All along the route, heralds let loose with mournful horns to alert those ahead of the sad display approaching.

When that had been done, Ravencrest's corpse was set along with those of all who had perished in an area separated by some distance from the living. It fell to Malfurion to ask of Korialstrasz a terrible favor, one to which the dragon readily agreed.

With hundreds standing near enough to see but not be in any danger, Korialstrasz unleashed the only fire certain to burn despite the dampness pervading everything.

As the bodies of Lord Ravencrest and the other dead became an inferno, Malfurion sought seclusion. However, one figure would not leave him, that being the young female who had attempted to rescue Tyrande. Shandris, as she called herself, constantly pestered him with questions concerning when he would go after the priestess. Malfurion, sadly, had no answers for her, and finally had to get the other sisters to take her under their wing if only to keep from tripping over her.

Lord Stareye, proclaimed commander by his counterparts, had scoured the army for other traitors. Two soldiers associated with the assassin had been executed after fruitless questioning. Stareye now considered the matter closed, and moved on to the next stage of the struggle.

Krasus and Rhonin, accompanied by Brox and Jarod

Shadowsong, tried to convince the host's new leader of the need to turn to the other races to create a combined force, but their pleas fell on ears deafer than ever.

"Kur'talos laid down his edict on this subject and I will honor his memory," the slender noble said with a sniff of white powder.

That ended the discussion, but not the concern. The Burning Legion would not be long in recovering, and Archimonde would quickly send them back against the night elves. There was no doubt in anyone's mind that the demon commander would unleash a fury even more terrible than any the defenders had thus far faced.

And even if the night elves held the invaders in check or pushed them back to the very gates of Zin-Azshari, none of their success would matter if the portal stayed open and the Highborne and demons managed to strengthen it further. A thousand thousand demons could perish and the night elves could storm the palace itself . . . but all would be for naught if Sargeras stepped through to their world. He would sweep away their army with a wave of his arm, a glare of his eyes.

That, in itself, made the decision for Krasus. The others gathered with him, he declared the only thing that might be done to stave off what appeared almost inevitable.

"Ravencrest was wrong," he insisted, defying the memory of the dead, "and Stareye is blind. Without an alliance of all races, Kalimdor—the *world*—will be lost."

"But Lord Stareye won't speak with them," Jarod pointed out.

"Then *we* must do it in his place . . ." The mage eyed each of them. "We cannot count on the dragons for now . . . if ever. Korialstrasz has gone to see what has become of them, but I fear that as long as Neltharion holds the disk, they can do nothing. Therefore, we *must* go to the dwarves, the tauren, the furbolgs . . . and we *must* convince them that they should help those who disdain their assistance."

Rhonin shook his head. "The other races may see no reason to ally themselves with ones who'd almost as much as the Burning Legion prefer to see them all wiped out. We're talking *centuries* of enmity, Krasus."

The thin figure nodded grimly, his gaze shifting to the direction of the unseen capital. "Then, if that is the case, we will all die. Whether by the blades of the Burning Legion or the malevolent power of the Demon Soul, we will all surely die."

No one there could argue with him.

Malfurion was the only one of the group not in attendance; these past few days, he had been on a hunt. It had started with a plan, a desperate plan, and there had been only one he could consider mad enough to join him on it. The druid wanted to go after Tyrande, still perhaps rescue her from the demons' evil. Only one other among the thousands in the host might see the matter in the same light as he and Malfurion had spent all this time searching for his intended partner in this suicidal quest of his.

But of his brother, Illidan, he could find no sign.

At last, he dared approach the Moon Guard. Pretending to merely ask for his twin's counsel on the upcoming advance, the druid sought the audience of the most senior of the sorcerers.

The balding night elf with the thin beard looked up as Malfurion neared. While the Moon Guard still did not trust his calling, they respected the terrifying results of his spells.

"Hail, Malfurion Stormrage," the robed figure said, rising. The sorcerer had been sitting on a rock, reading a scroll that no doubt contained some of the arcane knowledge of his own craft.

"Forgive me, Galar'thus Rivertree. I come seeking my brother, but I can't locate him."

Galar'thus eyed him uneasily. "Has word not been passed on to you?"

Malfurion's tension mounted. "What word?"

"Your brother has . . . disappeared. He went riding to investigate the volcanic regions created by the dragon . . . but never returned."

The news left the druid incredulous. "Illidan rode out there alone? No bodyguard?"

The sorcerer bent low his head. "Can you think of one of us who could stop your twin, master druid?"

In truth, Malfurion could not. "Tell me what you know."

"There is little. He rode out the night after the storm settled with the promise that he intended to return before daylight. Instead, two hours after night ended, his mount returned without him."

"Was there—how was the beast?"

Galar'thus could not look at him. "The night saber looked ragged . . . and there was some blood on him. We tried to trace it to your brother, but much magic still radiates the area. Lord Stareye said—"

"Lord Stareye?" Malfurion grew more upset. "He knows, and yet I wasn't told?"

"Lord Stareye said that no time could be wasted on one certainly dead. Our efforts must be made for the living. Your brother rode out of his own accord. I'm sorry, Malfurion Stormrage, but that was the commander's decision."

The druid no longer heard him. Malfurion turned and fled, stricken by the new loss. Illidan dead! It could not be! For all the differences between him and his twin, Malfurion had still loved his brother deeply. Illidan could not be dead . . .

Even as he thought that, a shiver ran down his spine. Malfurion halted, staring not at anything nearby, but rather *inside* himself.

He would know if his twin was dead. As sure as he felt the beating of his heart, Malfurion felt certain that if Illidan had perished, the druid would have known. Despite the evidence, Illidan had to be *alive*.

Alive . . . The druid eyed the smoldering lands, trying to sense beyond them and failing. If Illidan *was* out there . . . then where exactly was he?

Malfurion had the horrible feeling that he knew . . .

TWENTY-FOUR

The stench of the ravaged city did not in the least disturb the cloaked and hooded rider as he rode slowly along the ruined avenue. He eyed the overturned tree towers and crushed homes with mild, analytical interest. The corpses so very slowly rotting away he looked at almost with disdain.

His mount suddenly growled and hissed. The rider immediately clutched the two tentacles he held tight, forcing the felbeast to move on despite its reluctance. When the huge, demonic hound did not do so at a sufficient pace, the rider unleashed a wave of black energy that, instead of feeding the vampiric creature, filled it with awful pain. The felbeast quickened its pace.

On and on through the dead city, the hooded figure traveled. He sensed many eyes watching him, but chose to do nothing. The guardians were of no interest to him; if they let him be, he would do the same.

His reluctant mount, which he had seized two days outside of the city, slowed again as it came to a crossroads. This time, however, the rider knew that the felbeast slowed not because of reluctance, but because it knew that its brethren were closing.

They would not leave him be. They intended a trap.

They were fools.

The three Fel Guard charged him from in front. With their brutal, horned visages and blazing weapons, the giants presented a formidable sight. But they were not, he knew, the true threat.

From the ruins on each side of him, a felbeast eagerly leapt at the supposedly distracted prey. Their tentacles reached out hungrily as they prepared to feast on this naive spellcaster.

He sniffed, disappointed with their ambush. With one quick tug, he tore a tentacle from his mount, ensuring that it would understand not to join the effort. As the felbeast howled, he tossed its appendage at the three warriors.

The bloody tentacle stretched out as it flew at the trio, turning into a sinewy noose that snared all three around the waist. The bestial warriors tumbled forward, ending in a pile of limbs.

Even as the tentacle left his hand, the rider glanced at the felbeast coming from his right. The demon suddenly howled and burst into flames. It dropped several yards short, its burning corpse quickly adding to the thick odor permeating the area.

The second monster collided against his mount. The new felbeast's tentacles adhered to the chest and side of the rider and the creature began to feast.

Rather than devour the hooded figure's magic, however, the felbeast instead found itself *feeding* its prey. It frantically tried to remove its suckers from his body, but he would not permit it to do so. The felbeast began to shrivel, its skin sagging on its very bones. A creature of magic, it was almost entirely composed of energy that the rider now absorbed.

In but a matter of seconds, the deed was done. With a

mournful cry, the tattered felbeast collapsed in a mangled heap. The rider plucked the still-adhered tentacles from his torso, then urged his frightened mount on without another glance at either the dead hounds or the struggling Fel Guard.

He sensed others near, but no one else had the audacity to bar his way. With the path clear, it did not take long to reach his goal—a tall, gated wall upon which dour night elven soldiers glared down at him.

Reaching up, the rider removed his hood.

"I come to offer my services to my queen!" Illidan shouted, not to the guards but rather to those well within the palace itself. "I come to offer my services to my queen . . . and to the lord of the Legion!"

He waited, expression unchanging. After almost a minute, the gates began to open. Their creaking echoed through Zin-Azshari, the sound almost like that of the ghostly moans of the city's dead.

When the gates had ceased moving, Illidan calmly rode inside.

The gates closed quickly behind him.

CONTINUED IN
WAR OF THE ANCIENTS
BOOK THREE:
THE SUNDERING

ABOUT THE AUTHOR

Richard A. Knaak is *The New York Times* bestselling fantasy author of 27 novels and over a dozen short pieces, including *The Legend Of Huma* and *Night Of Blood* for *Dragonlance* and THE WELL OF ETERNITY for *WarCraft*. He has also written the popular *Dragonrealm* series and several independent pieces. His works have been published in several languages, most recently Russian, Turkish, Bulgarian, Chinese, Czech, German, and Spanish. He has also adapted the Korean Manga, *Ragnarok*, published by Tokyopop. In addition to the third volume of the WAR OF THE ANCIENTS trilogy, THE SUNDERING, the author is also at work on EMPIRE OF BLOOD, the final book in his epic *Dragonlance* trilogy, *The Minotaur Wars*.